Praise for

"Anything can happen, and does, in this rollicking farce, set in a sleepy south Georgia town where the Sweat family resides in the Garden of Eden Trailer Park. Jesus returns to earth as a Mexican forklift driver at the Majestic Chicken Plant, a NASCAR-loving redneck named Butterbean takes on corporate corruption, and the scales of justice swing every-which-way. If reading *Luck Be A Chicken* doesn't make you laugh out loud at least a dozen times, you owe me an RC Cola and a Moonpie."

-Cassandra King, author of *The Same Sweet Girls' Guide to Life*

"With *Luck Be A Chicken,* author Jameson Gregg has penned a masterful work of comedy, taking the reader on a hilarious romp through rural south Georgia, a landscape populated by unforgettable characters inhabiting a world that lies on the periphery of mainstream America. Gregg's forte is his ability to skewer for the reader the little eccentricities that define each of them and their environment, from the weighty denizens of the Garden of Eden Trailer Park to the faux finery of Honeysuckle Plantation. A most enjoyable read from a most talented author!"

-William Rawlings, author of *A Killing on Ring Jaw Bluff*

"NASCAR fans will enjoy this raucous tale about Butterbean Sweat, the good ole boy race fan who lives for Dale Earnhardt Jr.'s next win and idolizes Bill Elliott, aka Awesome Bill from Dawsonville. I know a thing or two about Georgia rednecks and *Luck Be A Chicken* is on the money. Bean is in the fight of his life against his crooked boss in this well-written and fascinating story."

-Gordon Pirkle, President, Georgia Racing Hall of Fame, and owner, Dawsonville Pool Room

Luck Be A
CHICKEN

Jim & Frida –
Jim – Best down
golfer in north Georgia!

All Best wishes

Sam & Cy

Luck Be A
CHICKEN

a comic novel

Jameson Gregg

Published by Ignatius Publishing, Dahlonega, GA

Library of Congress Cataloging-in-Publications Data is available upon request.

ISBN 978-0-9985348-0-0

Second Edition

10 9 8 7 6 5 4 3 2 1

TO MAUREEN

Contents

To those aristocrats and tycoons who domineer,
it is not your like-kind whom you should fear.
'Tis we who live on a pittance—'Tis I,
upon whose toil and sweat you rely.

The spoils of your greed are guaranteed for life, it would appear,
but never let our drumbeats stop ringing in your ear.
"Rise up, rise up, my Brothers!" we will cry, for we are strong.
Surely mankind shall rally to end this reign of wrong.

But who amongst us will stand tall and lead the coup?
'Tis I, the Common Man, the salt of the earth, that's who.
But how will we know if we are kindred spirits?
A sure way to tell: He sings the Butter Bean lyrics.

Just a bowl o' butter beans
Pass the cornbread, if you please.
I don't want no collard greens,
Just a great big bowl o' butter beans!

PART 1:
HELL OR HIGH WATER

Chapter 1

*B*utterbean Sweat raced his forklift down the backstretch approaching the last turn before his sprint for the checkered flag. The burly driver leaned out of the cab like a crewman on a heeling sailboat and squalled his tires around the corner past the nugget line.

"Chaps my ass," Bean muttered as he checked his watch. *If them Mexicans beat me to the lunchroom, I ain't never gonna get a cold Co-Cola.*

The deafening metallic grind of the chicken plant's *dis*assembly line rumbled behind him. Trucks roll in with live, plump broilers before deft hands tear them asunder and dispatch their frozen parts to feed the global masses.

Bean screeched his lift to a halt at his workbench by the shipping dock and grabbed his brown-bag lunch. An extra TGIF spring in his step propelled him toward the lunchroom in his 3XL camo T-shirt. He glanced around for plant manager Wilbur then pulled a pouch of Red Man from his jean's back pocket and jammed home a chew between cheek and gum.

"El Gringo," Angelo the gizzard puller shouted as he strolled in the opposite direction, "ju gonna bet on Earnhardt this weekend, mi amigo?"

Bean pointed at the #88 Dale Earnhardt Jr. cap on his head. "Podnah, does a fat baby fart?"

He continued his trek and the lunch whistle blew. The disassembly line rattled to a halt. *Uh, oh, here they come.* He glanced at the fresh sign above the entrance printed in Spanish then English…

THIS LUNCHROOM IS A PRIVILEGE
NOT A RIGHT
IT WILL BE CLOSED IF
NOT KEPT CLEAN!

The room brimmed with plastic picnic tables for the multitudes—skin pullers, bone poppers, lung gunners. Management spied in real time through the camera inside the plastic bubble on the ceiling.

Bean leapt through the doorway just ahead of the human wave. First to the Coke machine. *Yeah, baby. Victory Lane.*

"El Gringo," co-workers hailed. Bean inserted his dollar and a cold Coca-Cola rolled into his meaty palm. *Bingo.* He turned and nudged his way against the flow. Comrades pointed, patted his back, and whispered, *"Gracias, gracias."*

"Sweat, where are you?" The plant manager's voice rang out as he clawed through the crowd. Wilbur emerged with his haggard scowl and bad comb-over. Rage seethed in his good eye as he shook a blood-red paper in Bean's face.

"Look a-here, Sweat, this is a code red. Final warning. Next time you refuse to work overtime, you're fired. *Adios,* El Gringo." Translators whispered and a hush fell over the room. Wilbur clenched the paper in his fist and glared at Bean.

"Dammit, stupid, I just got my ass chewed over this. You ain't gettin' paid time-and-a-half. I don't care if you work a hundred-hour week."

Bean flushed and narrowed his eyes into slits. "This ain't just about me. We all deserve it, *and* law says you got to pay us time-'n-a-half if you work us over forty hours, and you know it."

Wilbur pointed his nicotine-stained finger an inch from Bean's nose. "Get the wax outta your ears, son. One more code red and I'll have the pleasure o' firing your ass. Lose your job and guess what? You'll never be able to afford to get your baby girl a..." Wilbur jabbed his finger into Bean's chest, "... club..." Jab. "... foot..." Jab. "... operation."

"You sumbitch," Bean growled. "Leave my baby outta this. And stop pokin' me or I'll rearrange your face."

"Oh yeah? You and whose army?" He shoved Bean's chest.

Bean pivoted and cocked his fist to deck Wilbur once and for all, job be damned. Co-workers clamped on and restrained him. "No, El Gringo, *mucho problema.*"

Wilbur crammed the warning into Bean's T-shirt pocket then wheeled, and a sea of immigrants parted as he stormed toward the exit. He whirled and pointed at Bean. "One more thing. I'm writin' your sorry ass up for chewin' tobacco inside the plant."

Bean grumbled as Wilbur stomped away. Bewildered Latino faces turned toward El Gringo. He snatched the paper from his pocket and fluffed his T-shirt where his boss had poked him then hollered, "I'll slap you so hard, make you forget who your mama is, you whomp-eyed, butt-kissin' cheeseball."

Chapter 2

Bean escaped the south Georgia dog-day afternoon sun in the long shadow of his singlewide. He shifted his blubbery bottom on a rotting bench seat from a long-ago pickup and bounced his baby daughter on his knee.

"Yeah, baby!" Bean whooped. "GO, JUNIOR, GO!"

Li'l Bit chomped her pacifier and giggled. He tightened his grip on her shoulder and reached for his tiny TV perched on a lawn chair. Quarter-sized rolls bunched tight across the back of his neck, and perspiration rolled down his arm. He cranked the volume, fighting to hear NASCAR's roar over the surround-sound of window unit air conditioners.

His BBQ charcoals smoldered. The aroma of cumin-laced pinto beans and sautéing onions wafted from the Mexican's trailer across the dirt cul-de-sac. El Gringo raised his nose and sniffed. His mouth watered—Sunday ritual in the Garden of Eden Trailer Park.

He studied the face of his ten-month-old baby, and she returned love with her big, hazel eyes. "Baby Girl, we gonna load our grill with chicken and cover it with Mama's special sauce, and our smoke'll show them dummies who's boss."

"Da-da-da." Li'l Bit flapped her arms.

"Now, Baby, listen up." He goosed her ribs with his paw as big as her torso. She cackled and pushed his hand away.

"Mr. Dale Earnhardt Junior is 'bout to go on a big-time winnin' streak, and Daddy's gonna win enough so we can get your foot fixed real soon, no matter what that mean man Wilbur says.

Ain't that right, Baby Girl?" He tickled the bare bottom of her good foot, and she spit out her pacifier and squealed.

Bean cupped her tiny clubfoot in his palm. Her foot twisted downward and inward, creating a sharp angle with her ankle resembling a nine-iron with toes. He released her foot, stared into her eyes, and stroked her wispy brown hair. He fought back tears and forced a smile while bouncing her on his restless leg.

He lowered Li'l Bit to the bench, struggled to his feet, then scooped up his giggling daughter and plopped her onto his hip. Pacing the yard, he whispered in her ear. "Daddy loves you, Baby. We all love ya. You our saint. You perfect and beautiful in every way. We don't care what nobody says, ya here?"

The bedroom AC sputtered and gurgled down, and the plastic window sash flew open. "Bean, you've had a case o' the jitters all weekend. You ready to tell me what in the blue blazes is yo' problem?" Ruby Sweat's silhouette dwarfed the window, reminding him of Jabba the Hut on his throne.

Li'l Bit perched atop bad news on the red paper crumpled in the pocket of his threadbare cut-off jeans. Bean couldn't put off telling his wife any longer. He scowled, socked his camo cap on backward, and turned down the TV.

"Honey…" He felt sorry for her, for what he had to confess, for what she was going through. The knife in his stomach twisted. Bile rose and burned his throat. He doused it with Budweiser.

He squeezed Li'l Bit tight to his chest, raised his clenched fist, and shouted over grinding window units. "Ruby, I'm gonna kill that sumbitch, Calvin Butler, with my bare hands."

"You hush up. You ain't killin' nobody. And stop cussin' on Sunday. Baby Girl's hearin' every word you say. With that last raise, you makin' good money. Who else is gonna pay that much to somebody who ain't got no technical trainin'? You bess not mess it up. Now what in God's name did ya do this time?"

Li'l Bit rode his hip as he lumbered hangdog to the window. "Here, take Baby for a while."

Ruby popped the screen off its hinges and pulled it inside. Bean passed Li'l Bit through the window then pulled Majestic

Chicken's final warning from his pocket and handed it over. The sash slammed, and the light within lit up.

He slumped back down on his bench seat to duck and cover from Ruby's fury, his mind roiling like a lava lamp.

She ain't gonna be happy.

Chapter 3

Ruby tossed Bean's crumpled paper onto the bedside table. She laid Li'l Bit on the bed and exhaled a heavy sigh. "Baby Girl, we got to see what Daddy done this time, but Lawdy, we got to clean you up first. Funny how Daddy hands you over every time you got a full diaper."

She spread a towel on the bed, and her skillful hands freshened Li'l Bit. She kissed her daughter on the forehead before settling the cooing child into the crib at the foot of the bed.

"Baby, it's nap time. There's milk left in yo' bottle. You drink then lay down and sleep, ya hear?"

Ruby un-balled her husband's red paper, tumbled back onto the bed, and propped pillows under her knees. Sun glaring through the blinds cast prison bars across her sheets. The window unit and oscillating fan couldn't plug her perspiration, and she was in desperate need of a catnap.

Dang you, Bean. Why in tarnation are you always gettin' in trouble?

She fished dime store reading glasses from the drawer. Her white pound puppy, Slippers, part toy poodle/part mystery breed, snuggled her side. She stroked her dog's dense, curly fur with one hand and held up the crinkled paper with the other. "CODE RED—FINAL WARNING" blazed across the top.

Clink, clink, clink arose from the crib. Li'l Bit's tiny voice sang in rhythm with the drumbeat of her spoon on her pot. "Ba-ba-da-da."

"Quiet now, Baby. Go to sleep."

Bang, bang. "Ooo-ooo-ooo."

"Li'l Bit, please. Let Mama read."

Wham, wham, wham.

Lawd o' mussy. What am I gonna do? 'Tween Bean and these young'uns, they's killin' me.

Ruby grabbed her inhaler from the windowsill, lipped it, and pumped twice. Like a seal dragging across dry land, she struggled to scoot to the end of the mattress and peered into the crib. Li'l Bit stopped drumming, and her gaze riveted on Ruby. Her eyes looked more like her father's every day.

"It's okay, Baby Girl," Ruby whispered. She slipped the pacifier into her infant's mouth, slid the wooden spoon from her hand, and picked her up.

Li'l Bit clutched her stuffed dinosaur and clamped onto her mother's side. Ruby crawled back to her valley in the mattress. The toddler nestled into Ruby's portside, and Slippers circled then flopped down at her starboard.

"Cover your ears, Baby... JUNIOR." The trailer walls rattled.

The bedroom door swung open, and Junior peeked around the corner, a miniature version of Bean with copper-penny hair and cheeks packed with Gummy Bears. "Whut?"

"How many times I got to tell ya to turn that dern TV down? You gonna be deaf as a doorknob."

"Yes, Mama."

"Take the slop bucket, and you and Daddy go feed his worms."

"But Mama, cain't I wait 'til a commercial? Big lions is huntin' them African deers."

"Okay, Angel, you can wait 'til the next commercial, but don't forget."

"I won't forget, Mama."

"And turn that TV down," she hollered as Junior closed the door.

Ruby patted Li'l Bit's head. "Everything's gonna be fine, Baby Girl..." She hit her inhaler and held up Bean's blood-red paper. "... unless your Daddy messes everything up again."

Chapter 4

*B*ean feared for Ruby, the threat of being fired looming large. *If Li'l Bit cain't get her operation soon, Ruby's gonna have a heart attack… or give me one.*

He knew how to cope with anxiety. *This is Sunday, after all, and God told us to rest. No more worryin'.* He took a slug of Budweiser and fired up a Marlboro. Sweating like a block of ice in the oppressive heat, he wiped his face and slung his hand. Mosquitoes buzzed his kidney-bean ears.

Elvis, his scrawny, mongrel yarddog, lounged in shaded dirt under the trailer, ambling out from time-to-time to drink from the kids' inflated pool. His lids hung at half-mast over bloodshot eyes, and his muzzle sported a fresh, port-wine gouge. Small price to pay for being the canine Casanova of the Garden of Eden.

Bean returned to NASCAR Nation and cranked the volume. The TV displayed more snow than show, and its raspy speaker fared no better. Illegally-spliced cable wrapped in camo tape snaked from under his bedroom window. He emptied a potato chip bag into his mouth, dregs fluttering down his face, and squinted at the screen.

Oh, yeah, baby! Dale Earnhardt Jr. was in the hunt and running strong. Bean fist pumped the sky.

Their air conditioner whined down, and Ruby's window snapped open.

"Why in tarnation are you always gettin' in trouble?"

"Butler kin kiss my ass. Oh, s'cuse me, it's Sunday. The bastard kin smooch my buttocks."

"If you don't stop cussin' 'round these young'uns…"

"Yep, his fancy warnin' system he learnt in college. Ten years and ain't never graduated. He can take his code red and stick it you know where."

"That attitude ain't gonna do yo' family no good."

"I'm pissed off, and I'm meetin' with Butler hisself after work tomorrow." He rocketed tobacco juice into the weeds. "Wilbur give me the paper Friday in the lunchroom so everybody could see. That plant used to run so smooth under old man Butler his dog coulda run it. He give the company to his son on a silver platter and the boy screws it up in five years. The old man would o' just sit ya down and talked it through. Now, cain't nobody even get near this punk's office or you get a warnin'."

"Bean, you listen to me. Don't you meet with Butler tomorrow. You gonna get fired, I can feel it."

"But I got to meet him. Since insurance won't pay to fix Li'l Bit's foot, overtime is our best chance o' raisin' the money. Butler just up and decided he weren't gonna pay overtime. It ain't legal, and it ain't right."

"You just gonna have to start workin' overtime for reg'lar pay like he orders. Lawd knows, we lose health insurance and we in big trouble. Plus, reg'lar pay sho' beat *no* pay. You done applied for every forklift job in town that carries insurance and ain't nobody hirin'."

Ruby raised the palm of one hand as a stop sign against his speaking while her other hand jammed the inhaler between her lips and pumped. "The doctor said Baby shoulda had treatments when she was one month old, when her bones and joints were real flexible. She'll be a year old in a couple o' months, and we still ain't done nuthin' 'bout it. Now she's gonna have to get an operation or else be a cripple for life. She'll be wantin' to walk soon and it's gonna be pitiful. You lose yo' job and it's only gonna be worse."

He pulled his last drag, toed out the butt in the dirt, and exhaled a cloud. "You ain't listenin'. Everybody's dependin' on me to fight this. Them folks at the plant cain't fight it since they don't speak no English. I got to do it for all of us. We all family at Majestic Chicken."

"They playin' you for a fool, Butterbean Sweat. They speak mo' English than they let on, and you know it."

"Honey, Cuz told me—"

"Hold on…" Ruby torqued and yelled. "Junior, I done told ya to turn that TV down… Whut? Wha'chu say?"

"Bean, you stay put. I'll be right back. That boy's gettin' a switchin'." Her window slapped shut and she shuffled away.

Dammit. He chugged his beer, smashed the empty can in his palms, and hurled it at the garbage can.

Chapter 5

*B*ean flagged in the scorching heat awaiting Ruby's return. He rose from the bench seat, paced the small yard, and gnawed his fingernails. Ham-sized biceps jutted from his sleeveless camo T-shirt wringing wet with perspiration, tufts of hair extending northward beyond the neckline. *It's hotter'n a jalapeño enema even in the shade.*

He couldn't concentrate on NASCAR… *fired from the chicken plant, lost pay, egg on my face, the hassle.* He smelled fight or flight, felt it oozing from his neck and pits. *I hate that sour smell.*

Elvis's gaze followed Bean's every move, his ears perked on high alert. He squatted on his haunches, panting tongue hassling away August's sweltering heat. His paws scratched, and his muzzle darted to his hindquarters, bared teeth gnawing skin, one step behind the fleas' covert advances.

Bean lifted his Chevy camo cap and raked his hand over his stubbled scalp, dispatching sweat down his back. Time was, Bean sported the finest mullet in the county, but Ruby gradually clipped his fins. His buzz-cut now resembled cinnamon dust.

Perspiration streamed down the hills and valleys of his legs' doughy terrain before disappearing into untied hunting boots. Citronella bug spray pulled double duty against the blitzkrieg of mosquitoes and reeking B.O.

He peered through the bedroom window, and his gaze followed Ruby's shuffle and her dejected flop onto the bed. He gulped Bud and squinted at the TV to check Earnhardt's standing. Before he could get a race update, Ruby's window whipped open. Her narrowed eyes flashed.

"Why does that boy always push me to the limit? Sometimes I think he's dumber than them worms you grow."

"As I was tellin' ya, Cuz told me Butler's got to pay us time-'n-a-half for overtime when ya work more'n forty hours. He told me we'd have a purty good shot at winnin' the case."

"Yo' cousin gonna let us go live with him when you get fired? He ain't nuthin' but a traffic court judge who don't know a law book from a cook book."

"Cuz knows more'n you think. 'Sides, I ain't so sure I want my job, anyway. I'd rather starve than fight them rats. I seen one the other day big as a coon and twice as mean. And Butler still ain't fix the roof leak."

"Everybody's roof leaks sometime. You don't think them Mexicans at the plant is afraid o' gettin' they backs wet, do ya?"

"Fun-ee. I done told ya, the leak's right over the packagin' line, and there's a million pigeons live on that roof. You like your chicken seasoned with pigeon poop?"

"Then what you 'bout to cook on that grill? Surely with all them gub'mint inspectors y'all got, they's watchin' to see the chickens is clean, don't you think?"

"Them inspectors is half-ass on a good day. If 'roof leak' ain't on they job description, they look the other way. All I know is, Wilbur claims everything's legal. He's such a brown-noser. Things is awful in that plant, and here I am feedin' them same chickens to my family. Maybe I *am* a fool, like you say."

"It ain't gonna matter when you get fired."

"If Butler fires me, *everybody'll* walk off the job and we'll shut him down. We'll get one o' your refrigerator-magnet lawyers, and we'll *own* us a chicken plant."

"Bean, don't be stupid. You think all them Mexicans and Vietnamese is gonna strike to support *you*? You think they gonna walk away from they paycheck and health insurance *for you*? They got families to think about. You better wake up and think about *yo'* family. You lose yo' job, and the wolves'll be knockin' at the door 'fore the month is out. You thirty years old now, and you need to start actin' your age."

He considered Ruby's words, pinched off the filter of a Marlboro, and fired it up. "Who cares? If he fires me, I could be a travelin' beef jerky salesman like that feller asked me that time at Git-N-Split."

"Punkin', if you was sellin' beef jerky, you'd eat all the profit. I done told ya, you ain't cut out for sales."

"Then I'll go to raisin' worms full time. Turn the whole side of our plot into a worm farm. I been figurin' how much money we could make."

"If all you do is sit 'round drinkin' beer and waitin' on yo' worms to grow, you couldn't make enough to pay for the beer, much less health insurance. You just gotta stay at the chicken plant and put it in God's hands."

"*God?* Where is God? Our baby daughter cain't get clubfoot treatments 'cause we cain't afford it, and now she needs surgery 'cause we waited so long. American doctors is travelin' to foreign countries fixin' clubfeet for free, but they won't do it in they own back yard? There ain't no God that's got time for the likes o' us."

"You think every unfair thing is God's fault. What about Satan? They's always a tuggin' match 'tween 'em. You got to do yo' best for yo' own life, and in the end, we all God's people and He shall prevail."

"Then what's *He* waitin' on?"

"We got a roof over our heads, ain't we? You thank the Lawd for what we got, and quit blamin' Him for what we ain't. The quicker you get that through your thick skull, the quicker things may get better 'round here."

Bean sighed and shook his head. *Oh, Jesus Gawd, if You is real and You up there, hep me get through this. We gettin' screwed down here, but she don't get it. Please don't never let her get it. Amen.*

"The coals is hot. I gotta put the chicken on."

A man's work ain't never done.

Chapter 6

Ruby landed on her bed with confidence that it would not give way. The first time she lay on it right out of the box, its reinforced support frame collapsed like a cheap umbrella. King box springs and mattress now rested flush on the master bedroom's floor, wedged into a corner and leaving a narrow path along which to maneuver. No regular particleboard floor for this trailer. Two layers of three-quarter inch plywood lay atop columns upon columns of cinderblock.

Her fretting mind sank into depression quicksand. Careful not to squish Li'l Bit or Slippers, she reached into the bedside chest and retrieved her chocolate chip cookies. She propped her shoulders on pillows, dug out a fistful, and munched one after another, her mind rapt in ecstasy. Feeding her sugar addiction triggered an endorphin flood and a sense of well-being she so craved. *Bye-bye anxiety. Hello warm inner glow.* She plundered another fistful.

Li'l Bit giggled as she and Slippers pawed at one another.

Ruby held out a cookie. "Here, Baby, you can have one, too."

Li'l Bit snatched the cookie and into her mouth it went in one seamless motion.

"Baby Girl, believe it or not, there's a skinny girl livin' inside me dyin' to get out. Doctor says Mama's got a granular problem and he promised he's gonna fix it."

Ruby clapped. Baby clapped.

"Soon we gonna have your operation, and you gonna be the fastest runnin' gal in school."

Ruby clapped. Baby clapped.

"Come on, let's try to nap-nap one mo' time. Maybe nobody won't wake us up this time." She raised her knees and feet onto pillows. Gout aggravated her joints. She tried every lotion and potion in a heavyweight bout against pain, desperate enough to try snake oil.

"Now lookie here, Baby, Mama needs to rest. You lay still and be real quiet, you hear?"

Ruby reached and twirled the rod on the blinds toward darkness and switched on her blue Zen light. She hit the clock radio's button and gospel music rang forth. *Drown out the noises and get into The Word.* She hummed along... *Angels is goin' to fly me to the Promised Land, fly me to the Promised Land...*

She inhaled deep and slow while stroking Slippers' coat—blood pressure lowering techniques she learned from *Oprah*. She stared at the Dale Earnhardt Sr. poster through eyelid slits and regretted the day she agreed to let Bean decorate the bedroom. *Thank the Lawd I decorate the rest of the trailer.*

Posters of the Daniels Family—Charlie and Jack—flanked Dale's poster. From the other wall, Dusty Rhodes, "The American Dream," decked out in red leather jacket and black Stetson, stared her down from a framed, autographed photo, a souvenir from Bean's birthday bash a few years back at a professional wrestling match.

Bean's most prized possession loomed overhead—the shoulder mount of an eight-point white-tail buck. *Why would anyone keep a dead animal in the bedroom? 'Sides, it cost us a whole week's pay to stuff that dern deer.*

A soft, blue glow lit the popcorned ceiling and danced off luminescent speckles embedded in the paint. Ruby gazed upward and slid into religious bliss, floating in the gentle sky.

She willed the gospel music and the AC's moan to drown out Bean's TV on her left, soccer-playing Mexicans on her right, and Junior's TV blaring through the living room wall straight at her head.

She laid one hand on Li'l Bit and the other on Slippers, closed her eyes, and as she lay suspended in dreamland, the gravity of the Michelin around her midriff stressed and strained her organs in a squeeze play.

A rap at the window startled her.

Dang you, Bean, you worse than a chil'. She sucked her inhaler and, mindful of Li'l Bit and Slippers, struggled to roll and rise to a seated position. She cracked the blinds and unwelcome sunlight flooded the bedroom. Peeking out, she saw the backwards cap on Bean's tree-stump head and his eyes gleaming from his moon-pie face.

"Open up."

She raised the blinds then unlatched and lifted the sash. "Wha'chu want? I got to rest. My knees is killin' me. I'm in a delicate way—I ain't had a BM all weekend. I got a fountain o' youth facial and four hair appointments tomorrow. I'm slap wo' out, and it ain't even Monday. Now what is it?"

"Got good news I ain't told you 'bout."

"It better be good."

"I got me a new account for my worms. One o' them Pawtell families bought the American Mart. I talked 'em into sellin' worms. I just made me a new sign." Beaming with artistic pride, he stepped back and held it up…

A smile crept across Ruby's face as she studied the poster. Li'l Bit popped up to see what the excitement was about. "Lawd, Bean, you gettin' better every time."

Li'l Bit bounced on her knees and laughed, "Chee-chee-oo." Slippers barked, "Yip, yip."

Bean pushed his bear paw hand around the screen and patted Li'l Bit's head. "That's right, Baby Girl. Daddy's takin' care of bidness."

"Bean, you lettin' skeeters in. Get yo' big arm outta' here."

He withdrew it, and Ruby jimmied the screen. She studied his sign again. "Wait a minute, we ain't got no thousand dollars to pay no re-ward."

"Think 'bout it." A philosopher's grin spread across his mug. "How's a fish gonna say what a worm taste like?"

"I don't know, I ain't never heard no fish talk."

"Egg-zackly. I done figured this thing out I'm tellin' ya."

"Since you done figured it out, when we pay off the dinette set, we need to buy Li'l Bit a real bed. This crib's to' up, and she's 'bout to outgrow it."

"Aw, Ruby. Cain't it wait a little while longer? I been lookin' at this used four-wheeler. I was thinkin' Santy Claus could bring it to Junior. We sho' could use it for huntin'."

"You gonna get a four-wheeler and send yo' eight-year-old boy high tailin' it 'round this neighborhood to get hit by some drunk driver. That's real good thinkin' on yo' part. Meantime, yo' daughter cain't even get no proper bed, much less get her foot surgery. This girl needs her own bed, and it's time she moved out of our bedroom."

Ruby watched as her words sank in and as his shoulders slumped. "Where is this four-wheeler, anyway?"

"Elmer's got it at Toot-Toot Motors."

"Good ole Honest Elmer, huh? Ain't his secret motto 'You can fool some o' the people all the time, and them's the ones we want?'"

"I'd just love for the boy to have a four-wheeler, that's all. I been wantin' one all my life, too."

"Bean, have you lost yo' mind? You know we savin' every penny for Li'l Bit's surgery. Only way I can see we can afford to fix her foot *and* buy a four-wheeler is for my case to settle. I'm gonna' call that dern lawyer first thing in the mornin' and find out what's happenin'. Prob'ly nuthin'."

Chapter 7

Sunday shadows lengthened, and like clockwork, Latinos gathered in the dirt cul-de-sac beside the Sweat trailer, turning it into a raucous MexFest soccer pitch. Spanglish chatter grew rowdy. *Machismo* trumpets blasting from a boom box grated in Bean's ears. To him, it was the sound of his failure, his inability to afford a place in the woods where they could live in peace.

Geeze-us. Chaps my ass them jalapeños choose my street to play in every stinkin' Sunday. They better not steal Ruby's hubcaps again.

Bean's action was on Dale Earnhardt Jr., #88, like all his other NASCAR bets. Oh, the Earnhardts...*can Dale Jr. ever live up to his daddy's success? Why did God take Dale Sr. anyway? 'Cause He needed a personal driver, that's why.* He tumbled back down on his seat and glanced at the race standings.

"Good-Gawd-Amighty! Junior's runnin' third!" *If he wins, we'll have groceries for a week. If he don't, my bookie'll be huntin' me, assumin' Ruby don't find out I'm bettin' and kill me first. Yessir, an Earnhardt runnin' strong on Sunday afternoon calls for a beer.*

He struggled off the bench seat, weaved around the satellite dish, and lumbered toward his chariot, a half-ton pickup—black, in Dale Sr.'s honor—sporting oversized mud tires and dual exhaust. "Mossy Oak" film covered the rear window camouflaging his gun rack. Decals covered the bumper and tailgate then turned the corner and crept up the side like kudzu.

They were fine looking wheels from afar, but upon approach, factory stench pervaded, a pungent reek from the ghosts of thirty million chickens. He fortified the bouquet each time he crawled in after a shift at Majestic. Dozens of deodorizer bombs and dangling spruce trees later, the odor was more stubborn than Ruby's gout.

Ruby's rusted red Lincoln with its donut spare tire languished beside Bean's pickup. A thick wrapping of Georgia Chrome covered holes in its muffler and a "Honk for Jesus" sticker adorned the rear bumper.

He lifted the lid of his truck bed's metal toolbox, opened the cooler hidden inside, and seized a Bud. He poured while studying his neighbor's dark bedroom window, the distance between the two singlewides less than a horseshoe pitch. He sensed the old goat peering from inside the shadows of his snooping post.

The neighbor's name was one of those foreign-sounding names with three or four syllables, so the Sweats settled on "The Ole Man."

Bean whipped his head to look into The Ole Man's den window. *Caught you, dirty ole pervert.* The silhouette of his neighbor's head disappeared in a flash.

Bean drained the can, crushed it, and stashed the evidence from Ruby the Baptist. He raised his Bud to the fading tribute Ruby had painted in silver nail polish on the driver's door...

He hustled back to the TV to crank up NASCAR's sonic boom. *Whack.* His snooping neighbor's window slammed open against its casing.

"SWEAT." The neighbor's graveled voice irked Bean. "Turn that damn thing down 'fore I call the cops."

Bean swung around and spotted The Ole Man's scowling face framed by a small, screenless window. An ancient eye patch sat askew and stretched around thin, greasy hair strands, matted and swirling on the side of his bed head. A tell-tale red crease etched The Ole Man's pale cheek revealing his recent whereabouts on the Naugahyde couch. Oxygen tubes snaked up his nostrils. He reminded Bean of Oscar the Grouch, the Muppet who lives in a trash can.

"Good mornin' to you, too, ole codger," Bean barked.

"I ain't kiddin'," The Ole Man snarled. "I'm gonna call the cops right now."

Bean stomped over. "First off, why don't you straighten that eye patch and cover up that hole in your head 'fore I hurl all over your trailer." A Marlboro danced between his lips as he spoke. "I'm gonna plug a cat-eye marble in it next time. Second, how you gonna call the cops when you ain't got no phone?"

"The hell I don't. I'm lookin' at it right now," The Ole Man screeched.

"They done cut it off two months ago, you ole fool."

"I don't give a damn, I'll call 'em anyway, you tub o' lard."

"Then go ahead and call 'em, you geezer, and I'll call 'em on you."

"Ye' ain't got a damn thing on me, son."

"The hell I don't. How 'bout I call 'em next time you too drunk to roll your wheelchair up that ramp? Let *them* push you for a while."

"I cain't help the idiot built my ramp too steep, but that ain't your worry."

"Maybe I tell 'em you been spyin' on little boys. Uh-huh, we'll see if you kin push that wheelchair home from the jailhouse, draggin' that oxygen tank behind ya."

"Oh, yeah. That's bullshit and you know it, Sweat. How 'bout I tell 'em you runnin' an illegal hair cuttin' business outta your trailer?"

Bean's face flushed and he shook his clenched fist. "You do that and you'll regret it, buster, I gar-ron-tee."

"Just turn that damn TV down. Cain't nobody get no sleep around here. You'll be sorry when I call the cops." The sash slammed with a *bam.*

Damn him. How dare him threaten to shut Ruby down. Why cain't folks just leave us the hell alone?

"Good Gawd, Junior's leadin'!" Chill bumps popped up his arms and scalp. He gyrated his tubby hips in a victory dance. "Luck be a Earnhardt."

Little E is winnin' the race. Tomorrow, I'm gonna win overtime back at the plant. Hey, hey, all the chips is comin' my way. Li'l Bit's gonna get her operation come hell or high water.

Chapter 8

The pride of lions worked as a team, stalking an impala herd on the Tanzanian plains of east Africa. The predators crept downwind, maneuvering behind sparse clumps of grass, bellies low and shoulder blades high.

Driven by kill-or-starve instinct, some lionesses lay in wait while others charged, stampeding the quarry towards ambush. Impala sprinted at thirty mph, weaving and leaping like ballerinas as graceful as their S-curved horns.

Junior sprawled in the luxury of his beanbag chair facing a forty-two-inch flat screen in the darkened living room of the trailer. His jaw hung agog, his lips painted Cheetos orange. He was mesmerized as he watched the pride work the herd. He leaned forward and popped more Gummy Bears.

Lionesses plotted to separate mother impala and calf from the herd. The hunters' charges created chaos for the faster impala. The cats tag-teamed in the chase, another always a few paces back, wearing down the prey, until… commercial break.

Rolling off the beanbag onto his knees, Junior grunted as he shoved up and slid into worn-thin flip-flops. He scuffed to the kitchen, opened the door under the sink, and grabbed the slop bucket. Raking his Cheetos-stained fingers through the bowl on the table, he snagged a fistful of cocktail peanuts.

He waddled to the aluminum front door and swung it open then stepped onto the stoop and shielded his eyes from the glaring summer sun a world away from the carnage on Tanzania's plains.

He performed a cautious, splayfooted, flip-flop shuffle toward the steps until his eyes acclimated. A flattop haircut accentuated dime-sized rolls padding the back of his neck.

The worm bucket swung as he lumbered down three wooden steps. His white underbelly peeked out and bounced below his camo shirt. The sun glistened off his flaming-red hair and bore down on a face splashed with freckles. He plodded through dirt and weeds toward Diddy, his meaty thighs rubbing together and his short, chunky toes overhanging his slides. He shook peanuts in his fist like dice and shot more into his mouth every few steps to top up the cud.

Diddy sat on the bench seat sipping from his cup, smoking a cigarette, and watching the race. *Prob'ly a Marlboro and Budweiser, the King o' Beers.*

He felt a pang of gas swelling in his nether regions. He squeezed his sphincter, dropped the worm bucket, and waddled on stilted legs toward his father.

"Diddy, Diddy, listen," he cried. *Whommp.* "That there's a ten," he hollered in his high, squeaky voice.

"That weren't no ten, Sugah. No way. I'll give you a five."

"I bet you couldn't poot that good when you was my age."

"You're wrong 'bout dat, son. I told ya, Grampa taught me how to cut 'em good and he won the fartin' contest at the county fair three years runnin'. The newspaper even wrote a story 'bout it. On your tenth birthday, I'm s'posed to pass the secret on to you."

"I know, Diddy, you done told me a hun-ert times. How 'bout a nine?"

"I'll give you an eight but you can do better. Now, if you wanna know what a ten sounds like, listen up."

Diddy pushed up from the seat, wheeled around, and perched on his knees. He bent over the seat's back and pointed his rear end like a Civil War canon. "You got to spread your legs just right... not too wide, not too close. You got to make your butt cheeks act like the reeds o' that duck call we got."

Silence, silence... "Listen now." He let fly one for the ages with excellent and sustained volume. It resonated through the trailer park like a bull moose during mating season. Junior fell to the ground laughing, holding his jellyrolls. The entire zone instantly smelled like an overturned septic truck.

Junior coughed and staggered to stand. He turned and scampered away, calling over his shoulder, "I'll give you a nine on that one, Diddy."

"When you kin top that, Son, I'll put my money on you, and we goin' to Hollywood."

He returned after the toxic plume dissipated. "That was a good un, Diddy."

"I think I burnt my underdrawers on that one." Diddy pointed to the TV. "Look, Sugah, guess who's winnin' the race."

Jiggling his peanuts, Junior glanced at the screen. "Dale Earnhardt?"

"Dale Earnhardt, *who?*"

Junior extended his doughboy arm and spread his sweaty palm. "Yon't some peanuts, Diddy?"

"No thanks, Sugah, I got me some in the truck. Now Dale Earnhardt, *who?*"

Junior threw his head back, drained the peanuts into his mouth, and wiped his hand on his shirt. He mumbled through packed jowls, "Dale Earnhardt, *Junior.*"

"Hot dog, boy, yer gettin' it." Diddy set down his beer and clapped. "I knowed you was gonna be a smart one. Our man is kickin' butt today. That's who you was named after, Sugah. You both named Junior."

"I know that, Diddy." He knew Diddy wanted to name him "Junior," as Dale Sr. named his son. Mama told him that in the excitement at the hospital, the birth certificate came out as "Junior Sweat." It should have been Darryl David Sweat Jr. He was eight now but Diddy hadn't gotten around to straightening out the paperwork with the government.

"I seen you got the worm bucket."

"Yep. Mama asked me to bring it to ya."

"You wanna feed 'em during a commercial?"

"Sure, Diddy."

During the next race commercial, father and son puttered to the trailer's far side. "Listen Sugah, some day I want you to take over the worm operation. With fishin', sometimes the wigglers is hot and sometimes the crawlers is hot. There's money in this but you got to keep your worms happy."

"How do you do that, Diddy?"

"You got to *think* like a worm. Always put yourself in they position, day and night, summer and winter. You got that?"

"Yes, Diddy."

At worm headquarters, Diddy reached under the trailer, unlocked the chain snaking around two fiberglass bath tubs, and slid off the sheet metal cover. Junior dumped half the bucket over the red wigglers and half over the night crawlers…

Chicken bones and apple core,
tore up poster of Al Gore.

Plate scrapin's and coffee grinds,
egg shells and watermelon rinds.

They covered the tubs and returned to the race. "Diddy, when we goin' huntin' again?"

Diddy ruffled Junior's flattop. "Huntin' season opens in a couple o' months and I'm building us a special stand at Fat Back Hunt Club. You and me's gonna be there for your first Openin' Day, Sugah. We gonna get us a big un this year. An eight-pointer, you wait 'n see. Now, where's your sister?"

"'Sleep with Mama."

"How's Mama?"

"She's aw-ight. Layin' on her bed."

"When you gonna learn to change Li'l Bit's diaper?"

"Diddy, I don't know how to change no diaper."

"What'cha watchin' on TV?"

"A nature show. Them lions is 'bout to catch one of them African deer babies."

"You hongry, Boy?"

"I'm real hongry, Diddy. When we gonna eat?"

"We'll eat directly. You got any school lessons?"

"Nah. I done my English, and I ain't got no more homework. I got to git 'cause them lions is 'bout to pig out."

Chapter 9

Ruby slipped back into bed for her last chance to nap. Li'l Bit and Slippers cozied her port and starboard. Her mouth draped open, and she snored like a foghorn as blessed pain relief engulfed her.

Ruby woke to the gentle touch of Li'l Bit shaking her leg, each push a pebble rippling a pond of flesh.

"Whut, Baby? You ready to get up? Mama don't feel good. I got to check my vitals. Just sit tight for a minute then we'll see 'bout yo' diaper."

Ruby struggled to sit upright, switched on the lamp, and grabbed her blood pressure cuff. She hit the button to inflate then release the cuff velcroed around her arm. Waiting for the readout, she stared at silver duct tape on the wall fluttering in the window unit's cool breeze. It hid a jagged hole where a grab bar once lived.

There ain't nuthin' that man cain't fix with Georgia Chrome...

Crack in the cabinet door, hole in the kitchen floor,
Busted window pane, roof leak against the rain.

Water pipe, toilet seat, extension cord,
Chair leg, coffee mug, Junior's skateboard.

The cuff's beep startled her, and she read the digital display. *Lawd o' mussy.* She separated the blinds and peeked out. She scanned the yard and spotted Bean putzing around his pickup.

She slid her window open and shouted. "Bean, come over here."

He ambled over, shaking his head. "Wha'chu want? I'm busy."

"Punkin', my blood pressure's done got up on me. Think you could cook the peas and Texas Toast?"

"No problem-o. I'll be happy to come inside in the air conditionin', but you and your lapdog haf'ta come out here in this heat and cook the chicken."

"Butterbean Sweat, you kiss my big white behiney." Ruby slammed the sash.

"Baby Girl, I'm sorry I done talked bad on Sunday. Maybe the Lawd will forgive me. I don't know what we gonna do with Daddy. Things sho' run a lot smoother 'round here when he's at work."

Chapter 10

Rust claimed the grill's underbelly and hot drippings joined the petrified gray stalagmite mountain below—a new periodic table element in the making...

Animal gore, fat, and blood,
BBQ sauce, ash, and Bud.

Morton Salt sleeted as Bean practiced his chefery, flipping chicken parts, his endorphins flowing and his mouth watering. Time for BBQ sauce—regular on one half, butt-burner hot on the other. His left hand slung Ruby's sauce while his right wielded a long-handled brush, painting with the skill of Norman Rockwell. Globs from the grill's belly plopped below.

Elvis haunched downwind of the grill, drooling and punchy with optimism. Bean periodically snapped his tongs at him to keep the beast at bay.

He replaced the top, and pungent smoke belched from all sides as if she were about to blow, tipping the scales in Sunday's battle for aromatic supremacy.

Take that, you chili-chompin' beaners.

Ten laps to go and #88 Dale Jr. held fast the lead. "Yeah, baby. Bring it home, Junior."

Across the road, the Mexicans' Ford roared to life and backfired. Bean flinched. The car belched and settled into a thundering idle. *Damn car's lost its muffler again.*

Elvis's ears shot up at the backfire. Hair on his thick neck bristled as he crept to the road's edge like a stalking lion—belly low, shoulder blades high. A guttural growl rumbled in his throat and oozed through clenched teeth and quivering lips as he poised for a surrogate INS raid.

Bean relished his great social experiment—counting how many Mexicans packed into the clunker. He danced a fleet-footed waltz past the satellite dish and around the corner then sidestepped Ruby's Lincoln in time to glimpse them piling in. *Six, maybe seven, too many young'uns to be sure.*

The Ford sputtered like a two-penny airplane, roared, lurched onto the dirt road, and blasted off. Four open windows exuded *bambinos'* caramel elbows and ebony hair glistening in the sun.

Elvis laid his ears back and peeled out, barking like a modern day Paul Revere—*The Mexicans are coming! The Mexicans are coming!* He accelerated and overtook the Ford.

Bean marveled at the rambling circus. Like a magnet dragged through metal shavings, the entourage grew as neighborhood mutts fell in one-by-one, keeping pace and barking to beat all hell.

Down the block, white, black, and brown color-blind children played together, gliding down a yellow slide and dashing back to climb three steps to do it again.

The Mexican's Ford—the pageant's grand marshall—braked behind a creeping Bobcat tractor, which was driven by a red-capped man who bounced up and down.

Old Salty prob'ly goin' to the store for cigs.

The Ford darted around the Bobcat, hit the highway, and zoomed away, leaving the dogs howling "good riddance." The pack dispersed and returned victorious, heads held high for review.

Bean shook his head as he returned to NASCAR Nation.

"SWEAT," The Ole Man screeched.

Bean stomped over. "Mornin', ole codger."

"Dammit, boy," The Ole Man snarled, "how many times I got to tell ya to turn that thing down? I'm sick o' all this shit. I'm gonna call the cops, and they gonna take you downtown, son."

"Ole fart, we done been over this twice today. Don't start anything with me. I done told ya it's a free country. You need to go check into one o' them ole folks homes if you want nuthin' but quiet. That's where you ought to be anyhow."

"You jest shut up, smart ass. Peaches and me can take care o' our own damn selves."

"I hate to be the one to break it to you *again*, but your wife died over six months ago."

"That's a damn lie."

"It ain't no lie, Ole Man, she's gone. We sat right behind ya at the funeral. We brung over fried chicken and 'nanner puddin' when your kids was here. Where're your kids at, anyhow?"

The Ole Man puckered his face for a moment as if pondering the question. "Sweat, you fool, what you need to do is get your butt down to Everlastin' Baptist and start acceptin' Jesus as your Savior? Did you know Jesus was Baptist? Do you fear God, son?"

"Ole codger, I sho' don't need to hear all that from you 'cause I get enough chapter and verse from Ruby. Jesus done found her, and He knows where I live. And Christ wasn't Baptist or Methodist. He was Jewish, Baptist, and all them religions rolled into one."

"Praise Him for His mercy. Come to Everlastin' Baptist, and praise God, and ye shall have everlastin' life'. Now, do you accept Jesus as your savior, or don't you, son?"

"I keep tellin' ya, Grampa, it ain't none o' your bidness. Besides, I've seen enough to know the only time y'all Baptists is really interested in ole Butterbean Sweat is on tithin' day when the preacher's Cadillac payment is due and baby needs new shoes."

The Ole Man shook his head. "You got a bad attitude, boy. Jest forget it. There ain't no hope fer you. Now, turn that TV down. And shut that dog up while you're at it 'fore I call the pound."

"You two-faced like most o' the rest. The Bible says never trust a man who don't own no dog."

The Ole Man wheezed as he sucked oxygen from the tube. "Yeah? What book's that in?"

"Palms sixty-five, verse twenty-four, or thereabouts."

"Palms?" The Ole Man looked puzzled. *"Palms?* You mean *Psalms*? I'll look it up right now… sixty-five, verse twenty-four… there ain't no verse twenty-four."

"Ole Man, I don't know. I don't tote no Bible, and I ain't got time to argue."

"Son, you ain't got no clue. Now, turn that TV down 'fore I call the cops." The Ole Man's sash slammed shut.

Bean rushed to the grill, lunged for the handle, and Frisbee-sailed the lid. Whirling dervish flames leapt around crackling and hissing chicken. He let fly his Bud with one mighty splash and the fire sizzled and sputtered.

"Two laps to go and Earnhardt clings to the lead, fending off one challenger after another. But can he hold on?" The commentator cried over screaming engines. "Others have pitted for a splash of gas, but not Junior. He's slowing to conserve fuel. Can he finish? Yessir, fans, it's a risky strategy."

"Whut?" Bean slapped the TV. "You got to be shittin' me! Don't you run outta gas. Don't you do that to me, Junior. Not today."

"ONE LAP TO GO AND HE'S DRIVING ON FUMES," the commentator thundered. "THERE'LL BE SOME FINGER-POINTING IF HE RUNS OUT OF GAS."

"Gawd-a-mighty. Say this ain't happenin'. Come on Little E. Come on, you can do it, baby."

"EARNHARDT IS HOLDING ON AROUND THE LAST TURN… BUT WAIT, HE'S SLOWING DOWN. EARNHARDT IS OUT OF GAS! HE'S COASTING. JIMMY JOHNSON PASSES HIM AT THE FINISH LINE. UNBE-LIEVABLE!"

Bean mashed the TV's "off" button, slumped over, and dropped his sweaty forehead into his palms. *Lawd, Lawd, the Landlawd.* "Why me?" He paced to and fro, trying to figure out the answer.

Shaking his head, he closed air vents on the grill belly and tonged two chicken quarters onto a paper plate. Shoulders drooping, he ambled over to The Ole Man's window and rapped. He heard shuffling from within and the sash flew open.

"What the hell you want now, Sweat?"

"Yon't some chicken?" Bean lifted the plate and steam wafted.

The Ole Man's eye grew as wide as a silver dollar, his gaze bouncing between Bean and the food.

"We don't take no charity in our family."

Bean held the plate higher and blew the sweet aroma into The Ole Man's face. "Take it or I'll feed it to my dog. Your choice. It don't make no difference to me."

"You ain't playin' no trick on me, are ya?"

"It ain't no trick, Ole Man. The gnats is tearin' me up. Now, take it 'fore I change my mind."

The Ole Man's shaky hands seized the plate, and he disappeared into the darkness of his trailer.

As Bean returned to the grill to harvest the chicken, he looked to the sky and pondered Heaven...

I bet you on the other side o' them clouds there's a NASCAR track... banks as high as the sky, bleachers as big as the ocean, a sea o' screamin' fans... all-you-can-eat chili dogs, burnin' rubber, the roar of stock car engines... The Daytona One Million. NASCAR angels floatin' overhead.

Jesus'll have His own skybox. I'll be ridin' wing man with The Intimidator, Dale Earnhardt Sr. hisself, inside car #3... in a dogfight with Richard Petty and Bill Elliott. We'll win in a photo finish... I'll hold the checkered flag high for the victory lap. And then—

"Bean." Ruby's voice jerked him back to earth. "We ready to eat."

PART II:
MAJESTIC CHICKEN PLANT

Chapter 11

Before roosters crowed on Monday, the headlights of Cal Butler's Jaguar tunneled through the darkness down Majestic Chicken Company's drive. His free hand massaged Winston, his AKC certified lap dog, who was sprawled across his muscular thighs. His black Gucci loafer gave it the gas.

Butler rolled into his reserved parking spot at the executive office. The instant he opened the car door, the reek of his chicken plant, only a slingshot distance away, flooded his nostrils. He shooed Winston out the door and grabbed his briefcase. The idle plant smell was horrid enough, but nothing compared to full operation and the stench of fresh, warm entrails of thirty thousand chickens a day.

He never understood why his father, Calvin Butler Sr., housed his office inside the wretched-smelling plant. It took no time after his father's death for Cal to build the freestanding office building. He preferred to arrive early so he could sequester himself inside his sanctuary before the plant cranked up, before his international cast of low-life employees poured into the parking lot like refugees.

He arrived extra early this day fretting over an urgent conference call with his legal team. Floodlights kicked on as he approached the building. He disabled the alarm, unlocked the front door, and waited for Winston to do his business on manicured Bermuda grass.

Butler purchased fabricated credentials showing Winston, a Welsh Corgi, to be a direct descendent of England's Queen Elizabeth II's favorite Corgi. The Queen owned at least four at all times. *If it's good enough for the Queen, it's good enough for me.* "Credentialed" Winston concluded his business, scratched the grass, and sprinted through the door propped open by his master's foot.

Cal hit the lights, locked the front door, and strolled past his secretary's desk to the antique French doors of his suite. The doors' industrial bolt-lock hardware looked as out of character as warts on a beauty queen's nose. *Safety first.* He inserted his key and punched a code into the security system. His idea to require key *and* code.

Inside his inner sanctum, he unzipped a pocket of his briefcase and extracted his French silver pillbox. Percocet, the narcotic pain reliever *du jour,* awaited. A dozen to be exact, one day's supply... for the nerves, for the courage. The task at hand was not for the faint of heart. His chest tightened as he pondered his mission.

It didn't matter that he was the high school quarterback who struck on a Hail Mary in the waning seconds to win the Georgia State Championship over twenty years ago. That night he earned his nickname, "Champ." He still maintained his athletic fitness and coiled-spring intensity, ready to strike anything or anybody within arm's length. He still had it, but it didn't matter. Physical strength could not overpower the noxious stench about to shock his senses.

Butler popped a pill and waited for the first of many peaks in his day. Butterflies tickled his heart and stomach. They flitted up his esophagus, through the roof of his mouth and into his head. Pyrotechnics exploded in his brain's frontal lobes then melted into a warm, euphoric glow. One moment his feet slogged through quicksand, the next, the buzz set in and every step was lifted by a cloud, rising higher and higher.

In early addiction stages, it was easy to climb the stairs and stand tall on the high platform of bliss and rapture. Stairs loomed higher as time passed, requiring more and stronger pills to soar. A sly grin seeped across his face as he floated.

Showtime.

The chairman locked his suite and exited the office building's side door where he flipped off his loafers and donned rubber boots and a special odor repellent overcoat. He pulled latex gloves over his fingers, careful not to chip polished nails. He fired up a Cuban *Grandisimo* cigar and hustled down the sidewalk to the plant, long and wide as a football field.

At the metal door on the side of the plant, he donned a rubber skullcap and goggles. Since he had to smoke, the task's worst part was not being able to wear his respirator to cover his nose and mouth. *Suffer the stench. Damn I hate this part of my job.*

His lips puckered, and his cheeks puffed the cigar like bellows as he unlocked the plant door and stepped inside. He unlocked the electrical panel, flipped numerous light switches, and began his work.

The chairman tried to avoid entering the God-awful plant altogether but conducted occasional early morning cigar blitzes. Inspecting during operating hours was out of the question.

His stomach lurched at the thought of being inside the plant during the shift—suffocating heat and roar of the assembly line, sights and smells of entrails and blood, standing shoulder-to-shoulder with his filthy immigrants. *No thanks.* He didn't know a fat scraper from a lung gunner from a yield checker. Wilbur Smith, plant manager, was paid to know all that.

The "no smoking" rule applied to all except the chairman. Ownership had its privileges. The aromatic cigar informed all that Big Boss is watching. Business 101: management-by-walking-around (MBWA). He'd lifted the idea from a magazine and put his own twist on it.

He wound along the plant's inner perimeter, puffing toward the head of the assembly line, swerving through both restrooms on the plant's east side and the maintenance shop where grease monkeys toiled. He cruised through the lobby past the receptionist desk that guarded walls covered with plaques and awards earned while his father ran the show. Then through the job center, a bustling spot given the plant's three hundred percent turnover rate year-to-year.

Sailing down the walkway to the receiving dock, Butler paused for a moment and listened to noises outside. A transport truck idling in the lot, another pulling in. Cages clanged as USDA inspectors examined live bird samplings and tallied diseased and dead on arrival.

He backtracked to the entrance of the live hang room but dared not enter the repulsive chamber itself, having heard about the appalling process that happens inside. He hustled to the killing chamber—puffing, puffing—where live chickens glide by hanging upside down on shackles. Electrical stunning enabled Oriental women with sharp knives to slice the carotid artery so the bird bled out and died before being scalded.

He passed scalding vats where birds were dropped into one-hundred-thirty degree water to loosen feathers before they glided to the plucking line—very important for final appearance.

Zipping along, he puffed toward the re-hanging line where feet were sliced off before carcasses were hung upside down again and sent down the evisceration line where the plant's lack of modernization was most evident. Upgrading equipment like the big players in north Georgia would enhance hygiene and create savings, reducing employees from one hundred twenty to thirty.

Cal's father delayed modernization, building a war chest to pay for new machinery in cash. Cal Sr. monitored technical advances and awaited production of the newest ground breaking equipment. He planned to retrofit the plant from stem-to-stern while fretting over his workers' welfare. Lost paychecks and benefits, the effect on the community.

Plans for Majestic Chicken's modernization died with Butler Sr. Cal had designs on that war chest. His father's death catapulted him toward the goal he set in college—to be a millionaire by age twenty-five. He accomplished the goal upon his father's death, ten years late.

At age forty, after five years at the helm of Majestic, I'm hitting my stride. He puffed his Cuban cigar with delight at the thought.

He had a daughter, Lizzie, and his three sisters, fellow shareholders, had several children. *But why modernize and spend good money today chasing the future? The next generation can fend for itself. Carpe diem—seize the day. Live in the moment.*

The old-fashioned evisceration line required an army of carpal-tunneled hands to split the birds and gut them with spoons. Some birds remained whole, some carved in various ways, others deboned and some carted to the nugget line.

Ah, the nugget line, where my cutting edge creativity shines. Majestic Chicken's only equipment purchase since Cal took over was a grinder capable of rendering most anything into a mush that could join the nugget mix, parts otherwise destined for lower grade products destined for overseas.

Wait... why are two pallets of product sitting at the head of the nugget line? They shouldn't be here. He approached, held his cigar behind his back and sniffed. *Gross me out. Dammit, these must have stayed out all weekend. Somebody is in deep shit.*

Butler finished his MBWA tour at the side of the plant closest to his office, the less odiferous side where refrigerator/freezers and the loading dock served as a buffer. *That troublemaker, Butterbean Sweat, drives his forklift in this zone, the backdoor where most theft occurs. Coincidence? I doubt it.*

He lingered in a Cuban cigar haze inside coolers stacked with pallets of meat-filled boxes then hovered over Sweat's workbench and jumbled the clipboards. At his meeting with Sweat after work today, he wanted him to know Big Boss is keeping a close eye on him. He dropped his cigar butt onto the concrete next to Sweat's forklift, toed it out, and rushed back to his office.

Chapter 12

Bean torpedoed his meaty hand through loose castings up to his elbow and explored. He scooped pay dirt to the surface—a tangled, slithering mass of red wigglers. The worms freaked, pelting his hand with slaps and pushes, pissing, corkscrewing, writhing for freedom.

Feisty little bastards.

He plopped the wigglers into a pint cup, heaped on extra dirt, sealed the lid and likewise harvested a pint of night crawlers. Bean laid both in his pickup's bed and shoved off to work.

Mardi Gras beads and spruce-scented trees swung from his rearview mirror. A rod-and-reel nestled in his gun rack. He could catch a mess of fish any time he wanted by following his formula—go often, go early, stay late. Bean filled his freezer every spring by heeding the generational family secret of the best time to fish—when leaves on the oaks are the size of a squirrel's ear.

Bean's pickup crept down Garden of Eden's main drag, its headlights illuminating ambling dogs doing their business and sniffing the business of others. The school bus would soon arrive. Lights in trailers flicked on. Joes and Janes, Julios and Juanitas, dressing for work.

A Latino stranger stood in the road holding jumper cables and pointing to his car. Bean eased his truck across the fellow's yard until his truck's nose was *mano-a-mano* with the nose of an ancient Dodge. He pulled the hood lever and idled while the *hombre* latched the cables, hopped into his car, and revved her up. The stranger unhooked the cables from Bean's battery and closed the pickup's hood.

"Muchas gracias, amigo.*"*

"No problem-o, Bubba."

Bean hit the highway, listened to country music on his radio, and fired up a Marlboro. *Damn the day Majestic Chicken went non-smoking.* He burned a chain, building up nicotine for the long, dry spell ahead. He barreled down the dark, sparsely populated black ribbon of road.

He spotted a jogger wearing a miner's headlamp just in time to swerve. *Damn fool. If he don't have a heart attack first, he'll get hit by a truck or bit by a dog.*

He gunned it for miles, watching for cops and cows in his headlights, singing *Country Boy Can Survive* with Hank Williams Jr. His brights illuminated fenced-in cows chewing cud as he rocketed by like a streak of lightning.

When the intersection loomed, he let up, and his Chevy crawled into the parking lot of Patel's Git-N-Split convenience store. Git-N-Split shared the building with a dentist whose vinyl sign on wheels broadcasted, "Got Teeth? Call 162-2166."

He strutted into Git-N-Split with two worm cups in hand and glanced at the live bait display case. Weekend sales were good. He'd bring more tomorrow morning. He plopped his cups down on the counter.

"Mornin', Pawtell." He couldn't remember or pronounce the Patels' first names. "One Canadian night crawler and one Georgia red wiggler."

"Thank you veddy much, guv'nor," Patell said in his high-pitched accent. The clerk opened each container then stuck his finger in and fished around. Butterbean cut his gaze to the Mason jar on the counter with a slit in the lid. Li'l Bit's photograph wrapped around the jar and coins covered the bottom. He tried not to look at it but could never control his eyes. He fought back tears. He never told Patel the girl on the jar was his daughter.

Satisfied with the count, Patel wiped his finger on his pants, reached up and slid out a box of Marlboros.

"Fishing must be good, no?"

"Hell yeah, Pawtell, does a bear crap in the woods? Cain't hardly keep no worm on your hook this time o' year if you know where to go. Speak my name in these parts and the fish shiver in their boots."

Bean pulled two lottery tickets from his T-shirt pocket and winked as he slid them across the counter to Patel who ran them through the computer.

"Bean lucky man today, heh? Lucky Sevens, one ticket... let's see, *winner,* seven dollar. Bingo, let's see... *winner,* one dollar. That eight dollar total. Veddy, veddy good."

The worm farmer leaned over the counter and peered in deep concentration, scanning ticket rolls behind thick, scratched plexiglass like a wild-eyed child in a candy store.

"Let's see, how 'bout one o' them Eight Ball one dollar tickets." Patel tore as Bean plotted a well-orchestrated transaction and tapped the glass at another roll. "And one o' them Cash Fiesta two dollar tickets. And for the grand finale, one o' them big Monopoly five dollar tickets. Thanks, Pawtell. I won't forget you if the Monopoly ticket hits five hundred grand. Man sells me a big winner, I'm gonna take care o' him."

"Thank you veddy, veddy much."

He tucked the new tickets into his pocket and wheeled to peruse the day's pastry options. His big paw reached out and snagged one strawberry and two apple crème pies. He threw in a tube of cashews, a Red Bull, and a Coke in a large Git-N-Split Styrofoam cup. He leaned on the counter and plucked a beef jerky strip from the jar, added a pouch of Red Man and paid up.

"Aw-ight, Pawtell, you make sure to tell your customers them's the fightenest worms in Georgia."

"Ah, yes, guaranteed to catch big fish, veddy big fish."

"Now you catchin' on, podnah."

Bean took a seat on the bench outside the store beside the ice cooler. By the light of neon signs in the window advertising money orders, ATM, and hot dogs, he ate a crème pie and guarded against Kamikaze moths. A lone white rooster strutted across the parking lot. He thought of Li'l Bit's jar and the shame of begging for money. A tear flowed down his cheek as he chewed.

On the next lonely stretch of highway leading to work, Bean gunned his pickup and fantasized about driving NASCAR. Red Bull kicked in, and he played drums on his steering wheel, trying to keep time with Charlie Daniel's fiery fiddle in *The Devil Went Down to Georgia.*

He daydreamed about the lottery tickets in his pocket and ran a finger over their fresh perforations. The gambler could have scratched them at Git-N-Split, but that was no way to stretch an entertainment dollar. He contemplated how he'd spend five hundred grand, many possibilities tickling his brain.

As the rising sun crested the horizon, the road ahead snaked through verdant, rolling pastureland, farmhouses and barns dotting the way. He whizzed past a stately pecan plantation with neat rows of tall, graceful trees, branches massive and crowns broad and rounded.

Majestic Chicken loomed in no time, a hulking, pale aluminum cube. Sharp metal roofline angles sliced the backdrop of white, bulbous clouds. Bean's truck fell in with other vehicles streaming onto Majestic Road like ants marching to a picnic. No sign advertised the turnoff.

"Don't want to ruffle PETA's feathers," he claimed.

He queued between a chicken transport truck and a banged-up, low-slung Ford sedan full of Vietnamese women. He studied the Ford in his rearview mirror and watched the women yak. He couldn't tell one from the next. They were mostly cutters and deboners. *Makes sense, I seen enough Kung Fu on TV to know you don't mess with knife-totin' Orientals.*

Cars closed ranks, but Bean kept his distance behind the truck and its flying poop. Squeezed into grilled cages stacked ten high, immature chickens fidgeted and squawked, their dirty-white feathers ruffled from the open-air drive. Some feathers floated in the air like snowflakes. The trailing odor, enough to gag someone with normal sensibilities, hardly registered with Bean. He felt the chickens' terrified, sorrowful stares. A few turned in circles, looking for more comfortable positions. *I wish I could tell 'em not to bother 'cause it'll all be over soon.*

Bean glimpsed Majestic's markings on the truck signifying that these birds were artificially conceived, incubated, and hatched at the company's hatchery. Biddies were raised in pens at Majestic's grow-out facility for six-and-a-half weeks, bred for meat and fed like queens on corn and high-protein soy diets, antibiotics aplenty. Now they were firm and fat broilers on the way to harvest, robbed of the chance to become roasters, the "big'uns."

Trucks for loading and unloading veered left, passenger vehicles right. He veered left with the transport and pulled alongside the graveled delivery lot to get a read on the day's work. Two other trucks idled in the lot, their payloads crammed inside cages, hunks of live meat with feathers and beaks and feet.

Typical morning start, he estimated.

Bean eased his Chevy into the queue and drove the hundred yards to the guard gate, a barricade that didn't exist under old man Butler. Bean viewed the guard gate as one of the few benefits ushered in by young Butler. *Now my bookie cain't cruise the employee lot on collection missions.* He scanned the road's shoulders leading to the gate, looking for the infamous red Camaro. *Whew.*

Traffic funneled through the gate manned by a US Border Patrol Officer. Not a *real* officer but a Latino wearing mirrored sunglasses and faux Border Patrol uniform with counterfeit badge—Butler's effort to keep out troublemakers and undesirables among illegals.

Decaled pickups, cars, and minivans streamed past the guard. The decal was simple under old man Butler: MC. Now, it sported the new Butler Coat of Arms with lion and unicorn grasping a shield. Bean rolled through the gate, fingers of his left hand thumping the truck's rooftop.

"*Buenos días,*" the guard mumbled.

"*Buenos* tacos."

Bean glowered at the executive office down the drive. He spotted the chairman's Jag and *just knew* Butler was down there cooking up his next crooked deal.

The employee lot was now a blacktop job with painted stripes. It sprawled behind a shiny, new, ten-foot chain-link fence crowned with barbwire—testament to Butler's obsessive fear of employee theft.

Bean cruised the lot before heading to the front corner where he always parked beside Pickle Joe and Joker, the only other English-as-primary-language plant workers. By unwritten rule, the trio had dibs on front-row spaces.

He idled a lap around the lot, waving and nodding like the mayor, throwing his transmission into neutral, gunning the engine, grinning and pointing at co-workers.

"Señor Bean. El Gringo," co-workers hailed.
Latino music blared from a jacked-up muscle car with fancy rims and a rear spoiler. Base speakers throbbed in the trunk. Bean rolled up his window to salvage his hearing as the pulsating music passed. The music reminded him of his favorite *restaurante Mexicano,* Amigo Gordo. His mouth watered at the thought of enchiladas verde.

A liver-puller, a skinny Latina gal with gold front teeth, waved him to stop, and she sashayed to his window. *"Buenos días,* El Gringo. *"*

"Buenos diaz to you, too, Sista Margarita. You ready to pull some livers?"

"Sí, Señor Bean. Rápido livers. *Ándale. Mucho* gizzards. Ju Chevrolet win at NASCAR?"

"Earnhardt didn't win, but at least a Chevy won. You catchin' on, Sista."

"Why ju like Chevrolet?"

"It's like this," Bean smiled and raised his fist. "Dale's daddy made his name racin' Chevys." Index finger up. "Dale made his name racin' Chevys." Stub of middle finger up. "Junior made his name racin' Chevys." Ring finger up. "So as long as I'm drivin', I'll be drivin' Chevys. Comprehend-o?"

"*Sí. Comprendo.*"

Another Latina gal, a fat-puller, strolled over and stuck her head in the passenger window.

"*Buenos días,* El Gringo. What is *Inglés* lesson for today?"

"Glad you asked, Sista Chimichanga. Remember, 'i' before 'e' except in Budweiser." He found an empty behind his seat and showed them the proof with a pontificate grin.

"*Gracias.*"

"No problem-o, Sistas. El Gringo at your service."

He pulled up to pole position and backed his truck in. Shania Twain sang to him and him alone on the radio as he set into another crème pie and laid his three scratch-off tickets across his thigh.

El Gringo examined the tickets—his future—and a surge of optimism coursed through his veins, a reasonable certainty that a winning streak would strike soon and continue indefinitely. As he scratched the tickets, sweat laced with fantasy and exhilaration oozed from his pits.

The gambler played a game within a game while scraping circles and squares. As he chewed his crème pie and cashews, the mounds of his cheeks rose and fell, obscuring his view in a suspenseful game of "now you see it, now you don't."

His heart pumped over the one-dollar ticket… *loser,* sped on the two-dollar ticket… *loser,* and raced for the big five-dollar ticket. *Come on baby. Come to Papa. Baby needs a new foot and Mama needs new shoes.*

Mesmerized and staring at the picture of the swimming pool overflowing with five hundred thousand American smackers, Bean imagined cannonballing off the diving board into all that money. Dopamine pumped in his brain and endorphins gushed forth like volcanic lava.

Scratch, scratch… *WINNER!*

He stared at his Monopoly ticket in disbelief. The final unscratched circle concealed his winnings. *Is this the five hundred grand winner? Is this the first day o' the rest o' my life?* "Luck be a lottery."

Before revealing his winnings, Bean glanced up to watch his co-workers trudge by. He wouldn't be back tomorrow if he won the big prize... or ever again. He felt melancholy thinking he may never see his *compadres* again. He'd miss the old-timers, those on the job a whole year, who like himself, invariably had mangled fingers.

Taco lolled past, his right arm stump peeking out and swinging from his T-shirt, the lower half having been ground into nugget mix and long since shipped out. Taco held his lunchbox in his only hand and twirled his stump at Bean who waved back. *I'm gonna miss you, Taco.*

Time to show me the money. Scratch, scratch... *"Another Ticket." Is that all? At least I live to scratch another day.*

Pickle Joe arrived in his purple Chrysler Imperial. Bean splattered tobacco juice on the pavement next to his truck as Pickle Joe backed in. PJ climbed out of his sedan with breakfast sack in hand and opened Bean's passenger door. Empty soda cans and McDonald's bags tumbled onto the pavement. PJ stepped over and climbed in. He grabbed a *National Enquirer* and jumper cables from the passenger seat, chunked them onto the junk heap in the back, and squeezed in his six-and-a-half foot frame.

PJ's peculiar, elongated build and neck reminded Butterbean of a giraffe. Standing pigeon-toed with arms at his sides, PJ's fingertips hung to his knees. As receiving dock manager, PJ's stock-in-trade was alive and clucking. Bean's stock at the loading dock was dead and frozen.

PJ settled in and flashed Bean an incredulous stare. "Can you believe Earnhardt runnin' outta gas?"

"Don't even go there with me." Bean held up his doughboy palm.

"Whatever you say, maestro, but the boy's got to win sooner or later."

Bean returned to his crème pie as the smell of warm grease wafted. "What the hell? You got a hot breakfast? You better brung me some."

"Last time I done that," PJ pointed with his fried egg biscuit, "you didn't show up for work, and you still owe me four dollars."

Bean wiped his damp face on his T-shirt and fired up a Marlboro. "You ate the food, didn't ya? I told ya, I ain't payin' for sump'n you ate."

They sat in a state of contemplative repose, windows down, doors propped open, each with a foot on his running board. PJ sipped coffee from his thermos cup. "You still seein' Butler after work today?"

"Yep, that bastard. He's pond scum."

"Did you tell Ruby?"

"Yep. She's some kinda' pissed. She don't want me to meet with him. 'Fraid I'll get fired. She's right 'bout dat, 'cause if he gives me any shit today, I'll rip his head off and spit in his neck."

"Think Wilbur knows you're meetin' with Butler?"

"Don't know and don't care. I cain't believe Wilbur sold us out. He'll do anything Butler tells him, right or wrong, legal or illegal. There ain't no use talkin' to a puppet."

"It'd sho' be nice makin' overtime pay again." PJ finished his biscuit and fired up a cig.

"You tellin' me?" Bean punctuated each word with a thumb-flick of his cig. "Hell, Butler's raised insurance so much, time he takes out taxes and everything, I almost got to pay him to work, and worms ain't makin' me no money. Overtime's the only chance I got to make a lick, and he's done took that away. It ain't right. I got fifty hours o' overtime in the last two months and he ain't paid nuthin' but straight time. No time-'n-a-half. No sir, I'd just as soon go to the house than work overtime at straight pay."

"You ain't tellin' me nuthin', but be careful. Next time you walk off the job when they wantin' you to work overtime, they gonna fire you."

"I don't give a rat's—"

"Hey, mi amigo." Rio, a lung gunner, trotted over. "El Gringo, my fren. Buenos días."

"¡Hola! My man Rio. What up, dawg?"

"This Venezuelan, Enrique. He pick fruit in California last week and need money to get family to Georgia. Want to know how to play lottery."

"We got a minute. Call him over. I'll show him now."

Rio whistled Enrique over.

PJ tapped Bean. "Where the hell's Venezuela?"

"I don't think it's part o' Mexico." Bean traced the atlas in his head. "It could be around Mexico. Or, maybe it's across the pond, the one shaped like a boot. Who can keep up these days? Around here, we got Mexican look-a-likes coming in from everywhere, comin' out da woodwork."

A short, sinewy fellow with oily hair and jet black eyes, dark for a Latino, sauntered over and smiled.

"What a greaser," PJ whispered.

"Yeah, I bet Goodwill wouldn't even take them clothes."

Bean leaned his head out the door. "¡Hola! In-Ricky."

"Mucho gusto."

"A Venezuelan? How 'bout we call you Veni?'"

Rio piped in. "He speak only little *Inglés*. He want to know about lottery?"

Bean glanced at Rio. "Tell him he can be rich overnight beyond his wildest dreams. Tell him that I've got a lot o' my eggs in the lottery basket."

Rio commenced rapid-fire translation. Veni grinned and nodded his head.

"Tell Veni, lottery rule one is, 'Ya' cain't win if ya don't play.'"

Rio translated. The immigrant shot thumbs up to Bean and rattled off a soliloquy of Spanish gibberish.

Rio explained, "He say his wife want him to play so chicken wing."

"Whut?" Bean asked. "Tell him ya don't play for chicken wings, ya play for cash money." He held up his hand and rubbed his thumb against his middle nub. "Moolah. Wampum. Greenbacks."

"That's right, Señor Bean. Che want him to play so chicken wing money."

"Oh, Lawdy, I get it," Bean laughed. "Yeah, baby. Chicken wing. I can wing. You can wing. We all can wing."

"Now you take this ticket right cheer." Bean held up a losing Mega Millions ticket and thumped it. "This is your big money ticket. Veni needs to play it. Just pick five numbers and match the Mega Ball and, boom, you'd o' won eighty-nine million dollars on Friday. We're talking American here, not pesos. You follow me, amigo?"

As Rio attempted to translate, Bean gnawed beef jerky between pulls on his cig. Veni knitted his brows, crinkled his face, and nodded as he listened.

"Now look a-here. I got two numbers right." Bean handed the ticket to Rio and pointed to where he had circled two of the five Mega Million numbers. Rio showed Veni and translated.

Bean pointed to an un-circled number. "Now add ten to this here number and, boom, you got it. This one, double and subtract one and, boom, got it, too. Gettin' hot now. This one is my baby girl's birthday—I should o' knowed that—boom, you got all five. Just match the Mega Ball and you're golden."

Rio studied the ticket then scratched his head and rendered a translation. A baffled look spread across Veni's face.

PJ punched Bean's shoulder. "How come you didn't win since you claim to know so damn much?"

"*Shhh.* I'm tryin' to teach the kid. You don't never know. It'd be just my luck if he won after givin' him my secrets."

"Señor Bean, he want to know how to pick Mega Ball."

"That's easy. Tell him to use his mama's birthday."

PJ pulled Bean back into the cab. "You so full o' shit, your eyes is brown. Besides, that poor taco-bender cain't afford to play the lottery no more than you can."

"Why don't you just shut up and leave me be, grandpa. My mama died two years ago and you tryin' to pick up right where she left off."

Bean turned to Rio. "Tell him it's a tradition at my house. We all in front o' the TV at eleven o'clock every Tuesday and Friday night for the live drawin'." Rio repeated in Spanish.

"You see, I just missed it. If I'd o' won eighty-nine million, the first thing I'd do is buy this shit hole." He pointed at the plant. "I'd tear it down and plant a big field o' wild flyers."

"Flyers?" Rio looked puzzled. "Ju mean *pollo*? Flying chickens?"

"Hell no, I mean flyers." Bean waved his arm across the horizon. "Like dandelions and daisies and roses, all colors o' the rainbow, blowing in the breeze."

Rio and Veni laughed when Rio explained while sweeping his arm wide.

Bean ripped up this morning's losing tickets and let them fly out his window.

"Until then, *yo no le importa una mierda*—I don't give a shit. Hey, I hear Joker comin', I got to talk to him. *Adiós.*"

Joker's corroded muffler rumbled long before the boys spotted his truck. The ancient, black pickup with red roof sputtered to a stop and backed into the spot next to PJ's car. Bean noticed a new, white spray-painting across the tailgate: "Beats walkin."

Bean pointed his cig. "You know, I was thinkin'. Joker's got the worst teeth o' any white man I know."

PJ nodded. "Hell, he ain't got no top teeth a-tall. I've seen better teeth on a jack-o-lantern. Claims he's savin' up for new ones, but he ain't even got enough to pay his fine so he can get his driver's license back. If the cops catch him drivin', he's up shit creek... without no teeth."

Joker hopped out and walked with an uncharacteristic spring in his step, looking light in his tennis shoes, his clothes hanging on him like a specter. If he had no Adam's apple, his body would have no shape at all.

PJ glanced at his watch. "He's walkin' like a ballet dancer. What the hell's his hurry? We got eleven minutes."

In his late forties but looking sixty, Joker measured his life events by rehab stints. On the wagon, off the wagon—AA is life. In the six months he'd been at the plant as a scale operator, two of his disability claims had already been denied. If his words were believed, sadly, most of his family and extended family had perished, one-by-one, since he started work. The funerals required a three-day-weekend whereupon he would return to work reeking of sour whiskey.

Joker stopped at the hood of Bean's truck.

"Hey, hey." With his thumb, he mashed one nostril shut and blew a snot rocket out the other. "Chicken Workers of the World handshake."

Bean and PJ blew the handshake out their doors. "Hey, hey."

Joker stepped to Bean's window. "You still meetin' Butler today?"

"Yep."

"Will you give him a message for me?"

"Maybe."

"Tell him he can kiss my bony, white ass."

"I'll be sure to tell him, Joker, anything else?"

PJ leaned his head over. "Hey, Joker, why you walkin' like your pants is on fire?"

"Ate at Bubba Chin-Chin's last night. Got to birth a Yankee 'fore the whistle blows. If I don't go quick, I'm gonna have to shit in the creek to keep from settin' the woods on fire."

PJ pointed. "You sure you ain't gonna' go hide in the stall and take a slug o' likker?"

"Hell no, idiot. I'm on the wagon. Come with me and stand outside the stall and you'll find out. I don't think you can handle the truth."

"No thanks. Why don't you show me some mercy and go to Bean's bathroom this mornin'."

Bean sat upright. "Wait a minute, Joker, please don't. Who gave you a beer last week when you had the shakes?"

PJ punched Bean's shoulder. "That was a big help to a man tryin' to stay on the wagon."

"Gentlemen, gentlemen," Joker interrupted, "I'm open to the highest bidder."

"Get outta here," Bean and PJ chimed in unison.

"Okay. But one of ya's gettin' punished." Joker dashed away, double time.

Bean snickered. "Don't he look all important and official, like some VIP hurryin' to a board meetin'?"

A gaggle of yackety-yak Mexican gals ambled across the lot towards Bean's truck.

PJ elbowed Bean and whispered, "Look at that one on the right. Them jeans is so tight, if she farts, she'll blow her boots off."

"Hey, El Gringo, is Obama going to make it better for us?"

"Sista, all I know is, I'm gonna buy me a case o' beer and drink it Obama self."

The girls giggled. One peeled away from the group and circled Bean's truck, examining bumper decals.

"*Hombre*, why so many stee-kers?"

PJ leaned over. "His old lady won't let him get no tattoos so he tattoos his truck."

"Real funny," Bean said as the girls waved over their shoulders.

A young Guatemalan saw operator stopped by.

"*Buenos días*, Señors Bean and PJ. I need some advice about my wife, *por favor*."

"What's the problem?"

"Che argue with me about every-ting. Tell me I not making enough money. I can't take no more. What should I do?"

Bean spewed smoke, hastening to beat PJ to the punch. "You ever tried hittin' her over the head with a phone book? It don't leave no bruise and you'll get her attention, especially if you can get a-holt o' one o' them big city phone books."

"Ah, Señor Bean, and you have done this to your wife?"

PJ piped up. "Hell no, he ain't. Ruby'd kick his ass all over the Garden o' Eden."

The employee bus pulled into the lot, a re-tooled yellow school bus with the Butler Coat of Arms on each side. It was chock full of Hispanics and others collected from various spots around the county. PJ gathered his things. "I got to git so I can clock in before the Mexicans. You sure you know what you doin' by meetin' with Butler today?"

"Hell yeah. I may file a complaint with the gub'mint if he don't pay overtime. It's Butler's choice. Cuz said I'd prob'ly win."

"Ain't your cousin just a traffic court judge?"

Chapter 13

A cloud of sweet fragrances welcomed Butler when he opened his office door after his management-by-walking-around plant tour. A hodgepodge of diffusers, potpourris, and time-released aerosol sprays disinfected and masked the obscene odor from next door. The air quality consultant warned of the sprays' toxicity, but Cal assumed the risk without hesitation. *That's a no brainer.*

He brushed and re-sprayed his thinning, coal-black locks, careful not to pull on the plugs. Punching buttons on the sound system, he started a continuous loop of Beethoven and Bach piping through a dozen speakers. He eased into his ostrich skin desk chair and tilted back as Winston jumped onto his lap. He collected his thoughts for the upcoming conference call.

He leaned back, Guccis kissing his sockless, white ankles. His feet swung and grazed the elephant hide rug under his monstrous, mahogany desk. One of his most prized possessions, commissioned by him for one hundred thousand dollars, the desk's dark leather top sported a Sun King gold inlay, emblem of Louis XIV, France's seventeenth century monarch.

King Louis ruled France for seventy-two years under "divine right," subject to no earthly authority. He was convinced his entitlement to rule came directly from God. King Louis believed, "The State is King, and I am the State."

Butler's edict: "Majestic Chicken is King, and I am Majestic Chicken."

"Only the best," he reiterated to his interior designers. Another prized possession hung in the lobby, his knockoff British royal

Coat of Arms. Crests and banners on the newly-carved heraldry told a storied Butler family history. A history invented by Cal.

Before the death of Cal's father, old man Butler caught a glimpse of what was to come. "Why spend company money flying on a private jet to Ontario to select black walnut paneling," his father pleaded, "when they're happy to deliver all the samples you want? Must the company buy you mahogany bookcases stuffed with leather-bound antique books you scoured Europe to collect but will never read? Why all the expensive play-pretties and doodads?"

His father may have seen it coming, but he transitioned power to Cal nevertheless, blood being thicker than any element in the periodic table. Cal stared at his father's warm, wise eyes in the oil portrait, assuming his father's gregarious smile marked approval of all he perused from the canvas. "Father, look what trophies and fame our money has bought."

Framed photographs hung among animal mounts on the walls—tarpon fishing with the senator, quail hunting with the governor, posing with Ted Turner in his box beside the Braves dugout at Turner Field. Nestled in the bookshelves was the photo from the day his wife, Charlotte, and he delivered their eleven-year-old daughter, Lizzie, to finishing school in London. A paunch belly showed in more recent photos, the result of Percocet-induced lethargy and constipation.

Animal heads loomed high on the walls, various stag and deer species and a portion of his African antelope quarry. Two bull elephant tusks formed an arch framing an oil portrait of him with the freshly killed trophy. A Masai warrior shield and two metal spears guarded the exhibit. On one wall, a taxidermied black marlin with a fly in his mouth soared through the air. A hole-in-one plaque from Augusta National adorned another.

"You see, Father, hard work should be rewarded. If I cannot enjoy the fruits of success, why did you even bother? Our family dynasty is secure, so let the family be glorified through me. We are no longer mere common folk. We have risen, in two generations, from proletariat to, well… me."

Over time, Butler Sr. transferred a debt-free company to his children and walked away, tired of all things chicken. His three girls married and moved north, their lifetime financial security—and that of their children—assured by his hard work.

Cal Jr. embraced what was rightfully his. With joy in his heart, Butler Sr. trained his only boy in all aspects of the operation. A man grounded in common sense but blinded by love for his son. He believed Cal would shepherd the company in the family's best interest.

Or did he?

Old man Butler's death by heart attack stunned the region. One of its most respected leaders and philanthropists gone. Overnight, Cal found himself at the wheel of Majestic Chicken Company, owned jointly with absentee sisters. With no parents left in life, his moral compass was free to seek its own bearing.

The moment they turned the last spade on old man Butler's grave, Cal set out to re-shape the company in his own image. Majestic Chicken printed money like the US Mint, and his fantasies and schemes were now flush with cash.

He could have sold the business after his father's death but wanted to control the money and power from the chairman's seat. He embarked on a course to carry on, vowing to his sisters that the company would thrive.

Why would my sisters think differently when our wise and beloved father placed full faith and credit in me and drummed into them that, if it spills across my lips, it is true by definition.

In a wing of his suite, Cal unlocked the closet door, which concealed a state-of-the-art monitor displaying multiple images. The hardwired system delivered in real time, fed by a dozen digital, high-resolution video cameras strategically located around the plant.

Six cameras nestled inside tinted, spherical bubbles attached to the plant's ceiling. Vandal-proof and in full view, all knew that Big Boss was watching.

The remaining cameras were hidden. Big Boss sees all.

A separate monitor scrolled images in and around the lodge at Honeysuckle Plantation, the two-thousand-acre Butler family retreat outside town.

Cal powered up the screen. He rewound scenes of his plant tour this morning then fast-forwarded to watch himself "smoke" the plant. *What a thrill to see myself in action. Father would be proud of my management technique.*

He tinkered with amateur surveillance cameras years before, envisioning creative uses. He later went to great lengths to make clandestine arrangements with a retired Secret Service agent in Atlanta whose company routinely recorded covert video of lofty men in low places. Cameras now surveilled Majestic Chicken Plant and Honeysuckle Plantation. But not home.

He knew Charlotte would chop off his balls if she found a spy camera in their home. He suspected his wife was cheating, but she wouldn't screw someone at their home, would she? If so, he'd like to watch but was sure the prude would never go for that.

Cal was determined to catch her cheating. He monitored home and cell phone logs and snuck into her email to read with great curiosity. The covert GPS device he planted on her Mercedes revealed the car's whereabouts at all times. He maintained a record of any place she'd been for longer than fifteen minutes and personally checked out each.

The thought of her infidelity enraged him, and he imagined that she chose inconspicuous places to rendezvous with her boy toys. *I know she's getting nailed by her personal trainer, that young stud. Muscle Man is probably leading her down a trail of rose petals into the "massage therapy" room and having his way with her. The yardman is taking her to the shed. Her acupuncturist is poking her with more than needles.* He slammed his fist into his thigh.

Cal closed the doors to his network, crossed the office, and settled into his desk chair in a pleasant Percocet fog. *I bet her Bible study group is gay. She's going to force me to bug her phones.*

Grandisimo cigar smoke floated toward the cathedral, pecky cypress ceiling with its massive cross beams and past the taxidermied twelve-foot alligator lurking there. The gator's eerie eyes and monstrous head served to intimidate all who entered Cal Butler's cloister.

His anger boiled as he focused on the problem *du jour*. Worries and hassles of running a business were closing in. *Damn government pricks are making it impossible for me to make a profit.*

Radford Campbell, golden boy of the local Bar and Majestic's lead counsel, called Butler *at home* last night. An underling at the Atlanta USDA office tipped-off Campbell to a "surprise" inspection scheduled for this afternoon.

Those bastards would love to padlock my business. Dammit to hell, I cannot let that happen. Time to make those lawyers earn their keep. He cradled Winston's head by the ears and looked him in the eye. "What a way to start the week. You and I, we'll get through this. We've been through worse together, right, old sport?"

His chest tightened, so he swallowed a Percocet and stared at his photo of a space shuttle launch at Cape Canaveral. He waited on his own dope-induced blastoff and his cobwebs to clear. He grabbed his gold Mont Blanc Meisterstück fountain pen and twirled it like a baton through the fingers of his right hand while leaning back and spewing cigar smoke. Ceiling fan blades whirled as the smoke and his brain swirled. He hit the speaker button on his phone and speed dialed Radford. Campbell's staff had yet to arrive, and Cal was taken aback when Radford himself answered.

"Cal, good morning, my man. We have some quick work to do. Kilroy & Russell is waiting on our call."

"As much as I pay them, they better have a plan. I've got to have some time before an inspection."

"Listen, we'll get it postponed one way or another," Campbell assured. "No need to panic just yet."

Butler listened as Campbell dialed Griffin Henry in the Government Investigations/Special Matters Division of the Atlanta law firm of Kilroy & Russell. "Griff" Henry, former general counsel for the USDA, was one of many in a long line who gave up top-level government jobs to earn obscene salaries with Kilroy & Russell representing the very companies they once regulated.

"Cal, let me say straight off," Griff hastened, "I don't want to know how you found out about this surprise inspection."

"Fine." *How ironic that the tipster is on this call and remains silent.*

Each man held a fresh copy of Majestic Chicken's failed USDA salmonella evaluation, its second consecutive failure in the fifty-one-day testing series. Cal's face reddened as Griff rambled at length about the infractions in the report and the implications, citing long sections of the Code of Federal Regulations and various USDA directives.

"A written action plan will be required then a third series of tests will be conducted. In addition, it's not shocking that a surprise on-site inspection is in the offing."

Cal's gut churned and his patience waned as he listened. Veins bulged in his neck. Winston popped to high alert in his bed, ears perked.

With each passing moment, Butler fumed over the money this was costing. *To support the silk-stocking bastards in their Atlanta high-rise is bad enough, but Campbell's bill is going to hurt.*

Campbell's colleagues in the state bar joked that he didn't know a damn thing about the law, but they marveled at his ability as a hustler and schmoozer. He was intimate friends with half the judges and politicians in the state, all fat off his fried shrimp and liquor—billed to select clients such as Majestic Chicken.

Campbell generally knew enough about law to fake it until he consulted someone from Kilroy & Russell. Switchboard operators at the firm were on strict orders to find a lawyer anytime Campbell called—no voice mails or phone tag for him. He represented half the who's who in the region and fed most business to Kilroy & Russell, producing more business for the firm than most partners.

Tapping into Campbell's vast network came at a stratospheric price, however. Cal was amazed at the man's gall for billing twice that of Kilroy & Russell, who did the work. Then again, Cal remembered his football days. *Campbell is the quarterback. He takes the snap, hands the ball off, arranges gourmet lunches when Atlanta lawyers come to town, and makes the occasional critical call to the right judge or politician.*

Cal listened to the two squires discuss legal minutia and realized he was wasting time and money. *Let the bastards discuss it among themselves and come to me with their executive conclusion.*

He stared at the glowing red bulb on the wall opposite his desk—the assembly line light. Similar to a traffic light, red meant the line had stopped. Green, of course, was the objective. He didn't like the negativity of "stop light," so it was the "run light."

His new Corporate Mission Statement resonated in his head: To be the most profitable medium-sized chicken producer in the South. Since he cut back to one shift to maximize profits, the assembly line had to move at full capacity at all times during the shift. *Straight forward enough for any dimwit plant manager to comprehend.* With all this inspection crap, he sensed that the red light would be his arch nemesis this week.

"Cal, since you exceeded their limit twice in a row," Griff summarized "you're a category one facility, a big blip on their radar screen. They don't treat salmonella lightly. It's typical in these cases to immediately send an inspection team to test for general cleanliness. One more salmonella failure and they'll shut you down. But they can also shut you down on sanitation grounds, not just lab tests.

"Something else, I don't know what's going on down there, but I've been told, in strictest confidence from a high level, they're also beginning to question the tally sheets of their daily inspectors assigned to your plant."

Oh, shit! Cal's eyes bugged.

"Bottom line, I don't see how we can prevent an inspection."

Butler had heard enough. Veins bulged. He bolted upright in his chair and slammed his fist on his desk. "Godammit! I don't give a shit what it takes, I don't want those sons o' bitches here right now. I have forms, reports, inspections, surveys, and studies coming out my ass from those people. Mr. Taxpayer—you and me—pay their salaries, for God's sake. You need to remind them of that."

"I'm afraid those arguments aren't going to—"

"Christ Almighty! What a joke these pricks are. Their line inspectors are slow as molasses. Ask a simple question, and you never get a straight answer. They all point fingers at somebody else. It's like trying to nail Jell-O to a tree. All useless."

"I hear you," Griff assured, "but I don't think you're hearing *me*. I'm telling you they can shut you down if this is a bad inspection."

"Bullshit!" Butler exploded. "That little weasel inspector who's running the tests is a liar. He has a hard-on for me and is trying to be the next Ralph Nader. That little Napoleon bastard doesn't know a damn thing about processing chickens or meeting a payroll. It's all government bullshit. I'm trying to make a payroll down here, and they just sit in their little cubicles in Atlanta dreaming up ways to delay and harass me."

"What do you expect?" Griff snapped. "You failed the test series twice in a row. Flunked them miserably, actually. Hell, we can't keep them at bay forever. What do you—"

"*God Almighty.* All I'm asking for is some time. I don't pay you to tell me 'no.'"

"Okay, okay," Radford Campbell jumped in. Couldn't let one of his best clients get into a row with Kilroy & Russell. "We can figure this out. Somebody in the Department just needs to table this inspection for a while, that's all. Cal, how much time do you need?"

"Hell, I don't know. I'm about to fire my plant manager. I can't believe he let this happen. The bastard knows better. I'm going to find a good man who'll come in and straighten all this shit out. Listen, it's not nearly as bad as they try to make it. It's going to be okay, just buy me some time."

"I don't know how we can do that," Griff replied.

"We'll find a way," assured Campbell. "I'll call the governor and explain it to him if I have to. Your plant is too important to our region's economy to let some overzealous kid from USDA foul it up. I think the governor will understand. Your being such a big financial supporter will help our cause."

"Fine. Let me know ASAP. I'm going to stop production this morning and have everybody clean. It'll cost me a damn fortune to shut down with a plant full of workers. I've got to go now." With that, he reached over and smacked the "off" button on his speakerphone. He wanted to stop the bleeding from prattling lawyers. *Jesus, what if the blood-sucking government leeches do come today and give me a real inspection?*

Cal sprang from his chair and swung his foot to boot the leather trashcan across the room but kicked his desk instead.

"*Dammit to hell.*" He slumped into his chair, pain radiating up his leg. "Shit! This is unbelievable. Did I break my toe? Look what they made me do, Winston."

He lifted his foot to the ottoman, leaned back, groaned and patted his thighs. Winston jumped onto his lap, circled, and plopped. Cal ran his fingers through the dog's coat and massaged his warm skin.

"Dammit, Winston, this whole world's going to hell in a hand basket, but we have no choice. It's like your namesake, Mr. Churchill, said to the British when they were being bombed in WWII: 'Carry on.'"

Chapter 14

Bean locked his truck and began his march to the plant entrance, ubiquitous Git-N-Split cup in hand. His dungaree bottoms scraped the pavement. He glanced at his Timex as he sauntered along in his stained but clean undershirt, his boots and camo cap decorated with last night's BBQ sauce.

Gravity tugged his and his co-workers' heads and shoulders as they neared the plant, the same puppeteer pulling *all* their strings. Every day brought new faces. Most came and went before he got to know them. He could spot new ones, apprehension in their faces when entering, panic-stricken when the line cranked up.

As Bean approached the double-door mouth of the beast, by reflex he rubbed his thumb against the stub of his right middle finger. He fought his flashback, trying not to relive the incident, trying to trick his mind. The harder he tried, the more inevitable the memory that choked his throat.

The trouble started six years ago, in his younger days at Majestic as utility man, ready to step into any short-handed line position, even live hang.

He despised live hang—*¡pollo vivo!*—as did everyone, but the job had to be done. He could hang with the best on a normal day, but this morning arrived early after a hard night of bowling, chilidogs, and beer.

His request for a different assignment denied, he somberly picked through the gear outside the live hang room hoping for good fits.

Friday morning and a week's worth of rancid poultry stench—blood and guts, piss and shit—hung heavy in the air. His stomach gurgled and lurched. *This'll be a true test of manhood to hold my guts when the action starts.* Perspiration beaded his brow.

He sat on the bench with three greenhorn Latino live hangers with fear in their eyes. *Not good.* He untied his boots and guided his stocking feet into neoprene hip boots then stood and tied his rubber apron.

A truck ready to dump its feathered payload idled at the receiving dock, its rumble vibrating the men's feet. Chickens in cages stacked on the truck's bed clucked low and nervous, their fate drawing near.

The foreman, a short, middle-aged Latino, tapped Bean on the shoulder. "Grab, flip, hang," he explained, flipping one finger up at a time. "Grab, flip, hang." Three fingers again. *"Comprendo?"*

"Yes, I comprehend-o," Bean snapped. "This ain't my first rodeo, podnah."

The foreman turned to the other three live hangers and flipped *uno, dos, tres* with his fingers. *"Agarre, volcarse, colgar*—grab, flip, hang. *Pronto, pronto, pronto."*

"Sí, sí," they replied.

Classroom training complete, the foreman suited up, ready to assist the novice crew. Bean slipped into a rubber smock, wet some rags in the sink, and zippered them into his pocket.

6:55 a.m.—*Gather remaining accessories and open door to room. BAM. Wretched odor slams men. Bean gags as he steps into room and turns head to distance his nose from smothering stench.*

Bloodstained room is sweltering and dark, save one stark, blue light bulb in ceiling covered with metal basket. Darkness and heat calm birds, if only for an instant, benefitting live hangers.

Eyes acclimate. Bean dons tattered rubber cap and pulls it down over ears, secures claustrophobic mesh painter's mask over nose and mouth and stretches tight-fitting goggles over eyes. He wiggles hands into thick rubber gloves and guides them through hard plastic cones that protect arms from striking beaks.

6:56 a.m.—*Diesel engine of disassembly line power drive in adjoining room roars to life in fits and starts before settling into ear-splitting drone. Men flash apprehensive glances at one another as they squeeze plugs into ears.*

6:58 a.m.—*In dull light, four live hangers assume positions beside idle rubber conveyor belt at floor level. Abutting one conveyor belt side, room's wall rises, making escape to left impossible for beltway passengers. Knee-high wooden barrier guards other side, discouraging renegades from jumping off belt yet allowing human access.*

Second conveyor suspends from ceiling behind them at shoulder level. Every foot, pair of vertical, metal shackles with grooves hangs empty. Conveyor lurches forward and glides from live hang room into kill line at pace which will dictate existence of every man and woman in plant for next eight hours or more.

Humming of forklifts resonates. Loud Hispanic voices and clanging of metal bars echo. Chicken chatter escalates. Sweat drenches Bean.

7:00 a.m.—*Belt beside feet jolts into action, crawling and grinding like moving sidewalk. Trap door flies open and first clucking customers glide into room.*

Showtime!

Grab. *Seventy dazed chickens per minute stunned by tranquility of darkness and warmth. Quickly wrap hand around chicken's neck and jerk into air.*

All hell breaks loose. Shock, panic, rage. God-awful squawking. Chickens scratch attackers, clawing for skin but scoring only rubber and plastic.

Flip. *Grab thrashing legs and release neck while turning and stepping to shackle line. Blood, feathers, piss, and shit fly. Chickens flail, twist, and speed-peck tormentors.*

Hang. *Jerk convulsing, upside-down chicken up and forward. Jam legs into grooves of moving, metal shackles. Limbs break. Organs hemorrhage. With luck, shackles hold.*

Turn. Repeat.

Bean's goggles fog.

Turn. Repeat.

Dizzy. Oozing sweat. Too hot. Too much spinning. Chickens piling up. Butterflies tickle inside of stomach.

"¡Rápido! ¡Rápido!" Foreman waving arms and shouting. "Faster! Faster!"

Workers can't keep up. Bean is faint. Grabs chicken and swings it too close to face. Chicken and Bean make eye contact in flash before it pecks goggles, shattering plastic and splattering blood and shit in his eyes.

Furious, he lunges forward and slams bitch chicken's legs into shackles. Shackle breaks. Sharp metal point impales gloved, middle finger of right hand, just above middle knuckle. Conveyor yanks hand and he side-hops and screams for help. Conveyed until shoulder hits wall, finger pulled as far as arm can reach. Upper half of finger r-r-

rips off and glides down disassembly line, never to be seen again.

Recoiling in pain and shock, falls to floor holding blood-gushing stump and wallows in chicken stew. Hurls morning breakfast. Last night's chili dogs go ballistic.

That was the day Bean joined the ranks of the mangled.

"I'll never be able to flip a bird with my right hand again," he oft claimed. "It's a deaf mutant. That's why I got that big disability check."

He rested at home for a week, eating ice cream and watching TV. The settlement money disappeared like smoke and left him with a pool cue finish on his nub. He massaged it now as he approached the mouth of the beast.

The earlier bottleneck at the entrance thinned, and a few fellow soldiers rushed to clock in. A Latina gal performed the ritual of the cross as she passed through the double doors. Bean sneered at the sign posted above, young Butler's sign written in Spanish then English: "DEMOCRACY STOPS AT THIS DOOR." Before crossing the threshold, he hocked from the depths of his lungs, pursed his lips, and sailed a glob into the dirt and weeds.

Chapter 15

Cal Butler surveyed live video of the employee parking lot and watched vehicles pouring in. *The plant is not ready for a government inspection. All these bastards are going to have to clean all morning. This will cost me a fortune. Government schmucks can kiss my ass.* He turned up the volume of his classical music to drown out thunderous mufflers and Latino boom boxes.

A rap at his door startled him. "Whaaat?"

Heloise stuck her head in. "Morning, Mr. Butler. Shall I make you a cappuccino?"

Butler's secretary tried to look her best in her well-worn Belk Hudson dresses that were long since stretched too tight. Heloise, a tall, big-boned country gal, wasn't the cheerleader type in high school but made a fine officer in the Future Farmers of America. She started at Majestic Chicken right after high school a dozen years ago as assistant to Mr. Butler Sr.'s secretary. She now earned more money than most at Majestic. She was paid for her loyalty. Paid to keep secrets.

"Yes, make it hazelnut. I'm ready for breakfast. See what quiche François is serving, and include fresh melon. But first, find Wilbur and have him report to me pronto *before* he goes inside the plant and gets stinked up."

Knowing a real inspection could occur that afternoon, Butler paced his suite, forced to focus more than he preferred. Hovering on a fresh Percocet buzz, he drifted in flight across the slate floor and Oriental rugs to the French doors. Winston shadowed him, his claws clicking on the slate. Logic clouded and proportionality skewed, Butler floated around the sitting area, glided past mahogany bookcases and coasted into the adjoining board room.

Call the governor? The Lieutenant Governor? The Senator? All would take an urgent call from me, and all would be motivated to help me. What about Kilroy & Russell? My highbrow Atlanta law firm has clout and sway. I'm a big enough fish for them to expend a chit or two.

Butler had no incriminating video on Griff Henry, Kilroy & Russell's lawyer—*yet.* He plotted to have him hunt at his Plantation this fall where Butler would gather blackmail ammunition. Then Henry would pull out all the stops to help him in the future.

His phone buzzed. "Yeess?"

"Wilbur is here. Shall I send him in?"

Shit. Think fast. Inspectors could be here today. "Yes, but I'm expecting a very urgent call from Radford Campbell. You need to make damn sure I take that call."

Plant Manager Wilbur Smith, looking weary and older than his sixty years, let himself in and ambled to his boss's massive desk. He sat opposite in the lone chair with its hard, wooden seat and stiff back. Butler had the legs shortened so he could look down upon any guest perched in his Seat of Inquisition. Wilbur squirmed in his baggy clothes and smoothed his tousled hair with nicotine-stained fingertips.

Cal noticed the bad comb-over and the right eye floating more freely than normal, independent of his good eye. *Looks like a chameleon. Behind the façade, though, is a glimmer of a brain. More than I can say about the other employees.* Wilbur made fleeting eye contact.

Hell, bloodshot eyes. I hope he's not on the sauce again.

Cal inherited Wilbur and suspected he'd have to fire him. Wilbur learned how to run the plant under old man Butler's by-the-numbers style but turned out to be re-trainable. *Funny how a man can get hooked on a paycheck.*

Protocol allowed Wilbur to meet in the executive suite only if he hadn't already entered the plant. Once anyone's clothes and skin were saturated with *l'odeur du poulet,* meetings were held on the rear terrace.

Butler decided not to stand, not to risk stumbling. He twirled his fountain pen and stared at Wilbur through penetrating, steel-gray eyes. "I walked the plant this morning, and Christ Almighty, there are two pallets of rotten product sitting at the nugget line. How the hell did that happen?"

"I don't know, sir. My line supervisor must have been asleep at the wheel on Friday afternoon, I guess, and forgot to get them to the cooler."

"You guess? You guess? You fool, I don't pay you to guess. You are ultimately responsible for this. What the hell you think I pay you for, to walk around and twiddle your damn thumbs? Listen here, friend, we lose that product and I'm docking your pay for half of it. You understand?"

"Sir, remember I left early—"

"Dammit. I said, do you understand? That calls for a yes or a no."

Wilbur sighed. "Yessir, I understand."

"We've got much bigger problems. We're not running the line this morning."

Wilbur focused his good, now alarmed, eye on Mr. Butler. Line stoppage at Majestic meant something drastic. "What's wrong?"

"We've got to clean. We may have a surprise inspection this afternoon from our friends at USDA. I want everyone to clean from stem to stern, double-time. We've got to sweep and bleach and rinse before they get here. We can't act like we knew they were coming so go easy on the chlorine. We need to be clean and running when they arrive."

Wilbur scratched his head and shot his boss a puzzled look. "How can it be a surprise inspection if... never mind. What about the live birds at the dock now and those that'll be comin' in today?"

"Let those already here, stay. Put all incoming trucks on hold 'til further notice." Butler drew on his cigar and spewed toward the rafters. "You can't tell anybody about the inspection. Tell our folks this is routine cleaning. Say nothing about an inspection, and act surprised when the inspectors get here."

"What about last week's lab results?"

"Oh, shit. We *have* to destroy those. These government pricks. We live in a police state, I'm telling you. Have Dr. Sanjay destroy all positive results—computer, hard copy, everything. You do the same, as will I. Have him find some good results and re-date to last week."

"Does Wimpy know about the inspection?"

"I don't know. If he is aware, he'll tell me. But we surely can't tell him that we know. We should have a few hours' notice, so make sure Wimpy's not napping on the couch in the lab when his bosses arrive."

"Yessir."

"Get everyone cleaning before you remove that rotten product. You see what those government fools are doing? Those chickens are now going to have to wait a few more days before they get processed. So get those pallets the hell out of here and onto a Majestic refrigerated truck, along with anything else that's questionable. We'll bring them back when this thing blows over. I'm already paying dearly to shut down to clean, so I damn sure can't lose any product. I have too many mouths to feed at this company, including yours. Do you understand?"

"Yessir." Wilbur looked away. "Shall I get busy now?"

"First, tell me about Butterbean Sweat. Why the hell's he coming to see me today? Can't you handle your people? He doesn't need to jump ranks and come to me every time the vending machine runs out of candy."

"He's got a bee in his bonnet about this overtime thing. I told him the company position. You don't *have* to meet with him."

"Aw, hell, I'll meet with him. I rather enjoy making the fat man squirm. It'll be comic relief."

"Sweat has a big mouth, and he worries me, sir. He drives that forklift like a maniac on speed, thinking he's a NASCAR driver."

"As long as he doesn't kill anybody with the forklift, the faster the better. But if his mouth gets too big this afternoon when I meet with him, you'll be looking for a new forklift man in the morning. For now," Cal waved the back of his hand, "chop, chop. We've got to move."

"Yessir." Wilbur made a hasty exit.

Over breakfast, Butler scrubbed bad lab results from his computer and shredded hard copies. He fumed each time he peeked at the run light and the glowing red bulb glared back.

His phone buzzed. He sighed and hit the speaker button. "Yeess, Heloise?"

"Wimpy is on the premises. Shall I send him in when he arrives?"

"Call me before sending him in."

Clyde "Wimpy" Pepper, the USDA daily inspector-in-charge at Majestic Chicken, paid a visit to the chairman's suite every day before assuming his regulatory duties. Butler doubted Atlanta would warn Wimpy of a surprise inspection for fear that he'd cover his own butt. *Maybe they're gunning for Wimpy's ass, too.*

After Wimpy rotated in as USDA inspector, it didn't take long for Cal to discover his hot buttons—cash and desserts. *Wimpy's beauty is that I cannot trust him, but at least I know it.* Cal scanned live videos, making sure his people were cleaning. The phone buzzed. *Dammit. No rest for the weary.*

"Whaaat?"

"Mr. Pepper is here. Shall I send him in?"

"Yes."

The pudgy inspector entered and made sure the door closed behind him. He shuffled to the chairman's desk on sore feet bearing slumped shoulders. His half-cropped, shoe-polish-black mustache reminded Butler of Adolf Hitler's.

Wimpy's necktie knot hung loose. Fresh sweat stains adorned the neckline and armpits of his crumpled khaki jacket, and product in his hair revealed fresh comb tracks. A worn portfolio tucked under his arm. All inspectors, except Wimpy, wore white, knee-length smocks, hard hats, and safety goggles. Wimpy had confided to Cal that he was tired of inspecting chickens and wanted to be an entrepreneur, a wheeler-dealer, and needed to look the part.

Cal remained seated with his feet on the ottoman, stroking Winston's neck with one hand and twirling his pen with the other. "Clyde, my man, how are you?"

"Exhausted." Wimpy's flabby bottom settled into the Seat of Inquisition with a thud. "This heat is killing me."

"I'll have them crank up the AC in the lab."

"Bless you, my dear man."

"I've got pastry surprises for you today." Cal knew how to keep Wimpy from snooping around the plant, knew how to make him use his imagination in filling out those forms in the comfort of the lab.

The lab morphed into a gourmet restaurant of sorts on Wimpy's account, complete with picnic table, microwave, and refrigerator. An important duty of François, Butler's Honeysuckle Plantation executive chef, was to keep Wimpy supplied with gourmet pies, cheeses, coffees, and cakes, including his favorite, cherry cheesecake.

Wimpy's duties far exceeded his ambitions, especially in this suffocating heat. "How can a civilized man keep his head in the game," he once explained to Mr. Butler, "and put his face in the cavities of all those chickens year in and year out?" Wimpy rose through seniority to daily inspector-in-charge, managing three other inspectors at Majestic. His activities these days dwindled to gathering test data from his staff and tallying the summary report while lounging in the lab, resting his arches, and nibbling cheese. The only "testing" Wimpy performed consisted of taste testing fried chicken nuggets, always the best samples.

Wimpy licked his lips and his half-moon eyelids rose at the chairman's proclamation of gastronomic surprises and cooler climes. "You are such a dear man. You know I cannot stand surprises. I shall go investigate."

Butler opened his desk drawer, slipped out a crisp one-hundred-dollar bill, and laid it in the middle of his desk. A hidden camera captured a clear image, like many times before, videos safely stored for a rainy day. A stack of hundreds with Wimpy's name on them lived in the safe and a one-a-day prescription kept the inspector healthy.

Wimpy stood on cue, seized the bill, folded it, and slipped it into his trouser pocket. "Thank you my good man. I shall gladly repay you today with a glowing report."

"Good day, Clyde. Let me know how you like the new topping on the cheesecake."

Wimpy departed, and Cal nudged Winston off his lap, stood, and grabbed deodorizer. He rounded his desk, aimed the can, and blasted the Seat of Inquisition and Wimpy's path of egress.

Acts like business as usual. I don't think he knows about the inspection.

Butler opened the surveillance closet and watched all hands filling buckets and brandishing brooms and brushes. High-powered hoses slithered and writhed. In the video, Wimpy shuffled away to the lab, apparently oblivious to the cleaning going on around him.

Pity the fool.

Chapter 16

Butterbean stepped into the mouth of the beast. Thick, pungent air hung heavy inside the building. When the wind was right, the stench escaping the plant triggered grimaces ten miles away.

The keys on Bean's retractable belt ring jingled as he strolled to the time clock. He was responsible for only two work keys but kept a few others on the chain to bolster his supervisory image. He snatched his time card from a slot along the wall and joined the last who beat the whistle at 6:59 a.m. *Perfect. I don't want to give Butler an extra minute.*

Line workers were to be in position by 7:00, but Bean needed only be ready when the first chickens hit his station at the end of the line. Those at the front, short-changed in the morning, were compensated at quitting time.

Bean hustled along the aluminum building's interior perimeter, around the disassembly line, and toward the loading dock. He noticed the overhead ice conveyer standing still. Two Latino ice shovelers waited outside the ice room in their coats and gloves, ready to enter when the huge, horizontal corkscrew piercing the heart of the floor started spinning. Line workers took their positions in aprons and hairnets, ready to don rubber gloves and goggles once the line chugged.

Good. The line ain't cranked up. Prob'ly another mechanical screw-up.

He made a restroom pit stop, two urinals and two stalls shared with half the plant's males. Fortunately, women outnumbered men three-to-one. He smelled Butler's cigar hanging in the air.

Butler's inspectin' the plant again. Wonder what all he looks at? Don't he know we can smell that cigar?

The supervisor lumbered to his workbench adjacent to two forklifts. Swinging aluminum doors of a gargantuan chill room and freezer towered down a nearby corridor. A cigar butt lay crushed on the concrete. *Butler's a damn pig.* The clipboards on the bench were in disarray. *What the hell's goin' on 'round here?*

As cooler manager and shipping checker, Bean managed one underling who beelined all day, forklifting finished product into the coolers. Bean took it from there, assembling and delivering pallets to docks A and B.

Managing an assistant granted him supervisory status, but it came with headaches. HR always sent him un-trainable stooges who had no business driving a forklift.

"How many Mexicans do you see in NASCAR?" Bean interrogated plant manager Wilbur. "Case closed. Give me a white kid from Dawsonville or the Carolinas whose grandaddy ran moonshine and is named something like Earnhardt or Elliott or Lebonte, and we'll move some pallets 'round here."

He led by example—pedal-to-the-metal. *Turn three hundred sixty degrees on a dime. Front, back, left, right. Let's see the NASCAR boys do that. Any monkey can turn left all day.*

His duties called for his initials on the shipping checker manifest each time he dropped a pallet at the loading dock. He knew his initials were crucial for accounting and government inspectors. *This is serious bidness, brother. It ain't high school no more.*

His T-shirt was already soaked from summer's heat and humidity, yet he donned his long sleeve camo shirt in preparation for inspecting his coolers.

Where the hell is Ricardo? I swear, soon as I get one trained, poof, he's gone.

Bean pushed through the chill room's swinging doors with clipboard in hand and began his daylong process of hot-to-cold-to-hot—Petri dish for catching a cold. Faint cigar scent lingered. *That sumbitch's been in here countin' pallets. He must be sharper than I thought.*

Bean's breath steamed the air as he walked the aisles recalling where pallets stood last Friday at quitting time. *Wait a minute. Things is different from what I left. Ain't no surprise. I know product moves after hours, after inspectors go home. Too much funny bidness 'round here.*

Wimpy, the USDA daily inspector-in-charge, sometimes shuffled through, but Bean was always forewarned to hide suspect pallets behind a sliding door designed to look like a permanent wall. Unlike inspectors in the past, Wimpy blew through like he had better places to be. He reminded Bean of Hardy in *Laurel and Hardy*. Even had the goofy mustache and wore a Sunday School jacket like Hardy.

Time to move product. He swung doors open and strolled toward his forklift, fiddling for the key on his chain.

Whoa. He didn't hear the grind of the disassembly line. He looked across the way. *It still ain't movin'. Great, maybe I can look at Auto Trader a while.*

He scanned the plant, looking for the cause of the shutdown. Wilbur stomped around the breading line, flailing his arms, pointing and gesturing, trying to communicate in lousy Spanglish. The plant manager turned and headed for Bean, waving a hand in the air. Wilbur loped faster than Bean had seen him move, his baggy shirt and long comb-over strands bouncing with every stride.

"Bean, Bean." Wilbur leaned forward, bracing a hand on the forklift, sucking wind, sweat dripping down his flushed face. After a breathing respite, Wilbur looked up, left eye in panic, right eye floating in its own little world.

"Quick. We got to clean all mornin'."

"Clean? Aw, man, I ain't paid to clean. I'm a forklift driver."

"Bean, you know you don't have to clean much. This is an emergency. You'll clean, or you'll get your walkin' papers."

"Yassir, Mr. Bossman, what's the occasion? We got company comin'?"

"You don't worry about that. Just get a mop and hose and get busy. Start with the worst places and hit the blood first."

"Where's *Ricardo*?"

"Hell if I know."

"You gonna get me somebody else who can drive before the line starts?"

"I'll see what I can do but cain't make no promises."

"You need to try harder than that. Maybe *you* need to come drive if you cain't find me nobody."

"I said I'll see what I can do. I'm under a lot o' pressure right now."

"I reckon so. Anybody got his head up Butler's ass far as you ought to feel somethin'. Must be suffocatin' up there."

"Shut up, Bean. I'm just tryin' to keep my job so I can feed my family, just like you. Boy, you already in enough trouble. Shut up and clean up, and don't think I don't know you're meetin' with Mr. Butler today."

"If you'd grow a sack and stand up for us, I wouldn't have to be meetin' with him."

"If you say anything to him to get me fired, so help me—"

"I ain't gonna try to get you fired 'cause I know it's comin' from Butler. He ain't nuthin' like his old man. But I'm telling ya, you goin' down a bad path. This plant gets busted and you know who Butler's gonna point the finger at, don't ya?"

"Last warnin'. Quit bumpin' your gums or you're fired. When I want your opinion, I'll ask for it. Now, clean."

"Okey-dokey. If you say so, John Wayne."

Wilbur spun and hurried away, working his way back up the line, pointing and barking orders as pressure hoses blasted and scrub brooms swept in a frenzy.

Ain't that some shit. Bean detested cleaning. Under old man Butler, cleaning was always part of the job. It wasn't so bad to clean along-and-along, before the mold and slime built up. Young Butler ordered cleaning on only two occasions—down times in the line or for an upcoming inspection.

El Gringo set out cleaning, cursing, and grumbling. *My boots is gettin' covered in bleach and chicken blood. Them deer are gonna smell me a mile away come huntin' season.*

Tired of cleaning, he decided on a mid-morning constitutional. *Ah, the luxury of being Supervisor.* Line workers had to get permission to go to the can except for break time and lunch. He made sure the coast was clear, inserted a Red Man plug, and stuffed a rolled-up *Auto Trader* in his pocket.

He kept a lookout for Cisco, the Latino reputed to be the fastest bone popper and thigh breaker in all of Georgia, and rumored to have Hepatitis C. Bean worried about catching it himself, whatever "it" was. The secret agent man in him made sure he never followed Cisco into the john.

No sign of him. Bean spotted a machine operator at the sink splashing water on his face. "What's the matter, amigo? Too many margaritas last night?"

"No, El Gringo. Blood pressure, I think."

"Hell, I can help you there. What you do is, get a sharp blade and knick your fingertip. Squeeze your wrist with your other hand like this. Drain some o' that blood off, and the pressure will come down. It's simple science."

"¡Gracias, amigo! I'll do it tonight."

Bean slipped into the stall—no lock—conducted his business then lingered a while, checking on Chevy trucks and bass boats in *Auto Trader.* Anything but mop.

He strolled back to his station where he spotted Wilbur pacing with a middle-aged Latino looking on.

"Where the hell you been?"

"Pinchin' off a loaf."

"I got a man here to drive for you. His name is Hay-Seuss."

The well-postured man of medium height was light skinned for a Latino. His black hair skimmed his shoulders, and a thick beard hedged his chin. His clothes were threadbare but clean.

The man smiled and nodded as Bean looked him up and down. "How you spell that?"

"'Fraid he don't speak too much English," Wilbur said. "He spells it J-e-s-u-s. Like in the Bible."

"You mean Jesus is coming to work at Majestic Chicken?"

"He ain't Jesus," Wilbur said. "He's Hay-suess. I wish he was Jesus."

"How you make a 'Hay' out a 'J'?"

"Beats me, Sweat, take it up with Mexico. Job center claims he can drive a lift. All you got to do is show him what to do."

"Guess I'll have to show him 'cause I damn sure can't tell him, now can I? How long has he been drivin'?"

"I don't know, Bean, ask him. You need to finish cleanin' cause we're probably going live after lunch. I got to go." Wilbur whirled and shuffled away.

Bean sized up Jesús. Clear, intelligent eyes. Sincere and agreeable attitude. Seemed anxious to work. Bean felt an odd compulsion to show this man respect.

"*Buenos días. Mi nombre es* Butterbean Sweat. *Mucho gusto. ¿Es usted de Mèxico?*"

"*Sí,* Señor Sweat. *Soy de* Veracruz."

Bean remembered last week's special at Amigo Gordo with great fondness—Chili Rellenos del Veracruz. *This feller cain't be all bad.*

Bean walked him over to the second Nissan forklift and pointed. "You know how to drive this?" Bean pretended to hold his hands on the wheel, turning left and right.

"*Sí,* Señor Sweat."

Bean released a key from his belt ring and tossed it to the new man, pointed to an open area, and twirled his wrist. "Drive around this area and do some stop-and-goes and turns. Comprehend-o?"

"*Sí.*" In seamless movements, Jesús mounted and cranked her. She beeped when he threw her into reverse then she glided like an ice dancer, cutting flawless geometric, loop-de-loop patterns, backward and forward, curving in perfect concentric circles.

Bean's jaw dropped. *The smoothest thing I ever seen on a forklift.* A tear welled up.

Jesús glided the lift beside Bean, stepped down, and nodded.

Bean tried to gather his composure. He started to speak, stopped himself, and stood in awkward silence. Finally he stepped close to Jesús and whispered. "Are you really Jesus? I mean Christ, like in the Bible, who come back like You said You would?"

Jesús smiled and shrugged. "*No comprendo.*"

"Come on, you can tell me. I won't tell nobody. I always knowed You was real. Really, I swear I did. I knowed You'd sneak back when we wasn't watchin', but I didn't think You'd be drivin' no forklift in a chicken plant."

Jesús shook his head. "*No comprendo,* Señor Sweat.*"

Bean studied genuine confusion in the man's face. *The real Jesus would know English, I'm purty sure.* He walked Jesús through the work routine in Spanglish then heard Wilbur's voice and turned.

The plant manager bent and rested his hands on his knees, disheveled and perspiring. "Come with me."

Bean motioned to Jesús like a puppy in training. "Stay. Stay."

"No, no." Wilbur corrected, "Both o' ya bring a lift. I'll ride with you, Bean." Wilbur stepped up and held on. "To the head o' the nugget line."

Butterbean and Wilbur took off, and Bean waved *Jesús* to follow. Wilbur rode shotgun in violation of the rule *he* laid down. Jesús tailed hot on their heels.

"We got two pallets up here that need loadin'. I need to show 'em to you. A Majestic truck should be waitin' at the dock."

Whatever, thought Bean. "What should I put on my log?"

"Don't worry, I'll handle the paperwork on these two."

Bean's eyebrows shot up. "My orders from Master Butler are to put *everything* goin' out the door on my log, no exceptions."

"People in Hell want ice water, too, and that ain't gonna happen either. You need to dig the wax outta your ears, Sweat. I said I'll handle the paperwork. This ain't outgoin'. We're just sendin' 'em for testin'."

"Testin'? Wha'chu talkin' 'bout? We got our own testin' people here. Your nose is growin', Pinocchio."

"Bean, shut up, and don't give me no trouble on this. Just get these damn pallets on that truck, you hear?"

"Yassir, Mr. Bossman. Whatever you say." They screeched to a halt by the pallets and hopped off. Bean's head snapped back when he inhaled the stench. "Good-Gawd-Amighty. Them things need to go in the dump."

"Just get 'em on the truck and don't give me no lip." Wilbur hustled away.

Bean and Jesús each forked a pallet and high-tailed it back to loading, gagging downwind of the rotting chicken. They dropped the pallets into the belly of the waiting refrigerator truck and parked their lifts.

"Dinnertime," Bean indicated by shoveling imaginary spoon-fuls into his mouth. He gathered his keys, snuck a Red Man chew, and bolted for the lunchroom to get a cold Coca-Cola.

Waiting at the door for the lunch whistle to blow, he postured like a runner at the starting line, ever on the lookout for Wilbur. His tongue massaged the tobacco and the sweet nicotine high kicked in.

Chapter 17

*B*utler's day wasn't going well. Never does when a USDA visit is in the offing. *Too much bullshit. Why can't things be simple? I need a quick diversion.* He popped a Percocet and logged onto his premium porn site while waiting on Heloise to bring lunch. The chairman scrolled through the menu of fresh videos, chose one, leaned back, and reveled in lust.

Seems an unwitting tourist's car broke down in shantytown. Four leather-clad bikers stepped forward to help "get her engine started." *Nice plotline.* He marveled at their equipment and the actress's ability to accommodate. *Mercy, she must be a contortionist.* The crazed bikers had their way with her. He imagined starring in the movie, getting his piece of the action. Testosterone pumped through his veins. He massaged himself knowing he would return to this video later, alone and naked. The phone buzzed.

"Whaaat?"

"We have your lunch. May we bring it in?"

He stopped his movie as Heloise and the assistant chef from Honeysuckle Plantation entered and hurried to set his dining table. "François sends his regards," the Chef said as he arranged with five-star flair—chardonnay poached salmon with dill dijon whipped cream, asparagus parmigianino, and fresh berries. *"Bon appétit,* Mr. Butler.*"* The chef bowed then snapped to attention.

"Thank you, dismissed. Heloise, stay for a moment. When is my next appointment?"

"It's at two o'clock with Mr. Parkman."

"Jesus, that's going to be painful. I'm afraid it's time for old Bob to resign from the board."

"That's too bad. He's been a director since your father founded the company."

"I know, but times have changed. To be perfectly honest, Parkman is stuck in a time warp. He's getting under my feet, so to speak, and it's time he moves on. I just hope he doesn't make a big stink. Dismissed."

Heloise nudged the bridge of her glasses up her nose and stared at him in silence then departed. He groaned when he saw the run light still glowing red. Big Boss took his tray to the surveillance monitor to dine while spying on his employees. Everyone still cleaned—receiving dock, evisceration line, re-hang—right down the line. After perusing the plant, he focused on the scenes in the men and women's restrooms, hoping for something entertaining. Nothing doing. Back to the biker video. Before he could rejoin the flow, Heloise buzzed him.

"Do you mind, Heloise, I'm trying to eat lunch. What is it?"

"I have Radford Campbell and Mr. Griffin Henry of Kilroy & Russell on the phone. You told me you needed to take this call."

"For Godsakes, yes. Put it through."

"Cal, we've got good news." Campbell's voice seemed to elevate an octave when he delivered good news and a handsome paycheck was in the offing. "We got the inspection postponed until tomorrow morning. Go ahead, Griff, tell him how we did it."

"I decided to call a friend high up in USDA Safety and Inspection in our region," Griff explained. "He worked with me on a big project when I was with the Department. Obviously, I had to be real careful about what I said."

"Yes, yes—" Butler intoned.

"This guy happens to be related to the governor's wife, and they know what a big friend and supporter you are. I explained, off the record, you had a personnel issue with your plant manager, and if any inspections happened to be planned for the next couple of days, could he please buy us some time. He was flabbergasted that I may know about their surprise inspection, but I didn't admit anything. He said the inspection team was driving down as we spoke, and he finally agreed to hold them off until tomorrow morning. He said he could fake it with his people once, but don't even think about making it a pattern."

"Hey, hey," Campbell piped in, "I told you we'd get it postponed somehow."

Butler breathed a sigh of relief but knew not to show it because Campbell wouldn't hesitate to double an invoice if he sensed a client's glee. "Is that all I get, a half-day postponement?"

"Cal, a half-day is a gift from God Himself, compliments of your lawyers. You have no idea how difficult it is to postpone an inspection in these circumstances. This is truly a legal miracle. You've got time to clean today and be running when they arrive in the morning."

Cal sighed, "Listen, pal, I hear you. But between us chickens, I'm disappointed that's all the time I get. If that's the best you two can do, let me go so I can act accordingly."

Butler signed off and paged his plant manager. He removed his Guccis, leaned back, and propped his bare feet on his desk. He grinned, re-fired, and savored the burn of a thrice-lit cigar. *Know the right people and grease the right palms. That's about the only way to make it in business now-a-days.*

He met Wilbur on the terrace and conveyed the news. "Douche bag inspectors will be here first thing in the morning. Wrap up the cleaning and get the line going ASAP. Those schmucks are costing me a fortune."

The chairman sauntered back inside and settled into his chair. A Percocet relieved his chest pressure. The phone buzzed.

"Dammit, Heloise, what form of woe are you going to burden me with now?"

"Mr. Parkman is due soon, and we have some things we need to cover. May I come in?"

"Yes, with a cappuccino and aspirin."

"Yes, Mr. Butler."

Heloise knocked and entered, balancing her boss's steaming cup on a silver tray with a portfolio tucked under her arm. She settled into the Seat of Inquisition.

Butler sipped, leaned back, and twirled his pen. He gazed at her and smiled. *I know my good looks are overwhelming you, especially compared to your redneck husband.* Many women, in fact, considered Cal Butler handsome in his cloak of wealth and power. "Well?"

"The jet company needs to know how many will be flying out next Wednesday so they can send the proper jet. Are rifles traveling?"

"Hell yeah, there'll be rifles. I'm not hunting grizzlies with a knife."

"Yessir. Do you know how many will be flying?"

Cal cocked his head toward the ceiling and focused. "Four. Tell them four."

"Thank you. Next, the taxidermist from Memphis called. They're ready to ship your mounts from the Colorado hunting trip. Would you like them shipped here, to Honeysuckle, or to your home—"

"Godsakes, don't ship them home, Charlotte would flip. Send them to Honeysuckle, and let staff know they'll be arriving."

"Fine. You're scheduled to meet with Butterbean Sweat after the shift ends."

"Aw, hell. I know. That tub o' guts always wants something. He seems to think he's the anointed one. I know he'll bitch about overtime pay, but does he have other issues today? Wrong candy bars in the machine, perhaps?"

"I don't know, sir, but remember last week, Wilbur gave him a code red warning under our new disciplinary system. One more violation and he's fired."

"That's right. I guess the big baby is sweating now. Ha, ha, pun intended. Hell, okay. But reschedule it, I've got a lot on my plate right now."

"Sir, last week you told me this afternoon would be okay. It's been on your calendar. He's called me three times to see if the meeting is still on."

"You know, that boy is dumber than a box of rocks. Butterbean is a perfect name for him. If he pushes me on this, he'll never work in this town again. Some people just can't appreciate a paycheck and benefits. He has most of his family on our insurance, and they're all heart attacks and diabetics waiting to happen. We lucked out by not having to add his daughter and her retarded foot on our policy. I may give him five minutes, so he'll have to talk fast. Call Mutt for backup."

"Yessir, Mr. Butler. That's all."

"Did Radford Campbell's office email a document that Parkman is supposed to sign?"

"I haven't received it."

The instant Heloise closed the door, Cal tapped his speakerphone button then speed dialed Radford.

A sweet young voice answered, "Campbell and Associates." He had heard that voice moan in ecstasy and tickle his ear at cheap, no-tell-motels around town.

"Melissa, darling, how are you doing this afternoon?"

"Just fine, Cal." She whispered. "How are you doing, sweetheart?"

"I've had better, but the thought of you in that fishnet outfit brings me back to life."

"*Shhh,* careful you little imp. You never know who's listening in. Do you need me or Mr. Campbell?"

"I always need you, but I need Radford right away."

"Okay, honey. He's in a meeting, but I'll pull him out. Hold please."

The chairman leaned back and propped up his feet. Through a haze, he focused on his bookcases along the opposite wall.

There, next to his black-tie photo with the governor, rested his favorite plaque...

A Feast is Made for Laughter, and Wine Maketh Merry, But Money Answereth all Things.

He bought the plaque in a pawnshop while in junior high. He later learned it was a Bible quote, and he twisted it to good use. Ever since, it's been near his desk, ingrained in his psyche, his Golden Rule. *Time to trade the Jag for another Mercedes.*

"Cal." Campbell's all-too familiar voice boomed over the speakerphone, "I told you we could buy some time with that inspection, didn't I? I'm waiting on a call from the senator as soon as they recess from committee in Washington. If he calls, I need to take it, believe me. What's up?"

"Parkman is due in my office soon. What about the document you wanted me to have him sign?"

"We're making changes to it right now. We'll email Heloise in a few minutes. Good luck on getting his signature. We could use it. I sure don't trust him anymore. I don't know how you'll get him to sign."

"Maybe I can convince him that signing will be in his best interest. I'll let you know how it turns out. Oh, the run light just turned green. I'm back in business."

The chairman hung up and gulped a sigh of relief. He gazed at the green run light with a smile then flipped his computer back to the biker gang-bang. He concentrated and tried to teleport himself into the action.

"Mr. Butler? Mr. Butler?" Heloise's voice was shrill on the intercom. "Are you there?"

Butler jolted to attention.

"Yes. What is it now?"

"Mr. Parkman is here for his appointment."

"Shit. He's early, isn't he?"

"Yes, sir, I mean no, sir."

"All right. Make sure the boardroom is clean. I don't want him snooping around any papers. Then usher him in and make him wait."

Chapter 18

*B*ean spilled into daylight the second the lunch whistle blew. One step out and he rifled brown juice into the dirt. He lit a cig and headed for his Chevy. Many co-workers ate in the lunch-room, either their own food or from vending machines, but not him. He needed to climb out of the beast, even if it meant getting drenched in sweat. *Oh, but for twenty minutes in my own world. Home away from home.*

"Bean, wait up." Pickle Joe wasn't far behind, walking in his awkward yet rhythmic gait.

Bean stopped and turned. PJ's neck undulated like a giraffe with each stride. While waiting, Bean drifted back to the time he discovered the truth about Pickle Joe Johnson.

"Hey, why they call you 'Pickle'?" He asked one day after hiring on at Majestic Chicken.

"I don't know. It's a name I got back in high school gym class."

Bean didn't pursue it, but PJ's answer intrigued him for weeks. *What's high school gym class got to do with it? Prob'ly his long neck.* Then, at Fat Back Hunt Club when Bean was a newbie, a beaver dam caused flooding.

"We got to bust that dam or it's gonna take out the road." Otis Odom, club president, declared by the bonfire at the annual meeting. "Any volunteers?"

"Why don't we get Pickle Joe," shouted one of the boys. "He can swing his dick like a wrecking ball and bust it. Ha, ha."

Bean caught on and his curiosity piqued. On morning break one day, he strolled toward PJ's restroom and hung out at the water fountain, thumbing through papers on his clipboard.

When PJ walked into the men's room, Bean followed and, trying to act natural, assumed the position at the urinal next to PJ. "Man, summer done come early again."

"What you complainin' 'bout, Bean? You in that cooler all day settin' on that cushy forklift seat. You ain't got no worries."

The men unzipped, pulled out their trouser snakes, and whizzed. Man Code prohibits roaming eyes at the urinal, but not this day. "It ain't no fun goin' from cold-to-hot-to-cold all day." He snuck a peek.

Shit!

He yanked his stare back. He heard PJ talking but didn't comprehend, his mind exploding into a million pieces over the image branded into his psyche.

That slab o' meat is hangin' halfway to his knees. Is it a optical conclusion? One more covert gander. Rotating his head ever so slightly, he cut his eyes like a lizard and saw urine flowing from the bottom of the telephone pole.

Good Gawd! It's real. Long as my forearm. A real donkey dick. PJ drained the tank and reached way down and shook it like an elephant's trunk. Bean tried to act normal as they parted. His mind traveled to places it had never visited as he wandered back to the cooler in a daze, bumping into people.

What a lucky sumbitch! If I had a pecker like that, I'll be damned if I'd be workin' in a chicken plant. I'd be in Hollywood. I'd be President. I'd be the richest man in the universe. I'd be...

He worked the list, stretching his imagination as he lay in bed with Ruby at night, holding his equipment in the cup of his hand, his shortcoming haunting him. Hell, he had to fish his weenie out and stretch it just to clear his pants when he peed.

A range of emotions cycled through him after that fateful morning. Wonderment and awe. Jealousy and envy. Anger at God. Humility and sorrow for himself. In time, he forgave PJ. Lady Luck had tapped him on the shoulder and inducted him into the lucky sperm club, a child of genetic fortune.

He fantasized about his staff being equal to PJ's before he made love to Ruby, arousing himself with the vision as he sashayed around the bedroom in his Dale Earnhardt boxers, working her up. *I could give it to her good if I had that rod.* As it was, by the time his Vienna sausage cleared his *and* her folds of fat…

Now he understood why PJ always wore baggy pants. *If it was me, I'd wear skin tight britches and be eye candy for all the bitches.* He grew to realize that word of such endowment is the worst kept secret. Bean heard countless off-the-cuff references through the years. Hints dropped, rumors circulated.

Even a preacher's daughter hopped on the fantasy train at the grocery store. She and Bean were in the meat section when she picked up a sixteen-ounce tube of breakfast sausage, caressed it, smiled and said, "So tell me, how's Joe Johnson doin' these days?"

Of course, Bean didn't exactly guard the secret when he was with the boys. "Pickle Joe's dick is so big, it gets an extra thirty minutes for lunch," he'd joke. Or, "His dick is so big, it still has snow on the top in the summer."

He forced himself to forgive PJ for his forgetfulness, knowing there wasn't enough blood in his body to feed both heads.

"It's like this," PJ explained to Bean when the topic finally surfaced. "I was given a choice—a big dick or a good memory. I cain't remember which I chose."

"Damn," PJ said when he reached Bean. "You been cleanin' all mornin' like me?"

"Yep. Somethin's up. You can bet your ass on that."

"We swept up so many rotten chicken parts, I liked to puke." PJ shivered. "Then Wilbur made me and a couple o' the boys go to the dock where they load parts headin' for the incinerator. We could hardly get through the flies to spray the maggots with poison. That was kinda fun seein' the bastards squirm. We covered 'em with sand and dirt."

Bean splattered tobacco juice on the asphalt. "Wilbur had me load a couple o' pallets o' rotten chicken onto the company truck."

"It's about time. Them things been stinkin' up the place, if that's possible. They was s'posed to be processed Friday and didn't make it."

"They gone now. Bet you money them pallets show back up when this is over."

They reached their vehicles on the shadeless blacktop, heat ribbons wavering off hoods. PJ cocked a thumb toward his Chrysler Imperial, a land yacht, a 1993 relic with 150,000 miles but still kicking. "We can eat in my car if you want."

"Same answer as always—I get a bellyful of Majestic and all things royal during working hours. I ain't sittin' in nothin' 'imperial' during my lunch break."

PJ grabbed his lunch sack from his cooler and joined Bean who idled his truck with the AC blaring. "Man, it's hot enough to melt ear wax."

Each spread his buffet over his thighs. Bean studied PJ's fare. "What'd your old lady make you?"

"Who knows. It's soggy as hell. Smells funny." PJ took a bite, cringed, and opened his door to spit onto the blacktop. "It tastes like a lard sammich." He guzzled Coca-Cola.

"That bad? What the hell is it?"

"Cain't tell." PJ hocked and spit again. "I'm gonna have to lick a cat's ass to get the taste out my mouth. I think she's tryin' to poison me."

"I thought you and your old lady made up."

"Naw, she's actin' weird again. It's like Granpa said, 'If it's got tits or tires, sooner or later you gonna have trouble with it.' 'Least I got some Fritos. What you got for dinner?"

"The one thing I don't need after this mornin'—Majestic Chicken I barbecued last night. Eat at my own risk, I guess. That and a Snickers. Here, you can have some chicken."

Bean reached into the back seat, found a bag of pork cracklings, and laid them open to share. The two scarfed.

PJ came up for air. "Speakin' o' my old lady, her beer belly is growin' by the day. It'd be nice to have a woman whose gut don't stick out past her tits."

Bean turned to stare at him, BBQ sauce smeared nose to chin like a hyena pulling its bloody face out of an antelope's gut.

"Wha'chu mean? That's more cushin' for the pushin.' You don't want to get bruised up by humpin' some bag o' bones, do ya?"

They set back into gobbling. Bean came up for air. "You ain't gonna believe who come to work for me today."

PJ paused. "Who?"

"Jesus."

"*What?*" BBQ sauce dripped down PJ's chin.

"I ain't kiddin'. Jesus is my co-pilot on the forklifts. He looks like the real thing and drives like only the real Jesus could. Wouldn't you know it, Christ comes back as a Mexican."

"Jesus? You ain't serious. Is this guy some kind o' religious freak?"

"I ain't sure. He pronounces it Hey-Suess. He's from Veracruz, somewhere in Mexico. He can drive a forklift better than anybody… 'cept me."

"Jesus is come back and workin' under Butterbean Sweat at Majestic Chicken. I guess you can kill me now since I done heard it all."

Bean reached into his back seat, fished out a *National Enquirer*, scanned the front page, threw it back, and fished out another.

"See, look at this picture of a enchilada. A lady in Tijuana saw the Virgin Mary in it. See right there? That tells me He could be Mexican when He comes back, but I didn't think He'd work at no chicken factory."

"PJ pointed to the *National Enquirer*. Only thing *that* paper's good for is wrappin' fish. But just in case, keep me posted. If he feeds the whole plant with five loaves and two fishes, you let me know." PJ dropped a gnawed bone into the trash bag and grabbed a drumstick. "What about Butler? You still meetin' this afternoon?"

"I reckon, unless he chickens out. I been figurin'. That boy was so young when he took over the company, he still had milk on his breath. Growin' up, his daddy prob'ly told him he could be anything he wanted so he decided to become an asshole."

"What if he fires ya?"

"I'll wait by his fancy car and give him sump'n good to re-member me by—some chin music. A good ole country ass-wh-uppin', that's what he needs."

"Call me tonight when you get home?"

"You know Ruby'll be workin' the phone, keepin' up with the latest gossip. I'll call you if he fires me. Otherwise, I'll tell you about it in the mornin'."

The heat rendered Bean's Snickers bar mush. He whipped out his hunting knife and sliced off the wrapper's top. He tilted his head back, aimed for his mouth, squeezed from top to bottom and deposited the entire contents.

Bean gnashed chocolate, nuts, and caramel. He cocked his eyes, saw PJ start to drop a half-eaten chicken piece into the bag, and grabbed his wrist. "*Whoa*, podnah, you finished with that chicken? You know they's starvin' young-uns in Africa."

Bean cleaned up the chicken while PJ turned his Frito bag upright to finish the crumbs. "Time to go."

They walked back behind a clutch of Vietnamese women who jabbered with extra gusto.

Bean cupped his ear to hear better. "Listen at 'em a-yingin' and a-yangin'. I wish I knowed what they was sayin'."

"Maybe they tryin' to figure out if Jesus could be Mexican."

"Naw, they wouldn't know nuthin' 'bout it. Them Orientals got a different Jesus. Buddha or Mohammed, somethin' like dat."

Chapter 19

 utler studied gray-haired Bob Parkman on the monitor and his angst escalated. The last of the old-line Majestic Chicken Company directors had become an obstructionist to his corporate vision. A killjoy. *He knows too much... is too close to my sisters.*

The boardroom's camcorder and microphone, hidden in a fake smoke alarm in the ceiling, had proven invaluable when Butler left the room after board meetings to allow directors to talk "in private" about his management. Parkman was not an ally.

Cal watched Parkman hang his jacket on the back of a director's chair, sip coffee, and stroll around the room looking at paintings. The aging director stopped and gazed at the oil portrait of the two Calvin Butlers.

Parkman played a key role in helping Calvin Sr. increase company revenue twenty-fold. They predicted the increase in demand for chicken so Cal Sr. started a chicken farm and feed mill.

Parkman then recommended that Cal Sr. build a chicken processing plant, one of south Georgia's first. They performed due diligence together, and Parkman's bank extended itself in making the loan to build the plant. Parkman advised changing the company name from "Butler Farms" to the loftier "Majestic Chicken Company." The senior Butler further vertically integrated the company by building a hatchery and grow-out facility and by starting a trucking line. He turned away many offers from big players to buy his thriving business to keep it as a legacy for his children.

Parkman and Calvin Sr. sat on each other's boards and were key civic leaders. Their families grew close. Vacations and holidays, births and deaths, always together. Parkman sat at his friend's side for the birth of the four Butler children. He mentored all four and knew them well. So he thought.

In this new era after his father's death, Cal neither needed nor wanted Parkman. He moved the banking relationship to his good friend, a fellow progressive. They sat on each other's board and, more importantly, each other's compensation committee.

Cal closed the surveillance closet door, returned to his desk, slid a Percocet home, and beckoned Winston to his lap. He turned the Corgi's head so they were eye-to-eye, man-to-dog. "I'm afraid it's time for Bob Parkman to move on. What do you think? You can tell me what you think. It's down to us. We're the chairmen. We own more than fifty percent of the company, you and me, and we can out-vote my sisters. The decision is ours. Do we boot the old man out the door? Come on." He extended his hand to Winston. "Give me your paw if you think we ought to boot him."

Winston extended his paw and they shook. "Bingo. Thank you, buddy. I agree. Let's go do this thing."

The chairman scooped up the document prepared by Radford Campbell and strutted from his office to the boardroom, making his grand entrance with Winston prancing at his heels. Wearing a nervous grin, he shook Parkman's hand.

"How are you, Bob?"

"Not well."

Butler laid his document face down on the table, sat, and raised his loafers and white ankles to rest in the adjacent chair. Winston hopped onto his master's lap. Cal leaned back and twirled his Mont Blanc fountain pen. "What's on your mind?"

"I'm sick."

"What's wrong?"

"I'm sick over what you've done to Majestic Chicken. I don't want anything to do with it anymore. I'm resigning as director."

Perfect, Butler thought. "You were always my father's favorite. To be perfectly honest, we'll miss you."

"Bullshit. You don't want me around here, and we both know it."

The chairman shifted and sat erect. Parkman had never spoken in such a direct manner to him. "Whatever," Cal said, "there's no need to debate."

"I intend to have my say, whether you like it or not. You're ruining this company and robbing your sisters blind. Each inherited one quarter of the company, like you. What you inherited was the result of your father's excellent work for over three decades. Now, you're strangling the goose that lays golden eggs."

"I don't need a lecture from you, pal."

"The hell you don't. You're paying yourself ten times what's reasonable, like you're running a Fortune One Hundred company. You would have been fired long ago if this company were public."

"Look, my sisters just sit on their asses by the mailbox waiting for gravy. I'm the one putting sweat and blood into this company. They didn't step up. I earn every nickel I'm paid. To be perfectly honest, they're damn lucky I'm looking after their interests. They *should* kiss the ground I walk on."

Parkman edged his chair forward, crossed his arms on the table, and stared straight into Butler's eyes.

"You've lost contact with reality. Why do *you* think you deserve to have your ownership increase by twenty percent a year through stock grants at the same time you're driving the company into the ground? Then you have the audacity to gross-up your salary so the company pays the tax on the grants. It's unconscionable. Did you learn that lesson from Wall Street?"

Parkman shook his head. "You've gradually reduced the dividend from a dollar per share to a nickel, and your bank should have stopped that months ago. During that time, your compensation has tripled. You've cozied up with your new banker friend, and he lent you a whole lot more than he should have. He let you suck out the equity, and I don't know how the company will ever pay it back. The shame of it is, very little of the money went into the business. It's gone to your salary, trips around the world on private jets, Honeysuckle Plantation, and God knows what else. This is narcissistic entitlement at its worst. It's outrageous. I am certain your father is turning over in his grave. What kind of man would steal from his own family? They're your sisters, for Chrissakes. You owe them better."

Veins bulged on the chairman's neck, and he jerked upright in his chair then stomped his feet on the floor. "You're a fine one to be talking." He huffed and his heart pounded. "You and your bank sure made a ton of money off my family through the years. Helped build that fancy house you live in. You seem to have lost sight of that fact. Seems to me, you aren't paying proper respect to the family that helped you so much."

"Oh, my young friend, that's exactly what I'm doing. I'm standing up for your sisters and your father's memory. You take your director buddies on whirlwind private jet vacations, and they rubber-stamp anything you do. Now, with the help of your little weasel lawyer, you own two-thirds of the company and net income is approaching zero."

"Are you opposed to giving a chief executive officer incentive? Last I checked, you own a very healthy interest in that bank of yours."

"Earned through performance. I've grown it from a community bank into a regional power. You know your father bought my stock at two dollars a share and, with various stock splits, it's now worth a hundred dollars a share. But in your case, Majestic Chicken is nose-diving. The plant is filthy. You're on the USDA watch list and could be shut down over one more infraction. Morale in the plant is at rock bottom. You and that little smart-ass lawyer can't keep skating on thin ice forever. You're stabbing your sisters in the back, and you know it—"

"Wait a second. Let me tell you, pal, we've got our problems, but money isn't one of them. As for my sisters, I'll handle them.

They understand this is a family business. Like my father said, "Family comes first."

"Oh please. I'm going to throw up."

Cal fidgeted, chuckled and shook his head. *How dare he.* "Look, I'm fucking this duck. Go fuck your own duck."

Parkman stood. "This is all very wrong, morally, even criminally. I'll have no more part. I'm resigning from the board and informing your sisters as to the reason."

Cal Butler bolted to his feet, head spinning in a buzz. He stared Parkman down, gathering his nerve, lips pursed in a smile.

"Resign? I have super-majority voting rights, and you are fired as of right now."

Parkman grabbed his jacket. "I wash my hands of you, you egomaniac."

"You will not talk to my sisters. They are housewives who can't be bothered, and that's how they will stay. "

"I have a fiduciary duty to tell them what's going on here. I owe it to them and to your father. You can't prevent my talking to them. I've known them their whole lives, and I'll talk to them whenever I please."

"Bullshit."

"Who's going to stop me?"

Cal sat, flipped over his lawyer's document and slid it across the table.

"What the hell is this?"

"Confidentiality agreement, hold harmless, release of all claims, indemnity, whatever else Campbell thought to throw in."

Parkman picked up the document, scanned it and shot it back across the table. "You're crazy. I'm not signing this. I'll be bound by existing law on these issues, not some one-sided document Campbell conjured up."

"Somehow I thought you may say that. Wait here. I'll be right back." Cal stood and stars filled his eyes as he tried to walk a straight line. He strutted into his office, regrouped, and returned with a PC. He scrolled to a file, queued up a video, and shoved the screen in front of Parkman.

"Sit down and pay very close attention." The chairman interlaced his fingers behind his head, licked his lips, and leaned back.

Parkman looked bewildered and glared at Butler with knitted brows. He sat and stared at a grainy video Butler recorded when he was an amateur learning the nuances of spy cameras.

An empty bed filled most of the screen in an aerial shot. Distant voices and laughter wafted in a drift of electronic snow. Wooden rough-hewn bedposts towered toward the ceiling. The quilt was unmistakable—the distinctive Honeysuckle Plantation logo embroidered in the center.

Parkman's brows shot up. His jaw dropped, and he flushed fire engine red. He sat upright and covered his mouth with his hand as he continued to watch. A door closed and a couple tumbled onto the bed. The woman wore a tight-fitting, low-cut blouse. The man... Parkman gasped when he saw himself on-screen.

The couple groped and embraced in a long, moaning kiss. The woman pushed him back and slid off her blouse. Heavy, rounded breasts bounced. The man buried his face into her cleavage, lips smacking, tongue gliding over her nipples.

Parkman sneered at Butler and pointed his finger. "You son of a bitch."

Cal stared into Parkman's eyes, into his soul, and grinned.

The woman pulled his head away from her breasts and pushed him onto his back. She unbuckled his pants while he unbuttoned his shirt. The man raised his hips as she slid his pants down to his knees. He groaned when she straddled him.

The director pushed back from the table. "Stop it. Turn the thing off, you bastard. I can't believe it. You set me up with that hooker, and you *recorded* it. You low-down scum. You're not the son of the man I knew for forty years. You're the son of Satan. I shouldn't be surprised. It was illegal for you to record that without my knowledge, and no court in the land would allow it as evidence."

Cal grinned. "Who said anything about court, pal? Right now, this is just between you and me, and that's the way it'll stand if you wish. Or, we can involve your wife and three children. Your choice."

"You son of a bitch. Are you trying to blackmail me?"

"I don't want a nickel from you. All I want is your silence. All you have to do is sign your name and live by this agreement, and it will remain our little secret. Radford Campbell doesn't even know about this video."

Butler felt a surge of magnanimity over his control and discretion. He *really* wanted to share the video with Campbell and others, to laugh at Parkman for being such a gullible fool and a lousy lover to boot. He wanted to gloat about his brilliant spy work but realized the value of a well-kept secret.

Parkman slumped back into his chair and held his face in his trembling hands. He dropped his hands and glared at Butler.

"If my family ever sees or learns of this, so help me God, I will kill you. Do you hear me? I will hunt you down and kill you."

Butler held up his palms. "*Whoa*, pal, calm down. This is business. I'm just trying to look out for Majestic Chicken Company's best interests."

"Bullshit. In five short years, you have destroyed this business and your good family name it took a generation to build. You, my friend, are going to burn in Hell for eternity."

"Whatever. Now, are you going to sign? I have other appointments this afternoon." Butler wasn't worried so much about appointments as getting to his Percocet, stress having flatlined his buzz and tightened his chest.

"What are you asking me to do?"

"Just zip your lip. Keep your mouth shut about Majestic Chicken *and* me. That means to my sisters, other directors—" Cal flipped fingers into the air as he ticked off his list "– the press, the government, your friends, your best fishing buddy, the waitress at the corner diner, your priest, your shrink, et cetera. To be honest, just keep quiet, and you've got nothing to worry about."

"You bastard. If I sign, I want the original movie and all copies."

"Can't do that, Bob. I need to keep a copy to enforce this agreement. You have my word. If you keep quiet, nobody will ever see this."

Parkman bowed his head and shook it. "Your word is worth about as much as a bucket of warm spit." He reached out, scribbled his name on the document, and rose from the table. The defeated warrior stomped out without a parting glance.

Chapter 20

The disassembly line cranked up after lunch for the first time that day. In a blink, chickens were moving through the plant—hung, stunned, bled, scalded, decapitated, eviscerated, cut-up, deboned, processed, packaged, labeled, chilled, and shipped.

Plant workers scurried in their usual rhythm—heads bobbing, shoulders, arms, and hands working in repetitive motions. A river of chickens signaled life back to normal to Bean's relief. *That's poultry in motion, right there.* Bald, upside-down, and gliding down the line. He imagined their muscular drumsticks as weightlifter's arms in the final act of a clean and jerk.

Supervisor Bean and Jesús cranked their forklifts and moved pallets in unison, bouncing around like spheres in a pinball machine. Jesús seemed to possess bat sonar, a sixth sense as to when Bean's forklift may race around the corner or burst through the coolers' swinging doors.

Sista Margarita stopped the supervisor during break. "El Gringo, we heard ju meeting with Señor Butler today about overtime pay."

"Yup. Right after work."

"*Muchas gracias,* El Gringo. *Vaya Con Dios*—go with God." She crossed her head and shoulders in ritual.

"Thanks, Sista.'"

Rio sought him out. "Mi amigo. Good luck with Señor Butler. We behind you."

Why is it me *seein' Butler again?* Bean pondered. *Am I the smartest English speaker or the dumbest? Maybe Ruby's right, maybe*

I am bein' played for a fool. Everybody wants to piss in my pocket. Too late to back out now.

Bean headed back to his station and heard his name called by a familiar female voice. He saw someone rushing toward him in "executive" plant gear, covered head-to-fingertip-to-toe. The half-face respirator with two black, protruding filters reminded Bean of a giant insect.

"Them outfits is for astronauts, for Pete's sake," Bean oft proclaimed. "Young Butler counts his money all day, but he don't want his sissy nose bothered. 'Lay me golden eggs, but I ain't touchin' the goose'."

He watched the lady's gait. *Heloise.* She reached him, huffing, and removed her respirator and earplugs then spoke in a hushed tone.

"Bean, I got to tell you something."

"Butler ain't gonna like it when you go back smellin' like chicken guts."

"I'm not going back today. I'm leaving early to run errands."

"You came all the way here to tell me that?"

"No, idiot. Listen. I wouldn't push Mr. Butler today. This stays between you and me—he's acting crazier and crazier these days. Strange things are going on."

"Heloise, I'm sure he can see you from that camera up yonder on the ceilin'."

"I don't care. I'll say I came here to tell you the side gate at the office will be un-locked for you this afternoon. He says if you cause trouble, you'll never work in this town again. He's loony enough to do it, believe me. You don't need that."

"Baby, thanks for the warnin', but if he fires me, I got four different jobs waitin' on me tomorrow. He don't scare me."

"You ain't in high school anymore, Bean. You've got a wife and two kids. It's time to grow up. Don't be stupid today."

"Speakin' o' that, you think Butler knows we dated in high school?" Bean knew Heloise wouldn't risk her plum job as Butler's secretary unless there remained a soft spot in her heart for him.

"I don't think he knows, and I intend to keep it that way."

"Ruby don't know either, and I intend to keep it that way, too. But look here, Butler's doin' us wrong, and he knows it. Everybody knows it. You know it, too. You know he s'posed to pay time-'n-a-half for overtime, don't ya?"

"I don't know. He's got lawyers crawling everywhere. I just do my job, and passing out legal opinions ain't part of it. I've got to go. I'm just telling you, in my opinion, don't do anything stupid. Oh, by the way, Corporal Hightower will be there, too."

Heloise squeezed her earplugs in, pulled the respirator back on, turned on her heels, and rushed away throwing a "bye" over her shoulder.

Bean wheeled and stomped away. *Don't be stupid today*, echoed in his head as he cracked his knuckles. *Hightower? What's he got to do with this?*

For the balance of the shift, Bean rehearsed the meeting as he and Jesús moved pallets. Scheduling it was easy, felt good. Now, rubber was about to meet road. Armpit saddlebags bled on his T-shirt.

The shift whistle blew. Bean dawdled at his workbench then ambled to his Chevy, his mind in a daze. He fired up a cigarette and popped his sweaty knuckles. *I'll kill a little time before the meetin', get some fresh air, smoke a few cigs, practice my speech.*

"Bean." It was Joker. "Wait up."

"Wha'chu want? I got to go."

Joker extended his arm and opened his palm, exposing an orange medallion.

"Borrow it for good luck."

"Whut is it?"

"It's my eight month recovery coin from AA. It always brings good luck."

"Joker, I ain't no alchy and got no addictions. All that AA crap gives me the creeps."

"No. God is with you. Just put this in your pocket and it'll make you remember you're not alone."

"Listen. I 'preciate it, but I ain't into superstition."

"This ain't superstition. It's religion. They're different."

Bean thought of Ruby's similar words and decided to play it safe. He held his hand out. "O-Kaayy." He examined the medallion. "What's all this writin' say? I ain't got time to read it."

"It's the Serenity Prayer: 'God grant me the serenity to accept the things I cannot change, courage to change the things I can, and wisdom to know the difference.' I'd be up a tree without a paddle without the Serenity Prayer."

"That's the dumbest thing I ever heard. I'm s'posed to accept things I cain't change? Listen, I don't think I'm gonna change Butler, but I ain't gonna accept it, either."

"Why don't you come to a meetin' with me and we can talk about those things. My sponsor's a genius. He'll know the answers."

"If your sponsor's such a genius, how come he's caught up in AA?" Bean patted Joker on the back. "We'll see, but there ain't no need savin' a chair for me. Anyhow, Ruby told me to rely on what The Good Book says—'Yeah, merrily, even though I'm gonna walk through the shadow o' death, I ain't gonna fear no evil.'"

He stuffed the medallion in his pocket and plodded to his Chevy to sit behind *his* steering wheel… to breathe deep, marshal his thoughts, and visualize victory over the Devil himself.

Chapter 21

Calvin Butler leaned back in his chair with Winston in his lap. His video ingenuity paid off as he stared at Bob Parkman's signature on the confidentiality agreement. He rolled a fresh Cuban cigar around in his fingertips and ran it under his nose to enjoy the rich aroma.

He punched the speaker and speed-dialed Radford Campbell.

"Campbell and Associates."

"Melissa, Sweetheart, how are you?"

"I'm tired," she whispered. "It's been a hectic day."

"How about you take off the last Friday of next month and we'll take the jet up to Memphis for the weekend. There's some poultry convention up there. I don't have to attend, but it'll provide an alibi. We can do some shopping. How'd you like a couple of new outfits?"

"That sounds wonderful. I'm putting it on my calendar right now."

"Sweetheart, I need to talk to Radford."

"He's on his way to a meeting, but let me see if I can reach him on his cell phone and patch you through."

"Fine, I'll hold."

Cal closed his eyes and listened to elevator music. *Whoever thought orchestras would play Beatles tunes?* He stroked Winston's coat and thought of Melissa and her fine, young, tight body. *I love young ones, those who have not had babies, those not stretched in important places. Need to check my Viagra supply. I'll try to keep her in bed in Memphis as long as I can. More sex, less shopping.*

Butler slid open his desk's top drawer and removed a velvet pouch containing a ring. He slipped it onto his finger, held it out, and admired the diamond from his deceased mother's engagement ring. As his parents' executor, he decided to take the diamond and mount it in a masculine gold setting.

"Cal." Radford Campbell's voice startled him. "How'd it go with Parkman?"

"No problem. He signed."

"What? You're shittin' me. I always thought he was smarter than that."

"Well, I can be very persuasive sometimes. Any update on the inspection? They didn't show up today, thank God."

"They drove down from Atlanta and are staying at the Holiday Inn. Look for them first thing in the morning. Remember, you need to act surprised when they show up. Did you get the plant cleaned up today?"

"Somewhat. Good enough to pass those pricks' inspection, I think. Don't want things to be too clean. Don't want to tip them off that we knew they were coming, you with me? We shut down the line all morning and cleaned. I had to crank it back up after lunch. Missing a half day's production is going to kill my numbers. I couldn't afford to shut her down all day. Those bastards."

"Cal, I'm sure you're correct. Good luck in the morning. Call me if they get out of hand, and I'll drop what I'm doing and come right over."

"Will do. I've got to go."

"Hey, good job on shafting Parkman. Someday you'll have to give me a lesson on getting people to sign one-sided documents."

Slim chance of that, buddy boy, until I get your smooth ass on video. Then my technique may be revealed to you.

Cal hung up and smiled while packing his briefcase for home. The day's many stresses compelled him to take more Percocet than normal. He was tired but pleased with how the day went. *Dodged a surprise inspection. Fired Parkman, the biggest thorn in my side. Life is good.*

He glanced at his antique Austrian wall clock. Fifteen minutes until his meeting with Sweat. He toyed with skipping out—didn't want the hassle of listening to Mr. Fat Ass bitch and moan. *What the hell, I'm on a roll. Might as well stay and face it. Put an end to it once and for all.*

The chairman reached into his briefcase and pulled out a Vicodin. Though in the same category as Percocet, he could detect the subtle difference. He stepped to his wet bar, poured a healthy shot of Jameson Irish Whiskey, popped the Vicodin, and killed the whiskey, doubling down his fun. *Down the hatch.* He wasn't worried about fine Celtic elixir on his breath. *It's my company, I can do whatever the hell I want. The cigar will hide it, anyway. I want Sweat to smell my cigar, for that numb-nuts to associate it with power and authority—namely me.*

His laughter echoed through the cypress rafters as the whiskey and Vicodin swirled in the cauldron of his brain. Stars floated across his vision. *Here come the butterflies. Five years at the helm of Majestic Chicken and I've mastered it with ease. I need some entertainment. Maybe I'll have some fun with Sweat and make him earn his name.*

He decided to check Heloise's computer until Sweat arrived, hoping to discover visits to porn sites. Though not attracted to Heloise, it aroused him to think of confronting her about surfing porn. *If I catch her, maybe I'll have her demonstrate what she likes best.* Dildos, vibrators, handcuffs, and more lived in his desk drawers. *Maybe I'll sneak onto her computer during office hours and visit a porn site to frame her.*

Engrossed in Heloise's computer, Butler flinched at the rap on the front door. He looked up and saw Corporal Mutt Hightower, Georgia Department of Natural Resources, waving through the door's side window.

Butler logged off Heloise's computer and unlocked the door. Hightower, a short man with a body builder physique, strode in wearing tight-fitting DNR green. Cal knew him to be a gym rat and figured his leathered face came from a lifetime of sunburns. A shiny, silver DNR badge pierced the chest of his polo shirt next to a pack of cigs bulging in his pocket. DNR adorned his baseball cap and a holstered pistol rode high on his hip.

"Mutt, you made it. Have you seen Sweat?"

"Good afternoon, sir. No I ain't seen fatso. He's due any minute."

"Let's go to the camera and watch him on the terrace, see if he tries to steal anything."

Chapter 22

Bean locked his truck and smoothed his T-shirt, which was dotted with bleach stains from this morning's whitewash. A clean shirt lay on the backseat, at Ruby's insistence, but the maverick balked.

Screw Butler, I'm up to my elbows in it all day. Let him smell the roses, same as our noses.

He took a deep breath, cracked his knuckles, and lit one last cig. Time to walk the plank to Butler's office. The sour fight or flight odor he detested oozed from his neck and pits. *Ruby told me not to do this. What if I am fired? Boom, we got no insurance.*

He gnashed his teeth at the implications while walking from the employee lot to the main drive. Bean always turned left to drive home and it now felt weird turning right to head to Butler's office. He knew he'd never enter the building—reeking of entrails or otherwise—his meeting place was always on the back porch.

El Gringo clinched his jaw trying to steel his nerves. *Come on, get pissed off. This asshole is screwin' everybody.* The elastic in his drawers was shot, and he ran his hand down his backside every few steps to pull them up.

His stomach churned as he turned into the office parking lot. Butler's Jag and a Georgia DNR pickup truck held pole positions. Bile rose in Bean's throat as he stepped on round pavers sunk in fancy grass. He rounded the building's corner and approached the tall, black chain-link fence with creeping plants weaving through its gaps. He pushed through an unlocked gate and spotted red clay barrel tiles on the patio roof looming ahead. *New roof since I been here last.*

Perspiration trickled down his forehead. He purposely left a divot when he dropped his cigarette butt in the grass and toed it out. El Gringo scanned the surroundings. Nobody in sight. He hitched his britches and stepped onto the brick porch.

A breeze from dual ceiling fans made palm fronds quiver in huge urns in the corners. Red and white flowers stood in a vase on an ornate glass top table surrounded by plush cushioned chairs. Soft music wafted in from several directions. *Them orchestra boys don't know how to play the fiddle. Charlie Daniels needs to give 'em lessons.*

Gurgling water captured his attention, and he whipped his gaze toward a cement pond, another new addition. He walked across the shaded porch to the pond. Fishing line crisscrossed the top like a net. The angler spied a plump fish gliding along, big as his forearm, white with large orange spots.

Damn. That'd be a piece o' cake to catch with my bare hands. Another glided by, white with black spots like a Dalmatian. *I ain't never seen nuthin' like them fish. They look like they'd be good eatin'.* An orange giant with white spots rolled. *That does it. I'm sneakin' back here one night with my cooler.*

He strolled to the glass-paneled twin doors, which were topped with an arched glass clearstory. *Them doors look ancient. Wish Ruby could see 'em.* One door was ajar, and sweet fragrances seeped through the crack. *Smells like Ruby's beauty parlor on Friday afternoon.*

He turned his cap backward, pressed his face to the glass, and peered inside. He'd never seen the interior. His jaw dropped. *Only time I seen candles like that was in a Catlick church.* The office resembled a museum, his brain dizzy trying to take it all in. Shelves packed with books and doodalia. A huge, shiny fish with a long bill and a fin like a sail. Stuffed ducks, geese, dove, and quail everywhere.

He recognized elephant tusks forming an arch and jolted when he spotted a huge stuffed alligator crawling across the ceiling. Many animals mounted the walls, some he recognized from African nature shows. Black horns—some short, some long, some straight, some curved. The shoulder mount of a white-tail deer, larger than he'd ever seen, peered down at him from above the fireplace. *Man, if only Junior could see this. Wonder if I can hunt like that when I get to Heaven?*

A thought struck him. He shuddered and touched his neck. *A human mount is the only thing missin'. Bet Butler would like* my *head on that wall.*

Chapter 23

Butler and Corporal Mutt Hightower scanned the images on the surveillance monitor focusing on the terrace. They watched Sweat wander into the camera's eye and observed his movements as he stepped onto the terrace then stopped to scout surroundings.

"What's he waitin' on," Hightower grunted, "a greetin' party?"

Sweat headed straight to the koi pond, and the two men chuckled as they watched him gawk and ogle.

"He ain't the brightest crayon in the box, sir. Bet you he's wonderin' what kind of fish them carp are."

"They aren't carp. They're koi, and they cost a damn fortune."

Sweat glanced around then ran a hand down the back of his jeans.

"What the hell was that move?" Butler reversed the video and they watched again. "Did he just hide something in his pants?"

"Looks to me, sir, he just scratched his ass and pulled up his drawers."

They monitored Sweat as he drifted from the fish and strolled toward the French doors. Pressing his face to the glass, Sweat cupped his hands over his eyes and peered into the office.

"Look at lard ass. His belly's tighter'n a four-day tick," Mutt laughed at his own humor. "Bet you he don't know half them animals he's lookin' at."

Neither do you, buddy boy.

Sweat straightened, wiped perspiration from his brow, slung it, and leaned back into cupped reconnaissance.

"Isn't it ironic, a cosmic coincidence, that his appellation matches his inclination?"

"Beg pardon, sir."

"Sweat, I'm talking about sweat. Never mind. You better go out there before fat ass breaks something. Put him on the bench. Don't let him sit on a cushion—I'd have to burn it to get the smell out. I'll be out in a minute."

Hightower patted the pistol on his hip. "Sir, shall I wear my gun for the meetin'?"

"Hell, yeah. Can't be too careful when dealing with these crackers."

Mutt rolled up his shirt's tight sleeves, exposing menacing biceps and the horned tail of a dragon tattoo. He hiked his belt and sprinted to the French doors. Butler watched on screen as Sweat startled and jumped back.

Hightower jerked open the door, stepped out, and motioned Sweat to take a seat on the wooden bench.

The chairman strolled to his wet bar for another shot of Jameson Whiskey then into his restroom to splash cold water onto his face. Admiring himself in the mirror as he patted dry, he forced himself to wipe the saucy, high-times grin away. He combed his hair and noticed the bags under his eyes. *All this stress. Cost of being a captain of industry.*

Let's do this. He winked at himself and walked to the French doors. Outside, Mutt towered over Sweat. The DNR Corporal looked official, arms crossed, biceps looming large. Butler snapped at Winston. "Come on, boy, let's go have some fun. Get him, boy! Bad man. Bad. Get him."

Cal opened the door and Winston shot out, barking like a crazed man-killer. With teeth bared for blood, he charged Sweat and skidded just short of his reach.

"Winston, come back here." Winston swallowed his bark to a low, rumbling growl as he strutted to his master with eyes trained on the stranger.

"Well, if it's not El Gringo himself. Sorry about that, Sweat. To be perfectly honest, I don't know what got into old Winston. Must have seen something he didn't like."

Cal scrunched his face when he caught wind of Sweat and grabbed a box fan hugging the wall. He cranked it toward Bean and winked at Hightower. "Damn. Smells like a bouquet of ass-holes out here."

Hightower chuckled.

"You don't mind the fan do you? No offense, El Gringo. It is the infamous El Gringo, isn't it?"

Hightower grinned, flashing crooked, yellow teeth and repositioning himself upwind.

Butler eased into a cushioned chair, stars exploding in his vision from the sudden drop in elevation. Winston leaped into his lap. The chairman slid on his sunglasses and fired up his Cuban, blowing smoke into the fan and onto Sweat. He propped his loafered heels on a neighboring chair.

Sweat held his camo baseball cap in hand. *A commoner begging royalty,* Butler thought. He noticed stubble and a tan line across Sweat's face. *No doubt the lummox always wears that filthy cap. His kidney bean ears look tight and bloated—too much fat, not enough skin.* He studied Sweat's belly. *Much hard eating and investment to grow that bread basket. Impressive.* He watched perspiration bead and trickle down Sweat's face. *Now he's earning his name.*

"So, Sweat, what's on your mind?"

"Overtime pay."

"Son," the chairman gritted his teeth and looked up at the ceiling fan blades. He took deep breaths as veins bulged in his neck. "Sweat, why do you keep making trouble? If I wanted to hear from an asshole, I would have farted." Butler shot a grin at Hightower.

"You ain't doin' your people right. We s'posed to make time-'n-a-half if we work over forty hours. Your daddy used to run two shifts and—"

"Listen, dammit, don't come in here telling me how my father used to do things. That was then, and this is now. Times have changed. You either adapt to change or get run over by the competition. And I'm surprised to learn you're an expert at running chicken plants."

"I just know it ain't right not to pay overtime."

"I'm tired of hearing this shit about overtime. I'm generous to pay ten hours straight time for a job which should be done in eight. Enough excuses. Finish the work quicker."

"How can you blame us when a machine breaks down that ain't had no maintenance?"

"There you go with excuses. Look, Sweat, to be perfectly honest, I'm already paying above industry standards." Cal grinned at his bald-faced lie, but there wasn't another chicken plant in the area, so his folks couldn't compare pay stubs on Friday afternoon at the local watering hole. "You should be kissing the ground I walk on for giving you such a good job and benefits, especially in these dire economic times."

"I'm just tellin' you what the law says."

"So, you're a lawyer now, too? I'm sure you're stirring the pot in the plant, being the lawyer for all your third-world cohorts."

"No, I ain't no lawyer, but I know a good'un."

"Are you threatening to sue me?" Butler jerked to an upright position. Winston jumped down and growled at the stranger.

"I didn't say one way or the other."

Butler bit down on his cigar and stabbed a finger toward Sweat. "Let me tell you something, buddy boy. If you repeat this, I'll deny the hell out of it. Officer Hightower is my witness that I never said it. You file a complaint, and for starters, you'll never work in this town again. I guarantee that. But forget about *you*, dammit. How about your cousin at my hatchery? You wouldn't want her to lose her job, would you?"

Sweat's neck flushed crimson. White coronary lines crept up his face. He sat up straight and stiff. "She ain't got nuthin' to do with this, dammit."

Hightower shot out of his chair and stood between Sweat and Butler, one hand on his revolver, the other pointing a finger at Bean like a cocked gun. "Look here, Sweat. Show Mr. Butler the respect he deserves."

Butler smiled. *It's fun being the smartest person in the room.* Hightower backed down, and Butler continued. "What about your good friend Joe Johnson, the one they call 'Pickle'? He's been here longer than you. He doesn't give me any trouble. How would you feel if he lost his job?"

Sweat grimaced and stared. "You kiddin' me? You wouldn't do them things just 'cause I asked you to do what's legal."

Butler laughed until he bent over coughing, acting the showman. He leaned forward and pointed his cigar. "Did they elect you in Spanish, Vietnamese, or are you self-anointed? Listen, have you been talking to those union bastards again? Is that what this is about?"

"I ain't been talkin' to them union boys. I'm just representin' my own self."

"So you're trying to get money out of me for yourself. Are you looking for a payoff to keep quiet?"

"I ain't lookin' for nuthin' for me that everybody in the plant don't get. Everybody who works overtime ought to get time-'n-a-half."

"Look, Sweat. These folks are making twenty times what they could make in their third-world countries, and they have health insurance. I don't hear them complaining. Do you think you're helping them by attacking me? Go ahead, run me out of business and see what that does for your comrades. Tell you what, if I have to pay time-and-a-half, first thing I'll do is eliminate a dozen jobs. You go back and tell them their jobs are lost compliments of El Gringo. Is that what you want?"

"Well... no."

"Listen, pal, I'm out of time. Do you want your job, or not? If you do, then go back to work and shut the hell up. If you don't, I've got a stack of applications a foot high. This is not complicated. Don't waste my time like this again."

Sweat socked his cap on backwards then reached into his back pocket.

"FREEZE." Hightower drew and aimed his revolver at Sweat.

"*Whoa*, cowboy, I'm just gettin' some Red Man."

"Slowly raise your hands," Hightower growled.

Sweat pulled out the rolled pouch and waved it in the air. He pinched a healthy plug and jammed it home in his cheek. He stared at Butler. "Is that the way it's gonna be?"

"Afraid so." Butler puffed his cigar. "Furthermore, one more violation in your ninety-day probation, buddy boy, and you're on the street. Some days you're the pigeon, and some days you're the statue." He winked at Hightower. "Tell me this—are you still a Fat Back Hunt Club member?"

"Yep."

"I thought so. You tell those boys to keep their damn dogs off my property, you hear?"

"I hear."

"Something else. How did Joe Johnson get the name 'Pickle'?"

"I don't know. I reckon 'cause o' his long neck."

Cal knew Sweat was lying. When he overheard the rumor around the water cooler in the executive office about Joe Johnson, he spent countless hours reviewing men's restroom video until he came upon a scene with Johnson at the urinal.

Johnson swung around with his middle leg dangling before zipping up. *Stunning! Could do some kidney damage with that thing.* Butler zoomed the image and watched slow-motion replays a hundred times, lapsing into envious daydreams, fantasizing about owning such fine equipment and how ladies would bang his door down for their chance to lay him.

"Meeting adjourned, Sweat." Winston crouched and growled.

"But, but..." Sweat stuttered then stood. He scratched his head and turned to walk away.

Butler waved him off with a royal backhand. "Don't let the door slap you in the ass on the way out, buddy boy."

Sweat stepped off the terrace onto the grass, Hightower a few paces behind. Sweat's neck snapped forward, and a brown stream rocketed through the air onto the blossoms of the lone, pink Japanese Camellia, Cal's prized perennial.

"Asshole," Butler shouted.

Hightower glowered at Sweat. "What a jerk. Should I go search his truck, sir?"

"Nah, Let him go. Lock the side gate then return. We've got bigger fish to fry."

PART III:
RUBY'S CURL UP 'N DYE

Chapter 24

Homer Flay was *the man,* manager of Garden of Eden Trailer Park, collector of lot rent. He stood on the parcel next to the Sweat's lot and surveyed the situation with Ruby and Bean at his side. Homer towered above them.

"It's an Airstream, a Flying Cloud." Homer waved his hand at the abandoned travel trailer, its distinctive silver-domed aluminum body coated with years of dirt and algae. Knee-high weeds concealed its underbelly and rotten tires.

"A 1963 model, I think. About a twenty-two footer, maybe twenty-four. She could be a beaut, but that fella let her get run down. He was a weird one. He up and hauled his singlewide off but left this piece o' shit—'scuse my French, ma'am—as a tip for me, I guess. Got no papers, but if you want her, she's yours. Otherwise, I'm hauling her to the dump."

Ruby covered her mouth to hide her surprise. *For free!* She composed herself and turned to Bean. "Wha'chu think?"

"Man kept dogs in there. We better have a look inside 'fore we say 'yes'?"

"Be my guest." Homer fanned his arm.

Bean opened the door, and the stench of a hundred ancient dog turds slammed his face. "Ladies first," he motioned to Ruby.

Bean braced her from behind. She pinched her nostrils and mounted the cinderblock then stepped up into the trailer with one foot. It tilted and teetered. She squealed, flailed her arms, and stepped back. "Mercy!"

"*Whoa,*" Bean hollered as he and Homer rushed to hold the Airstream's side. "Try it now, Darlin'. We'll brace it. If we take it, we'll have to block it up good for support, like our trailer."

She held her nose again, stepped inside, and glanced around. Fleas crawled up her legs, biting and heading for higher ground. She scratched her ankles with her feet and stepped down.

As Bean took his turn, Ruby visualized her dream—styling chair in front, shampoo and nail stations in rear, mirrors everywhere. *I could make it look first class.*

Bean stepped down, scratching and turned to Ruby. "Well?"

After high school, a tall and stocky Ruby Strickland started her first job, apprentice nail technician at a salon in the mall. She put in her training hours, passed exams and became a certified nail technician. Next, esthetician—eyebrows, lashes, wax jobs, and neck massages. Framed certificates cluttered the wall and Ruby's parents beamed with pride. She progressed to apprentice cosmetologist and, after more training and testing, a full-fledged cosmetologist—shampoos, dyes, cuts, and facials.

Then one day a gorgeous, big-boned, camoed hunk of a man named Butterbean strolled in for a mullet trim. They were soon married, and in no time, she was pregnant with a boy they would name Junior. Due to a sluggish thyroid, she gained weight as if quintuplets were brewing. After Junior weaned, she returned to her mall salon and improved her craft, clipping her way toward cutting edge master cosmetologist.

She became pregnant with Li'l Bit, and her legs and feet couldn't handle standing any longer. She hung up her blow dryer knowing she would one day return to the profession.

Now faced with Li'l Bit's clubfoot, she knew this was the time. *This trailer is a sign from God.* She could tend her baby and manage the household while working at home. Besides, she always wanted to own her own beauty parlor.

Ruby gazed at the Flying Cloud and tried to restrain her excitement. She glanced at Bean. "I think we can make it work."

Bean turned to Homer. "We'll need a week to move it?"

"Deal."

Voilà—Ruby's Curl Up 'N Dye was born then and there. They celebrated their acquisition that evening, Bean with Bud and Ruby with juice. "Here's to bein' lucky enough to be in the right place at the right time."

"It ain't luck," Ruby corrected. "It's Providence. This is God showin' His favor on us for bein' good Christians. He's lookin' out for us."

Bean removed the dog turds and set off multiple flea bombs inside the Airstream. He strung hoses, scrubbed, and sanitized. "Finished," he declared but Ruby made him do it again. And again.

With help from Pickle Joe Johnson, Bean roped the giant silver bullet to his truck bumper and dragged her onto their lot, flat tires trenching through the dirt. Out came the jacks and a half-ton of cinderblock found a home underneath.

"All I want is the shell and bathroom," Ruby instructed. "I need every inch for the parlor."

Bean and PJ gutted the built-ins—half-walls, double bed, table, bench seat, kitchen cabinets, counter, sink, and oven.

Bean eyeballed Ruby's girth. "Darlin', I'm 'fraid you ain't gonna fit through that bathroom door."

"It ain't for me, Punkin', it's for my patrons. I'll walk outside and around to our bathroom."

Bean had a revelation. "I'll cut a door in the Flying Cloud and a hole in our trailer's kitchen wall and marry the two. That way, you can get inside our whole trailer without walkin' 'round."

"That's brilliant, Honey Bun."

They cut new doors and clamped them together. PJ welded a metal cover to keep out water and cockroaches.

Bean ran a hose to the Flying Cloud's freshwater tanks, and Ruby made him agree to dump the gray water from the bathroom and maintain the chemicals. PJ made some electrical modifications, and two heavy-grade extension cords kept the Airstream flying—one to the window unit and one to the battery which ran all else.

Ruby rested her head on Bean's belly one night in bed and revealed her vision. "This is our new beginnin', Punkin'. It's like

God said to Noah, 'Whenever the rainbow appears in the clouds, I will see it and remember My everlastin' covenant with all livin' creatures on Earth.' You see, there's a rainbow straight from God to our Flyin' Cloud, and it's gonna be a new day."

"Since the two o' you talk, think He could slip me some lottery numbers?"

"Bean, stop playin' the fool."

"Why? Joker says you ain't never too old to say sump'n stupid. Okay, if you want to be serious, you think you can compete with Candy's Cut & Curl?"

"Everybody knows Candy is the grandmama 'round Garden of Eden Trailer Park. Where you think I been gettin' my hair done? Half her doublewide is nuthin' but her shop, and she's got two beauticians workin' for her now. But you know whut? Candy and her ladies cain't hold a candle to me."

Ruby arranged to borrow a thousand dollars from her rich uncle to buy used fixtures and new supplies.

"Over my dead body," Bean decreed. "The last thing I want is to be obliged to your uncle."

Loan proceeds in hand, Bean and Ruby drove to Tallahassee and returned with a brimming pickup—hydraulic styling chair, shampoo chair on wheels, sink, bubble dryer, and nail station with manicure table and two chairs.

She bought combs and scissors, rollers and creams, dyes and hairspray. She put her first-class touch on the inside—zebra wallpaper and lamps, mirrors with gold flecks, a boom box, silk plants. She arranged her prized Jesus and Virgin Mary figurines by Li'l Bit's tip jar. Above the tip jar hung her faded, framed print of Jesus with flowing brown beard and hair in a Mt. Sinai backdrop.

Ruby enjoyed exciting days working pencil and calculator.

"Punkin', good Lawd willin' and the creek don't rise, I figure we can make enough in six months to start Li'l Bit's foot treatments."

An awful thought came to her mind. "What we gonna do 'bout the gub'mint?"

Bean looked up from the TV. "Wha'chu mean?"

"I ain't figured taxes and fees and gub'mint things in these numbers."

"We won't tell 'em."

"I remember from workin' at the salon in the mall, I had to take a state test and pay fees every year and hang my license on the wall."

"We just won't tell 'em."

"I remember my boss complainin' 'bout competition from all the ladies stylin' hair outta they kitchens. She called 'em 'kitchen-ticians'."

"Kitchen-tician? Okay, I reckon that's what you can be."

"That's what Candy is, I know. They ain't got nary a certificate on they walls. Should we file taxes with the IRS?"

"Hell no." Bean drained his Bud and glared at Ruby. "Once you show up on the IRS radar screen, they'll be on you like cockroaches on a ham sammich. It ain't right. Let's keep it simple, like our parents and grandparents, without a bunch o' gub'mint red tape. Just do some hair for a few friends and neighbors, that's all. The gub'mint ain't got no business interfering with that."

"What about sales tax?"

"Same. Ain't none o' their damn bidness. Darlin', since you was up, can you hand me a Bud?"

"You know I told Sue Flay that her daughter, Tootsie, could come work for me when she finishes high school if I got enough bidness. Should we take taxes from her pay?"

"You ain't catchin' on too fast. No way. We'd have to get a bookkeeper to figure all that up, and you'd spend all day fillin' out gub'mint forms. Who knows how much all that would cost? Next thing you gonna tell me is we need insurance in case you screw up. Darlin', if we did all that, we'd lose money every time you flipped the light switch on."

"I guess we'll have to just keep it kinda' quiet."

Bean scratched his stubbled chin and flashed a sheepish grin. "They's sump'n I ain't told ya."

"Whut?"

"PJ told me the county makes you buy a bidness license. Says they charge five hundred dollars right from the git-go, and after they got your money, they'll prob'ly say you cain't put no bidness in here next to a bunch o' homes. If it's approved, you have to pay the gub'mint every year, and they'll come snoopin' 'round all the time, wantin' you to do things like build a wheel-chair ramp."

Ruby was shocked by that news. "Good gracious, if it ain't one thing, it's sump'n else."

Bean swigged his beer, smiled, and continued. "But I done figured it out. You cain't hardly see the Flying Cloud from the street, but I'm gonna put some lattice up so you cain't see it a-tall, in case them gub'mint inspectors drive by. Might not be best for bidness, but we cain't put up with them leeches suckin' us dry. Don't worry, I'll make it look real nice."

Ruby shook her head. "The cotton-pickin' gubmint is every-where. They's sump'n I ain't told *you* 'bout. Sue Flay told me it's against trailer park rules to run a bidness. Homer didn't know we was gonna run a parlor outta the Flying Cloud when he let us have it. Sue is purty sure that he'll turn a blind eye since their daughter will be workin' here. She says not to worry 'bout it, she'll take care o' Homer. Says she has her ways and means. Says she'll be my number one customer."

"Folks been cuttin' each others' hair since caveman days, and ain't nobody got bidness gettin' 'tween you and your custom-ers."

So, Ruby became a kitchen-tician.

She couldn't advertise with a proper sign, so she found red scripted decals for the sides of the mailbox...

$$\mathcal{R}$$

"Soon enough," she predicted, "folks'll see the 'R' and automatically think 'Ruby's Curl Up 'N Dye'."

She crafted a flyer, made a good many copies, and passed them around Garden of Eden. Word-of-mouth sure enough got around. Nowadays, she had plenty of business.

Thank You, Jesus.

Chapter 25

Ruby's Monday morning alarm jarred her slumber. Bean had left for work. She heard Li'l Bit stir in her crib, and she struggled to sit up.

Ruby changed Li'l Bit's diaper and perched her on her hip for the few steps to Junior's room. She opened the door and flipped on the light.

"Wake up, Angel. Time to get dressed for school. I'm gonna make us a good breakfast."

"Okay, Mama," Junior's voice croaked.

Ruby cooked in her tank top, pajama bottoms, and flip-flops. The beginning of another day of tortuous standing. Li'l Bit banged her cup on the high chair making joyous music.

Searing Spam and baking biscuit aroma permeated the trailer. Slippers poised at Ruby's feet, on high alert for spillage. A pot of grits simmered. Eggs sizzled in the skillet.

"Junior, come on. We ready to eat."

Junior lumbered in wearing jeans, camo Crocs, and a T-shirt with his back pack strapped on. "Mama, do I have to go to school today? Why cain't I stay home and play with Baby Girl?"

"Sorry, Angel. The law says you got to go to school. 'Sides, I got good news. Lunch today is your favorite, sloppy joes and tater tots. I put some trail mix in your bag to tide you over 'til then."

Ruby crumbled a biscuit into Li'l Bit's bowl of baby mush. She tied a bib around her daughter's neck and laid the plastic bowl and spoon on the high-chair tray. "Eat up, Baby. Yum-yum." She served up heaping portions for Junior and herself, which they engulfed. Li'l Bit spooned food in and around her mouth while banging her free hand on the tray.

"Baby, you better be careful." Li'ls Bit's bowl sailed onto the floor, and Slippers scarfed the bounty.

"Lawd, hep me."

"You better hurry up, Junior. The bus'll be here in four minutes. You behave yourself today. Remember, you one step away from gettin' suspended. You don't want Daddy to have to spank you, do you?" *Lawd, Lawd. Just like his daddy—one step away.*

"No, Mama. I'll be good today."

"You promise?"

"I promise, Mama. You put a treat in my bag?"

"You know I did. Don't look 'til lunch time, and let it be a surprise. Now, you come here and give Mama some sugah then you better git."

Junior hugged her neck and shuffled to the door. He paused and looked back then said, "Later, sweet potater."

Ruby nibbled on a Snickers Bar. "Nibbling" was her new weight-loss technique. She needed a morning pick-me-up as she prepared for the flow of parlor patrons.

"Baby, they's two things important 'bout my work today," she said as she cleaned the kitchen. "First, we raisin' money fast as we can for your foot treatments." Ruby wiped Li'l Bit's face and hands.

"Ba-ba-do-do."

She turned the stove's dial to simmer the hot dogs. Li'l Bit banged her spoon, and her spare hand clutched her stuffed purple dinosaur.

"Second thing, I'm buildin' a bidness that you can take over one day. I want your future to be secure. I'm gonna teach you to style hair and run a beauty parlor better than anybody in these parts. We gonna get us a double-wide someday, and one whole side will be for our parlor, just like Candy's Cut & Curl, 'cept we gonna have us a tannin' bed. You gonna be rich and famous."

Bang, bang, bang.

"Come on, Baby." She snatched up Li'l Bit. "Mama's got to get dressed."

Ruby chose a chartreuse muumuu dress with a parrot theme and matching parrot hairclip. She struggled to slip on tube socks and Velcro her orthopedic sandals. She dressed for comfort Monday through Thursday, but come Wild Thing Friday, she'd dress to slay.

The Flying Cloud creaked but held firm under her footsteps as she plopped Li'l Bit into her playpen in the corner. Ruby turned on the lights, raised the blinds, and unlocked the entry door. She turned on the AC window unit and took a hit off her inhaler. They wheezed in concert. She smacked the unit until it stopped its whining. *Lawd, I cain't wait for fall.*

Ruby teased her shoulder-length, Cleopatra-black hair with a master's touch, training it off her face. She then covered her eyes and sprayed a cloud of Bed Head volumizing hair spray. She stroked crimson blush up the apples of her cheeks, emblazoned her lips ruby-red, and lined her eyes Kohl black.

Dress may not be so important, but hair and makeup is. Got to look professional to show my patrons how it's done.

She raised her nose and sniffed. Passion fruit perfume… the Flying Cloud's door flew open. Tootsie ducked and breezed in wearing white, cat-eye sunglasses edged in rhinestones. She patted Li'l Bit's head and tucked her bag in the corner.

"Mornin', Miss Ruby."

"Mornin'." Ruby shot a glance in the mirror at Toots and continued working a mascara wand on her lashes above puckered lips. "Ain't we lookin' purty today."

Fresh out of high school, Tootsie's face still suffered acne's red splotches. But today, her painted porcelain face smiled in stark contrast to what lay underneath. Designer jeans and a spandex tube top revealed a wisp of a waist and a pair of natural mammaries that made grown men ogle.

"Why, thank you, Miss Ruby." Laying her glasses aside, Tootsie batted false eyelashes as big as a geisha girl's fan. She displayed her long, electric orange nails to Ruby and adjusted her month-old engagement ring.

"Like my nails?"

"My word, chiiil', you got a rhinestone on each nail. Way to go. Now *that's* the way to sell manicures, honey."

Tootsie stepped to the playpen and showed her nails to Li'l Bit who gripped the side of her playpen and struggled to stand, placing her weight on her clubfoot's outer edge. "Ooo-ooo-ooo."

Tootsie held her engagement ring close to Ruby's face. "Remember we couldn't tell last week, but if you look with a magnifyin' glass, you can see it's a real diamond."

"They say diamonds is a girl's best friend." Ruby sighed and tidied her makeup. "Maybe someday I'll know firsthand. Did ya have a good weekend, Toots?"

"It was interestin'. I rode with Mama and Daddy to Uncle Gomer's funeral over in Waycross on Saturday. He was a plumber. I didn't know he was so popular."

"How were you related?"

"Daddy's brother."

"Homer's brother? Homer and Gomer?"

"Yeah. Anyway it was a mess. It took thirty minutes and a bunch o' jumper cables to get all them cars and trucks cranked for the procession."

"Sakes alive, I know that routine. Bean always makes sure we got the cables 'fore we go to any weddin' or funeral."

"You know Miss Ruby, sittin' in the back seat by myself most o' the weekend, I had time to think about this business."

"Yeah?"

"It's the craziest thing. Seems like women with straight hair want curls and women with curls want straight hair."

"You better believe it, Toots. That's how God made us women, and that ain't never gonna change. That's why you picked a good profession."

"Miss Ruby, 'fore I prep my station, where's Li'l Bit's tip jar? I'll put it out."

"Thank you, Tootsie. It's in the den. 'Preciate it. I got a few mo' chores, and my feet is already killin' me. I got Bunny comin' in for stylin' at nine, and you got Jessie for nails."

Toots retrieved the gallon pickled sausage jar with a slit in the metal top. She set it next to the figurines below the picture of Jesus. Li'l Bit's photograph was taped on the jar. A placard read, "Please help Li'l Bit's foot. Thank you. God Bless."

Ruby made sure not to obscure the tip jar's bottom. Patrons needed to see money inside so they'd be nudged into action. She dumped each day's take into a canvas bag but kept her "seed" money in full view—a few ones and fives and a ten.

"Honey, this time tomorrow we may have Bean on top o' us."

"Why's that?"

"He's meetin' with Calvin Butler hisself, the owner o' the chicken plant, after work today to complain 'bout no overtime pay. He's gonna lose his job any day now, I feel it, and I don't know what's gonna happen to us." She sucked a hit from her inhaler.

"Oh, Miss Ruby, you know the Lord will take care o' ya."

"I know that the good Lawd is tryin'. But Bean seems to fight Him every step o' the way."

Tootsie turned and spotted the product shelf jammed to capacity.

"Holy dog crap! The new shipment must o' come in. I ain't never seen so much product."

"*Shhh!* Please, Toots, watch your language in front o' Li'l Bit. Now lookee-here. Last week I hocked the title to my Lincoln to buy all this. See this special box? All the money from product sales goes in this box 'til I get my car outta hock, you hear?"

"Yes'm."

"We got shampoo, conditioner, hair spray, and this special hair oil from Morocco." Ruby held up the oil in admiration.

"Where's Morocco?"

"Morocco?" Ruby traced the atlas in her head. "I think it's south o' Mexico. But look here, we got more. We got perfume, acne-peel, anti-aging cream, and aromatic candles. The price is marked top o' each bottle. Anything you want is half-price, but it's for your use only at that price."

"I know, Miss Ruby."

"Look at this." Ruby held up a tube of Tummy Flattening Gel. "We finally got some more. I bought two cases, and they gonna go fast, gonna be hotter'n blazes. See, says 'flattens abs and tightens thighs.' Says here, 'Miracle Gel, the eighth wonder o' the world.' Says 'just apply it to your waist and tummy and watch 'em shrink before your eyes.' Word gets out and we gonna have a stampede at our door."

Chapter 26

Ruby cranked the Flying Cloud's window unit all out and set in to organizing for her nine o'clock with Bunny—combs and brushes, perm rods large and small, chemicals for thin, limp hair.

Tootsie prepped her nail station—bowl of soap and essential oils, polish remover and buffer, clippers and emery boards, creams and lacquers. She shoved the special of the week to the front, glittery vamp violet polish.

"Tootsie, I read in *Styles and Smiles* that hair this year is all 'bout 'change.' Short hair is the rage. It's so versatile. Dress it up, dress it down. We in modern times now. Attention-grabbin' tiger stripes, too." Ruby clawed the air. "It's good for bidness—our patrons will be comin' every other week for touch-ups. Talk it up, you hear? I'm gonna shorten your hair and add more highlights and lowlights so you can lead the catwalk."

My stars, Ruby thought, *with a body like Toots's, it don't matter how I style her hair. Ladies is gonna say, "Gimme what she's got."*

"What'd they say 'bout nails?"

"Nails is big and bright this year. They an extension o' your personal image, a way to express yourself without gettin' a tattoo. And a whole lot cheaper. Explain that to our younger patrons."

"Yes'm." Tootsie held her hands up to admire her rhinestone-studded nails. "Jessie's comin' in this mornin'. I wish she'd let me do her nails like mine, but all she ever wants is a French manicure."

"That's okay, Toots. Bidness is bidness. What she really needs is a long sit in my stylin' chair to get her hair retexturized."

Tootsie jumped up and snagged Li'l Bit from her playpen. She kissed and cradled her on her hip. "Yes'm. What about this pretty baby I got in my arms?"

"Hey, Li'l Bit." Ruby puckered her lips like a fish in an air kiss. "Mama *loves* her baby girl."

Li'l Bit flailed an arm and bounced in Tootsie's grasp.

"Her diaper should be okay. Get her a cup o' Cap'n Crunch when you put her back in the pen."

"Yes'm, Miss Ruby. Anything you want in the kitchen?"

"I got hot dogs simmerin' on the stove. Hep me keep an eye on 'em. Buns, mayo, and ketchup is on the counter. Hep yourself. We just gotta save a couple for Junior for his after-school snack."

"You got the blood pressure machine workin'?"

"Yes, wonders never cease—Bean finally fixed it." She held up the camo-taped cuff. "He's quite handy sometimes with duct tape, I have to admit. Everybody gets a compliment'ry pressure check. It's our main value-added service once again. We got to stay one step ahead o' Candy's Cut & Curl. They tryin' to steal our patrons every day, count on it."

Ruby's initial value-added service, a weigh-in with the results charted for all to see, never gained traction.

Ruby switched on the boom box, and country music teed up ambiance. She sashayed around in her tube socks, muumuu swaying as she checked inventory and rearranged product. Cramped quarters inside the Airstream caused her to stand in one spot and sway side-to-side like an elephant in a cage.

"I took my pressure this mornin'," Ruby said. "It got up on me yesterday, but it come down now." She lit a scented candle and organized *National Enquirers* by date. "It always gets up when Bean is home. I'm fixin' to take your pressure in a minute, Toots."

The Flying Cloud's door burst open. Blue-haired Bunny crouched, grabbed the handle, and entered in her new, white walking shoes for seniors.

I cain't wait 'til we draw social security, Ruby lamented. *I'll buy new shoes all the time, too.*

"Mornin', Bunny, how you?"

"Poorly." She raised the back of her hand to her forehead. "I'm doin', but I don't know how."

Ruby pulled up a chair. "Good heavens, girl, sit down. Has your bowels moved today?"

Bunny slumped into the chair. "Barely."

"You prob'ly need more fiber and water." Ruby glanced at Tootsie. "Get her a cup o' water. Bunny, sounds like you comin' down with a cold."

"Naw, I think my gallbladder's flarin' up again."

"Hold your arm out and let me take your pressure." Ruby slid the cuff up her arm and pumped the bulb, duct tape stretching and creaking.

Bunny breathed slow and deep. "I didn't see you in church yesterday."

"Couldn't get Bean up. But I went to pajama church and saw a good sermon on TV."

"You know you cain't let Bean nor nobody else interfere with the Word."

"Praise the Lawd. If Bean had his way, we'd be members o' the church o' C & E—Christmas and Easter."

"There's a tent revival comin' up next month, you know."

"Gosh dog." Ruby hit her inhaler. "I'm afraid it'd take a mule team to drag Bean to another revival. I might take Junior."

"I'll pray for Bean's soul."

"Thanks, Bunny. While you're at it, would you mind prayin' for Li'l Bit to get her foot fixed?"

"You bet'cha, Darlin'. A special prayer for Li'l Bit."

Ruby's brows knitted as she read the digital results. "Your pressure's a little high on the top side, okay on the bottom. Watch your salt intake, Sweetheart. Now, I got you down for a shampoo and perm. Any special concerns?"

"You dern tootin'. I'm goin' to my niece's weddin' this weekend, and my hair just ain't got no get up 'n go." She held up a clump of gun-barrel blue hair and let go. It flopped like a dead squirrel. "Look at it. It's puny." She pulled a tattered magazine page from her purse, unfolded it, and handed it over. Ruby knew the picture well, having gone through Bunny's routine many times—Farah Fawcett in her prime, thick, vibrant hair with huge, bouncing curls.

Bunny grinned and poked an arthritic finger at the page. "That's what I'm thinkin' 'bout."

"Honey, you in luck. We gonna volumize your hair and give it more body than Arnold Schwarzenegger. Make Farah Fawcett jealous, Lawd rest her soul. Toots will give ya a good shampoo while I tend to Li'l Bit. Want a hot dog?"

"Maybe after while." Bunny pointed to the burlap-covered card table in the corner and its pottery and jewelry display. "I'm thinkin' 'bout buyin' somethin' original as a weddin' present."

Ruby held out her thumb. "Check this ring out. It's called Moonstone. It's the hottest thing goin'. Adjustable, so size won't be a problem."

"I like it, but I prob'ly ought to get sump'n for 'em both. I guess I'll take one o' them decorative bowls."

Tootsie guided a staggering Bunny the few steps to the shampoo chair. "You walkin' a little woozy, Miss Bunny."

"I'm so dizzy, I don't know which end is up."

"Honey," Ruby patted her back, "you better hurry up and figure it out 'cause Toots is 'bout to wash one of 'em."

Bunny eased her head back into the sink, a towel noosing her neck. Warm water flowed over her scalp, and she lapsed into a slack-jawed snore.

Ruby tied a five-and-dime polyester cape around Bunny's neck then reached for her latex gloves. Elvis barked from underneath the trailer.

"That dog is barkin' at somethin'," Toots announced.

Ruby motioned her head, "Look see."

Tootsie peeked through the cube window. "A taxi is parked next door."

"'Scuse me, Bunny." Ruby stepped to the window and peered out while wrestling on her gloves. "It's The Ole Man, bless his heart. He cain't hardly get around. His legs is so skinny it looks like he's ridin' a chicken. Lost his wife six months ago and sometimes he don't remember. It's pitiful. We bring him food, but we cain't take him in. Lawd knows I cain't keep up with what I got."

The Ole Man wheeled himself onto the stoop and locked his door. The taxi driver positioned himself behind the wheelchair and eased it toward the ramp built at an angle twice as steep as county code.

The wheels inched past the start line. The driver leaned back for leverage. When the rear wheels hit the ramp and the full weight of The Ole Man and his chair came to bear, the chair broke from the driver's grip and took off like a runaway train. The Ole Man's head jerked backward sending his hat flying. Wheels hit the dirt, snapping his head forward, and the chair spun a one-eighty.

Ruby's eyes flared. *Oh, my!* She returned to her styling chair and Bunny's hair.

Moments later, the Flying Cloud's door swung open. Jessie stooped and entered wearing well-worn cowgirl boots and a loose-fitting yellow dress, stains bleeding into a collage on the front. A tattooed dove flew up her neck.

"Mornin' everybody." The ball on Jessie's pierced tongue glistened as she spoke.

Bunny opened her eyes. "Hey, Jessie."

"Hello, Miss Bunny. How you doin'?"

"Oh, I've felt better, but it costs too much."

"Sit down, Jessie," Ruby instructed as she wrapped Bunny's hair around big curlers. "Toots will take your pressure then give you the best manicure this side o' the Miss'ippi."

"So Jessie," Bunny said, "you datin' anybody?"

"I cain't find a decent man."

"Blood pressure's great." Tootsie removed the cuff and guided Jessie's fingertips into a bowl of warm essential oils.

"I'm thinkin' 'bout savin' up and gettin' plastic surgery on my nose. What do y'all think?"

"The devil you say, child." Bunny sliced her hand through the air. "Don't start down that road. You cain't never stop. My sister-in-law's face stays so bloated she always looks like she's swole up from bee stings. She's a botoxaholic is what she is. She's had so many face lifts her ears flap when she blinks. It's all my poor brother can do to work two jobs to keep up with her plastic surgery payments. They on a five-year payment plan, for Pete's sake, and I ain't makin' that up. You a pretty girl. Don't start, young lady."

"Did y'all hear 'bout Candy over at Cut & Curl?" Ruby chimed in as she outlined Bunny's hairline with cholesterol cream. "Her daughter got arrested at Walmart this weekend for stealin' chicken wings and a dog sweater."

"Kids these days." Bunny shook her head. "Did I tell you about my nephew's weddin' last year? Did I tell you about it? His sister is the one gettin' married this weekend. They the wild side of the family. Anyway, my nephew's weddin' got a little rowdy, and a neighbor called the cops. My nephew, the groom, ended up gettin' tasered. I seen it with my own eyes. Knocked him clean 'cross the road and they hauled him away. That kinda' broke up the party."

"That sounds as wild as my weekend." Jessie laid her hands on a towel. "I went to a motorcycle rally at a farm. I was some guy's 'bitch,' as they call their women. Believe me, there ain't no lack o' lovin' at them rallies. Glad my mama wasn't there, if you know what I mean."

Bunny's jaw dropped. "Holy Moses, that's more story than I needed. Ruby, you got any smellin' salts? I'm feelin' lightheaded. The Bible says eat and be merry but not *that* merry." As Ruby worked chemicals into her hair, Bunny reached for her purse, fished out a coin and flipped it to Jessie. "Take this nickel, young lady, and hold it 'tween your knees next time." Bunny closed her eyes and soon snored in harmony with the window unit.

Slippers rose from her bed and scratched the door.

"Toots, please let Slippers out."

Jessie stared at the dog. "Miss Ruby, how'd ya come up with a name like 'Slippers'?"

"Shoot, that was easy. *The Wizard of Oz*, my favorite movie. Dorothy wore ruby slippers. I'm Ruby. She's Slippers. Get it?" Ruby clicked the heels of her sandals together. "There ain't no place like home. Right, Baby Girl? There ain't no place like home."

"Ma-ma-ma-ma." Li'l Bit clapped her hands.

"Ooww!" Jessie cringed. "I got cramps. My monthly's 'bout to come."

Bunny appeared to be dozing in the comfort of Ruby's chair. Eyes remaining closed, she spoke. "Listen here, honey. Goin' to them motorcycle rallies, you need to thank the Lord each time Aunt Flo pays a visit." Bunny relapsed into her stupor, and Jessie tiptoed out when her nail job was complete.

After the chemicals had done their work, Ruby woke Bunny and walked her over for a rinse. She blotted her hair with a towel then massaged in neutralizer. Ruby changed Li'l Bit's diaper then removed Bunny's rollers and rinsed again. She helped Bunny back into the styling chair where she trimmed and blow-dried.

Bunny stood and admired herself in the mirror, patting her new curls. She swung around. "What do y'all think?"

Toots clasped her hands under her chin. "Holy smoke, Miss Bunny, that's the best perm I ever seen. Them curls got more bounce than a trampoline."

Bunny beamed. Ruby winked at Toots and admired her own work. "Sugah, you gonna steal the show from the bride." Ruby cashed her out. "Li'l Bit, say goodbye to Miss Bunny."

Li'l Bit clapped and bounced in her playpen as Bunny stepped over and patted her head.

"Chee-chee-ma-ma." Li'l Bit giggled.

Bunny slid several ones into Li'l Bit's tip jar. "I'll drop by later this week and pick out a bowl for the weddin' present. Toot-a-loo."

Chapter 27

Sue Flay's head draped back in Ruby's styling chair, towels swaddling her hair and shoulders, round cucumber slices covering her eyes. Ruby smeared and patted green secret-formula fountain o' youth facial paste onto Sue's cheeks, moving quickly before it dried.

Earlene, a new patron, sat at Tootsie's nail station soaking her fingers. Quivering hands triggered ripples in the warm essential oils. A tattooed Playboy Bunny tramp stamp peeked out where her blouse rose up her lower back. Swollen, red eyelids hung at half-mast, and premature wrinkles creased her brow. Car keys and a pack of Camels lay beside the bowl.

This one looks rode hard and put up wet, thought Ruby.

"Miss Earlene, where you live?" Sue Flay's lips, the only exposed part of her face, moved like two worms making love.

"Two streets over," Earlene cotton-mouthed a reply. "A girl friend and me rented us a Horton singlewide."

"You must o' met my husband, Homer, when you rented the place."

"That was your husband? He sure is handsome."

"Handsome?" Sue lifted her head, and cucumber eyes stared Earlene down. "You must be seein' something I ain't. You prob'ly the first person who's called him handsome since his mama. Do I need to keep an eye on this—two single ladies livin' down the street?"

"Oh, no ma'am. I didn't mean it like that." Tootsie guided Earlene's hands into a towel and massaged them. "I was just tryin' to be nice. Besides, I'm married, but my husband and me is separated."

Ruby looked up from her work. "Bless your heart. I'm so sorry."

"It's awful. He's got our baby boy and is using him as blackmail. He don't even change my baby's diaper 'til it's so heavy it's draggin' the ground."

"Sounds like my husband, Bean. He's field-dressed a hun-ert deer but says he ain't yet figured out to change a diaper."

"I need a lawyer," Earlene said, "so I can get a divorce and get my baby back, but I don't know any."

Ruby's gaze met Tootsie's in the mirror. Ruby winked.

Sue trained her cucumber eyes at Earlene again. "You done come to the right place, honey. Ruby here has had dealin's with about every lawyer in town."

Ruby rinsed her hands and dried them on a towel. "That ain't true but I know who you ought to talk to. Y'all 'scuse me."

On the way to the kitchen she paused at Li'l Bit's playpen and ran a finger down her diaper. *Ain't too bad.* She ducked and stepped into the trailer. She heaped potted meat onto saltines and munched while scanning magnetized lawyer advertisements on the refrigerator. She peeled off a Wizeburger & Garcia advert. Back in the parlor, she laid the magnet down at the nail station in front of Earlene. *Another value-added service.*

"Simon Wizeburger is who you need."

"Is he any good?"

"Any good? Honey, if he takes your case, he'll pick your husband's bones clean as a buzzard on road kill. But don't never pay no consultation fee."

"Thank you, Miss Ruby. I'll call him."

"Tell him Ruby Sweat sent ya and you need a discount. After every divorce, them lawyers is the only ones livin' happily ever after."

Sue laughed and cracked the green mud on her cheeks. "Hey, y'all know what's black and brown and looks good on a lawyer?"

Earlene looked up. "I dunno, a suit?"

"No, a Doberman."

Sue cracked more mud laughing at her own joke.

"Oh pa-lease." Toots waved her emery board. "You've told that one a thousand times."

"Earlene, did you know the young lady workin' on your fingernails is my daughter."

"Oh, Mama, you don't have to tell all our secrets."

Ruby ladled touch-up paste in Sue's cracks. "Now you quit laughin' so the beauty can set in." Li'l Bit cried in her playpen. Slippers pawed the door for potty time. Tootsie's orange fingernails tickled her cell phone keys.

"Toots, will you stop typin' on that phone and tend to Li'l Bit and Slippers."

"I declare," Ruby whispered to Sue. "She's a good girl, but I don't know about young'uns in general these days."

Tootsie finished typing and laid her cell phone aside. "Miss Ruby, we need to get us a computer in here. I need to be Facebookin' my friends."

"Chiiil', I cain't afford no computer and don't need one, either. If we had a computer, I'd never get any work outta ya."

"Facebook is where the action is," Earlene chimed in. "I get propositioned all the time by guys I ain't even met."

Sue mumbled through her mud. "You hear that, Tootsie? Don't you get hooked on Facebookin'. I don't want my daughter to marry some computer pervert. Hey, I wanna see Facebook. Wonder if they'll let you see it at the library? That's where I use the computer."

"See, Mama," Tootsie chirped, "if I had a computer you could look on mine."

"I don't think the library'll mind," Earlene offered, "long as you don't surf porn or nuthin'."

"Holy Moly, Ruby, I'm glad you ain't checkin' my pressure now."

Ruby dried her hands. "Junior showed me how to use the computer at his school open house this year. I'm sorry, but it ain't sump'n I need in my life right now."

Li'l Bit bawled and Ruby stepped to the playpen. "Y'all mind if I let her crawl for a while?" She plunked Li'l Bit and her stuffed dinosaur onto the floor.

Li'l Bit crawled to Earlene, the new face, as hunched-over Tootsie pushed back the lady's cuticles. Baby Girl dropped her dinosaur, grabbed the leg of Earlene's jeans like the two were old friends, and struggled to stand while holding on to the patron's knee. Li'l Bit stared up, her big hazel eyes gazing in wonderment. She listed toward the side of her clubfoot.

"Hey, little girl. Ain't you got purty eyes."

Tootsie sat upright and raised Earlene's hand. "The ends o' your fingers is puffy and starting to cover your fingernails. I think the book calls it 'drumstick disease,' but I thought that's what alcoholics get."

"Tootsie!" her mother chided through mud. "You need to be a little more delicate."

"That's all right," said Earlene. "I reckon each of us has our own little red wagon."

Smiling, Li'l Bit slapped Earlene's knee.

"I see you purty girl." Earlene looked to Ruby. "Poor child. What do the doctors say is wrong with her foot?"

"They call it clubfoot."

"Can it be fixed?"

"Yes, Lawd. That's why we all here now. My husband's insurance won't pay for the treatments, so we savin' up just as hard as we can."

"Seems like insurance ought to pay."

"They prob'ly woulda if Bean ain't messed the paperwork up."

"Oh, bwutha," Sue mumbled through petrifying mud. "Youu gotta heear thisss."

Ruby sighed. "At the chicken plant, when a new baby is born, you got thirty days to enroll it on insurance. I kept beggin' him to take care o' the paperwork, but the idiot waited thirty-three days. The insurance said they wouldn't take her on the policy 'cause the time had done run out. Bean said he didn't know nuthin' about no thirty-day rule. I got two different lawyers, and sure enough, it was in the paperwork on page sixteen. Each lawyer said there weren't nuthin' to fight after they saw that."

"Damn!" Earlene knitted her brows and shook her head. "That just plain sucks." She looked at Ruby. "Wonder what makes a child get a clubfoot in the first place?"

Ruby froze then laid down her towel and capped her bottles with trembling hands. She turned to Earlene, lower lip aquiver and a tear rolling down her cherubic cheek.

"A mean nurse at the hospital said it was prob'ly *my* fault cause I ate so bad when I was pregnant... y'all 'scuse me a minute." She sucked her inhaler. "Tootsie, watch Li'l Bit. Sue, I'll be right back. Sorry."

Ruby covered her face and dashed from Flying Cloud into the trailer. Her rapid footsteps reverberated. She collapsed on her bed and buried her face in her pillow, wailing with shoulders heaving.

Dear Lawd, can you ever, ever forgive me? But it ain't 'bout me, it's 'bout Baby Girl and what I done to her. Please hep her. Please, oh please, Jesus.

She gathered her wits and returned to her parlor, eyes wet and puffy, cheeks streaked with mascara. "I'm sorry, y'all."

Tootsie and Earlene watched through wet eyes as Ruby returned. Li'l Bit nestled in Earlene's lap.

"Miss Ruby, I'm sorry I opened my big mouth. I didn't know no better."

"But everything's gonna be okay," Tootsie jumped in. "Li'l Bit's gonna get her treatments and everything's gonna be just fine."

"RRRR," Sue pleaded under her plaster.

"Jesus, Mary, and Joseph. Sorry, Sue." Ruby peeled off the hardened paste exposing skin red as a beet.

Tootsie bid their last patron goodbye then reviewed the appointment book. "Oh, no, Mrs. Lipshitz is comin' in tomorrow."

"Honey, she's one o' our best patrons." Ruby reclined in her styling chair with Li'l Bit on her knee as she fanned them both with a Last Supper hand fan.

"I see she wants a pedicure. Do I have to? Them crooked toes gross me out. And her toenails look like Fritos."

"Listen, Toots. If you gonna be a nail technician, you got to take the good with the bad. I done her toes a-plenty. You got to learn. Just be very careful with them tender spots."

"But she don't even tip."

"Not tippin' is the least o' my worries. You know to be careful. She's bad about findin' the littlest thing wrong then wantin' the whole thing for free. Before you give anythin' away to her, you talk to me first, you hear?"

Ruby collapsed on her bed and propped her aching legs and feet on pillows. She dumped out Li'l Bit's tip jar… surprise, a twenty-dollar bill!

Praise Jesus.

Chapter 28

Inside her playpen in the parlor's corner, Li'l Bit's hand grasped the top rail as she struggled for balance and swayed like a town drunk. Toys and stuffed animals crowded her feet. Her other arm clutched her favorite, Kee-Kee, a stuffed purple dinosaur.

Li'l Bit gazed through plastic prison bars surveying Mama's parlor full of jabbering ladies, blaring music, sweet smells, and loud machines. She held tight, sucking a pacifier, watching Mama work and glancing from lady-to-lady. A burning need made her heart flutter. Her head pounded, and the room spun. Nobody paid her any attention.

Bobbing up and down in her infantile effort to jump, she was certain someone would notice. Nothing. She spit out her pacifier. "Me-da-ba-bo."

Mama cut her eyes and smiled but kept twirling a lady's hair.

She looked lady-to-lady. Nothing. *Not fair.* She plopped onto her butt, grabbed her pot and wooden spoon and pounded out a rhythmic beat. Slippers hurried over and stuck her nose through a gap in the prison bars.

Mama waved. "It's okay, Baby Girl. We see you. We love you, Baby."

Li'l Bit sobbed then wailed. Slippers withdrew her head, looked at Mama, and yelped.

Mama put down her gun and stepped to the playpen. "Baby, wha'chu cryin' for? I just changed your diaper."

Mama ran a finger inside. "Ain't yo' diaper." She pushed past the playpen and into the kitchen where she filled a nipple-tipped bottle with cold, dark liquid. "Here, Baby." Mama handed her the bottle.

"Listen here. Mama's got to work. You behave yourself now. We'll eat dinner after while then Junior will be home from school and you can play with him, you hear?"

Li'l Bit cast Kee-Kee aside and grasped the elixir with both hands. The nipple slid between her lips and she sucked with vigor. *Ahhh.*

Mrs. Lipshitz's curler-laden head rose from her magazine. "What's that child drinkin', Ruby?"

"It's just Co-Cola. If I don't give it to her, we'll hear fussin' all mornin'. It's easier to give it than fight."

"Ain't it the truth." The lady in Mama's chair hollered. "It's the same with my old man. Without his Pepsi in the morning, he's meaner 'n a snake."

Mrs. Lipshitz frowned and shook her head. "Speaking of husbands. Remember Ruby, if you see my husband, Marty, don't tell him how often I come to your salon. I pay you in cash so he won't know. He thinks we're still holdin' on to the first dime he ever made."

"Not to worry. As a professional, I'm sworn to secrecy. How are your feet today?"

"Sensitive as nitroglycerin. Hope your lady will be careful."

"Not to worry. Tootsie always uses TLC." Toots glanced up from her feet-soaking preparations, spied Ruby in the mirror, and wrinkled her nose.

Li'l Bit sucked her bottle and watched through the bars as Mama blew the lady's hair with her gun. Everyone talked, but nobody talked to her.

Li'l Bit laid the empty bottle aside and grabbed Kee-Kee. They had to escape prison. She struggled to her feet and clutched the playpen's top rail. Swaying back and forth like a monkey, she cried and yelped with gusto. "Aiii."

Mama was on top of her like lightening. "Baby, you got your diapers in a bunch over sump'n. You hush or you're gettin' a spankin'."

She plopped onto her bottom, and tears streamed down her little cheeks.

"Why don't you let her outta her playpen, Ruby?" the lady in the styling chair asked. "She ain't gonna bother nuthin'. We'll all keep an eye on her."

Mama looked around. "You sure?"

Tootsie nodded. Mrs. Lipshitz shrugged.

Mama grabbed Li'l Bit under her armpits and lifted her like a feather. Kee-Kee joined her on the floor. "Now you behave yourself, Baby," Mama wagged her finger, "or you're goin' right back in the pen, you hear?"

Li'l Bit hugged Kee-Kee and flapped her free arm. Her caffeine-stoked brain studied every detail from her vantage point on the floor...

Undersides of chairs and ladies' clothes,
Shuffling feet and wiggling toes.

She crawled to the magazine table, pulled up, and stood, proud that she was now a big girl seeing the world from higher heights.

She watched Mama taking money from the lady with new hair. Mama turned to her. "Li'l Bit, say 'bye, bye.'"

She smiled in rapture at the attention. "Ba-ba-ba." The lady dropped money in the jar and left. Li'l Bit scrutinized Mrs. Lipshitz who was now under the bubble dryer and still staring at a magazine.

She plopped to her bottom then examined Mrs. Lipshitz's trouser legs and her sandaled feet. Nearby, Tootsie prepared a footbath. Baby Girl's eyes continued to scan the room... but wait. Something wasn't right. Her gaze swung back to the lady's toes.

She crawled over for a closer look and stared in confusion. Thin sandal straps exposed the lady's toes. Slippers trotted up and took a sniff. Nails—yellowed, curled, and flaky. On each foot, the second toe overlapped the big toe at a ninety-degree angle then wrapped downward like the claw of a hammer.

Her big toes is playing peek-a-boo.

Li'l Bit gawked from all fours, having seen nothing like it. Junior would laugh at this. She looked up at the lady and saw only the back of the magazine and heard the bubble dryer whine. She gazed again at the funny toes, smiled, rocked, and looked at Mama.

Mama glared back, shook her head, and mouthed, "No!"

Intoxicated by the hilarious sight, Li'l Bit grinned and feasted her eyes on Mrs. Lipshitz's toes. *What would Junior do?*

She remembered the county fair not long ago—the excitement, smiles, and laughter. She'd never seen Mama and Daddy and Junior so happy. Junior tried to win a prize by slamming a long hammer. He didn't win. Then Daddy stepped up and grabbed the hammer. He twirled it around his body then over his head in one fluid motion and slammed it down so hard the ball shot up and knocked the bell clean off the pole.

Daddy embraced his baby and let her choose the prize. She scanned the stuffed animal faces. Then, as though it was alive, a purple dinosaur called to her: Take *me*. Take *me*.

Li'l Bit pointed at the purple dinosaur. "This one?" the tattooed man behind the counter asked.

"That one, Baby?" Mama pointed. "The purple dinosaur? You sure?"

"Kee-kee."

The man handed the dinosaur to Li'l Bit, and she hugged it tight, her new best friend. Daddy patted her head as his tears flowed. Kee-Kee never left her side again.

Li'l Bit looked at the lady's strange toes, inched forward, raised her little fist like a sledge hammer, and slammed it down like Daddy at the county fair.

Chapter 29

Ruby scurried about the Flying Cloud distributing fresh towels and aprons. She heard the roar of a parking car. *Obviously, Polly ain't fixed her muffler.* The parlor's door popped open.

"Hey, everybody."

"Mornin', Polly." Ruby held the door. "Come on in, sugah. It's just me and you and Li'l Bit right now."

Polly turned sideways, sucked in her gut and scraped through the door, panting and sweating. "Oh, Lawd, that AC feels good." Though shorter than Ruby, she made up for it on the bathroom scales. She dropped her shoulder bag in the corner and squeezed into the shampoo chair.

Li'l Bit pawed at her sneakers.

"I see you, Li'l Bit." Polly reached down and patted her head. "Chiiil', you gettin' bigger by the day. And purtier, too."

Ruby draped a towel over Polly's shoulders, guided her head back, and massaged warm water through her hair.

"Where's Tootsie?"

"I give her the mornin' off." Ruby kneaded shampoo. "She got engaged and went to Walmart pickin' things out for her bridal registry."

"Oh, how marvelous. What's her fiancé do?"

"He's a sanitation engineer for the city."

Polly chuckled. "Yeah, like I said, what's he do?"

"He's a garbage man. He used to hang on the back o' the truck, but now he's a driver. Claims he's gonna be mayor one day and Tootsie believes him."

Polly rolled her eyes as Ruby rinsed. "Yeah, right. If everything Barrelhead promised over the years came true, we'd be livin' in a mansion, and I'd be drivin' a Rolls, not that rattletrap outside."

"You got nuthin' on me, darlin', with all them tales Bean keeps dreamin' up."

"I think registering at Walmart is smart." Polly sat up as Ruby toweled her hair. "When we was married, Barrelhead had us register at Bass Unlimited and 'bout all we got was camo clothes and fishing lures—not the first dern thing *I* could use."

"Your husband ain't no different from all men." Ruby patted the seat of her styling chair. "Bean's such a Romeo, for our ninth anniversary last year he took me to Subway in Walmart and we got meatball sammichs. How romantic is that?"

"I think they got the best meatball sammichs in town." Polly climbed the styling chair's step and squeezed in. "I would o' liked that. 'Least he didn't take you to wrastlin' like Barrelhead took me last year."

"Actually I would o' liked wrastlin'. Li'l Bit, too. Right, Baby Girl?"

Li'l Bit clapped as she sat cross-legged on the floor, glancing back and forth between Mama and Miss Polly, following the conversation like a tennis match. She laughed when Mama laughed, cringed when Mama cringed. It was her birthright, a rite of passage, learning the fine art of conversation and gossip, loading her private bag of tricks for later in life.

Polly fanned her perspiring face with a Last Supper fan. Ruby said, "Sugah, you seem extra hot. Has your bowels moved today?"

"Knock on wood, that ain't a problem today. It just takes a lot outta me to get from point A to point B these days. And you, Ruby, my feet ache just thinkin' 'bout yours. I don't see how you stand all day."

"It ain't just my feet, believe me. My knees is about to give out any day." Ruby combed and clipped Polly's wet hair. "I try not to complain to my patrons, but you such a good friend. My doctor put me on a special diet I'm gonna start next week. Says I got a granular problem. Says I ought to find another line o' work and to start takin' exercise, too."

"Exercise?" Polly chuckled. "Girl, we ain't in no shape to take exercise. Every time I hear that dirty word, I wash my mouth out with chocolate."

Ruby succumbed to temptation, reached inside the supply station's hidden compartment, and snatched a bag of cookies. She gave Li'l Bit a couple, took several for herself, and passed the bag to Polly. "You're right, there ain't no use fightin' it. There's a skinny girl inside me tryin' to get out, but I shut her up with cookies. Let's eat these 'fore we get hungry. Ain't no sense gettin' hungry and lettin' ya energy get low."

They both laughed. Li'l Bit laughed and slapped her knees as she munched.

Polly crammed a whole cookie into her mouth and chewed. "They's good. I ain't worried 'bout it. Cain't blame me if God made me too short for my weight. My luck, time I'm thin, fat'll be back in. 'Sides, my fat's done sot in. But listen, Barrelhead's been fussin' at me lately 'bout my weight, so what happens with us sistas stays with us sistas, right?"

"Our little secret, Girl Scouts' honor." Ruby laid down the comb and scissors and fluffed Polly's hair with her fingers. "Wha'chu think? I may need to cut some more. Shorter hair is in this year. Versatility is the key."

"Keep feedin' me cookies, and you can give me a mohawk for all I care." Polly pointed to the product rack. "Don't let me forget to get another tube o' your Tummy Flattenin' Gel. I cain't tell for sure, but I think it's startin' to work."

"You better get 'em while they last. I think it takes a few tubes to get goin'." Ruby combed and clipped. "Heard anything new 'bout Calvin Butler? Bean challenged him on overtime pay earlier this week and liked o' got fired."

"I hear he lives a purty fast lifestyle," Polly spoke with authority. "I feel sorry for his wife. I hear some wild things go on at their plantation outside town now that his daddy is gone. I know this, he ain't nearly the man his daddy was."

"Dad-gummit." Ruby fired up her drying gun and spoke louder. "Butler was born with both feet in the trough and look how he's actin'. Let him come live in my trailer for a week and he'll 'preciate what all he's got."

"I wonder 'bout his sisters. Do they know what he's up to? Mark my word, Ruby, he's gonna get tangled up in his own dark web."

The telephone rang. Ruby looked at the caller ID and laid down her brush. "'Scuse me, Polly... Hello... Hello, Miss April... Monday? Let's see. How 'bout two o'clock? Okay, see you then."

"That weren't April, the piano teacher, was it?"

"Yeah. She's ninety-two and still gettin' around. Bless her buttons, she ain't got the hair of o' anchovy but she keeps on comin' in."

"She still givin' piano lessons to Junior?"

"Oh, Lawd. He came home after the third lesson with a note that said, 'Tryin' to teach Junior piano lessons is a waste o' your money and my time.'"

The phone rang again. Ruby looked at the caller ID. "Lawd-a-mussy, speak o' the devil. It's Tadmore Elemen-tree. What in the world has that boy done now? Hello... Yes... Yes, this is Junior Sweat's mama. What's wrong... Suspended! What in the world? Why... nine-one-one? Uh-huh... Uh-huh... You kiddin' me... Okay, we'll come pick him up soon."

Ruby hung up, collapsed into a chair, and sucked her inhaler. "Lawd hep me, that boy's killin' me. He got suspended for the week. The cops and a fire truck came, but Junior's okay."

"Cops and a fire truck? What on earth? It'll be okay, honey." Polly patted Ruby's knee. "Wha'chu want me to do? I'll go pick him up if you want."

"No, a parent s'pose to get him. I got two more appointments comin' up. Bean has to go pick him up, that's all there is to it. Them chickens is just gonna have to wait." She called the Majestic Chicken Company front office.

"I need to speak with my husband, Butterbean Sweat. It's important… yes, I'll hold…"

"Polly, you mind pouring me some Co-Cola. Refill your glass, too.

"What? Cain't find him? This is his wife and it's an emergency. They need to look harder… Yes, I'll hold…

"They say they cain't find the idiot."

"Oh, he's prob'ly just in the bathroom or somethin'. They'll find him, honey."

"They better, for Bean's sake. Junior learns all this crap from his daddy then his daddy ain't never 'round to deal with it.

"What? Still cain't find him? You got to be jokin'… no… no, I cain't wait for y'all to call back. Just tell him to forgit it. Bye." She slammed the receiver into its cradle.

"His truck's there, but they cain't find him. He's prob'ly cuttin' the fool somewhere 'round that plant. I'm gonna strangle him. I'll have to go get Junior myself. Polly, do you mind terribly stayin' here with Li'l Bit and I'll be back soon?"

"Child, I got your back. Li'l Bit and me will have us a big ole time."

Ruby grabbed her purse. "They's more hot dogs on the stove and buns on the counter. You and Li'l Bit eat. She needs sump'n in her tummy. If I ain't back when my next patron gets here, give her a Co-Cola, and tell her I'll be right back."

Ruby rolled into a visitor parking space at Tadmore Elementary School, the donut spare tire on her Lincoln squeaking and squawking with every revolution. She rushed to the office with her muumuu flapping in the breeze.

She entered the door marked "Principal" and saw Junior sitting in a chair on the room's far side. A receptionist sat behind a desk. "May I help you?"

"I'm Ruby Sweat here to see 'bout my young'un over there, Junior Sweat." Ruby wagged her finger at him.

"Yes ma'am, Principal Patton has been waitin' for you." The lady knocked then ushered them through the door. Ruby scowled at Junior. He stared at his shoes and adjusted his bulging backpack.

"Mrs. Sweat." Mr. Patton stood and motioned to the two chairs opposite his desk. "Please sit." His white shirt collar rode high and stiff up his neck, and his eyebrows formed a bushy "V." "You too, Junior, next to your mother."

Ruby's brows knitted. "What's this all about?"

"It appears that your son and two other boys cooked up a little scheme and played a trick with the pay phone in the hallway. It's unclear who pushed which numbers, but they collectively managed to dial nine-one-one. My secretary actually saw them from a distance and thought they were just checking the coin return slot—the usual. Moments later, police cars and fire trucks descended upon us with sirens blasting. We were forced to conduct an emergency evacuation of the entire school."

"But Mama, I only pushed one button."

"Junior Sweat! You ain't stupid. You know'd y'all was callin' nine-one-one. Don't you lie. Your daddy's gonna tan your hide when he gets home."

"But Mama, Billy just asked me to push the 'one' button and that's all I—"

"Young man," Mr. Patton interjected. "You are clearly a co-conspirator, and claiming ignorance will not hold water. Mrs. Sweat, he is suspended for the rest of the week. It will be the family's responsibility to obtain his assignments from his teacher. Young man, you must keep up your work during your suspension. You may return Monday morning."

"He's learnt this type o' nonsense from his daddy."

"Let's just hope the authorities don't levy a fine. They take nine-one-one calls from schools seriously these days, in case you don't watch the news. They can levy a fine for the manpower involved in a prank alarm. It could be several hundred dollars."

"Jesus, Mary, and Joseph! Junior Sweat—"

"But Mama…"

Chapter 30

Friday couldn't roll around fast enough at Ruby's Curl Up 'N Dye. WTF, that is, Wild Thing Friday.

Ruby pushed her size-ten feet through the loops of her leopard leotard and pulled up the legs. She stood, waggled, and stretched it up her body, overcoming one cottage-cheese bulge after another—settling thighs, drooping hips, inner tube mid-section, sagging boobs—spandex stretched to the snapping point. Three hundred pounds of sugar bulging from a two-hundred-pound sack.

Leopard spots melted to cover her mass like a primitive hunter's pelt, her answer to Bean's camo. This was her one outfit she knew always kindled Bean's lust. She waited until he departed for work to pull it on, not wanting to distract him before another big day at the plant.

Tootsie had painted Ruby's fingernails and toenails masai red the day before. With a heavy hand, Ruby applied her makeup—ecru foundation, twilight black mascara and brow pencil, red glitter eye shadow, moulin rouge, all in keeping with her color palate.

As was the WTF custom, Tootsie arrived early to do Ruby's hair. She traipsed through the Flying Cloud wearing black stilettos and skin-tight, cheetah-print jeggings. Her snug, white baby doll tube top exposed ample chasm and flesh.

Ruby did a double take. "For the love o' Christmas, we got to cover them boobs up. We don't want to make our patrons *too* jealous."

Li'l Bit crawled around the Flying Cloud as Ruby settled into her own styling chair and pulled the lever on the side to prop up her bare feet. "I want you to fluff it and volumize it good, Toots. It's lookin' tired as I am."

Under Ruby's watchful eye, Tootsie pulled up handfuls and teased Cleopatra-black tresses downward with a comb. Needing a free hand for hair spraying, she slid the comb down her tube top's front and into the valley.

"Honey, you ought to stop storin' your tools 'tween them twin peaks. When you go for the cosmetology test and stick your comb in there, you'll lose points unless, of course... oh, never mind. Remember to put down an hour in your trainin' log.

"Toots, I been thinkin'. We got to do sump'n to separate us from the herd. They's too many kitchen-ticians 'round here. We got to show some spirit and make our ladies feel special today. We got to be classy. Candy cain't compete with us on Wild Thing Friday. Any patron who shows up today in a Wild Thing outfit, whether they's gettin' a treatment today or not, is gettin' a free Ruby's gourmet hot dog, chips, and drink. We creatin' a party atmosphere."

Now that's value-added.

Tootsie finished her masterpiece and crowned Ruby's head with a hair band showcasing a big, red "R" on one side. "What do you think, Miss Ruby?"

"I suwannee, young-un, you gettin' better and better. Just in time, too, Dorese is due any minute."

"Wha'chu gonna do with Junior today?"

"I ain't wakin' him up. Long as he's sleepin', that's one less thing I have to worry 'bout."

Ruby cranked up the boom box. *Wild Thing* by The Troggs led off her WTF song medley. Despite Slipper's protest, Ruby stretched a leopard-print dog sweater over her tight curls. Like mama like mutt.

"Come here, Baby Girl, we gonna bring back Halloween." Li'l Bit clapped when she saw her pumpkin outfit. Ruby said, "Today you gonna be a wild punkin'."

Ruby stood at the mirror and applied arousal red lipstick—"replenishing, anti-oxidizing, and silky smooth." She slipped into sparkling, rhinestone flats, her feet overflowing the sides like bread dough in an undersized pan.

She pulled out a giraffe-print apron and handed it to Tootsie. "Here, wear this. It ought to cover up most o' them boobs."

The Flying Cloud's door swung wide. Dorese ducked and entered with a zebra scarf around her shoulders and a grin across her pale face. Dorese's fame was being the only remaining original resident of the fifteen-year-old Garden of Eden trailer park.

"Well, look a-here." Ruby pointed. "We got us a wild zebra a-loose in the house."

Dorese stared at Ruby. "Sugah babe, ain't nobody gonna top your outfit today... or any other day."

"Thank ya, honey. Bean says we goin' to Mardi Gras next year and wants me to march in this outfit. But I'll be too skinny to wear it by then." Ruby patted the shampoo chair. "Come on and have a seat while I check your pressure. Tootsie, get Dorese a hot dog, chips, and a drink. Wha'chu want Dorese, sweet tea or Co-Cola?"

"Hit don't matter. Surprise me, Tootsie, I'm feelin' wild today."

Dorese ate a plateful of WTF fare then Tootsie shampooed her. Ruby guided her to the styling chair and tied a five-and-dime cape around her neck for chemicals. She would re-cape her for her trim in silky WTF tiger-stripe. "Dorese, after the perm you gettin' today, you gonna walk outta here lookin' like a million dollars."

"Cain't I just have the million dollars?"

Ruby motioned Toots to the side.

"Honey, I'm gonna highlight Dorese's hair. Take these bottles of emollient and hydroxide and mix them in that red bowl then stir in this lye powder. Try not to spill none."

Tootsie coughed as she mixed the potion. "Miss Ruby, can I open the door? This stuff is chokin' me."

"Sorry, honey. It'll be hotter'n sin in here in no time if we open the door. You'll be okay."

Ruby began brushing Dorese's hair when—"*Aargh!*" Tootsie screamed. "*No!*"

"What's wrong, Toots?"

"My new false eyelash fell in the bowl. *Look*, it's bubblin' and disappearin'." Tootsie looked up in horror with asymmetrical eyes, one eyelash dark and enormous, the other pale and puny.

"*Shhh.* Don't panic, honey. Let it go. We'll get you another eyelash. You in the right place for that."

The Flying Cloud suddenly vibrated from the trailer's TV speakers.

"Y'all 'scuse me a minute." Ruby threw down her towel and marched to the trailer's living room. Junior lounged in the bean-bag chair eating a bowl of Cap'n Crunch with a game show blaring.

Ruby's eyes flashed fire. "Junior Sweat, I suwannee, you ain't gonna live to see your next birthday if you keep it up. You on suspension from school, and I told ya there ain't gonna be no TV." She slapped the TV's "off" button.

"When you finished eatin', you gonna study your school books, and that's all you gonna do, you hear me?"

"Yes, Mama, but..."

"There ain't no 'buts' today. I should o' sent your butt to work with your daddy. I got a busy day in the parlor. Now, unless you want your rear end blistered, you better not give me no more trouble today, you hear?"

"Yes, Mama."

Ruby stomped back to the parlor and sucked her inhaler. *That boy's done got my pressure up good, I can feel it.*

Tootsie massaged Ruby's shoulders. "It's okay, Miss Ruby. Don't worry, be happy. It's Wild Thing Friday."

"You right, honey."

Dorese lay sprawled in the styling chair, her shoulders covered with a towel. Tinfoil-wrapped spikes of hair stood erect. Ruby stood back and smiled at her handiwork. She whirled the styling chair around so Dorese could look in the mirror. "Thunderation,

Dorese, like my grandaddy would say about WWII, you lookin' like you tryin' to radio Tokyo Rose."

Waynelle eased through the door, baby carrier in tow, wearing a coonskin cap.

"By golly," Ruby cried. "Y'all look at Waynelle. What a purty baby, and she's been huntin' coons. Is this Wild Thing Friday or what? Tootsie, take her pressure, and get her sump'n to eat, will ya?"

Ruby glanced at her watch. "Waynelle, you early, ain't ya."

"Yes, is that okay?"

"No problem, sugah. Enjoy your hot dog, hep yourself to some tea or Co-Cola, and make yourself at home. They's plenty o' *National Enquirers* on the table."

Waynelle stepped to the tea pitcher, poured herself a glassful over ice, and took a swig. "Wow, Ruby, I see you take a little tea with your sugah."

"Funny, honey."

Waynelle pawed the magazines on the table as she ate her hot dog. She motioned to Ruby who tiptoed over barefoot. Waynelle whispered. "Things ain't happenin' in the bedroom with Cletus, if you know what I mean. Can I look at your special magazines?"

Ruby frowned and nodded. "Oh, honey, I'm so sorry. But don't feel like the Lone Ranger—Bean ain't egg-zackly knockin' the lights out."

Wild Thing pulsated in the background.

Before Li'l Bit's need for foot treatments, when Ruby could afford to buy slick magazines, she clipped articles on the Big O— the female orgasm. *Redbook, Cosmopolitan,* and—of course—*O, Oprah Magazine.* She grabbed the shoebox housing her dog-eared special collection library and rested it on the table.

Wild Thing love filled the air.

"Sugah, you study these, and if you want, pick one or two to take home, long as you bring 'em back." *Another value-added service. Let Candy compete with that.*

Ruby grabbed a bottle of passion fruit perfume and held it out to Waynelle. "And there's sump'n else. You need to get this.

Drives men crazy. One patron told me she ain't done it in a year with her husband. Once he got a whiff o' this, his britches was off 'fore they could make it to the bedroom."

Dorese looked in the mirror and straightened her zebra scarf. She fluffed her new highlights, light sparkling on the bleach-blond streaks like diamonds in a showroom. "You right, Ruby, I feel and look like a million dollars."

Ruby turned to Li'l Bit. "Say bye-bye to Miss Dorese."

"Bwa-wa-Kee-Kee."

Dorese slid a bill into Li'l Bit's jar.

"Thanks, sugah, see ya next time." Ruby closed the door behind Dorese and turned to the others. "Y'all 'scuse me for a minute, please."

Like a leopard stalking an antelope, Ruby tiptoed through the kitchen and paused before turning the corner into the den. She heard low volume TV and Junior chuckling. She bent her knees, rocked back, and pounced around the corner.

Junior lay spread-eagle on the beanbag, TV remote in hand.

"*Junior Sweat.*"

He dropped the remote and scrambled up, spilling Goobers across the rug, then darted for the door with Ruby smack on his heels.

"But, Mama…"

"YOU STOP RIGHT THERE."

Junior bolted out the door just beyond Ruby's grasp. He bounded down the steps and across the yard, his naked belly flopping up and down. Ruby gave barefooted chase, mountains of leopard-skinned flesh bouncing with each step.

"STOP, JUNIOR, STOP."

As the distance between them lengthened, Ruby slowed then stopped and gasped for air.

"But, Mama…" Junior shouted over his shoulder.

"Junior Sweat, you in big trouble. You wait 'til yo' daddy gets home. He's gonna switch your rear end 'til it blisters."

She turned and huffed back to the trailer and locked the door behind her. *If he wants back in, let him come through the Flyin' Cloud. Then, I'll catch his butt and clobber him a good'un.*

Waynelle's turn. She positioned the carrier on the floor so her baby could watch then settled into the styling chair. Slippers rushed up to sniff the baby. The Flying Cloud burst open, and the crew welcomed Bunny. She wore her walking shoes for seniors and a tiger-print blouse.

"Well, butter my biscuits, if there ain't a wild tiger on the loose." Ruby motioned her in. "Bunny, you a wild child."

Bunny studied Ruby's leopard leotard. "'Fraid I cain't compete with you, sugah. I got to sit. That weddin's tomorrow, and I don't know if I'll make it. I'm plum wo' out. But I'm gonna get a decorative bowl just in case."

Ruby stepped over and patted her shoulder. "It's okay, honey. Toots'll get you a hot dog. You lookin' for a wax today?"

"Yeah, if y'all can squeeze me in. I'd rather pay you ten dollars than rip that tape acrost my lip myself. I just cain't do it. Makes a grown woman weep."

Tootsie served Bunny a hot dog and chips and slid the cuff up her arm. "Ruby, you ain't gonna believe what I heard. Candy got a blood pressure cuff, just like you."

Pop. Ruby clapped her hands. "See, every idea we come up with, Candy steals it. I think she's sendin' a spy in here to watch us."

All four ladies cut suspicious eyes at one another.

After the last patron, Ruby scooped up Li'l Bit and collapsed in her styling chair as Tootsie swept the floor. "Lawd-a-mussy, my feets is killin' me."

PART IV:
Openin' Day

Chapter 31

*'Tis the night before Openin', and all through the trailer
not a creature is stirrin', 'cept Ruby and her inhaler.*

*Camo is spread 'round the den with care
in hopes that a big buck will answer my prayer.*

Butterbean Sweat

As deer season drew nigh, Bean grew plum giddy, so many good things culminating at once. The worst of summer's oppressive heat was over, and NASCAR's Chase for the Cup hung in the balance. The county fair and Halloween were approaching. Ghosts and goblins haunted Garden of Eden trailer park yards, and trick-or-treat candy filled the Sweat family cupboard. *Most important—time to get back to the woods.*

Everything shouted, "PARTY."

The days leading up to deer season flowed like molasses. Rare insomnia plagued Bean as he chomped at the bit to end his hunting dry spell. At Everlasting Baptist Church the Sunday before, he negotiated a private deal with God, laying out things he'd do to be a better Christian if only He would plop a trophy buck in his lap, eight-point or better.

Kinetic energy ricocheted through the Sweat trailer on Opening Day Eve as Bean's adrenals pumped like a locomotive. The mother of all celebrations was underway at Fat Back Hunt Club, and he was missing it. He'd partied at every one since joining a dozen years ago at age eighteen, the minimum Fat Back age.

Now his heart was torn asunder. Junior was too young to witness the mayhem at Fat Back, yet Bean didn't want to abandon him. Couldn't take him, couldn't leave him. Therefore, couldn't go. He'd miss the party tonight, but father and son would be in the woods before daybreak.

Junior shadowed Bean in the deer stand a few times, but this would be his first Opening Day hunt. He had yet to witness a kill. One day his son would score his own kill, and Bean would smear his face with deer blood, a rite of passage as old as mankind.

The den morphed into camo central as they laid out clothes and supplies. Bean made his list and checked it twice. He polished his twelve-gauge Mossberg shotgun and slid it back into its sock. *What a beaut'.*

He emptied and cleaned his camo tote bag—can't invade the deer stand reeking of melted chocolate and stale beer. He tossed trash, took inventory, changed batteries, added food. Added more food.

"When I was your age, Junior, I'd hunt with no more than a shotgun, a couple o' extra cottages in my pocket, and a knife on my belt. But now, I've seen what a man may need in the woods, and I'm tellin' ya, there ain't nothin' more important than your tote bag." Moderation gave way to excess, and Butterbean now carried a fifty-pound general store.

Junior packed his camo knapsack, a pygmy version of Daddy's...

Dale Earnhardt race car, Snickers bar.
Bag o' peanuts, cream doughnuts.

Bug spray, cake from his birthday.
Couple o' Co-Colas, box of Crayolas.

The time arrived for the Sweats to take a short autumn nap. To connect with the call of the wild, Bean opened the bedroom window for fresh, crisp air. His head collapsed onto the pillow. "Night, night, everybody."

"Night, night," Ruby cooed. "Ma-ma-ma," Li'l Bit added from her crib.

The family nestled snug in their beds while visions of an eight-pointer danced in Bean's head...

The monster buck, the biggest ever seen in these parts, crashes through the swamp, and I make an impossible shot. The boys carry their new hero on their shoulders and shower me with beer. My trophy's photo hangs on the wall at Fat Back, on bulletin boards at work, on mirrors in Ruby's beauty parlor, at the butcher's, on the in-law's refrigerator... an endless list. Now famous, I sign autographs Saturday mornings at a card table outside Walmart...

A car rolling into the Mexicans' yard across the road awakened him. Headlight reflections split the blinds and danced into Bean's bedroom. The image of an eight-pointer raced across the sparkling blue ceiling, a sure sign that this morning would be his finest hour. He imagined his shotgun's blast ringing in his ears. He smelled gunpowder. *Yes!*

Ruby grunted and shifted. "Honey, what's wrong?"

That ain't gunpowder I smell. "Ruby, you need to stop eatin' them pickled eggs 'fore bedtime."

"I ain't had but two."

Liar, liar, panties on fire. "Get on back to sleep. I ain't got one wink all night."

Chapter 32

Honeysuckle Plantation buzzed with energy on Opening Day Eve. Another VIP mother lode was poised to join the long and storied guest list. Thousands of annual man-hours required to maintain two thousand acres of pristine habitat for white-tail deer was about to pay off. Calvin "Champ" Butler Jr. set the stage for a record harvest—corn-fed deer and the souls of three men. He knew well his guests' weakness for flesh, prisoners to mortal compulsions, Achilles heels lodged in their crotches.

Seize the day. Champ swaggered to the bar for a pre-guest nip. *Advance my interests and trust nothing to the future.*

Though Honeysuckle Plantation could accommodate twenty, the guest list for the night was intimate by design. Proper etiquette dictates discretion when coupling married politicians with ladies of the evening.

Butler met his guests and ushered them toward the lodge's baronial great hall. He had refurbished it after his father's death—his twenty-first century gothic fantasy, royal trappings without the peerage. A slate corridor wound past floor-to-ceiling bookcases and paintings in niches.

Laughter echoed through the great hall's exposed rafters and ricocheted off conquests mounted on red sandstone walls. A massive, two-tiered antler chandelier clutched the vaulted ceiling's apex. Bigwigs migrated to the fire and sank into plush armchairs upholstered in African pelts. Boots scuffed a Zebra-skinned ottoman as Georgia's lieutenant governor—the Bulldawg himself—nestled into the largest chair. A gooseneck lamp cast ambient light over his broad physique and eavesdropped on state secrets through a clandestine microphone.

Under the ellipse of an enormous stone fireplace, an aromatic hickory inferno crackled. A Canadian grizzly flanked the hearth and reared eight feet high on its hind legs. Butler's latest commission hung above the native cypress mantel—an oil portrait of himself posing as an English squire.

Pungent cigar smoke drifted upward past exotic taxidermied trophies from around the world then swirled to oblivion under fans hanging from cypress beams thirty feet up. Elephant foot ashtrays cupped butts and ashes.

Four massive antique English doors embellished with wrought iron framed each corner of the hall. Each led to a bedchamber. Stones formed twenty-foot arches above copper-grilled glass spanning three enormous bay windows. Two grand magnolias dominated the front lawn, and a verdant panorama of two-hundred-year-old live oaks graced the horizon.

An old black man entered the room through a side door, grappling a six-foot log. He shuffled across the slate with his green cap riding high on his forehead. A twisting honeysuckle vine and the letters "HP" adorned the cap's crown. The old man stepped inside the firebox and laid the log onto the flame and across English andirons. He turned, removed his cap, and with warm but anxious eyes, faced Mr. Butler.

"'Scuse me, Mr. Butluh, I been axed to tell you da oysters be ready in 'bout fi-deen minutes."

"Thank you, Thaddeus." Butler waved the old man away with the back of his hand.

"Yessuh, yessuh." Old Thaddeus bowed and shuffled away.

Butler studied the three men twirling amber liquid in cut crystal glasses and sipping Scotland's finest single-malt whiskey or Kentucky's finest single-barrel bourbon. *They all talk at once, each trying to top the other's story.* Acting as the consummate host, Champ monitored their social lubricant, coaxing carelessness and unwitting cooperation in his plot yet stopping them short of messy over-served.

He sipped a Heineken and tried to relax. Champ admired his recent purchases—Italian hunt boots, tweed trousers, and Penfield vest. But the old red-and-black plaid Mackinaw Cruiser jacket had belonged to Calvin Butler Sr. *If only Father could see how chic I look wearing his down-home clothing now that it's hot in the metrosexual camp.*

For the second consecutive year, Butler's guest of honor for Opening Day was the lieutenant governor. The Bulldawg pushed three-hundred pounds, but his large frame moved athletically, just three steps slower than his first team all-conference football days at the University of Georgia. His family's peach farm outside Macon was now fourth generational. Charisma and a slick public relations firm had propelled the country boy a long way. But now, ethics accusations hung around his neck like a lead shackle.

The Bulldawg dressed sensibly—khaki briar pants, zip-up snake-proof boots, and a plaid upland shooting shirt with leather shoulder patch. He tested the armchair's limits by shifting his frame forward to better wave his arms and cigar to illustrate his points. His jowls billowed and jiggled, keeping time with every gesture. His huge head twisted from man to man, commanding eye contact to stress his stories. Champ had seen him drink all night and was confident he wouldn't embalm himself before all the acts of tonight's play were complete.

Butler recruited two eager locals to help entertain the Bulldawg—the sheriff and the executive director of the chamber of commerce. He hoped these hayseeds wouldn't embarrass him but was crestfallen when they arrived together, both kitted out in camo, ignorant of proper fashion for high-class hookers.

An armchair swallowed the squat chamber director, Buddy "B. S." Birdsong. Broken capillaries streaked across his cheeks and bulbous nose like lightning bolts, and sparse wisps of ginger-red hair curved over from ear to ear. Champ had repeatedly invited B.S. to fly with him in the company time-share jet to visit his personal hair dresser in Atlanta, perhaps even get a toupee.

"Maybe next week." Birdsong's pat answer to most requests for action. He sucked his cigar, cocked his head back, and spewed smoke toward the chandelier.

"Champ, this cigar sure is smooth," B.S. opined in his Irish lilt. "My compliments to you, lad. Must be a Cuban."

"Indeed. Montecristo Double Corona, arguably the finest cigar in the world." Butler puffed. "A box of those and other treats await you each in a Honeysuckle Plantation duffel bag in your room, compliments of Majestic Chicken. Now, B. S., the Lieutenant Governor asked how you got your nickname. Tell the tale."

"Bloody hell, if you insist." He turned to the Bulldawg. "It was twenty years ago at a chamber of commerce retreat, and I was the new assistant director. The board allotted me fifteen minutes to present my ideas for increasing tourism dollars. My brilliant soliloquy far exceeded the level of thought previously known to them. After an hour, they stopped me, their brains unable to process further information."

Champ and the sheriff broke into laughter and Champ continued the story. "One board member told me they listened to old Buddy and when he left the room, they boiled down what he said, blew the smoke away, and realized he hadn't said one thing you could sink your teeth into—'Like a bird's song, he'll chirp all day and never say a damn thing.'"

The sheriff jumped in to finish. "He's so full of bullshit, his eyes is brown. You just wait, he's gonna explode one day, and shit'll fly everywhere. So they decided to call him 'Bullshit Birdsong.' But since we cain't say 'bullshit' in mixed company, they named him 'B. S.' Most folks assume 'B. S.' stands for 'Birdsong,' but we know better."

"There you go," Birdsong rallied in defense. "Some folks don't know shit from Shinola. But it didn't take them long to name me executive director, now did it lads?"

"Hell," the Bulldawg chimed in, "sounds like you ought to run for state Senate."

Butler knew Birdsong had enough Irish in him to hold his liquor until tonight's feat was a *fait accompli*. Birdsong was the lowest priority of his three targets.

Sheriff Roscoe Pitts presented Champ's biggest challenge. Roscoe had two speeds: all out or asleep. His eyes flared when he spoke, and his crooked nose and scar across his cheek signaled that he was unafraid of a scrap. His ears stuck out so far that Butler wanted to pin them back with chicken wire. Roscoe always wore a cap, thinking it made his ears less noticeable. He was right, for without it, greeting eyes zoomed in on his Dumbo ears. A camo "HP" cap now perched on his head.

Sheriff Roscoe switched to bourbon and Coke, and his low-hanging bottom lip alternated between sipping his drink and dribbling tobacco juice into a white Styrofoam cup. At the rate Roscoe was drinking, Butler worried he'd be drunk as a fiddler by the time the action started. For now, Roscoe was still sober enough to kiss up. "So tell us, Bulldawg, what's the first thing you gonna do when you become governor?"

"Probably build a proper wet bar in the governor's mansion. That teetotaler living there now thinks happy hour is a time to drink milk and study the Bible."

Butler clapped his hands. "All right gentlemen. Refill your drinks, it's time to walk to the fire pit." He stood and reached for the sheriff's glass. "Roscoe, let me top off your bourbon. You finish those fried shrimp."

"Sounds like a plan." He handed his glass to Champ, shifted forward, and rocked to get his belly heading in the right direction for standing. On knock-knees and splayed feet, he ambled to the dining table and its hors d'oeuvres where his arm and jowls worked in rapid-fire fashion.

Birdsong poured himself vodka. "Champ, what time the skirts gettin' here?"

"Around nine. Can you wait that long, my man?"

"It's gonna be close. My blue balls are aching, so tell 'em to come on. I'm ready to give 'em a good old fashioned chamber of commerce welcome."

"They're coming," Butler laughed. "Pun intended."

Birdsong strolled to the dining table to graze with the sheriff. Butler refilled Roscoe's drink with mostly Coke then added a healthy measure of bitters in hopes he wouldn't detect the dilution.

Champ lingered behind the bar and snuck another Percocet from his silver pill box. He wanted to push it close to the line tonight himself, to celebrate, but he had to remain alert. He needed to reach that narrow zone—enough dope and alcohol to calm his nerves, to give him courage for tonight's stunt, but not enough to make him loopy. As years of prescription drug abuse turned into decades, that perfect zone narrowed, difficult to achieve and maintain.

"So," boomed the lieutenant governor, slapping Champ on the back with his huge paw, "is Monika coming tonight?"

"Bulldawg, after you get hold of her, I'm sure she'll be coming. Roxie said she's picking up Monika in about an hour. She'll call again when they're *en route*. But don't you worry, if Monika doesn't make it, Roxie will bring a top drawer substitute."

"Man, I hope she makes it." The lieutenant governor smiled and shook his head. "I have wet dreams remembering her from last year. She's so tight, you can put a fifty-cent piece in that thing and she'll spit five dimes back at you. You understand what I'm talking about?"

Butler whistled. "Damn, Bulldawg, that sounds special. Frankly, no, I haven't experienced that since high school, but back then I didn't know how special it was. Don't you worry, you can count on Roxie to deliver."

The Bulldawg squeezed behind the bar, faced the bookcase along the wall, pulled his reading glasses, and scanned cracked leather bindings with bas relief designs and gold leafed titles. "Champ, let's see what light bedtime reading you've got." He canted his head and called out: "Napoleon... Shakespeare... Prince Machiavelli, whoever that is. Damn, you one cultured sumbitch."

"I need constant mental challenge," Butler lied about books he purchased only to impress. "You ready for a martini? We're about to walk to the fire pit. Let me light your cigar." He whipped out a torch, and working as a team, they re-fired the stogie.

Champ delivered the sheriff's drink so they could speak in private. "We were talking about the two dog hunting clubs bordering Honeysuckle."

The sheriff took a sip. "As I was sayin' yesterday, I sent a deputy to visit each club to warn 'em not to be runnin' dogs on the plantation."

"Those redneck bastards pack into those little hunt clubs." Champ pointed toward the distance. "They're like sardines in a can. They only use shotguns or they'd kill each other, which would be okay by me. They'll run their dogs in here, you can count on it. I'm going to sic my lawyers on them and get the bastards kicked off that land. Or else I'll buy the land myself and then you can go kick them off. Wouldn't that be fun?"

Roscoe looked askance at him. Butler knew the sheriff had friends in both clubs and a cousin in Fat Back. He wanted word to get out—*don't mess with Champ Butler.*

Calvin's father purchased Honeysuckle Plantation ten years earlier before retiring from the chicken business. Its two thousand acres were part of a larger antebellum cotton plantation once worked by legions of slaves. Now, the upland grew managed rows of slash and loblolly pine with its tracts cut and replanted on a twenty-five-year rotation.

After a long career of round-the-clock chickens, old man Butler could finally walk away knowing he had provided for his four children... and their children. For five decades, he arose before sunrise to work his chickens—on the farm as a young man then at the plant in waning years. He built the lodge as his retirement home where he could do what he loved—relax, hunt, manage his pine trees, plant vegetables, and be a gentleman farmer.

When his wife of forty-five years passed, he became a recluse, fresh air and nature his new companions. He was in his little workshop cobbling duck boxes when a fatal heart attack struck. The region lost a respected leader and philanthropist.

As Champ had planned for his father's eventual death, his trophy collection-in-waiting grew each year. When he took over Honeysuckle, he removed his father's paintings and memorabilia from the lodge and replaced them with his own international hunting and fishing trophies. He humored his sisters into granting him free reign. *Needed for business.*

Champ implemented his own secret plan for Honeysuckle, in development since the day his father bought the property. He loved the privilege and refinement of hunting red stag and grouse on English estates. *It is time for the Butlers to leave our own footprint on American history.* He set out with borrowed funds to purchase that legacy.

He commissioned an architect to draw plans for a replica of the "white house," which had long since burned down. The "white house," hub of the 1800's plantation, had slave cabin rows in the distance. Negroes arose at dawn to work the cotton and tobacco fields. The visionary in Champ vowed to restore the plantation to its glory days.

Majestic Chicken Company held title to the land, a mere technicality to Champ. He owned so much of the company now that the distinction between his property and the company's blurred. Majestic paid the plantation's upkeep and management and would pay for the new white house project. Cal would establish his main office there to make it fly with the IRS.

Unlike his father's more passive, natural approach to game management, Champ hired experts and triggered an aggressive regimen. Fields for quail and dove and habitat for wood duck and snipe were crafted and pruned. He built horse stables with a ten-acre turfed paddock. A putting green replaced his father's garden, and a swimming pool replaced his workshop. The over-arching goal, though, was to enhance the trophy quality of the white-tail buck.

Members of adjoining hunt clubs claimed sightings of monster buck larger than these parts had seen. It was the stuff of fantasies.

Chapter 33

Shortly after retiring as railroad supervisor fifteen years ago, Mr. Otis Odom formed Fat Back Hunt Club, named after his beloved slab bacon. A paper company clear-cut and replanted a four-hundred acre slash pine tract bordering Honeysuckle Plantation. Mr. Otis gathered his friends, secured a year-to-year hunting lease in his name, and presided as president and supreme commander. No bylaws—only Mr. Otis's laws.

The boys hauled in an old doublewide trailer as the clubhouse and spray-painted it camo. After taking the club's blood oath at initiation, new members added their own paint—green, brown, tan, black—resulting in an ever-changing camo montage.

Opening Day at Fat Back took on spiritual significance.

Bean and the boys had suffered through another sweltering summer, panting for the cool, stimulating fall air. Time to commune with nature in the evergreen pine forest where campfires and twinkling stars hypnotize. Time to bag food for a year, to hunt white-tail deer, God's most majestic creature.

Opening Day Eve parties grew wilder and wilder and Bean fretted over missing this one. Sleep was impossible as he ruminated and listened to Ruby's rhythmic snoring. He would be snockered and stumbling around the clubhouse, bumping shoulders, going to the trough for thirds at the field and stream feast.

Specialty game bagged throughout the year is served up, from gator to rabbit, possum to rattler, bream to shark, duck to pigeon, and a few threatened species to boot.

He rolled over, scrunched his pillow into a new ball, and remembered the variety of meats on his palate last year. The boys ate and drank like their Viking ancestors, planting benches and lawn chairs in the dirt around the flames, following the smoke to thwart mosquitoes, repositioning with each wind shift like seagulls on the beach.

Bean's belly pleasantly ached after the feast. He swilled Bud and got lost in the fire's glowing embers. As the night marched on, all manner of combustible and not-so-combustible objects found their way onto the bonfire. Chairs scooted back and shirts came off, some boys with their bushy-haired backs looking like kissing cousins of *Homo erectus*.

"Hey!" Mr. Otis leapt from the clubhouse waving his arms. "Knock that shit off 'fore you melt the damn trailer."

Early evening last year, beer flowed freely as a Stonehenge ring of deep-fryers and grills cranked up. These were not your typical store-bought grills, but industrial strength on wheels towed behind pickups. Shark jaws and other painted images adorned some grills like WWII fighter planes. Others were plastered with Georgia Bulldog stickers, though most boys did well to finish high school. *Go Dawgs!*

Smoke belched from grill bellies and frying pots. The aroma of greasy cornmeal and roasting meat hovered over camp. Giddy men scurried about as sunset washed the scene in gold.

The club's annual meeting followed the feast. The boys ambled to the skinning shed, filled the bleacher, and gathered around as Mr. Otis donned his antler helmet and held court. He led everybody in chanting the secret oath then called for committee reports, apologized for a dues increase, and handed out assignments for the coming year. For the grande finale, the club cast secret ballots for the one man out of ten applicants who would fill the year's only empty slot.

Business concluded, the boys cut loose. As empty beer cans and liquor bottles piled up, some staggered to palmetto bushes to woof custard and decorate their boots.

The posse migrated into the clubhouse where they ogled at hunting videos, high-fiving and whooping at the kill. Late into the night, someone pulled out a skin flick, and the complexion of the evening changed. Once the ice was broken, stag films stacked up in the queue like quarters in a crowded pool hall.

Pickle Joe inserted his favorite flick. Slack-jawed boys clapped as two well hung studs alternated putting the pile-driver on a buxom redhead, manhandling her like a rag doll. "Yes, yes," she moaned, "please give it to me."

The horny throng catcalled and whistled as heat in the room skyrocketed. In the doublewide amphitheater, hunters stood on the couch rubbernecking over those who stood on the floor who gazed over those kneeling who gawked over those sitting.

Bean remembered in vivid color what happened next. The wild Poindexter boy had already put them all on edge. He was on probation with the law and on thin ice with Mr. Otis for his prior Opening Day Eve indiscretion of rousing at pre-dawn and pissing a river on the bedroom wall, putting a literal spin on "wee hours."

Peanut pointed at Poindexter and slurred, "That redhead looks jest like yor wife." Time stood still as the comment's implication sank in.

Whack. Poindexter cold-cocked Peanut with his beer bottle and pounced with the jagged glass neck. When Poindexter was finally restrained, Peanut lay in a puddle of blood.

"Give me your key right now, Poindexter," Mr. Otis decreed, "and get your shit, and don't never come back." They duct taped the gash over Peanut's eye and, luckily, somebody was on the wagon and sober to drive to the hospital. When the dust settled and the blood wiped from the carpet, the boys replayed the incident repeatedly, the tale improving with each telling.

Truck lights set a dirt track ablaze, and footraces broke out to blow off steam. Whisky flowed, and wagers flew over two-by-two relays. Bean lost a day's wages, misjudging his opponents' sobriety as well as his own.

Wrestling matches erupted and carried on past midnight until Mr. Otis put a stop to it. In the wee hours, Bean dozed in his lawn chair, swatting mosquitoes with one hand and holding a bourbon in the other, when some wisecrack threw a pack of bottle rockets into the fire. One of the whistlers screamed into Bean's chest and the boys doused him with beer to quench his flaming jacket.

Now, Ruby's rhythmic snorts and snores finally lulled Bean into essential sleep. Moments later, he snapped upright.

Huntin' license! Dammit! He sprang from his bed and woke Junior. *Walmart, here we come.* They dressed and packed with such excitement and clatter that Li'l Bit cried, wondering what was the matter.

Ruby rose to make sure they didn't forget their sausage biscuits, ten for her hon and five for her son...

Now dash away, dash away, my great huntsman.
You teachin' a fine art to our young'un.

You a killin' machine, Sweetheart,
Fly on the wings o' Earnhardt.

Ruby heard him exclaim, 'ere he drove out of sight,
"Y'all take care, aw-ight."

Chapter 34

Champ met the lovely Roxie five years prior when she worked one of his private jet junkets. What a fine attendant she turned out to be.

After he took over Majestic Chicken Company, he began to avail himself of private corporate jet travel. *Mix in a little business and I can fly anywhere in the world on the company. Five-star accommodations. Throw in a week of hunting or skiing and the jet whisks me home. Part of my executive benefit package. So what if my perks exceed that of most Fortune 100 company CEOs. Why shouldn't they? My sisters owe me that much for running this godforsaken chicken business. Let the bean counters come up with paperwork to make it pass muster with the IRS.*

He became acquainted with the pilots in the jet time-share company. After a flight to Manitoba, Canada, to fish for walleye, pike, and salmon, he and the pilot bantered on the tarmac beside the jet as they watched Champ's limo clear security and roll towards them. The flight attendant stepped to the jet's doorway to bid farewell.

He elbowed the pilot. "She's a babe. Man, I'd like to get into her pants."

The pilot cocked his brow and turned to him. "Mr. Butler, we can hire a special flight attendant for you." The pilot flexed his fingers in air quotations around "special."

Champ's eyes came to life. "You're kidding me, right?"

"No, sir, I'm not kidding. Actually, for a select few customers such as yourself, we can arrange just about anything you want."

"Can we initiate this service on my flight home next week?"

"Yes, sir, Mr. Butler. There'll be no extra fees due our company. Please tip the lady cash, whatever you think is fair. That way, there's no record. Our company has no involvement. Once you're in flight and that cockpit curtain is drawn, we let consenting adults do what they wish. We hire the prettiest ones we can find. They'll be flying the route anyway, so why not let them pick up a little extra? They're happy. You're happy. We're happy. That's good business. Now, what's your pleasure?"

"Let's see, how about if we start with beautiful and naked?"

"You've got it. I've got you flying back to Georgia Friday morning, right?" He handed Butler his card. "Please call me if your schedule changes. Otherwise, I think you'll have a pleasant surprise."

"Great." He could not believe his good fortune. *This is the best news I've had in ages.* He reached into his coat pocket, peeled off five hundreds, and slipped them into the pilot's palm.

Champ couldn't concentrate on his fishing that week. Even though his guide arranged for exceptional female entertainment for his two fishing mates and him while in Manitoba, there was something intriguing about the concept of sex at twenty thousand feet.

He settled into his limo ride to the airport at week's end, palms sweating, groin tingling. As the stretch rolled across the tarmac toward the jet, he spotted her stepping from the fuselage onto the jetway. Long, shapely legs flowed from a tight, black leather miniskirt.

Damn!

He feasted his eyes. She had red hair, which she had tucked under a black beret. She wore a white silk blouse, black spike heels, and white gloves. The limo stopped, and she sashayed down the jetway stairs to his door. Her blouse gaped open in a triangle from shoulders to belly button. Her supple, pendulous breasts danced and swayed with every step.

She opened his door, bent over, and extended her hand. "So nice to meet you, Mr. Butler. My name is Roxie, and I'm here to serve you in *every* way."

He gawked at her dangling, plump melons, her wide, emerald eyes, and her chiseled jaw—beauty beyond that of a mere mortal. *Ecstasy.* A pageant winner in her day, Roxie was now aging, but her beauty endured. He fell forever hopelessly in love.

"Please call me Champ."

Once airborne, the co-pilot closed the cockpit curtain, and Roxie changed into her flight uniform: a black beret, stilettos, a starched white collar and cuffs, and nothing more. Champ soon joined the mile high club.

The experience was life changing, beyond simple erotic desire. He never again loved his wife, not even for a fleeting second. Turned out, Roxie lived just down the road in Jacksonville, and without leaving the ground, he began racking up frequent flyer points with Air Roxie.

The four gents strolled with drinks and cigars, their footfalls crunching on the pea gravel walkway that wound through the master gardener's manicured grounds. Sheriff Roscoe pointed at the dozen cherub sculptures lining the path to the fire pit. "Damn, Champ, what's up with all the statues of babies?"

"They aren't babies, pal, they're cherubs. I practically stole them from a vendor in France while on holiday earlier this year."

"Better be careful," Roscoe guffawed at his upcoming joke, "we keep a pedofile watch list in my office, and you may be on it come Monday mornin'."

Jesus, Butler lamented, *the dumb bastard's probably never been out of Georgia.*

They meandered through the compound—swimming pool, two guest cabins, tennis court, manager's office, game-cleaning complex, supply cabin. Dusk approached and brass oakleaf path lights illuminated their way. A fresh insecticide cloud settled along the walkway and fire pit to fend off mosquitoes.

Efficient staff greeted their arrival with steaming Brunswick stew and fresh cocktails. Flames raged at the core of a teepee of five-foot logs inside a low, circular stone barrier in the complex's center. Logs vertically embraced one another, and smoke filtered through an oak and pine canopy. Up-lights perched high in the trees created spectacular ambiance.

Chairs, benches, and tables surrounded the fire in tribal symmetry. Across the way, a man donning an "HP" cap leaned forward, raking and flipping oysters lying atop a glowing sheet of iron. Smoldering coals pulsed orange in the earthen trench below. He pulled croaker sacks from a tub of saltwater and spread them over the oysters. The steaming aroma of shell and sea wafted towards the guests.

A roofed, open-air structure hovered over the buffet line. Two chefs manned deep fryers ready to cook shrimp, catfish, and hushpuppies. Flames darted through slits in the grill's grate, preparing to sear beef tenderloin. Two ladies scurried, stocking the salad and condiment bars.

Champ and his guests eased onto benches and gazed at the dancing flames. He watched his head chef straighten his jacket and smooth his hair. François, crowned by a starched white chef hat, snapped into a pompous French military posture and paraded at a rapid gait toward the guests. His white chef's coat was trimmed in black with black pearl studs down the front. "Honeysuckle Plantation" was embroidered in French scroll across his heart.

"*Bonsoir, Monsieurs, bonsoir,*" Chef François sang out. The foursome stood. "*Comment allez-vous? Comment allez-vous?*" He pecked an air kiss on each guest's cheeks. "*S'il vous plait. S'il vous plait.*" He motioned for them to sit.

Butler acquired François while quail hunting on a nearby west Georgia plantation. Cordon Bleu credentials and his Parisian accent carried the cachet Honeysuckle Plantation needed, no further due diligence required. He hired François that very weekend, right under his host's nose. *Carpe diem.*

"I want you to speak mostly French in the presence of guests," Champ instructed François, "and ramp up your presentation. Put some *umpff* into it."

"Yes, sir, Meester Butler," François responded in Franglish. "Hell, I do zee can-can dance if you weesh." He folded into a deep, flamboyant bow.

Butler was quite chuffed with his coup but doubted these hicks tonight could appreciate his chattel.

"*Les huîtres un moment, oui, oui, un moment. Les huîtres magnifique!*" François cast his fingertip kiss to the wind.

The three grinning, puzzled guests knitted their brows.

"Oysters," Champ interpreted. "The oysters will be up in a moment, and they are magnificent." Champ cast his fingertip kiss to the wind.

"*Oui, oui.*" François wagged his head. "*Ahh, Anglais, ah, 'larsters?' Ah, 'histars?' Ah…*"

"Oh, hell," Roscoe boomed, laughing and slapping his thigh. "It's *oysters! Oysters!* Damn, son, we're gonna have to teach you some Anglish."

"*Oui, oui, Monsieur.*" François folded into a dramatic bow. "*Excusez-moi. Pardon. Bon appétit.*" He quickly left the stage. Champ couldn't conceal his smile as his guests shrugged and chuckled.

"Looks to me like the boy may be light in his loafers," Roscoe observed. "We ain't eatin' no prissy soufflé tonight, are we?"

"Let me tell you something," chided the Bulldawg. "That Frenchy can probably teach you boys a thing or two about *really* making love to a woman. As for the Bulldawg, the French take lessons from *me.*"

"I hope they're good at something," Birdsong said, "'cause they ain't worth a damn at fighting wars."

"They're like me," roared the Bulldawg. "They're lovers, not fighters. That reminds me of our opening joint session of the House and Senate earlier this year. The governor had to be out-of-town, so I delivered our agenda. I was at the podium just before my speech. The Democrat opposition leader, Boo Boo, a close friend, walks up to me and says, 'Bulldawg, you know if a man ain't thinking 'bout pussy, his mind is wandering.'

"He then guided my eyes to his young aid sitting at a front table. She's the only gal in the whole chamber showing any cleavage, and she's wearing this short dress. I'm staring right down the barrel of those gorgeous legs. She smiles and uncrosses 'em, and damn if she ain't going commando—no panties. That Venus flytrap is talking to me. Boo Boo slaps me on the back and whispers, 'That thang's dripping like a hot buttered biscuit.' It shook me up so bad, I left out two whole pages of my speech. The governor was pissed, but when I told him what happened, he vowed we'd get 'em back."

"*Les huîtres,*" Chef François broadcast from the oyster table. "*Bon appétit.*" Steaming oysters tumbled onto the table with a thud.

"Good Gawd Amighty." Roscoe rubbed his hands together. "There ain't nuthin' better'n fresh oysters. Viagra of the sea. We eat all them oysters, these gals will have to ride the hog all night. Their chimneys will be smokin'."

Guests gathered around the table, wiggled their hands into thick cotton gloves, and commenced cracking and slurping. Birdsong held up a big, juicy one. "Yep, slick and gooey, just like the real thing."

"Champ, ain't you eatin' any oysters?"

"Fellows, I'm allergic, so y'all eat up while I pop down to the gate and check things out. I'll be right back."

Butler watched for deer as he sped his Range Rover down Honeysuckle's mile-long blacktop toward the entrance gate. He recalled his father paving the road and how a century of travelers dealt with ruts, mud bogs, and corduroy bumps.

He slowed when his headlights illuminated his antique wrought iron gate with its black, hand-forged bullet finials. Ten-foot brick columns flanked the grand entrance, which was crowned by a brick arch befitting a plantation so rich in history. Suspended in the finials on each side of the swinging gate, an encircled "H" and "P" heralded civilization amongst the sticks and hicks.

A hunter green Chevy pickup sat idling inside the gate on the gravel lay-by. The faux Butler coat of arms adorned each truck door.

A lanky man wearing the "HP" cap and a service revolver holstered at his side stood beside the truck chewing on a cigar. Champ pulled up. His window whizzed down and cigar smoke billowed out.

"Evening, Freddie. Any action down here?"

"Hello, Mr. Butler. Hunters are barreling up and down the road, but all's quiet on our boundaries."

Freddie, one of Roscoe's deputy sheriffs, doubled as head of security at Honeysuckle, spending as many hours on one job as the other. He, and fellow deputies whom he hired part-time, patrolled the plantation for poachers and trespassers. They kept a special eye on the two neighboring clubs that hunted with dogs. It was a premium side job for lawmen who'd rather be in the woods.

"You think my fifteen-pointer will show in my field tonight?"

"If he does, our cameras will catch him." Freddie nodded in assurance. "He's been coming to your field some evenings, but in the mornings, you can set your watch by him. I think he likes to carouse at night and then come home for a good breakfast."

"Did you talk to Gonzales? Did he get the feeders right?"

"Yes, sir. He's gonna sneak into your field tonight and fill them as instructed."

"Good, I've been feeding that boy for at least four years. It's harvest time come morning."

"Yes, sir, Mr. Butler. I can't wait to see him hanging at the barn to get a close look at him."

"Now listen up, all three guests for the evening are here—the lieutenant governor, B. S. Birdsong and Sheriff you-know-who. Our ladies will arrive in a gold Mercedes in about thirty minutes. Have the gate open, and look the other way when they come through."

"Yes, sir, Mr. Butler."

Champ winked. "Then lock the gate with our special lock so Mrs. Butler doesn't come barging in on us, you follow me?"

"I'm with you, sir."

"We've got to protect the lieutenant governor. That boy could be governor in a few years. Who knows what crazies with cameras may be prowling, trying to get some goods on him."

"Yes, sir. I've got three men in the woods right now and a couple on-duty deputies watching the highway in both directions."

"Radio those men in the woods to stay away from my field tonight. I don't want to spook my buck."

"Yes, sir, boss."

"We've got more hunting guests arriving at five o'clock in the morning. I'll have the girls out by then. I want you manning the gate by four-thirty."

"I'll be here, Mr. Butler. You can count on me."

"I know I can."

The Range Rover's window zipped up and Butler sped back to the fire pit. *I've got to babysit those yahoos so they don't get too snockered.*

Chapter 35

By the midnight light of a crescent moon, Stag bedded down among a fallen pine's branches and needles. Each side of his rack sported a brow tine and six points, thick, long, and well spread. It was ideal symmetry, save for a lone drop tine protruding from the left side's main beam.

He swirled in early-rut euphoria. In pursuit of an estrus doe, he strayed far from home into territories unknown. Testosterone boiled his blood. White heat consumed his loins.

Extreme danger loomed. Canines barked nearby and worse— the sounds and scent of man. Lust overruled his instinct for safety.

Stag heard the bleat, locked onto airborne estrus pheromones at midday and gave chase. Following the scent, he abandoned his protected turf and coddled existence at Honeysuckle Plantation and crossed the swamp. He now rested on the lands of Fat Back Hunt Club, though he knew not man's boundaries.

He tried to doze, ears erect for any sound. Yelping canines and man's noise agitated him.

Front and rear legs tucked under, Stag tilted his rocking-chair antlers back and thrust his black nose high, sniffing with an olfactory acuity one hundred times that of man.

The king of the forest bowed his head, chewed regurgitated nut grass, and dozed in thirty-second increments, head bobbing in and out of fitful rest. He longed for the safety of his home— his jungle thicket of dense saplings and tangled grapevines surrounded by thick switch grass near a white oak stand with large acorns.

The impressive rack, stallion stature, and Brahma bull neck were no accident for this prime six-year-old. Thanks to his bene-factor at Honeysuckle, spinning feeders dangling from trees showered amber corn and rice bran onto the earth at designated hours. Fields of soybeans and clover, wheat and oats, alfalfa and chicory served as whitetail feasts. Salt licks abounded. He gorged at wooden troughs heaped with wheat, milo, rye, and oats, obliv-ious to surveillance by Swiss binoculars and motion sensor cam-eras capturing daylight and nocturnal patterns.

This pampered king had been spared. Never the hunted—until now.

Chapter 36

Guests hunched over the oyster table cracking shells and slurping salt-water goo. Champ watched his three stooges gorge themselves. The attendant served up another shovelful, delivering a steaming facial to his guests.

The Bulldawg raised a finger in the air and spoke with a mouthful. "Podnah, you got any raw ones left?"

"Yessuh, yessuh, got one whole basket left."

"Bring 'em raw, please."

The man nodded and turned to retrieve the basket.

"Are you sure you won't have any, Champ? Let 'em slide down your gullet, and they'll harden your pecker like a brick bat. Ain't that right, boys?"

"Yes, sir, damn right," Sheriff Roscoe and Birdsong affirmed in unison.

Champ knitted his brow at the thought. "Can't do it, Bulldawg. I've got business with Roxie tonight. You don't want to put me out of commission, do you?"

"Oh, hell no. That's aw-ight. These boys probably need extra, anyway."

Guests tossed slick aphrodisiacs down their gullets as Champ flitted between his culinary staff, Range Rover, and office like a caffeinated water bug, anxious for the evening's crescendo.

He rejoined his guests to escort them to the buffet. They struck in a gluttonous frenzy, turning dinner into a culinary orgy. Roscoe and Birdsong vied to keep up plate-for-plate with the lieutenant governor as a matter of civic pride.

Finally, mercifully, the Bulldawg pushed back. "Boys, I'm pot full. Listen up, leave the apple pie and eat the à la mode. There ain't many feelings better than ice cream seeping into the cracks and crevices of a full belly." He nudged Roscoe. "*Capiche?*"

"Capeesh?" The sheriff looked puzzled. "That's frozen yogurt, ain't it?"

The Bulldawg guffawed. "Forget it."

Each guest twirled around on the picnic bench, leaned back against the table, stretched his legs, and balanced a bowl of ice cream on his gut.

"*Ooo-wee,*" Birdsong sang out, "I cain't hardly eat no more."

"I done died and gone to Heaven," Roscoe declared.

The Bulldawg said, "What a way to go. My tombstone will say, 'Ate himself to death. Died a happy man.' Yessir, some folks eat to live—I live to eat."

They lit cigars and staff topped up cocktails. Champ's cell phone rang. He looked at the caller-ID and gave a thumbs-up as he answered.

"Hey, Babe… okay… right… see you soon." He turned to the boys. "Okay, they're thirty minutes out. Showtime! And Bulldawg, good news, Monika is coming."

"Hot damn," the soldiers cried, answering the call to arms as they lumbered back to the lodge to prepare for the tarts' arrival. Each headed to his rustic bedchamber, where the walls and bedposts were made of cypress harvested from the plantation, rough-hewn and ready for action. Sheriff Roscoe dispensed condoms and Viagra to all.

Hidden low-light video cameras and microphones covered each bedchamber's entirety. Retrofitted smoke detectors doubled as infrared illuminators. The cameras' lenses were embedded in eyeballs of trophy wall mounts—Blue Marlin, Cape Buffalo, Kudu with its corkscrew horns. Eerie eyeballs seemed to bring the animals back to life. Champ trained multiple cameras at different angles on his own four-poster bed.

He was satisfied with his surveillance contractor, the retired Secret Service agent who also wired the chicken plant, but he was more pleased with himself for conceiving the idea. Charlotte, his wife, questioned him about the new lockbox in the lodge's master closet. "Security," he clipped.

Champ opened the lockbox. The panel contained four equal sections, each with video screen and controls. He flipped switches to activate all systems then locked the panel and popped another Percocet.

He dabbed some Hermès cologne behind his ears then pulled down his tweed trousers and sprinkled his bikini drawers as a courtesy to Roxie.

All four married hunters strutted to the brick veranda to await their quarry. The ladies were due any moment to roll onto the circular drive and around the eighteenth-century fountain. The Bulldawg strolled to a cane-back rocking chair and flopped down. "Boys, I got to take a load off my arches."

"I got to go water the horses," Sheriff Roscoe announced. He ambled down the steps to the hedges with drink in hand and unleashed a yellow cascade onto Butler's ornamental shrubs.

Butler sneered. *You cornpone, you have no idea what it takes to create and maintain a place like this. You shall pay for that, my friend. And wearing camo for these high-class girls... please. They'll be real impressed, I'm sure.*

Headlights flashed, and pea gravel complained under the tires of Roxie's Mercedes as it entered the gate guarding the plantation's fifty-acre inner sanctum.

"Good Got-a-Mighty, Roscoe," the Bulldawg hollered, "put that little ole pecker back in your pants. Here come the girls."

"If them girls see this loggerhead," Roscoe called over his shoulder, "they ain't gonna be happy with any of y'all tonight."

Champ straightened his shirt's tuck and fluffed his hair, careful of the plugs. He rolled his eyes at the redneck banter. *No damn wonder our country is going to hell in a hand basket. These idiots are running the show.*

Birdsong rushed down the steps, careful not to spill his cocktail. "The Bulldawg gets Monika, and we know who gets Roxie. Roscoe and me need to see who gets first pick between the other two." He produced a quarter, flipped it, and slapped it against the back of his hand. "Heads or tails?"

Roscoe zipped up his pants. "Hell, that's a tough one. I'm goin' for some head *and* some tail tonight. I'll start with some head, so I'll call heads."

Birdsong uncovered the coin. "Tails. Sorry, Sheriff, chamber of commerce gets first dibs."

Birdsong and Roscoe turned just as the Mercedes rolled to a stop.

Champ cringed at the unfolding scene. Roscoe and Birdsong, camoed Casanovas, panted as they watched the doors of the Mercedes open. Champagne bubbled in a sweating ice bucket on the back seat. Four ladies whispered a giggled toast and clinked their plastic flutes.

Girls in the rear topped up their champagne as Roxie and Monika slid from the front seats. They waved to Champ and the lieutenant governor as the men walked down the steps to greet them.

Now a brunette, Roxie wore an African safari outfit—khaki shorts and shirt unbuttoned to the navel, chukka boots, expedition hat—compliments of an Abercrombie and Fitch gift certificate from Majestic Chicken. She could have been the girls' mother, but she minded her health and wore her age well. Roxie removed her hat to hug and kiss Champ. Her demi-cup bra, a size too small, amplified her bosoms just as he liked.

Wow, she's beautiful. I'm glad I went to the tanning booth this week.

"I thought I'd wear my bush clothing," she whispered in his ear. "Pun intended." She grabbed Champ's hand and guided it inside her shirt to her chest.

"I've missed you, baby." He popped the bra cups off her breasts and caressed. They were full, more than his hand could hold, something he craved and cherished. Sometimes he wondered why he married his frigid, flat-chested wife.

Monika's blond ponytail swished as she sashayed to the Bulldawg. Her pink sweat suit looked sprayed on. The Bulldawg's arms engulfed her, and the top of her head pressed below his shirt pockets. Her hug encompassed but half his girth.

She looked up at the Bulldawg with her big, brown eyes. "It's '*Moan*-ika' tonight for you, big boy, 'cause you're gonna be moaning."

The Bulldawg picked her up and perched her on his hip, which she straddled like a child. "Sugah, I'm gonna break you in half tonight." He turned and headed up the steps.

Candy draped her long, shapely legs out the rear door. They were wrapped in skin-tight, white spandex clam diggers. Thin black straps vined up her ankles like ivy. A red-and-white striped candy cane tattooed the length of her calf. Spandex accentuated her split and folds. Her smile flashed a gold bead on pierced tongue.

Birdsong elbowed Roscoe. "Jackpot!"

Candy stood, and her spike-heeled espadrille sandals hiked her curvatious hips and well-rounded ass into the air. A silver halter-top stretched to cover her firm apples, leaving a foot of exposed torso, flat and smooth. Her pierced navel iced the cake.

"*Aye,* I'm definitely an ass man." Birdsong whispered. "That's what you call a moneymaker, my sweet lass."

Babs stepped out of the car and stumbled, sloshing then guarding every sparkling drop of champagne. The bottle-blond leaned over in her ocean blue sundress, her neckline grazing the top of her rosy nipples, exposing a bounty of rich, creamy flesh. She licked the side of the flute from stem to rim and scooped brimming bubbles with the tip of her tongue.

"Gentlemen, meet Boobs, I mean Babs." Champ led a round of hearty laughter.

"Hubbahubba!" Roscoe's jaw dropped. "Would you get a load of them knockers."

Bab's udders were in danger of overflowing her dress, and her cleavage cast a magic spell. Two tiny strings bolstered the bodice and tied in a bow at the nape of her neck, strings just begging to be yanked like a ripcord so the dress would tumble to her ankles. She slinked toward the two camoed men, shoulders back in an exaggerated posture. Overhead lights set her milk wagons ablaze as they danced like two puppies fighting in a burlap sack.

Roscoe advanced for a hug. "Hell-ooo, Dolly Parton."

Roscoe and Birdsong bear-hugged and kissed each of the girls and exchanged first names. Birdsong raised his glass, his Irish lilt now a thick Celtic brogue... *Sláinte.*

> *Here's to you and yours*
> *and to mine and ours.*
>
> *And if mine and ours*
> *ever come across you and yours,*
>
> *I hope mine and ours will do*
> *as much for you and yours*
>
> *As you and yours are about to do*
> *for mine and ours.*

The girls giggled. "We love the way you talk. It's so sexy."

Roscoe nudged Toastmaster Birdsong and motioned him to the side. "Okay, Shakespeare, which one you want?"

Birdsong rubbed his chin as if pondering which lobster to choose from the tank. "I'll take Candy's candy."

Roscoe yelped. "You shittin' me? Man, I'd take Babs a hundred times out of a hundred. Perfect." They shook on it. The two camoed Romeos claimed their prizes as they whispered and kissed and giggled.

"*Ooww.*" Babs ran her hand over Roscoe's crotch then threw her head back and laughed. "Sheriff! Is that pistol loaded, big boy?"

"*Cocked* and loaded!"

The couples strolled to the great hall's dark corners to further acquaint and smooch. Soft jazz wailed through the rafters as Champ toasted Roxie. He slipped her an envelope stuffed with company cash—the tab for the evening's *affaire d'amour.*

"I've got a present for you," he whispered as he tickled her ear with his tongue. "Close your eyes." He reached into a drawer and extracted a silk pouch then French-kissed her long and deep as he tucked the pouch into her cleavage.

She opened her eyes and removed the pouch. A blue pouch. Tiffany blue! She opened it, covered her mouth, dangled the gift in the air, and squealed. "A diamond tennis bracelet!"

Other couples rushed over to see what happened. She showed off the tennis bracelet and squeezed the Tiffany pouch. "Girls," she looked into her companions' eyes and gripped the pouch, "this is Tiffany blue. It's the best jewelry on Earth. Count your lucky stars if you ever get any."

The couples retreated to their nests, the girls cocking their eyebrows at their johns, as if wondering what jewelry may be in store for them.

"Oh, Champ. You shouldn't have. It's stunning! I've never owned anything like this. You are too much." Tears welled in Roxie's eyes, and she slurped a hungry kiss ending with a loud smack.

"Baby, you're worth it. It was nothing."

Actually, it was better than nothing but certainly not genuine Tiffany. He bought the bracelet from a pawn dealer in Atlanta, a counterfeit artist skilled at replicating the Tiffany stamp. He pinched the pouch from his home safe where his wife's authentic items resided. He provided no provenance papers to Roxie, a concept unknown to her.

"Here's to poor white-tail deer," Champ toasted. "Their rut only lasts a few weeks whereas mine lasts year round."

"You imp." Roxie laughed as she slapped his shoulder. "You're such a savage. Screw anything that moves." A bosom bounced out amidst the laughter.

Champ and Roxie refilled their champagne flutes and nestled into a leather love seat. She spread his legs, dropped to her knees, and massaged his manhood through his trousers. He moaned and leaned back while taking note of his guests.

He peeked at the Bulldawg laid out on a window seat with his shirt off, Monika atop, kissing his chest. On a sofa, the sheriff's face lay buried in Bab's naked chest, his big ears flared out, perhaps the only thing preventing his fall into the fleshy abyss. In a neighboring love seat, Candy straddled Birdsong's leg, her writhing hips and undulating abs rolling like the sea to the beat of plaintive jazz.

Guests and escorts wandered to their bedchambers. *Showtime.*

"I know these girls are expensive, Champ, but you said bring the best. You think they're worth it?" she whispered.

Before Champ could answer, the headboard in the lieutenant governor's room started banging against the wall. They giggled and raised their flutes.

"My dear, the Bulldawg's music answers all."

Chapter 37

Bean's truck headlights bore through pitch-dark on the high-way to camp, a sheriff's car tailing him a while. He saw head-lights at Honeysuckle Plantation's entrance and slowed. Iron gates yawned open, and a man stood guard under the light of gas lanterns atop brick columns. A gold Mercedes with its back door open idled outside the gate. The car's interior light illuminated a Broadway blond pouring champagne bottle remnants onto the pavement.

Sumbitch! Bean caught a fleeting peek and spotted three more painted ladies. Eyes bulging and mouth agape, he almost drove his truck off the road.

"Diddy, who was them ladies back yonder?"

"Looks like Mr. Calvin Butler had some company last night."

"He's the man that owns the chicken plant, ain't he?"

"Yassir, that's him."

"What do them letters on that gate mean?"

"HP? It s'posed to stand for 'Honeysuckle Plantation' but it really means 'Horse Pee.'"

"Horse pee?"

"Yeah, like what comes out of a horse's tallywhacker."

Junior giggled. "Does Mr. Butler hunt deer?"

"He hunts deer but not like us. He sits still in a box way up in the air and hunts without no dogs. That's too boring for me. He feeds his deer and makes 'em real big which is good 'cause one o' them suckers is gonna come visit you and me this mornin'." Bean pinched his fingers as if holding a dainty china teacup and spoke in a high-pitched voice. "They hunt in silk stockings, and that ain't my cup-a-tea, either."

Junior chuckled, and his jowls jiggled. He was Bean's number one target for mirth and merriment. A rapturous father and son bond developed, but as Junior aged, Bean regretted having to teach responsibilities. It interfered with their fun and games. *Ain't that sump'n, responsibility to teach responsibility. Thanks, Ruby.*

"Sounds borin' to me, too, Diddy, huntin' without no dogs."

A few miles later and an hour-and-a-half before sunrise, Bean and Junior curved onto Fat Back's dirt road. It was flanked by two wooden posts. The metal gate was propped open and draped in chains laden with padlocks. They rolled through and bumped along a half-mile of corduroy until they hit the camp clearing.

Bean stopped and cut his lights to get the lay of the land. Two dozen jacked-up pickups encircled the camp, headlights setting the scene ablaze. They were mostly small trucks, many sporting long whip antennas and dog cages. Men scurried about preparing as flashlights popped on and off like firefly drills. A naked bulb swung like a drunkard above the clubhouse door.

Junior gawked at the spectacle. "Diddy, they sho' is lots o' trucks and lots o' men."

"It's aw-ight, Sugah, it's Openin' Day. This is how it s'pose to be."

Bean pulled up, parked in a slot, and hopped out. Junior hopped out débuting his new "3D" hunting coveralls with dangling camo "leaves." Bean stretched, Junior stretched. Bean farted, Junior farted.

Junior shined his flashlight on a camo four-wheeler tricked out with mud tires, two dog boxes on the back, and two shotguns strapped onto a rack. "Diddy, when we gonna get us a four-wheeler? I want one like dat."

Bean's brows arched mid-whistle. "Don't get your hopes up, Sugah. That's a nice'un. We cain't afford nothin' like that right now, but maybe one day we'll get us one. Now come on, we got to check in."

They wormed between pickups toward the open-air skinning shed, Junior trotting to keep up. The shed's tin roof, hose spigot, and concrete floor rendered it elaborate by many clubs' standards. Under the roof, a lone bleacher loomed large. Its three rows of wooden benches made room for nine hunters to view skinning and gutting and doubled for club meetings, weddings, and other social gatherings.

Junior's eyes flared at the macabre contraption of ropes and pulleys hanging from the ceiling cross beam. Metal T-bars swayed in the air, each with sinister-looking meat hooks on the ends.

"Wh-whut's that, Diddy?" Junior shuddered.

"Remember, them is what you hang the deer on to raise 'em in the air to skin 'em out."

They stood before the grandstand, and Junior pointed at the plastic chair bolted to the top bench with stenciled letters on its front. "Diddy, what's it say on that chair up yonder?"

"It says 'TOP DOG,' saved for the man who kills the best deer. We gonna be sittin' in that chair later this mornin'. You hear what I'm sayin', Sugah? We gonna be sittin' right yonder."

"Yep, Diddy, I hear ya."

They strolled past the outhouse with deer antlers nailed above its plywood door. There had been talk for months, but only talk, of digging a new hole and moving it. Junior recoiled. "*Yuck,* Diddy, that stanks."

"*Shhh.* Shut up, boy. You need to be thankful you gonna get to hunt. If all you gonna do is complain, I'll leave you in the truck while I hunt. You soundin' like a sissy. I'll leave you at home next time, and you can help with the dishes and do homework. Maybe play dolls with your little sister. Is that what you want?"

"Sorry, Diddy."

"Come on, then."

Buckshot, the camp's legendary dog driver, scrambled around his beat-up, mud-caked pickup. Bean and Junior sauntered up as Buck adjusted a dog's collar while whispering in its ear. The driver couldn't afford a better truck, but his hounds could fetch a king's ransom. Other caged dogs in his pickup's bed whimpered and yapped, their bodies shivering and ready to run. They, too, had waited nine months for this day.

Like his father before him, Buck drove the best deerhounds in the region, his dogs invariably leading the cry. Years ago, his kennel numbered twenty, all blueticks and redbones. He was now down to four chase dogs for deer and two Pit Bull catch dogs for hogs. He'd run two chase dogs this morning and the other two this afternoon.

Buck turned his gaze to Bean and Junior. "Well lookee what the cat drug up. If it ain't ole Butterbean hisself. Bean, I thought you was bringing Junior. Whar is Junior?" His head swung left to right.

Bean winked at Buck. "Beat's me. He was here just a second ago."

"Hey, I'm down here."

"*Oohh*," Buck cried. "I couldn't see you, boy, in that fancy camo outfit."

"I got it for my birthday," Junior beamed, "and Diddy's got a new shirt, too. Mama give it for his birthday."

"I see," said Buck. "Nice. You gonna get you a big'un this mornin'?"

"Yassir." Junior nodded. "Diddy, can I pat them dogs?"

"Not now, Son, they're too keyed up, and they might nip ya." Bean patted Junior's head. "Let's not start the bleedin' 'til the hunt. Buckshot, you ready, my man?"

"Chompin' at the bit. Got me a new motor on the four-wheeler, and my dogs is about to come out they skins. Maybe Missy here, my ole bitch beagle, can do somethin'. Old Dixie, my black and tan, is read-dy."

"Hope they flush some big'uns this mornin'. Good luck, my man. Come on, Junior."

Bean waved to Angus, another dog driver, preparing his hounds across the way. A mountain of a man, Angus towered 6'8" and boasted three hundred pounds and change.

"See that feller over yonder," Bean whispered. "Back when I was in high school, Angus was a *real* professional wrastler. One day on this very spot, I asked him if wrastlin' was real. He got me in a headlock and put the Texas pile driver on me. Like to broke my dern neck. I missed a week o' school.

"Look at them cauliflower ears. If it weren't for him, I'd a-won the club arm wrastlin' tournament two years runnin'. I beat everybody else but him. Let's go say hello.

"Hey, Angus, who won arm wrastlin' last night?"

Angus stood erect and raised his right arm bent at the elbow. "Who the hell you think won? Where was you last night, anyway?"

Bean pointed at Junior's head. "I was with my little man here. This is his first Openin' Day."

"Hot damn, Li'l Buddy." Angus palmed Junior's head. "Good luck this mornin'. With your pa, you gonna need it. Now look a-here, this season you gonna go with me one day, aw-ight, and you gonna' learn about runnin' dogs. You wanna' do that?"

"Yassir. I'd like that a lot. Is that okay, Diddy?"

"Well, you gotta' start somewhere, so yeah, that'd be great, you can start with Mr. Angus."

Junior pumped his fist. "Hot damn."

Bean whacked his head. "Son, I'll put a pop-knot on your noggin, you talk like that again. Where'd you learn to talk like that?"

"Oowww." Junior rubbed his head. "Sorry, Diddy."

Angus turned his back, shoulders heaving up and down in silent laughter.

As they walked toward the clubhouse, Junior kicked an empty beer can and looked up at his father. "Diddy, I wanna be a wrastler."

"Son, you cain't be a wrastler *and* a NASCAR driver."

"Why not?"

"Later, Sugah."

An ancient El Camino rested its front bumper inches from the clubhouse trailer. The driver's door hung open. In the ambient light, an old man's shaking hands draped over the steering wheel. Smoke floated from a cigarette dangling from his lips.

"That's Sergeant Walker," Bean whispered. "Don't be 'fraid o' him. He cain't speak right."

Bean glanced into the El Camino's bed—spare tire, walker with tennis ball shoes, and rusty shotgun atop a ratty quilt. He guided Junior to the car's open door, hands on his shoulders. Sgt. Walker's head bobbed. His eyes were closed. He wore his ubiquitous green Army fatigues with his pant legs tucked inside black military boots.

"Whut up, Sarge?" Bean called.

The veteran's dreary eyes opened and he stared at Junior. He removed the cigarette from his lips and inserted the filter into the laryngectomy hole in his neck. Pinching his nostrils, he inflated his lungs and the business end of the cigarette glowed red. He removed the cigarette and exhaled. A perfect smoke column billowed from his neck hole.

Junior's mouth gaped wide as Sarge flashed a gnarly-toothed grin. The veteran reached for his handheld mechanical larynx, switched it on, and pressed it to his neck. He spoke with a slow, robotic twang. *"Hey, Bean."*

"You okay, Sarge?"

Walker pressed the voice box to his neck. *"Damn yappin' dogs kept me up all night."*

"You huntin' today?"

Sarge twisted his neck to look Bean square in the eye and returned the box to his neck. *"Hell yeah, I'm huntin'. You think I'm here to teach Sunday school or somethin'?"*

"Naw." Bean shuffled his feet. "It weren't meant like that. I jest… you know… I'm jest askin'…"

"Son, you can live dyin' or die livin'. Hell yeah, I'm baggin' me a damn deer today." The old vet lapsed into a hacking cough. A string of green phlegm flew from his neck hole. It flopped over and stuck to his skin like glue.

"Diddy," Junior pointed, "he's got—"

"Quiet, Son." Bean waved to Sarge. "Good luck," he hollered as he scooted Junior along.

Behind the clubhouse, the generator rumbled in its shed like an alien drone, and gas fumes wafted. They rounded the front to the scene of last night's gluttony and carnage and saw cold barbeque grills and empty lawn chairs. The camp truck claimed squatters' rights in the yard, its bed brimming with fresh refuse, brown juice oozing under the tailgate, bluebottle flies swarming. Fish heads, rib bones, and such were scattered on the ground having missed their target. Junior covered his mouth and nose.

Some boys mingled by the fire's remnants—ashes and glowing coals, charred mattress springs, half-melted asphalt shingles, and the like. Cigar and cigarette butts dotted the yard.

Pickle Joe and Peanut lounged on a bench, their elbows resting on their knees, staring into the pulsing embers and sipping coffee. Flames flickered here and there like jesters waving their arms—*Now you see me, now you don't.* The boys looked up as Bean and Junior approached.

"Would ya lookee here," Peanut pointed. "Junior, you gonna show your pappy how to hunt this year?" Ever since Poindexter's beer bottle attack last year, Peanut hid his scarred left eye by turning his head askance for a right-eyed focus.

"Yassir," said Junior. "I gonna try."

The two men howled, and PJ winked at Peanut. "Maybe you can teach your daddy to shoot straight."

"Okay, smart ass." Bean stabbed his finger toward PJ. "Put your money where your mouth is. Twenty bucks, you and me, on who brings in the most points this mornin'?"

"Bean, it ain't my policy to take candy from babies."

Bean chuckled. "You been hangin' around chickens too long 'cause you done turned into one. Maybe you ought to join a women's hunt club."

"Okay, Daniel Boone," PJ winked at Peanut again, "but I want to hold your twenty bucks."

"Hell with you." Bean guided Junior to the trailer door. "You still owe me from last year."

"The hell I do!" Pickle Joe jerked erect. "Remember that first bet we made when—"

Bean felt his retort rumbling inside his gut. He flexed his oblique muscles, moving the gas along the flatus factory assembly line and into his lower chambers. He nudged Junior through the clubhouse trailer door. As he crossed the threshold, he loaded the firing chamber and squeezed his nether region. A thunderous moose call delivered his parting shot.

Chapter 38

Champ Butler's headlights bore through the darkness down Honeysuckle's blacktop at 4:30 am. He hoped Roxie and her girls would gather all strewn shoes and panties at the lodge.

His lights lit the entrance's backside. Freddie, his chief security man at Honeysuckle, stood on guard inside the gate. The Range Rover's window zipped down.

"Morning, Freddie."

"Morning, Mr. Butler."

"Did Mister fifteen-pointer show last night?"

"No, sir, at least the cameras didn't catch him. I'd say he's due back soon, exhausted and hungry."

"Hope you're right, Freddie. Keep your fingers crossed. Is Gonzales here?""

"He's due in about thirty minutes. Should I send him to the lodge?"

"Yes, but right now, we've got to get these girls out. Is the coast clear?"

"Clear at the moment, Mr. Butler. We'll see to their safe passage to the state line."

Champ dialed Roxie. "Hey, babe. All's clear, come on… No, the Bulldawg's just kidding. He knows Monika can't stay another day."

Freddie opened the gate, and the two men waited while watching pickup trucks fly up and down the road.

"Look at those rednecks. They're pumped up, aren't they?" Champ fired his cigar. "Remember, if any of them have so much as a taillight out, I want your deputy buddies to nail them, you hear?"

"Yes, sir, Mr. Butler. They have their instructions."

Roxie's headlights appeared in the distance. Freddie walked to the far side and looked away. The Mercedes stopped, and Champ bent down to peek in. Roxie's girls were settling into naps. He kissed her and whispered, "I love you, baby, more than you can imagine. You'll never know how much this means to me."

Roxie flipped on the interior light and held up her wrist, displaying her "Tiffany" tennis bracelet. "Darling, thank you for this. I'm finally a Tiffany woman and feeling great about it. You call me anytime. Come down next week, and we'll do our usual."

Champ reached in and squeezed her breast. "It may have to be the following week, gorgeous. I'll call you. You need to ease on out, more hunters are on their way." They kissed again, and Roxie rolled through the gate. Freddie returned.

"In approximately thirty minutes," Butler instructed, "expect three additional hunters, as discussed. Once they're inside the gate, lock her up tight."

"Will do, Mr. Butler. Break a leg this morning. We'll have the cameras ready to document your fifteen-pointer."

Butler climbed back into his Range Rover and sped back to the lodge where fresh coffee and buttered pastry aromas swirled. B. S. Birdsong, Sheriff Roscoe and the lieutenant governor nestled in armchairs in the great hall, clutching mugs of steaming latte. Chef François was whipping up egg and ham puffs in the kitchen, regularly waltzing into the great hall with coffee pot in hand. "*Le café, oui? La pâtisserie un moment, oui. La patisserie, c'est magnifique!*" François threw an air kiss. "*Magnifique!*"

"Boys," the Bulldawg spoke in muted tones, the same tones used during Senate recess when legislators huddle to discuss state secrets. "I don't know about y'all, but my ball sack couldn't give another ounce if you paid me."

Roscoe laughed. "I'm gonna have to wash my face or them deer will smell Bab's love juice for miles around."

Birdsong cleared his throat. "Laddies, say what you will, but Candy was best in show. If you're lucky enough to be Irish, then you are lucky enough."

Butler grinned at the macho banter. *Talk is cheap, my friends, but I'll soon watch video and see who's a player and who's a pretender.*

Pea gravel crunched under tires announcing three new arrivals. The men strolled into the great hall. Gonzales introduced himself as Honeysuckle's game manager and certified wildlife biologist. He worked year-round grooming bird fields, horse pastures, and deer plots; building deer stands; and nourishing wildlife. The biologist briefed guests on the particulars of the stand each would soon mount. The hunting party studied aerial maps and gawked at recent photographs of prize buck roaming the plantation. The images whipped them into a frenzy.

Game on, Gents. Let ole Champ show you how it's done.

Chapter 39

Bean and Junior shuffled through the clubhouse door. There was no step up, no running water, no utility lines, no slab, no ground anchor system—just a steel, aluminum, and particle board shell plopped on bare dirt. Under the toilet lid, only a plastic bag separated one from mother earth. But this was the closest thing to a "lodge" these boys would ever know.

Chatter rang from the kitchenette as a noxious odor hit the Sweats. The cleaning lady was a year overdue. The air was dank, the collective impact of wall-to-wall hunters who were overweight, overfed, over-beveraged, and escaping their wives' supervision…

Mold and mildew,
last night's barbeque.

Grandpa's feet,
musty smell of boiling meat.

Broke wind worthy of Hercules,
worse than rancid goat cheese.

Years of b.o.,
decay of many a wino.

Two dozen men with night sweats,
nicotine from a million cigarettes.

Soiled underwear,
sordid rotten egg affair.

Their eyes teared. Junior wrinkled his nose and looked up. Bean shook his head and mouthed, "No."

A naked light bulb beamed from the ceiling. Chairs jammed the wall, and ruffled sleeping bags hogged floor space. Duffle bags, clothes, and boots lay strewn to the trailer's four corners. Bean noticed porno DVD cases on top of the TV. *Hope Junior don't see them.*

Homer Hayes's sign hung on the wall behind the TV...

WHAT HAPPENS AT FAT BACK STAYS AT FAT BACK!

The lone work of art, the club's most valuable chattel, hung crooked above the couch. A monster white-tail buck, a god of a deer, loomed large in black velvet relief. Airbrushed antler tips formed a ten-point base for the glowing halo perched atop his head. Chiseled muscles rippled in his neck and shoulders. The image resonated and towered over members' collective psyche year-round, climaxing this day.

Thumbtacked to the opposite wall was the second most valuable chattel—a faded and dog-eared poster dating back twelve years to the club's inception. Otis Odom listed the Top Dog for each year—the man who kills the best deer, as voted by members.

"Right up yonder," Bean pointed, "is where me and you is gonna be this year. Can I get a amen from somebody?"

"Amen, Diddy."

A large pickle jar of raccoon pecker bones rested atop a side table, each shaped like a curved fishhook.

Junior picked up the jar. "What's this, Diddy?"

"*Whoa*, put that down. You gonna break it. Remember, it's part o' the club initiation. The new man has to walk out at night, kill a male coon, walk back, skin it, carve out the pecker bone, and drop it in the jar."

Junior squeezed his tallywhacker through his coveralls. "We got us a bone like that?"

"Nah, we ain't that lucky. Some calls 'em 'Texas toothpicks.' They bring good luck to the club."

Bean stepped to the hall where Homer's favorite sign hung…

LIFE IS A COBWEB, NOT A FLOW CHART!

He peeked into the two bedrooms where cots and sleeping bags covered the floors. The second bedroom reeked of fresh barf. A man lay on a cot in the fetal position, his ass's hairy crack greeting Bean.

"Hey, knucklehead," Bean called out, "you gonna hunt or lie there like a pantywaist?"

"Shut the hell up, Bean, or I'm gonna get up and puke on *you.*"

"Geeze-us, man. Can't blame this one on me."

Bean guided Junior's shoulder as they rounded the corner to the kitchenette. While the skinning shed served as the social gathering hub, the kitchenette served as Fat Back's nerve center.

Four men squeezed around a folding card table shrouded in cigarette smoke haze, drinking coffee, pinching pastries, and shooting the shit. Steam rose and twirled above the simmering pot on the stove.

The counter was heavy-laden with liquor bottles with names like "Clap o' Thunder" and "Liquid Fire" and unlabeled mason jars of 'shine. Opening Day tradition dictated bringing a bottle for the community bar then drinking whatever you wished. An inherently flawed system, the boys brought the cheapest liquor they could find, hoping to trade up. Rotgut hangovers resulted.

"Bean," Mr. Otis Odom greeted, "you made it, my friend. And would you look at Junior."

Junior beamed as he ran his hands over his new coveralls.

"Lawd o' mussy," yelled Lumpy, spraying cocktail peanut cud across the table. His cheap dentures took repose in a glass on the counter. Wise hunters avoided standing in Lumpy's line of fire when he ate. He pushed himself from the table and high-fived Junior. "I ain't never seen nuthin' like that get up." He grinned, exposing a wad of smashed peanuts. "Hell, I cain't hardly see ya, boy. *Ha, ha...*"

Homer the sign-maker reached over and rubbed the "leaves" dangling from the coveralls. "Damn, Junior, you look like the swamp creature from Camo Lagoon."

Purvis, the fourth man at the table and unofficial club vice president, belched violently. "Son, we'll see how long you can keep that outfit in one piece." Purvis pointed to Bean's camo jacket and the duct tape covering the hole from last year's bottle rocket incident. "Your papa here, his jacket is good and broke in." The boys snickered.

Bean straightened and puffed out his chest. "Purvis, it's like the Good Book says, it ain't the talent o' the clothes on the man, it's the talent o' the man in the clothes."

"Here we go," Mr. Otis piped in, "he's quotin' the Good Book on us again."

Bean tapped Lumpy. "Hey, big fella', wha'chu know? Still on the wagon?"

Lumpy shoved more peanuts into his mouth. His bulbous, purple-veined nose had been earned from decades of heavy drinking. "Yeah. 'Fraid so."

"Sorry 'bout dat," said Bean. "Such a pity."

"Why is it such a pity?"

"If a man cain't take no drink, that's a pity. Life is short and ain't meant to be so shitty."

The four men at the table glanced from one to the other then howled.

"Bean," Mr. Otis said, "you just got yourself elected the first poet laureate of Fat Back Hunt Club. Congratulations."

"Whatever that is, what's it pay?"

"You can sit in the Top Dog seat when there ain't nobody around."

"Thank ya," Bean said, snarling the corner of his upper lip, Elvis-style. "Thank ya very much."

"Bean, y'all eat some food." Mr. Otis grabbed the cookie sheet off the table and passed it. "We got venison meatballs and fried coon strips left."

The Sweats scarfed it down.

"This is great," Bean mumbled through stuffed jowls. Junior nodded his head, chipmunk cheeks bulging.

"Yon't peanuts?" Lumpy offered.

Bean held up his hand. "Cain't make no good turds off peanuts."

"I guess that's in the Good Book, too?"

"Nah. Figured that one out on my own. Anything else to eat?"

"Purvis made an excellent road kill soufflé this year," Mr. Otis said, "but we done sold out." He motioned to Purvis who leaned over, grabbed the handle of the pot on the stove, and brought it to the table.

"But we got some hog oysters. We saved some for y'all."

Bean reached for two toothpicks in the box on the table, stabbed a slice of hog ball with each, popped one into his mouth and handed the other to Junior.

"What's hog oysters, Diddy?"

"It's a treat, Son. Eat it and thank Mr. Otis." Junior complied.

"Bean, you goin' to your new platform, ain't ya?" Mr. Otis's pencil hovered over the spiral notebook on the table.

"*Yuck*, Diddy, this tastes like dirt."

Bean's right hand clamped Junior's shoulder like an eagle's claw.

"Diddy, that *hurts*."

Bean spun Junior around to face him eyeball-to-eyeball. His eyes and nostrils flared as he pinched Junior's cheeks.

"Eat and shut up, ya hear?"

Junior nodded his head with a horrified look and took another bite. Tears welled in his eyes.

Bean winked at the boys around the table. "Sorry about dat. Yeah, o' course we're goin' to our new stand." Mr. Otis made the appropriate entry as Junior darted from the room.

"What's ole Champ Butler up to at the chicken plant?" Mr. Otis inquired.

"Same shit, different day. Ain't too many folks 'round the plant like him worth a damn."

"He's givin' me hell about our dogs," Mr. Otis said. "Says they're takin' over his property. He called the cops on us yesterday, that sumbitch."

Purvis lurched in his chair and scowled. "Damn Butler." His nostrils flared, and his nose hairs quivered. "That sumbitch thinks he owns the whole damn planet. He don't own that property. God owns it, and dogs is one o' God's natural creatures."

Purvis's stare intensified. Bean felt like *he* was on trial—guilt by association. Purvis slammed his fist on the table. "Tell me this, they put their britches on one leg at a time like we do, don't they?"

"As far as I know, but I ain't never seen any of 'em put they britches on." Bean chuckled.

Homer the sign-maker chimed in. "Riddle me this… their shit stanks just like our shit stanks, don't it?"

"Luckily, I cain't answer that, either," Bean grinned. "But I'll go out on a limb and say 'yes,' final answer."

"We had six dogs turn up missin' last season," Lumpy said before firing up a cig. "I know those sumbitches at Honeysuckle are killin' 'em. I think it's the three S's when they see our dogs: shoot, shovel, and shut up."

"Boys, I wouldn't put anything past Butler, but I will show you *this*." Bean pulled a paper folded many times from his back pocket and unfolded it. He spread it on the table and stepped back for all to see. The men went popeyed, jaws dropping at the treasure map—Honeysuckle Plantation's roads, deer fields, lodge, stables, barns, and more. An artist's fancy rendering portrayed the grand entrance with its wrought iron gates and the Butler family crest.

"Holy shit!" Mr. Otis said as he examined the map. "Where in the hell'd you get this?"

"I got my ways." Bean nodded. "Let's just say Butler's got enemies within, the most dangerous kind."

Hunters pointed, mumbled, and shook their heads in wonderment.

"There ain't many stands on the whole west side," Purvis pointed out. "We could drop some dogs on the far side over here, and they could drive right at us."

"Problem is," Lumpy rubbed his stubble and pointed, "remember this part of Honeysuckle was clear-cut a few years ago after the fire, and there ain't many hardwoods left. May not be many big bucks in there."

"Anytime you want me to hep run some dogs over there, I'll do it," Bean said. "I ain't skeered o' him. He's bein' a asshole at work. Won't even pay overtime, *but...* he just got back from huntin' in Canada. Company paid for a private jet to take him and pick him up."

"Wow, what a jerk," Mr. Otis muttered. "Thanks for the map, Bean. I reckon we ought to table this conversation and saddle up or the sun'll come streamin' through that window and blister our asses sittin' inside this clubhouse. Good luck, boys. Everybody got their huntin' license?"

Shit, thought Bean. *Why couldn't anybody at Walmart this mornin' work the license machine? They screwed me. Oh well, the warden ain't showed up in a long time, so the odds are with me. If he shows, I'll just be a caught sumbitch.*

CRACK. Crashing and tinkling glass shattered the moment. Bean spun and dashed to the living room with four men fast on his heels.

Junior stood with a flushed face and his hand covering his mouth. A broken pickle jar lay at his feet, a hundred raccoon pecker bones scattered.

"Slipped," he mumbled.

"Geeze-us, boy," Bean yelled, "whut's gotten into you?"

Mr. Otis grabbed a cardboard box and handed it to Junior. "Just pick 'em all up, and we'll get another jar. Do it quick 'cause we got to go."

Bean and Junior knelt and picked up glass and pecker bones as others gathered their gear. The job completed, Bean clamped his hand on Junior's shoulder and guided him out and toward his truck. Men cranked their trucks as dogs bayed, bawled, pissed, jumped, and spun around, rattling their cages and whipping the hunters into a frenzy.

As if God's invisible hand waved a green flag, engines revved and trucks and four-wheelers peeled out into the darkness in all directions like spokes of a wheel.

Chapter 40

Stag knew by instinct that it was time to flee. Canines bayed an ominous symphony nearby, their pitch rising. Sunrise was approaching. It was time to leave the camouflage of his transient bed in the branches of a fallen pine. His rack towered as he arose and hosed the area with urine.

There was no wind this morning. No pine needles swishing, no breeze knifing through shrubs. Good. He could smell and listen in all directions, reducing the chance of a down-wind surprise in this strange and treacherous land.

The buck stretched his neck and head into the air on high alert, sniffing for the estrus doe of his loin's desire. Other deer milled about and grunted, none in estrus, then… another ripe doe. A small herd of doe crept across the forest floor, growing closer.

Stag bawled, signaling his desire for company. Then he grunted and slipped from his bed. He chose a spot under an adolescent pine to leave his mark. He pawed the earth and scraped the dirt with his antler tines. The king deposited scented glandular secretions with his forehead then straddled the scrape, lowered his hindquarters, and urinated.

Stag picked his way toward the doe herd, lowering his snout to the ground as he tracked. When he discovered the estrus doe's urine, he shoved his muzzle into it, raised his head, and worked his tongue around his nose and mouth to spread the urine. He tilted his head back, flared his nostrils, and curled his lip. The urine made contact with the auxiliary olfactory organ in his mouth, his sixth sense. He locked onto the doe's pheromones, and his testosterone jets fired.

The estrus doe bellowed. She was ready now. He'd be a savaging brute if he could mount her, ramming his seed deep within.

Barking canines were on the move. He stood motionless, listening and sniffing, getting the lay of the land as the sun painted the sky. He monitored the doe herd as it drifted away.

Stag sensed canines drawing closer, and his anger boiled. He was desperate for the estrus doe, but instinct urged him to assess his escape options.

He needed to move so the rising sun was at his back, better to see the path ahead and to hinder predators lying in wait. But canines barked from the direction he needed to go.

His loins boiled. Danger and confusion turned to rage.

Chapter 41

Dust swirled in the taillights' red glow as the Sweats raced along the bumpy dirt road. Junior gripped the door handle. *Diddy's driving like a wild man, still mad about the busted coon pecker jar.* Tall grass slapping their bumper in the headlight beams scared the boy. *What's hidin' in that grass? A big hole? A pig? We gonna crash.* Spooky eyes stared back at him from the darkness behind trees whizzing by—*come into the forest, little boy.*

"Diddy, I think I jest seen a spook back yonder behind that tree."

"Son, you ain't got nuthin' to worry 'bout. There ain't nuthin' out there. You know we done walked these same woods last month and ain't seen nuthin' but birds and squirrels. Remember?"

"I remember."

"You just think 'bout that big ole buck we gonna see soon."

Junior took solace in his father's voice. He thought about that big ole buck he wanted Diddy to get. "We gonna get us one today, ain't we?"

"You bet your bee-hiney. That big ole buck is restin' up right now, and soon he'll run right by our stand. That's when we gonna go *boom* and get him."

They slowed as they ventured deeper into the forest, riding in silence until Diddy spoke. "Now, remember, once we get out da truck, you only whisper real low but don't talk a-tall if I put my finger on my lips like this. When we walk to the stand, walk softly. Pretend you a ninja warrior sneakin' up on somebody. The ole buck could be restin' close by our stand. You got dat?"

"Yes, Diddy." Junior envisioned them on foot, face-to-face with the monster buck in the picture in the clubhouse.

"Remember, no sudden moves. They won't see you 'cause o' your camo, but they'll see movin'. So if you have to scratch your nose or somethin', do it reeeeal slooooow, like a robot in slow motion. You understand?"

"Yes, Diddy."

"You know whut to do if I put my finger to my lips, but whut if I throw the gun up to shoot, wha'chu gonna do?"

"Don't talk?"

"No. I mean, yes, don't talk, but you got to hold your ears 'cause I'm 'bout to shoot. You got that, plug your ears with your fingers."

"I'll do it, Diddy."

The further they traveled, the worse the ruts in the road. Junior held on as the truck listed right and left and bounced along. At each fork, Diddy didn't hesitate. It was like he was driving home in the trailer park.

"I built this stand 'cause Mama wants to hunt this season, and she said she ain't gonna stand in no water. I made it with heavy-duty materials."

"How come Mama didn't come today?"

"Son, Openin' Day at Fat Back is for men only. You ain't seen no women, and you ain't seen no young'uns just then at camp, did ya?"

"No, Diddy. I ain't seen no girls or kids."

"I figured you was ready to hunt on Openin' Day, but I ain't too sure after you busted that jar o' coon peckers. Are ya?"

"Are I what?"

Diddy rolled his eyes. "Ready to *hunt*?"

"I'm ready, Diddy, I promise."

Diddy stopped the truck. "We need to get out and take a leak one last time 'fore we get into the stand 'cause once we're in the stand, there ain't no peein'. Deer can smell your pee a country mile away."

They took positions in the grass on opposite sides of the idling truck. Junior unzipped his 3D coveralls, dug out his weenie, and strained. *Is that a bear hidin' behind that tree? I just heard a rattler crawlin'.* He couldn't get a flow started for all his troubles. He heard Diddy zip up and crawl back into the cab. He did likewise.

"Did ya go?"

"Yeah," Junior lied.

"Another thing, no stinkies."

"But what if I have a stinky, what do I do?"

"Hold it."

"Mama says I'll get a tummy ache if I hold it."

"You can hold it a little while. Farts is just as bad as pee. Them deer smell everythin'."

The road narrowed until there was no road. *The woods is gonna swallow us alive.*

Diddy turned the truck off and killed the headlights. "Just sit still, and let's listen for a minute."

Junior's eyes acclimated to the crescent moon. Menacing darkness lurked all around. Diddy's breathing quickened. Junior's breathing quickened. Diddy flicked on his flashlight and shined it in Junior's eyes.

"You ready, Son?"

"I'm ready, Diddy," he lied.

Diddy produced two camo chewing gum sticks. Shadowing Diddy, Junior folded and poked it into his mouth. "It camoes your breath and creates a natural scent."

"Diddy, where's Bessie?"

"She's waitin' on us at the stand. I can feel it in my bones, Bessie's gonna be our good luck charm today. Now, when we get in the stand, I'll untie her and carry her to a spot I got picked out. You jest stay in the stand by yourself. You can watch my flashlight then I'll be right back."

"They any wild cats or bears out there?"

"Nah, don't worry. You's with me. Just be real quiet."

Diddy gathered sausage biscuits and other sundries and jammed them into his tote bag. Junior perched his knapsack on his lap. Diddy slid the sock off his 12-gauge. *I don't remember the gun being so big. It's as long as I am.* Diddy slid four red cartridges into the gun's belly and whispered, "Okay." He slowly opened his door and Junior followed suit.

They slinked out. Diddy gently pushed his door closed. Junior slammed his, and the bang echoed through the night woods. Diddy hustled around the truck, leaned face-to-face, pinched his cheek, and hissed, "Don't ever slam your door like that."

"*Ooowww.*"

Diddy pinched harder. "*Shut up*, you hear?"

He pushed Diddy's hand away and rubbed his cheek, tears flowing. *I cain't wait to tell Mama what he done to me. She'll kick his ass.*

Swoosh, swoosh. Diddy sprayed himself with doe urine scent then sprayed Junior. Each gripped his flashlight and bag, Diddy cradling the shotgun. They began their trek through the woods, creeping like ninjas, Junior staying on Diddy's heels.

Diddy's flashlight shined occasional orange day-glo tape tied to a bush or tree. *What the hell is he doing that for?*

The grim wood's dark spirits hovered. Long grass brushed Junior's face, and he thought it was snakes hanging from trees. He heard a wildcat scream then a bear growling at his heels. He lunged, clutching Diddy's leg with both arms. They tumbled to the ground.

Diddy hissed through gritted teeth. "*What the hell, Junior?*"

"I heard sumpin' back yonder." Junior pointed. "I think it was a *bear!*"

"*Shhh.*" Scrambling to his feet and gathering his bag and gun, Diddy hissed and grumbled. "Would you be quiet? It ain't nuthin'. Get up and come on."

Briar thickets pricked Junior's face and hands. *I'll never make it.* Stickers gripped his coveralls and wouldn't let go. If he was to keep up with Diddy, he had no choice but to suffer scratches. He pinwheeled his arms with chopping hands like a ninja.

As they neared the swamp, their boots splashed in low, wet spots up to Junior's ankles. He trembled and feared stepping on an alligator head or a cottonmouth moccasin.

Without warning, the stand appeared before them. *Praise Jesus.* A low-slung, rectangular platform grazed Junior's belly. They tiptoed up three steps and cozied into plastic chairs. Junior's eyes were level with the top of camo netting stretching from corner post to corner post.

Diddy lowered his tote bag to the floor and headed back down the steps, shining his flashlight ahead of each footfall.

"Where you goin'?"

"*Shhh.* I'm gettin' Bessie, remember. Just sit tight."

Junior marveled as his superhero father's hulking silhouette lumbered down the steps. Light shown underneath the stand followed by sounds of rope and Bessie's hollow plastic.

The light beam swung away from the stand and lit the path as Diddy walked towards the swamp with the life-size decoy under his arm. Several trailer lengths out, Diddy stood Bessie up and worked her side-to-side until her feet stuck in the mud. *Look at Diddy kissin' the top o' Bessie's head,* he chuckled.

The light beam swung toward the stand. *Thank you, Lawd, he's comin' back.*

Diddy tiptoed backwards up the stairs spraying doe scent over his tracks—*swoosh, swoosh.* Gasping for breath, Diddy settled into his chair. He laid his shotgun across his thighs and cranked a cartridge into the chamber.

The great hunters settled in as a pink glow rose on the horizon to shed light on their white-tail fate.

Chapter 42

Champ Butler gunned his Range Rover over the elevated dirt road, hauling butt to the grassy parking spot near his field as Freddie and Gonzales ushered guests to their stands.

Champ strapped his rifle across his shoulder, an antique Austrian .275 caliber with an oxblood stock and bluing barrel. Hand-engraved scenes flanked the gold trigger. Arabesque scroll swirled around a leaping European red stag on the left and an attacking grizzly on the right. The Swarovski scope worked well in low light, but it was nothing like the gun he left in the Range Rover.

That rifle, his night gun, a .270 caliber Weatherby Mark V Deluxe, was equipped with state of the art U. S. military accessories, including a sound suppressor. The mounted light flipped from a white spotlight to infrared to aid his night-vision scope. The rifle would stay in his Rover for now, for use on those nights when he had no guests, to role-play as a commando taking out terrorist deer. Since the practice was illegal, he built a night shooting range for cover. His mantra matched that of the U. S. military—rule the night.

He grabbed *The Wall Street Journal* and his latte thermos and sauntered away. Moonlight cast an eerie arc on the shadow-pocked road. He knew the woods around his plot would be teeming with deer. This was confirmed by telltale hooves snapping sticks on the forest floor.

"Cut off the corn in all feeders within a half-mile radius of my field," Butler had instructed Gonzales. "Double-up on the special grain mix in my trough and cover it with molasses." Shooting baited deer was illegal when Champ began the practice, but with him and others pushing for a change in DNR's regulations, it was now legal in south Georgia.

Gonzales, a wildlife biologist, at first protested this and other illegal practices at Honeysuckle but soon learned the cash value of a blind eye.

Champ's field wasn't your basic food plot. A plush meadow surrounded an acre of green sorghum, sundangrass, and millet. A wire fence around the meadow was sufficient to keep hogs out, but deer jumped it with ease. He walked the fenced perimeter toward the tree house that loomed in the sky ahead. When he arrived, he tiptoed up fifteen wooden steps, unlatched the door, entered, and latched the door behind him.

Freddie had prepared for his arrival—opening louvered, hunter green wooden shutters, coating the sills with fresh bug spray, arranging freshly-cut black-eyed Susans in a vase on a corner table, stocking the cooler, and dusting.

Champ rested his rifle in the rack and settled into his leather recliner. He sipped latte, took repose, and listened to strange pre-dawn wails and cackles of the deep forest. He slipped on night-vision goggles and scanned the forest's edge around his field with an infrared light, watching in misty light as one deer after another approached with caution.

Birds' ode to joy welcomed dawn and awoke the day. *Showtime, you fifteen-point son of a bitch.*

Chapter 43

Father and son listened to the world awaken as the sun burst through. Bean's heart pounded.

From time to time, he unscrewed his water bottle cap, pressed the bottle against his lips, and dribbled tobacco juice. Junior ran his hands over his coverall leaves.

The morning was still, not a ruffle through the trees or bushes. Early light sparkled on swamp water before them. Arthritic cypress knees appeared to arise from plate glass.

Bean scanned the alluvial world of snakes and gators and inhaled the must of coagulated swamp slime, watching for ripples, ears peeled for a hoof splash or a twig snap.

"*Hoo, hoo.*"

Junior flinched. "What's that, Diddy?"

"It ain't nuthin but a hoot owl. *Shhh.* Keep your trap shut. Look at them stars disappear, Sugah."

Light split the horizon on their right and flickered on the water like a candle in a mirror. Junior tapped Bean on the arm and pointed.

"Diddy, I think the sun's comin' up on my side."

"*Shhh,* got-a-mighty, boy, o' course it is. Knock it off."

They sat motionless. Bean scanned his eyes side-to-side. Junior leaned into his father, and Bean watched his eyelids drift shut and his head list as he nodded off. Silence prevailed but for the nasal whistle of Junior's breathing. Stomach cramps prompted Bean to shift, looking for relief. Ruby's sausage biscuits called to him. He passed foul air in stealth.

Junior's head snapped up, nostrils flaring. He tugged his father's sleeve. Bean looked down at his boy in the dim light and noted the quizzical look on his face. Bean raised his eyebrows, grinned, and shrugged as if to say, "I couldn't help it." Junior caught on and covered his mouth as his shoulders bounced up and down in smothered laughter.

A brewer's fart crept up the crack of Bean's ass and burst like Louis Armstrong's trumpet. Junior lost it, laughter sputtering out the sides of his hands. Howling, he leaned over and returned fire. A cacophony of farts like horns in a traffic jam exploded as they held their sides in laughter.

Calm settled in. *"Shhh."* Bean detected splashing and a faint, familiar *oink* in the swamp. He held his breath and listened. *Yeah, Baby, come to Papa. I'll get me a hog AND a buck today.* Rumbling grunts echoed, and Junior snatched Bean's shirt sleeve.

"Diddy, did you hear that?"

"*Shhh.* They's hogs."

A rising chorus of snorts announced a panic-stricken pork parade tromping through the swamp and rushing toward the Sweats. Junior lurched forward in his chair.

"Diddy," he yanked Bean's sleeve so hard the collar jerked his neck. "Can them pigs get us? You sure them ain't bears?"

"*Shhh,* them ain't bears." Bean punched Junior's leg. "Now hush 'fore I tan your bottom." Bean fingered his shotgun's trigger, and the hair on his neck bristled. He had witnessed wild hog carnage.

A marauding sounder of ambushing raiders barreled straight toward them, squealing and crashing through the water.

Junior shivered and bear-hugged his daddy's leg. *"I'm skeered."*

An alpha boar and his sows hit high ground at full speed like Marines charging the beach at Iwo Jima, hooves pounding and quaking the earth.

Oh, damn. They's headin' straight for Bessie.

Junior's shivers turned to tremors as he buried his face in his father's lap. Bean wrapped one arm around his son and squeezed him tight. He released the boy and braced himself then steadied his shotgun and prepared for the onslaught as adrenaline prickled up his spine.

Hogs stampeded the platform in a flash then veered around at the last instant. Squeals deafened like Hell's gate ripping open. The platform groaned in seismic shudders.

WHAM. A hog crashed into the steps, and its ear-splitting cry caused the drift to shriek in chaos. The platform reverberated, and Junior tightened his death grip on Bean's legs. Another slammed into a corner post fueling pandemonium. Junior dug his nails in and sobbed.

The sounder shifted its path and departed in a thunderous exodus. Clamor ebbed then faded to silence. A feral musk odor invaded the hunters' nostrils.

Bean hadn't dreamed of this scenario when building the platform. *I'm glad I built it to Ruby's specs, or our ass would be grass.* His heart slowed its frantic pace. Junior's tremors subsided to mere quivering then he fell asleep. Bean embraced his shoulder, listened to his raspy breath, and beheld the dawn. The dimming moon hid behind a pristine, moss-draped stand of bald cypress piercing an orange sky. He heard wood ducks whir overhead.

A mosquito buzzed his ear. Another dive-bombed, and the blitz was on. Junior flinched as a brazen one battled through the deet haze to plunder his target-rich neck. Comrades swooped in, and Junior sprang up, slapping and swatting.

"Shhh," Bean pulled him back down to his seat. He grabbed bug spray, blasted his hands, lowered his head, and spread the juice over his neck and face before passing the can to Junior.

Father and son gazed in wonderment as the great fireball bubbled up on the horizon. Nature's film developed before them like a photograph in a darkroom—three dimension, real time, in the woods, in the trenches, on the front line, in the game.

"Conditions are perfect and it's Openin' Day, by God," Bean whispered.

"Shhh." Junior pressed his finger to his lips. They muffled a chuckle.

The unfolding of morning in the forest stood in stark contrast to dawn in the Garden of Eden trailer park. Youthful longleaf pine saplings with green punk haircuts emerged in perfect rows beside them. Ahead, ancient bald cypress waded in tea-colored swamp water, their boughs draped by moss windsocks glistening like gold when struck by the sun.

Bean strained his eyes searching for Bessie. He spotted her resting in a clump of chokeberry shrubs, her legs pointing to the sky, a swine stampede victim.

Oh, crap, that'll bring in a big buck, an upside down plastic doe.

A squirrel scampered down a tree. They watched it stop, ruffle its tail, and announce its squeaky wake up call. They heard low, steady rustling from the rear.

Junior tugged Bean's sleeve and whispered, *"It's a bear."*

"Shhh, it ain't no bear. It's a ah'madilla."

The miniature armored tank grubbed the earth weaving close to the stand then scudded away. Buzzing mosquitoes attacked their heads, testing the deet wall of defense. Bean heard the faint bay of dogs. He grinned and nudged Junior then nodded and signaled with two fingers pointing at his eyeballs—*be on the lookout.*

As they listened, Bean unbuttoned his shirtsleeve and rolled it up to expose a bald spot on his hairy forearm. He unsheathed his skinning knife and ran his thumb down the blade, testing its razor edge. Pressing the blade to his forearm, he scraped and hair floated to the planks. He winked and nodded at Junior's bulging eyes and re-sheathed the knife.

The racket from the dogs swelled. Bean grinned at his son, and their breathing grew shallow. Bean's trigger finger twitched as he kept his eyes peeled.

Junior tugged on Bean's sleeve, a sheepish look on his face. "Diddy, I got to pee."

"No, cain't you hear dogs is chasin' 'em right to us?" Bean whispered. "It's showtime, Sugah. We been waitin' all year on this."

Baying and barking echoed louder. Bean couldn't believe his fortune, every deer hunter's dream, the pack heading his way. Junior tugged again. Bean gritted his teeth and turned. His enraged eyes locked onto Junior's.

"*Whut?*" he hissed.

"I got to pee."

"You hold it until this hunt's over. The dogs is settin' us up. I ain't gonna let you blow it."

Clenching his jaw, Bean zeroed in on howling dogs driving from the left and running towards the sun. *Perfect, the deer'll be blinded.* The barking and yapping intensified. Bean gripped his shotgun, thumb on the safety, as he scanned the terrain.

Three panicked doe leapt through the pines and galloped along the swamp's edge. Bean shot a thumbs-up then locked his thumbs, spread eight fingers like antlers, grinned, and winked at Junior.

Junior yanked Bean's sleeve. "Diddy, I *got* to pee!"

Bean glared at Junior, shook his head and mouthed, "No."

Junior's eyes welled with tears as he nodded, "Yes."

"No." Bean frowned and shook his head.

"Yes." Junior nodded.

Bean shrugged, reached into his tote bag, grabbed an empty water bottle, and passed it to Junior. He retrained his eyes on the swamp.

Junior whispered, "What am I s'posed to do with this bottle?"

Bean whispered without taking his eyes off the tree line. "Stick your weenie in it and pee."

Junior jerked Bean's sleeve. "No way."

Flabbergasted, Bean held a knuckle sandwich under Junior's chin. He hissed through clenched teeth, "It's real simple. You either hold it or pee in the bottle. I ain't lettin' you ruin this hunt. Hold it or use the bottle."

Bean focused again. Hounds were closing in, and he scooted to his chair's edge, eyes scanning side-to-side.

Junior whimpered. Bean turned to see his boy's arms wrapped across his chest, tears streaming down his cheeks, shoulders quaking up and down with each sob.

Urine dripped underneath Junior's chair. Then a steady stream splattered the platform before spilling through gaps in the planks and showering the earth below.

Chapter 44

Stag faced the frenetic baying canines, armed to fight, to assert his rightful dominance. He was a regal and imposing foe with a broad chest and a massive neck, fifteen spears atop his head eager to gore, spry legs prepared to charge, and sharp hooves ready to slash. The rising sun shimmered on his chocolate-brown coat and highlighted his white markings.

The king tilted his head back and curled his lip to freshen the estrus doe's pheromones in his muzzle. He heard her faint bleat but allowed the doe herd to wander from sight.

Needing to satiate the burning in his loins, he sounded his tending grunts repeatedly to signal to the estrus doe that he would join her soon. He had to be on guard so another buck wouldn't mount her. He monitored the movement of the doe and the canines.

The great buck strutted to a cedar sapling with his head held high and his chest inflated in pomp and circumstance. He brandished his rack and savagely decimated the tree—first twisting and ripping branches and limbs off then scraping the trunk's bark. He stepped forward and massaged his glandular forehead on the moist, exposed wood.

Stag turned and focused his fluted ears towards the canines then detected another buck's danger snort. He felt the hoof vibrations of an approaching deer on the trot and spotted an oncoming eight-point buck, grunting and tailing *his* estrus doe's scent. The approaching buck spotted the behemoth staring him down and stomping his front paw.

The two buck sniffed, wheezed, and grunted as they circled each other. Then they reared up on their hind legs and slashed with lightning-fast forelegs. Stag, three feet longer and seventy-five pounds heavier, outclassed the smaller buck who backed away and licked a gash across his snout.

They lowered their heads and laid back their ears then lunged forward and crashed racks. Their antlers locked. Stag's rack sliced the smaller buck's neck, and blood gushed. The king grunted and shoved his opponent backward until the lesser buck's hind legs buckled. The contender regained his footing, lifted his tail in a white flag of surrender and ran, sounding the alarm.

Having dispatched that challenge, Stag homed in on the canines' wail and bark, closer now and locked onto his path. He stood his ground in angry defiance, chest bulging, testosterone pumping, furious over a rut interrupted. Sunlight glinted off his blood-splattered antlers.

Chapter 45

Sunlight illuminated mighty live oak boughs beside Champ Butler's tree house and confirmed what he knew from infrared—deer were feeding at the trough like ants at a picnic.

The field's wooden box paralleled his line of vision. He could clearly see both sides, and more important, have a shot at anything feeding.

As the sun pulled its tail above the horizon, deer gracefully leapt the fence from all directions. They reminded him of the dancers in *The Nutcracker*. *Belly up to the trough and take repose, frolic in lush grass then return for dessert. What a fine petting zoo I could start.*

Deer gorged on his "special mix," which was spiked with grain alcohol and beer. Their dulled and faltering motor skills made for hilarious comedy as they busted their asses trying to jump the fence again.

Two drunken, clumsy eight-pointers locked antlers and battled with fatal intent. Amongst the many doe and young buck at the trough, three other eight-pointers and a ten-pointer broke bread, engrossed in the battle while grinding grain, their heads and necks upright on high alert.

Butler's eyes scanned the wood's edge outside the fence, looking for his fifteen-pointer. *Dammit, where is the bastard?* Over the last three years, they witnessed the buck grow from ten-to-twelve-to-fourteen points. His Boone and Crockett score climbed towards one hundred eighty, state record territory for "typical" deer. Then the drop tine appeared this year, a lone six inch stalactite below fourteen stalagmites.

So what if the drop tine made him a "non-typical" deer, it transformed him from a trophy to a dream buck, still grain-fed and growing. A prominent spot on the lodge's wall awaited.

Morning unfolded with no sign of his buck. *Seems my old friend is wily for some reason. Don't double-cross me, you prick.* Champ marveled at the three-ring circus in the field below as shots rang out, echoing reports from the harvests of his cronies.

Chapter 46

Stag stood fast, eyes and ears trained toward the advancing canines. He grunted, pawed the ground, and bowed his neck. He'd rip them all to shreds.

He knew he could outrun them with ease, but instinct associated canines with man. His survival impulses kicked in, and he weighed conflicting urges of fight or flight. Barking approached, and he spotted a lone canine galloping toward him. More followed in headlong pursuit.

The king turned, flagged his tail, and ran full tilt along the swamp's edge, weaving around grapevine tangles and blackberry thickets and ducking his rack under branches. He bounded over a ten-foot wide swale without breaking stride and maintained his speed until the canines were out of sight.

He paused occasionally and turned his head, aiming his ears to monitor the enemies' path. He outpaced them at will, allowing them no closer than his vision's range. Two lesser buck on the run crossed his trail.

The great buck veered into the swamp, massive sheets of water spraying around each plunging hoof. He maneuvered cypress knees, swam, and pounced across trampolines of peat. After loping through the swamp for a stretch, he paused to listen. The canines still trailed.

He pivoted toward higher ground where he knew he could outrun anything alive.

Chapter 47

Junior whimpered, head bowed, arms clenched across his chest. *Drip... drip...* Bean smelled his son's urine as it pattered underneath his chair. *He's too young for Openin' Day. I knowed it, I knowed it.* A wave of guilt flushed Bean's face. *He must feel horrible, poor boy. Why didn't he pee in the bottle?* He leaned down to make sure his own boots steered clear. It was too late for Junior's boots. Urine dripped from the leaves of his coveralls.

"Damn, Sugah," he whispered, "why didn't you pee in the bottle?"

Junior didn't answer, didn't raise his head. His sobbing reverberated through the swamp.

Barking grew louder, closer. Bean's head popped up when he heard splashing. He spotted an apparition leaping over cypress knees and crashing through swamp water. Antlers flashed in the sunlight.

Got-o-mighty! "Luck be a buck," he whispered as he elbowed Junior, raised his barrel, and shifted to the edge of his chair.

The mammoth buck exploded out of the swamp and bolted straight toward them. Its galloping hooves sounded like a train in the wilderness. Its candelabra antlers bobbed up and down.

Are my eyes playin' tricks? Is that a moose?

The king rose as tall as a quarter horse, muscles chiseled and rippling in his neck and shoulders. The sun glistened off its white antler tips like the Hope diamond in showroom lights.

It's the buck in the pitcher on the clubhouse wall, thought Bean, *even bigger!*

It happened fast, but it felt like slow motion. The giant buck charged in a full-bore sprint... 75 feet... 50 feet...

Bean sprang to his feet, shouldered his gun, and fired in one fluid motion.

Chapter 48

Stag bounded to high ground and stretched his distance from the canines. He galloped toward sapling pines and scanned unfamiliar terrain for danger.

He chanced upon a strange, grotesque, upside-down doe. An overwhelming, sickening scent of man hit him. He recoiled and jumped backwards.

BOOM.

Earth splattered where he just stood.

MAN!

He froze then raised his flag and bolted in the opposite direction.

BOOM.

Earth exploded behind him.

He turned and raced a blue streak along the swamp's edge.

BOOM.

Swamp mud detonated and splattered him.

Running at full tilt, he spied movement in his peripheral vision, a bulky object with a pole and a squatty version of same. MAN!

Flash… fire from the pole… *BOOM.*

Stag heard the hiss and felt the heat from buckshot flying over his shoulder then sprinted unscathed as his tail's white underside bade farewell.

After a herculean sprint, the king halted to glance back, listen, and breathe. He did it. He confronted man on hostile terms and escaped the scare of his life. He didn't realize his good fortune, that the huntsman never learned the art of leading a moving target.

BOOM.

Fire pierced the buck's chest, and pain exploded...

Stag leapt over the Pearly Gates and ascended into Heaven.

Chapter 49

The buck disappeared in a puff of smoke—gone! Bean's body shook like a gigantic Mexican jumping bean as he cranked more cartridges into his shotgun. Spent gunpowder tweaked the air.

He stood at the ready as a tear rolled down his cherub cheek, his first tear since Dale Earnhardt Sr.'s death.

Junior stood in his pee-soaked coveralls and looked up at his father. He'd never seen him cry and didn't interrupt. Bean slumped into his chair, dumbfounded and mute. Junior shadowed him. Bean spoke in a hushed tone.

"Did you see him, Son? His rack? My Gawd!"

"I seen him, Diddy. He was a big'un."

"Lawd. He weren't just a big'un. I ain't never seen nuthin' like it, even in pitchers. His antlers reminded me o' candles I seen at a Jewish church when me and your mama was walkin' around Savannah."

The pursuit dogs approached. Junior peered over the camo netting.

"Look, Diddy, there's that dog we seen at camp."

Old Dixie, Buckshot's black and tan, crashed through the swamp, running hot on scent, swimming, crawling, jumping. Missy, the yapping beagle, trailed.

Old Dixie and Missy rocketed down the buck's precise path. A moment later, the woods exploded with the barking, frothing pack bounding down the same path.

Boom. A shotgun reported from the direction of the buck. Barking morphed to baying and moiling like hounds fussing over a downed deer. *Damn. Somebody else done got him.* Bean turned his camo cap backwards, leaned forward, and guided a long stream of tobacco juice between his boots and through a gap in the planks.

They sat in silence, listening to commotion down the line.

"I'm cold, Diddy."

Bean gathered himself and the tote bag. "Come on, let's fetch Bessie then you can take a dip in the swamp to wash the pee off."

"Was she our good luck charm today?"

"Yeah, she was. You seen her bring in that great big buck. Drawed him right in, you seen it."

"Yes, Diddy, I seen it."

The hunters trudged down the platform's steps like camo aliens sauntering side-by-side down the jetway of a spaceship.

They rested their bags at the base and shuffled off to rescue Bessie, Junior walking with legs splayed. Bean retrieved her and discovered her shattered side.

"I'll jest wrap her with duct tape. She'll be aw-ight." Bean cradled Bessie, and they walked back to the stand where he tied her underneath.

"Now, let's walk to the swamp, Son, and clean you up." At swamp's edge, Junior squinted at the dark water.

"Any gators in there?"

"No, Sugah. I ain't gonna let no gator get ya. Now go on, wade in to your waist."

"Remember, I'm s'posed to wear this for Halloween, too?"

"I remember. We gonna wash it, and we ain't gonna tell nobody. Now git."

Junior inched into the murky water. Mud and peat oozed around his boots. With each step, he struggled to free his foot from suction.

When waist deep, he gyrated his hips like a washing machine agitator, the leaves on his upper body flapping back and forth. His legs sank deeper into the muck with each writhing rotation until water rose to his armpits. He struggled to break the grip but bogged deeper.

"DIDDY, I'M STUCK. QUICK, I'M GONNA DROWN IN QUICKSAND."

"No, you ain't, jest—"

"I'M GONNA DIE."

"No, you ain't. Jest lean—"

"DIDDY! DIDDY!"

Geeze-us. He's yellin' so loud, everybody's gonna hear.

Bean jumped in feet first and bear-hugged Junior. He yanked and pulled and pulled and yanked. Junior shot out like a champagne cork into Bean's arms and they heaved over backwards, back-flopped, and submerged.

Bean came up gasping and cussing. He grabbed Junior's collar and dragged him up the bank. They collapsed on their backs and sucked air. As they gazed through the bald cypress canopy at drifting cotton ball clouds, their gasps turned to wild laughter.

Chapter 50

Georgia DNR's Corporal Mutt Hightower limped toward the Chevy pickup deep in the woods on Fat Back Hunt Club property. He was suffering a slow, agonizing death by bunions in boots that pinched. *Flip-flops is what I need.*

Steroidal biceps bulged under his green, tight-fitting polo shirt as he flexed to restrain Tazer, his Rottweiler. The black, muscular, broad-necked dog heaved against his shoulder halter.

Hightower passed by several pickups and four-wheelers on Fat Back property searching for Sweat's vehicle. He now recognized the truck—camo rear window, bumper stickers galore, hand-painted "3" on the door. He inhaled the all-too-familiar Majestic Chicken plant stench as he circled the truck. Tazer sniffed the scene and urinated on the tires.

The Warden pressed his face to a window and peered inside. The backseat looked like a tornado hit a Goodwill store. *No one else could possibly keep such a trashy vehicle.* He fired a cigarette and scribbled down the license number. "Come on, boy, let's go check it out."

Corporal Hightower and his Rottweiler returned to the DNR truck. He accessed his laptop, and sure enough, he identified Sweat as the pickup's owner. *Darryl David Sweat, ole Butterbean, that trouble-makin', smart-ass pest at Majestic. I thought so.*

"Mr. Butler instructed me to keep a close eye on him, Tazer. Time to perform for our boss. If I can work my way into full-time employ at Honeysuckle Plantation, I'll quit the government. You'd love that." Tazer barked.

Mutt's grin reflected in the laptop's glow as he continued his search. "Let's see... no huntin' license sold to Sweat this season. Interestin'. Let's double check... yep, no license." He removed the stalk of grass from his mouth as laughter stretched his leathered cheeks.

Maximum for hunting without a license? He checked his computer. "Yes, sixty days. What a shame, Fatso, you ain't gonna like the food in jail too good." He grabbed his ticket book and started scribbling.

He radioed his operator. "Corporal Hightower here. I may have a perp hunting without a license and will pursue on foot... roger that." He gingerly stepped out of his vehicle, donned his state trooper-style DNR hat, and clipped his portable radio to his shoulder strap. The Warden buckled his equipment belt around his waist and grabbed a Remington semi-automatic twelve-gauge shotgun. He knew that law enforcement should prepare for the worst when busting a hunter deep in the woods, especially when the hunter is a known rabble-rouser.

"Come on, boy," he tugged the leash. "Let's go have some fun with this bastard."

Hightower circled the pickup again, barrel perched on his shoulder, the Rottweiler leading the way. Ants feasted on strawberry crème pie remains. Hightower gave the okay, and Tazer scarfed the pie. A Snickers wrapper lay on the ground by the passenger door.

Littering—ten days. This is private property, and littering fines are limited to public property. But, hey, throw shit at the wall and see what sticks. Put the burden on that son of a bitch and see if he's smart enough to figure it out.

His equipment belt—Colt .45 pistol, bullets, Taser gun, handcuffs, pepper spray, flash light, and baton—slid down his hips as he circled the perp's vehicle. He hiked it up as he approached the rear of the pickup and started reading bumper stickers...

Squirrel-It's What's For Dinner
Keep Honking-I'm Reloading

If Heaven's Got Possum-I'm Bringin' My Shotgun
Wishin' I was Fishin'
Beer is Food
I'm Not Speeding, I'm Qualifying
This Truck Insured by Smith & Wesson
Hung Like Einstein-Smart as a Horse

Perverted redneck. Then he saw the sticker that sent him into lunar orbit...

Welcome to Georgia
Owned and Operated by the DNR

That bastard. He'll be lucky if I don't whup his ass right here on the spot. Mutt covered one nostril and blew a snot rocket onto the sticker. "Wake up, boy." He jerked the leash. "We got bad people. *Bad people.*" Tazer growled and bared his teeth.

The Warden examined boot prints in the dirt and fresh-trodden grass leading into longleaf saplings. Honeysuckle Plantation's swamp stretched beyond. Tazer snarled and pulled, begging to pursue. Hightower yanked him back, popped the perp's tailgate, and jumped up to sit and rest his feet. He smoked a cig, basked in the mid-morning sun, and waited.

Tazer's ears alerted, and a growl rumbled in his throat. Hightower twisted the leash around his wrist and gripped tight. He heard voices then recognized Sweat's bulky silhouette a hundred yards away, emerging from the pines and laboring to carry his bag. A half-pint version wearing swamp-thing coveralls hustled to keep up.

Hightower perched reflective aviator sunglasses on his nose, slid off the tailgate, hiked his belt, and spread his legs in a gunslinger's stance. His silver DNR badge reflected sunlight like a laser. One hand gripped the neck of the twelve-gauge resting across his shoulder, and the other grappled with restraining Tazer. "Easy, boy."

Sweat and the boy approached. The Rottweiler barked and lunged, his halter pulling him off his front feet so he balanced on his hind legs. Hightower let him bark until the hunters neared. "Heel, Tazer."

"Mornin', Sweat, we meet again. Been swimmin' in the swamp?"

Sweat's gaze shifted between Hightower and the dog. The boy hid behind his father. "Mista', you better hold that dog."

Hightower grinned and flashed his bad teeth. "He's just helpin' me enforce the law. If you ain't broke it, you ain't got to worry. Now, I repeat, you go for a swim?"

"Wet clothes, you mean? That's a long story. Hey, I know you from the plant. We work together. How you doin', ole buddy?"

"Sweat, I ain't your 'buddy.' I don't work *with* you. I work *for* Mr. Butler, and I don't do chickens. But today, I work for the Georgia Department of Natural Resources, Wildlife Resources Division, Law Enforcement Section."

Tazer's growl rumbled low and steady in his throat. He occasionally flared his lips, exposing menacing teeth. His neck and shoulder muscles bristled.

"Y'all had any luck huntin' this mornin'?"

"Oh, nawsir." Sweat lowered his bag to the ground. "We ain't been huntin', we jest scoutin'."

"You lyin' sack-a-shit. Hand me your shotgun, butt end first." Sweat's shoulders slumped and he passed his gun over the Rottweiler's head.

Hightower sniffed the shotgun's open ejection port then the end of the barrel. *Fired gunpowder. Lyin' bastard. Obstruction of justice—one year.* He dropped Sweat's shotgun in the weeds behind him, laid down his shotgun, and pulled his ticket book.

"Let's see… possession of a weapon that's been recently fired, comin' outta the woods on Openin' Day decked out in camo, and you're jest 'scoutin'? Do I have that right?"

"Yassir."

"Show me your huntin' license."

"I told ya, we wasn't huntin'. We jest been takin' target practice." Sweat winked and tilted his head toward the boy. "Jest tryin'
to teach the kid to shoot, you know. Ain't that right, Junior?"

"Yassir, we was jest shootin' at cans."

Conspiracy to obstruct justice—two years.

"Right, Sweat, save it for the Judge. Now show me your driver's license and huntin' license."

"All right." Sweat fished his wet wallet from his pocket and
pulled his driver's license. Hightower reached over his dog's head
and snatched it. Sweat scoured his wallet and pockets for his
hunting license.

"It's prob'ly somewheres in my bag or maybe in the truck. I
don't know, maybe at home."

"Then let's start with your bag."

"You don't want me to search the whole bag, do ya?"

Mutt shifted his sore feet and studied Sweat from behind his
reflective shades. *Pathetic bastard.* He snatched his cig pack from
his shirt pocket and fired one up. "Go ahead, I'll wait. Find your
license."

Sweat shook his head, and with a watchful eye on the Rottweiler, he dropped to his knees and started unloading his bag,
item-by-item…

Binoculars, sausage biscuits in Ziplock bags.
Disposable camera, last year's deer tags.

"And while you're lookin', we been havin' trouble over at
Honeysuckle Plantation with dogs that we think came from your
club. You know anything 'bout dat?"

"Nawsir, I ain't never heard o' no problems like dat…"

Walkie-talkies, Outdoor Life.
Orange vest, sheath knife.

"Listen here, Sweat. I'll deny I ever said this, but if your boys
don't knock it off with throwin' dogs over the fence to run Hon-

eysuckle, them dogs is gonna take a dirt bath and nobody will never know. You hear me?"

"Yassir... "

Coil of rope, stub from payday.
Flashlight, bottle of doe urine spray.

The assemblage from the bag piled in the dirt at the game warden's feet. Sweat fanned items around him in a half moon, taking his sweet time, Tazer scrutinizing every movement...

Thermos of Gatorade, spray can for bugs.
Orange tape, latest issue of Big Jugs.

A luscious milk maiden graced the cover of *Big Jugs Magazine*. Corporal Hightower did a double take when he saw the gal's melons. Magnificent, low-hanging teats, enough to make any heifer jealous, with nipples the size of silver-dollar pancakes. His face flushed, and his loins tingled.

The boy gawked at the cover, his eyes bugging as he studied the image. He turned to his daddy with a quizzical look. "Is that a pitcher of Mama?"

"No, Son, that ain't Mama. I don't know who that gal is."

The warden leaned over and picked up the magazine, exposing the dragon tattoo slithering up his bicep. He folded the magazine and stuffed it into his back pocket. "Damn, son. What kind o' sick puppy are you? I'll take that into evidence. Pitiful to have smut around a young boy." *Contributing to the delinquency of a minor—two years.*

Sweat blushed and continued rooting in his bag. Corporal Hightower stood grim-faced, his shotgun cradled as he puffed his cig from behind his mirrors. The boy hid behind his daddy and locked his gaze on Tazer.

Toilet paper in Ziploc bag (sign of a true outdoorsman), twine ball.
Compass, "bleat of doe in estrus" deer call.

Hightower was impressed by the expanding junk collection...

Pouch of Red Man, gloves, handkerchief, cap—all camo.
Bag of peanuts, two boxes of ammo.

"Son, we got a dollar waitin' on a dime here. You ain't got no license in there and you know it... "

Box of Marlboros, camo face mask.
Map of the hunt club, bourbon flask.

"Sweat, you been drinkin'? You know it's a felony to hunt under the influence." *Hunting under the influence—six months. Child endangerment—six months.*

"Nassir, trust me. I ain't had none. That's just for snake bites and things. You wanna smell my breath?"

Hightower considered the offer. "No thanks. Keep goin'. Where's your damn license? That's all I want to know. I ain't got all day..."

Pepper spray, Snickers Bar.
Handgun, cigar.

HANDGUN. Hightower flinched, clapped his hand on his revolver, and eased it out of the holster a touch. Tazer snapped to all fours, on point. "You got a license to tote that thing?"

"*Whoa,* cowboy, it ain't loaded," Sweat said. "My cousin give me that gun when he went from bein' a lawyer to a judge. He said a judge needs a lot more horsepower in his desk drawer than a li'l ole pawn shop derringer."

"I didn't ask you where you got the damn thing, although that may have to be investigated. I said show me your license to tote it."

"I didn't think I needed no license to tote this li'l ole pop gun in the woods when I'm huntin'."

"*Uh huh.*" The warden hiked up his equipment belt. "You just admitted you was huntin'. *And* you carryin' a concealed weapon without no permit. You in big trouble, boy. I'll take that pistol into evidence." *Carrying a concealed weapon—two years.*

Sweat was down to the scraps in his bag so he turned it upside down. Doodads and trash scattered into a montage on the ground.

"That's litter, boy." *Littering, second offense—20 days.*

Sweat labored to all fours then pushed himself up, stumbling before gaining his balance. "The damn huntin' license ain't here. It could be in the truck. We can go search that if you want. I coulda left it at home by accident with my wife and handicapped baby daughter."

"Lemme get this straight. You say you bought a license and just forgot to bring it. Is that what you tellin' me?"

"I'm purty sure but wouldn't want to swear to it."

"Where'd you buy it?"

"Hell, I don't remember. Prob'ly Walmart. Maybe the hardware store."

Hightower stood erect and motionless as he stared Sweat down from behind his shades. The perp shifted from foot-to-foot, mouth twitching, eyes cutting this way and that.

"You ain't the smartest knife in the drawer, are you, Sweat?"

"Yassir. I mean nawsir… ask that question again?"

"Point proven. Forget it. Pick all this crap up." He pointed at the boy. "You… walk over here with me."

The boy looked at his daddy who shrugged and nodded. Hightower kept Tazer on one side and the boy on the other as they walked out of Sweat's earshot.

"Now boy, you better tell me the truth. Is that your daddy?"

The boy stared into the Rottweiler's black nose and dark, almond eyes. The dog's head was broader than the boy's.

"Whut?"

"I said, is that your daddy?"

"Yassir."

"Your daddy's in big trouble, so don't lie to me. You understand?" Tazer snarled.

"Yassir." The boy blinked as his gaze shifted between the warden and the dog.

"Did y'all shoot a deer or not?"

"Nawsir."

"Boy, don't lie to me. Lyin's only gonna get your daddy in more trouble. Now, I'm gonna ask you one more time. If you lie to me, you and your daddy gonna spend the night in jail, 'cept y'all be separated. And the jailer is a real mean man, 'specially to little boys like you. Now, did y'all shoot a deer?"

The boy hesitated and looked over at his daddy scrounging on his knees, stuffing junk back into his bag. The boy shifted his weight from foot-to-foot, mouth twitching, eyes cutting this way then that.

"Well?"

"Yassir, we shot but we missed. We didn't kill nuthin'."

Mutt grinned. "Let me ask you this: Was that pitcher on that magazine really your mama?"

"Nawsir, it weren't."

"Does your mama look like that with her shirt off?"

The boy scuffed his boot in the dirt and hung his head low. "Yassir." Hightower's imagination soared.

They walked back to Sweat. "I'm writin' your sorry ass up. You in big trouble. Huntin' without no license, carryin' a concealed weapon, obstruction o' justice, conspiracy, contributin' to the delinquency of a minor, and litterin', twice."

"Obstruction o' justice? The hell you say. I ain't obstructed no justice."

"How about lyin'? Lyin' 'bout not huntin' and lyin' 'bout havin' a license? Them's two lies and no tellin' how many more you done told."

"Wait, officer. I didn't lie on purpose. It's Walmart's fault. Their machine was busted this morning, and I can prove it."

"Like I said, save it for the judge."

"Ain't no need to save it. My cousin who gave me that pop gun is Judge Ward Strickland. He can vouch for me, and you can call him right now."

Hightower stopped scribbling and looked up. "Wait a minute. You tellin' me that Judge Ward Strickland is your cousin?"

Sweat grinned and winked at his boy. "Yep. His mama is my auntie. We's kissin' cousins."

Hightower shifted his weight from side-to-side, bunions stabbing him. "Is that so? You ain't shittin' me, are you?"

"Nope, I ain't shittin' ya. Call him up. I'm sure he'll be happy to take you to supper any night you want."

Hightower clenched his jaw, hiked up his britches, and scribbled on his ticket pad. "You just tried to bribe an officer of the law." *Bribery—20 years!*

"That asshole cousin o' yours denied me a search warrant a couple o' weeks back. Cost me a bust. I'm addin' two more charges on your ass: bribery and drivin' with a broken taillight. I could impound your truck and keep it for evidence, but I ain't 'cause it stinks too bad. You better get yourself a good lawyer, boy, and give your cousin my regards."

Corporal Hightower ripped the ticket out of the book and flung it at Sweat. He picked up his shotgun and yanked at his dog's leash. "Come on, Tazer." As he limped toward his truck, the dog's stumpy tail waving goodbye, he yelled over his shoulder, "And tell that fat little kid o' yours it ain't good for deer huntin' to be pissin' all over hisself."

Chapter 51

Champ's blood pressure simmered as the morning yawned on and his fifteen-pointer didn't show. He couldn't wait all day on the bastard—he had guests. He trained his rifle's scope on a ten-pointer and several eight-pointers, all specimen white-tail. His crosshairs lingered on their bodies and faces. These trophies alone would constitute a bumper season for neighboring hunt clubs, but he wanted *his* fifteen-pointer, the king.

He was determined to show everyone that he was the Champ. A professional photographer waited at the barn. Thanks to the Bulldawg, the governor would see the photo of him posing with the fifteen-pointer, and it would make its way around the Gold Dome in Atlanta. *Maybe the governor will come next year.*

Alas, he harvested nothing, not even a doe, for fear of spooking his prize. *He must be lurking just inside the shadows at the forest's edge.* He gave up but not before pitching a tantrum and crushing the cut flowers under the sole of his boot.

Time to return to the lodge wearing a happy face to celebrate my guests' trophy kills. He would return that evening to harvest the king.

Driving back to the lodge, he popped a half dozen armadillos with his .22 rifle. He delighted when his bullet struck home and the little armored tanks jumped into the air like they'd been jolted by an electric prod. Each time, he'd stop the Range Rover, get out and find the downed armadillo. If it was still alive, he'd press his .22 barrel to its head, look into its dark, panicked eyes, and pull the trigger.

Chapter 52

Mr. Otis's ironclad rule at Fat Back Hunt Club required hunters to check in after the hunt, to make sure nobody lay wounded, or worse.

Bean's truck flew past pine trees, pothole to pothole. *Hell with the rule, I'm haulin' ass.* Junior bounced in the truck's bed like a bobble-head doll.

At the crossroad, he stomped the brakes and skidded to a stop. The Fatback gate and freedom beckoned on the right. Camp and humiliation called him to the left. Leave now and maybe get booted from the club? *In the history of mankind, has anyone been poet lariat or lasso or whatever for only half a day?* He leaned his forehead on the steering wheel to think then stuck his head out the window.

"Get in." He dug out a towel from the nest behind him and spread it across the seat. Junior climbed in, the urine and swamp water a refreshing relief from *stench du poulet.* He turned left and headed for camp.

"Diddy, that dog skeered me real bad. I wanna go home."

"We goin' home soon, Sugah, but you know the rule. We got to check in with Mr. Otis."

"Are we in trouble with the cops?"

"It ain't nuthin' for you to worry 'bout, Sugah, just don't say nuthin' 'bout that game warden when we get to camp, you hear?"

"Yes, Diddy."

Pickups and cars parked in perfect random surrounding the clubhouse and skinning shed. Two trucks backed up to the shed where four deer hung upside down. Men scurried about skinning deer, carrying buckets, and filling coolers. Some tended their dogs, but most stood around smoking and watching the action. Nine cackling judges and hecklers packed the bleacher.

Bean parked on the periphery. The crowd was in an uproar as he and Junior approached. Bean spotted Pickle Joe in the Top Dog chair smoking a cigar and waving a Budweiser.

Sumbitch. I knowed it.

Men whooped, cheered, and passed moonshine as father and son weaved through the crowd.

Bean saw the size of one of the hoisted deer. *Damn.* The monster's knees crammed the shed's eleven-foot ceiling, and its fourteen-point rack—plus one drop tine—scraped the ground.

Man, you could fit a Volkswagen inside that rack. Blood oozed from the gaping buckshot hole in the deer's side. A blood-soaked sweatshirt lay underneath to protect the antlers from chipping on the concrete.

Two doe and an eight-pointer hung next to it. The eight-pointer's rack cleared the floor by several feet and would secure Top Dog billing on a normal day. Not this day. It was an adolescent compared to the king.

Angus carved a doe with his gut-hook skinner knife. A helper sprayed the floor from time-to-time with a hose, sending bloody water flying off the slab into the dirt and onto spectators' pant legs. The aroma of blood and guts permeated.

Deft with a knife, Angus could separate a deer from its skin as fast and sweet as unzipping a lady's dress and letting it slide off her shoulders to pool on the floor. He was the best Bean had ever seen. Hunters were mesmerized by his quick and steady blade—pull, carve, pull, carve...

PJ told and re-told the story of his hunt, each more grandiose than the last. Hunters jockeyed to get a better look at the eye-candy. One hollered, "Cain't wait to see what he measures on the Davey and Crockett scale."

Two yard dogs, ears pinned back and tails tucked, darted in and out, licking blood from the nostrils of the hanging deer until the hose man blasted them with water. They skittered away only to return a minute later to hunters' bursts of glee.

A little four-pointer lay to the side, awaiting its turn on the hooks. A blue tick hound circled it, drunk with euphoria. The hound mounted and humped the dead buck. The boys howled at the spectacle. Between the monster buck and the dog-deer orgy, there weren't enough disposable cameras in Japan to capture all the action.

PJ spotted Bean. "Hey, there he is. Where you been?" All eyes turned on Bean. "My man. Thanks for the deer. I know any man shoot four times, he's tryin' to miss."

Hunters jeered, backslapped one another, and pointed at Bean.

"Now wait a minute," Mr. Otis hollered over the laughter. "Wait a minute." A hush fell over the crowd as many hands pushed Bean forward to center stage. "Pickle, did you say four shots?"

"Yassir, Mr. President. Four shots."

"Well, that's a serious infraction if it's true. Bean, how many times *did* you shoot?"

Bean pondered his answer. Knives stopped in mid-slice, all eyes fixed on him, the newest defendant in the Fat Back Hunt Club kangaroo court. He looked around at the blood lust in his comrades' eyes. He grinned. "'Bout four."

The crowd roared. "What a retard… Dick-brain… You need to join the Pollock Olympic Shooting Team… King o' the Texas brain shot."

Mr. Otis held up his hand to silence the throng. "Bean, what do you have to say in your defense?"

"To start out with, skeeters was so damn thick you had to take your fist and knock a hole in 'em just to spit."

Hoots and chortles.

"Okay, then what?" Mr. Otis prodded.

"Well, you see, the sun was jest comin' up, and it was in my eyes, and suddenly I seen this humongous buck in the swamp, biggest damn thing I ever seen. Like he was totin' a rockin' chair on his head. He disappeared like a ghost. Then, damned if I ain't seen him again. I throwed my gun down on him, and he done disappeared again. I looked up, and now he done appeared over yonder like a ghost. Every time I shot, he'd be three steps ahead o' me. It was an optical conclusion. It all happened so fast, in 'bout two seconds..."

Knee-slapping laughter erupted. Mr. Otis held up his hand again. "Tell us this—why are you and Junior so wet?"

Somebody yelled, "One a ya ain't pissed hisself, 'er he?" The throng roared.

"Nooo. He was jest playin' in the swamp, you know, like kids do and—"

"It don't matter," Mr. Otis decreed. "The Secret Committee done decided to invoke the Shirttail Rule today."

The president pointed to two hunters sitting in the bleachers. They stood and turned, their T-shirts revealing the absence of a backside. The crowd howled at them all over again.

"We done tried and convicted them for shootin' only once and not cuttin' a hair. Now gentlemen, here is Mr. Butterbean Sweat who missed four times. All in favor o' takin' his shirttail, say a'ye'."

"AYE," rang loud.

Four men stepped forth and grabbed Bean. Angus raised his knife like a scalpel. Junior went pie-eyed.

"Wait a minute," Bean protested. "The rule ain't s'posed to be for members. This is a brand new shirt. Take my T-shirt instead."

The four men held Bean and stretched the backside of his new camo shirt, the one with a button-down collar, the one Ruby had given for his birthday. Angus stepped forward with his blade.

Riipp.

"NO," Bean yelled, but it was too late.

Red-faced, he modeled his newly-aerated shirt for the roaring crowd. They cheered and clapped then turned their attention to another deer-laden pickup backing up to the shed.

PJ motioned Bean over. "Listen, we ain't layin' a knife to my deer 'til I take him and show some people. My wife and neighbor then to my brother's house. He's got a good camera. You and Junior wanna come?"

"Yeah, we'll go. We can take my truck."

"Hell no, I ain't hidin' this hoss in the bed o' no truck. He's goin' on the top of my Chrysler. I may cruise the mayor's house then drive to the television station then…"

Chapter 53

Champ followed his last guest to the gate to bid *adieu*. He strolled with Freddie to the road, and they watched vehicles whiz by as he briefed his security guard on upcoming guests.

A squeaking purple jalopy approached, creeping down the highway riding low on its shocks.

"There's something strange on top, Freddie."

"Yessir. Is that a deer on the roof?"

"Damn sure looks like it. Is it sprawled on its belly?"

"Danged if it ain't, boss. Men are grippin' each leg of the deer out the windows, and the head and rack are droopin' over the windshield."

"Look at the size of that deer, it's *huge*. Is that *my* deer? Can't be." Champ surveyed the rack… drop tine on the left! *Son of a bitch.*

HONK. A backseat passenger wearing a backward camo cap waved as the rattletrap rolled by.

"SWEAT, YOU ASSHOLE." Champ flipped a bird.

PART V:
FOWL PLAY

Chapter 54

Cal Butler reclined in his captain's chair, feet propped up on his leather Sun King desk. He massaged Winston's neck and spewed Cuban smoke toward the beams in the hinterlands of his office. The cloud mimicked the Percocet haze in his brain. With his head wrapped around Beethoven's Fifth Symphony, he floated around the room—he *was* the music—rising higher, defying gravity. Then he remembered the recent reprimand from his bank and snapped to attention.

Damn work always interrupts. God, I hate Thanksgiving. Everyone eats turkey for a week. To add insult, the plant shuts down for a day. At least I don't have to pay the bastards. Problem is, the bank's interest clock doesn't take a vacation. Turkey… the pilgrims can kiss my ass.

Cal lowered his Guccis to his elephant hide rug. "Hop down, Winston." He slipped over to the electronics closet, settled into his chair, and queued the video of last month's Opening Day Eve. He couldn't get enough. He had memorized the conversation, but he picked up new details with each viewing.

Butler smiled while watching his own performance. As he enjoyed Roxie, he played to the cameras, flashing signs— thumbs-up, A-OK, fist pumps. Roxie was none the wiser. *I love a good tale of romance… or is it tail of romance?*

Cal scanned the ill-gotten video of the lieutenant governor and B.S. Birdsong as they each fumbled with their women. Disgusting bellies, under-endowed, quick on the trigger. *Now we're in the comedy zone.*

Then there was Sheriff Roscoe—hung like a horse and humping like a crazed buck in rut. Cal loved it. *That's hard-core. Pity the poor buxom lass arrested in this county,* he fantasized. *If she's attractive and vulnerable, I can envision him administering his own brand of justice with the help of handcuffs and condoms.*

His desk phone buzzed. He killed the video, walked over, and hit the speaker button. "Yeees, Heloise?"

"Dr. Sanjay wants to know if he can see you about some lab results."

"I'm not in the mood. Why doesn't he drop off his report as usual?"

"He says it's urgent. Didn't give me any details. Just said you need to know right away."

"Aw, shit. All right, I'll see him."

"Mr. Butler, remember the employees are having their covered dish Thanksgiving luncheon in the lunchroom. Are you going to pay a visit?"

"No thanks. I have too many teeth and not enough tattoos for *that* party. I've ordered lunch from François."

The phone buzzed again. *Why can't these people just do their jobs and quit interrupting me?* "Yeess?"

"Dr. Sanjay is here. Shall I send him in?"

"Bring me an espresso first." Pressure was building, so he popped a Percocet. *This is sure to be a pain in the ass.* He dialed his chief financial officer.

"How are we looking today?"

"Not good, Mr. Butler. Just on bank interest and payroll, I project we'll be short about ten thousand dollars this week. Since the credit line is maxed out, I don't know where the money will come from. Do I short the bank or the employees? You know the bank has told us—"

"Calm down. I'll find the money. Your job is to find us more ways to cut expenses. I want you to dump five more jobs this week through attrition. Talk to Wilbur, and you two figure out where we can cut. These lazy bastards need to pull more weight."

"But Mr. Butler, you know—"

"Don't argue with me. Just do it, dammit."

Heloise rapped on the door and entered with Dr. Sanjay, a microbiologist from India. She served the demitasse and saucer as Mr. Butler trained her then departed. Dr. Sanjay slid into the Seat of Inquisition wearing his customary white lab coat and dark-faced frown.

Dr. Sanjay's usually neat black hair stood disheveled. His presence in the U.S. was due to recruitment by a U.S. employer—one Majestic Chicken Company—that sponsored his temporary work visa. Dr. Sanjay's dream of acquiring a green card and permanent U.S. residency status relied on the good graces of one Calvin Butler Jr.

With Kilroy & Russell's immigration team behind him, Cal recruited overseas for his chief lab tech and other key positions. In Butler's eyes, acquiring the power to yank a man's visa was a brilliant business decision. *Father would certainly applaud me for that.*

"Doc, what's the problem?"

"Three of my last six salmonella tests from post-chill are reading positive. Not good, sir." The young Ph.D. spoke in his high-pitched King's English. "When the USDA begins its next round of salmonella testing, the problem will surely be revealed, and that will be big trouble for us."

"Okay, Mahatma, what would you propose?"

"Drastic intervention. We need a comprehensive approach beginning with breeding then hatching and grow-out. The worst problems are here at the plant. We need to balance equipment performance. We should introduce more chlorine and other chemicals, but we need better ventilation. In the long run, these interventions are more expensive than correcting the root problem. Frankly, we need to re-equip the entire plant. Long term, it will be much less expensive."

"Dammit." Cal slammed his palm on his desk, veins throbbing in his neck. Winston tucked tail and scurried. "You're starting to sound more like *them* every day. What you want me to do is spend a fortune to comply with their barrage of red

tape. You sound like you're trying to put me out of business, just like *them*. If I go under, guess who'll be on the next flight back to India?"

"Sir, I am simply pointing out that the latest test results are yet another deviation from the USDA written action plan to which we agreed earlier this year."

"I know what's in the damn plan—I sealed it in blood. You just keep doctoring records and let me worry about the consequences."

Cal sucked on his cigar. "Do you know what made this country great? Well, I'll tell you—free enterprise, that's what. These government pricks are always doing their best to kill our great system—the system that produces their very paychecks. They just don't get it, so don't fall for every line of bullshit those parasites come up with. We both know a certain amount of salmonella and e-coli is inevitable in this business. Everybody knows that but do you think these bureaucrats in white coats accept that? Nooo…"

"Mr. Butler, I understand your feelings. I want you to stay in business, too. You say if we address the problem, we go out of business. I say if we don't address the problem, they shut us down. Either way, I will soon be on a flight back to India. Our future does not look bright."

"Listen, Doc, enough with your doomsday scenarios. I appreciate your input, but I'm calling the shots around here, and that's how it's going to work. I didn't bring you here from India to cause trouble. Cooperate with me, do things my way, and you are on your way to that green card. Do you follow me?"

Dr. Sanjay took a deep breath. "Yes, I follow you."

"Good. I'm not saying I won't modernize someday. The immediate problem is this—Wimpy told me today he has been ordered to start another fifty-one day series of salmonella testing on Monday. We can't afford to go through another cluster-fuck like the one this summer. That was a nightmare. We've got to find a better way for him to make test selections. We've *got* to find a way."

Butler stoked his cigar and stroked his chin. *Looks like now is the time.*

"Hey, Doc. The *random* nature of the testing is where the problem lies. I think I can remedy that. Here's what I want you to do. You test and find me salmonella-free product. Instead of Wimpy traipsing through the plant picking product at random to send for testing, we'll simply have him come to you every day for a clean sample. That should put an end to this bullshit."

"But sir, how are you going to get Mr. Wimpy to accept test samples from me and not randomly from the plant?"

"You let me worry about that. When Wimpy comes in to-morrow, I'll try to convince him to work with us. You just find some clean product. Keep looking and testing—there's got to be some in this damn plant somewhere. How quickly can we now test for salmonella?"

"Well, as you know, with traditional microbiological cul-ture, detection usually takes four-to-six days. Now, rapid test-ing protocols have been developed which rely on a single, en-hanced enrichment followed by an immunomagnetic capture that removes the need for selective enrichment relying on agar plates—"

"*Whoa, whoa*, Gandhi. Spare me the details. How long to run a test?"

"Twenty-four hours… if we have the proper tools."

"Then get the proper tools, *post haste.*"

Alone again, Cal hurried to his technology closet to check on his people. The run light mercifully glowed green. Big Boss pe-rused the screens, observing rapid movement on the loading dock, killing chamber, scalding vats, evisceration—right on down the line. Chickens, chickens, chickens. He loved chick-ens... but not to eat.

He loved chickens for the cha-ching each one placed in his pocket. When he took over the company after his father's death, he viewed each chicken as a dime in his pocket—over three-quarters of a million dollars a year. *Now my own damn bank has whittled me down to less than one lousy penny per chicken and has cut my perks to almost nothing. They're even threatening to yank Honeysuckle Plantation off the company tit... schmucks.*

Chapter 55

Streetlights shone through Bean and Ruby's bedroom blinds, and their popcorn ceiling sparkled like a blue Milky Way. Their mountainous silhouettes resembled beached whales, breathing in heavy cadence. Moisture glistened on Bean's face, and his lidded eyeballs twitched. Somewhere deep in his brain, things raced…

> *Thousands of chickens closing in—sick chickens with red wattles and combs bubbling with sal-vanilla blisters. Spindly legs snapped and dangling, they drag themselves closer. Like The Ole Man, each has an eye patch and pulls a miniature oxygen tank, tubes running into nostrils.*
>
> *They surround him. The circle tightens. I'm ready. Goggles, coat, gloves are on. Disassembly line shackles rattle behind him, longing for product. Here they come. Grab, flip, hang—agarre, volcarse, colgar. Pronto! Pronto! They keep coming. Too many, too fast. Peckin' my ankles, up my legs. Ouch, my chest, climbin' over each other to get at my eyes! Not my eyes! They got my throat and are flippin' me. Oh no! I'm upside down, ankles headin' for the shackles…*

"Bean, turn over." Ruby poked him. "You dreamin'. You sweatin' so bad the sheets is wet."

"Listen to my dream, you ain't gonna hardly believe," Bean said as he tore into a bag of cashews and Travis Tritt tore into his guitar on Bean's truck radio. PJ sipped coffee as each sat with door propped open, foot on running board, watching fellow workers shuffle by. "Sick chickens was closin' in, and there weren't nuthin' I could do. They picked me up, and I was headin' for the shackles. Ruby woke me up just in time. It's gettin' outta hand when I have nightmares 'bout this shit."

PJ lit a cigarette and flipped the match onto the asphalt. "Ain't never seen morale so low. Look at 'em walkin' by in a daze. Look like aliens marchin' to a death chamber."

"Rats outside the buildin' is big as possums, I been thinkin'." Bean lit his cig. "Been thinkin' 'bout talkin' to Wilbur 'bout a hunt. You and me could come out on a weekend with our four-tens and have a good shoot. But, then… I don't know, Wilbur would prob'ly make us pick up the dead ones. I'd just as soon the buzzards and ants took care of 'em."

PJ shook his head. "Nawsir, I ain't gonna try to help Butler. He don't give a damn about us or this plant. If we help him, we're just enablin' him. Nawsir, granpa once told me, 'the more you stir a bucket o' shit, the more it stinks.'"

Joker's truck roared into the lot then puttered up. He cruised past Bean's truck and angled for a spot close by. Joker shot a bird and they returned fire.

"Listen," Bean said, "before Joker gets here, I heard some interestin' scoop from my secret inside source."

"Yeah?" PJ's cigarette bounced in his lips as he squinted his eyes and poured more coffee. "What'd Heloise tell ya?"

"Butler holds the mortgage on Wilbur's house. And get this… Butler's lawyer put a clause in sayin' if Wilbur ever gets fired, the whole mortgage comes due. That right there may say a lot 'bout what's goin' on 'round this place."

"Obviously sump'n funny's goin' on—all them gub'mint inspectors seein' them dead chickens and rotten chickens and filth and stink, yet nuthin' ever happens. It don't add up. Sump'n ain't right."

"Here comes Joker," Bean whispered. "I'm sure he'll set us straight."

Joker walked to Bean's truck, covered a nostril, and blew a snot rocket. "Hey, hey. Chicken Workers of the World handshake. Mornin', boys. How's it hangin'?"

PJ spewed smoke. "Bean's havin' nightmares 'bout this place."

"Shiiit," Joker said, "it's an open secret around town that things are pretty ugly inside the plant. We in a mell of a hess, boys. What we gonna do about it, that's the question."

"I'll tell ya." Bean reached for his latest novelty purchase from Git-N-Split. He stretched and forced the yellow, rubber "WWJD" bracelet across his hand and onto his wrist. He held it up. "The question is, 'What would Hay-suess do?'"

"Cute," PJ said. "You'll see him in a minute, you ask him."

Bean cocked his head and rocketed a liquid scud onto the asphalt. "The rats and pigeons and cockroaches is takin' over. I think a large rat is signin' our paychecks."

"We're all nucking futs," Joker said, "and ridin' a runaway train to hell. Now gentlemen, I have to hurry along. To change the subject, can either of you show some love and spot me a fiver or tenner until payday?"

Bean chuckled. "What's the problem-o, Joker? Got barrel-fever? Monkey on your back talkin' in yo' ear?"

"Kiss my ass, Bean. I just got caught short on rent."

Bean whipped out a bill and handed it to him. "Take this dollar and invest in Mega-Millions tonight. Turn one dollar into twenty million," he snapped his fingers, "just like that."

PJ mumbled expletives and pulled a tenner from his wallet then unfolded a paper containing a list of numbers. He added "10" at the bottom and updated the cumulative. "Joker, this puts you up to fifty-one dollars. I cain't afford to go no higher." He handed Joker the list to initial before handing him the bill.

"Thank you, gentlemen. Now if you'll excuse me, I've got to go chuck a turd." Joker hustled away.

Bean snickered. "Told ya he'd straighten us out."

At lunchtime in the parking lot, Bean couldn't find enough time between mouthfuls of burrito to make his points to PJ. "When people quit, they ain't replacin' 'em all, have you noticed? They pushin' more chickens through the line… Doin' it with less people… Cain't hardly keep up… Couldn't survive without Hay-se-uss… Nuthin' is ever cleaned up anymore… Them inspectors must be blind… I agree with Joker… We in a mell of a hess."

Back in the plant, Bean and Jesús drove their forklifts hard, flying around corners like they were driving the Daytona Speedway. Wilbur appeared, waved Bean over, and stepped up for a ride.

"We need to go to the front of the line."

"Whut's goin' on?"

"We got some bad chicken we need to take to the dock. Inspectors told us to burn it."

Three pallets of chicken awaited, wrapped with neon yellow "CONDEMNED-USDA" tape. Bean's head snapped back. "Man, this stinks sump'n awful."

He hauled each to the loading dock, and a USDA inspector observed as Bean fork-lifted the pallets into the company truck.

At shift's end, as line workers were peeling off their aprons, caps, and gloves, Wilbur hollered for Bean. *Awe, shit. Here we go.* Wilbur hurried over, his comb-over a tousled mess. He propped himself on Bean's forklift, chest heaving.

"Bean, you gotta work some overtime."

"You pay me time-and-a-half, I will."

"Dammit, Bean. We've been down this road a hun-ert times. I ain't got time to play around. Now, get this lift over to the loadin' dock."

"How you know I ain't got sump'n important to do this afternoon?"

"Shut up, Bean. This ain't gonna take long. I'll hop on and ride with you."

"Dammit. You know it ain't right to work a man overtime at reg'lar pay. Hey, if we're goin' to the loadin' dock, don't we need to pick up some product first?"

"No. Just shut the hell up and drive. Don't ask no questions, and do what I tell ya."

They wheeled to the loading dock. Wilbur hopped off and raised one of the bay doors. A truck beeped in reverse, the same truck into which Bean loaded the condemned chicken earlier that day. It stopped, and Wilbur raised the truck's cargo door. Rotten chicken stench slammed them. Bean saw the same three pallets he'd loaded earlier, but now the "CONDEMNED" tape was missing.

"All right," Wilbur instructed, "get them pallets to the nugget line, *pronto.*"

Bean's brows shot up. "Them's the same three I loaded that were s'posed to be burned."

"No, they ain't. These ain't the same ones. Just do it and shut up, for Chrissakes."

"Wilbur, wha'chu doin'? You know this ain't right. Damned if I'm goin' to jail for you and Butler."

"You ain't goin' to no jail. All you need to know is that I told ya these weren't the same pallets. So quit yakkin' and askin' questions. If we don't get this done, we'll both get fired. And you need to stay 'til them pallets are processed so you can put 'em in the freezer."

Bean did as told, cursing under his breath. Fellow overtime workers awaited his arrival at the nugget line. Shaking his head, he dropped the pallets and motored back to his workstation.

"HEY." Wilbur's baggy shirt swayed as he approached. He caught his breath before speaking. "Listen, if you tell anybody 'bout this, I may just have to forget our little conversation earlier 'bout you not goin' to jail. You got dat?"

"Whut?"

"You heard me. Before you tell anybody 'bout this, remember that you just as guilty as me and Mr. Butler."

"I did whut you told me."

"You knew them were the same three pallets just as good as I knew it."

"Wilbur, you done turned into a snake, jest like Butler."

Wilbur shoved him with both hands. Bean stumbled backward and balled his fists, knowing he could take him out with ease. *Is this my time?*

"Get the wax outta your ears, boy." Wilbur stared Bean down with a wild look. "I said shut the hell up. I got plenty o' worries and don't need no lip from you. I'm tired o' your shit. Remember what I said. That little girl o' yours ain't never gonna get her foot fixed with you sittin' in jail, now is she?"

Chapter 56

"Hop down, Winston." Cal edged forward in his chair as Winston's claws clicked across the slate floor. Butler rolled his Cuban cigar between the fingers of one hand while the other worked the mouse. He browsed fresh video postings and clicked on "A Virgin's Tail." Heat flushed his loins as he watched a young lady satisfy two studs. *Virgin my ass.*

He then clicked "Naughty Housewife" and grinned as a shapely "housewife" in a skimpy nightgown greeted the TV repairman. Her nightgown *accidentally* fell open as she showed him the equipment, and the two were off to the races.

I wonder what the hell my wife is doing right now. He checked her car's GPS location. *Still at home. I've got to hide some cameras there. I don't care if she catches me. I've got to know who she's screwing.*

Cal pushed away from his computer, popped a Percocet, leaned back, and contemplated the coming day. Feeling the gravity of angst in his chest, he closed his eyes and concentrated on Bach's music, waiting to soar with eagles. His phone buzzed. *For God's sake.*

"Whaaat?"

"Wimpy is in the lobby. Shall I send him in?"

"Not yet. Give me a minute." He soared a bit longer then walked to his restroom to splash cold water on his face. *All the money I've paid to that dumb bastard… it's payback time.* He buzzed Heloise. "Okay, send him in."

Rotund Clyde "Wimpy" Pepper shuffled through the door, his shoulders drooping under a wrinkled khaki jacket. He tugged at his necktie and slumped into the Seat of Inquisition.

"Good day, Mr. Butler. I hope yours is going better than mine." His Adolph Hitler mustache danced as he spoke.

"Clyde, whatever is the problem?"

"My bursitis is flaring up, and home in bed is where I belong. But, alas, duty calls your faithful government servant. Unfortunately, I have used all my sick days and vacation days."

"I'm so sorry. Perhaps the pastries awaiting you in the lab will help ease your woes."

"You are so thoughtful and such a dear man. As you know, I have been ordered to start the dreaded random salmonella testing on Monday. It's such a wretched thing, to box up those samples and send them in every day."

Cal knew Majestic Chicken's very survival was at stake in this discussion.

"Ah, I wanted to talk with you about that." Cal winked at the inspector and leaned forward in his chair. Neck veins bulged as he spoke. "I want to make your life easier. Instead of your having to leave the lab and wander among all those disgusting chicken carcasses, why don't we just let Dr. Sanjay provide you with samples? Make it easy on yourself."

Wimpy's comtemplative face creased into a frown. "Sir, the thought is tempting. Don't think I haven't considered that before, but this directive is a rather serious one. True, I have been slightly bending the rules with my careless math 'mistakes' on the daily tally sheets. But this testing protocol for salmonella is a different animal."

"Look. I'm not asking you to assassinate the Pope, for Chrissakes." Butler stared him down. "Let us provide you the samples, and both of our lives will be easier. Look at the big picture. You and I know that you can find salmonella in ninety-five percent of the kitchens in this country. As a threat to human safety, salmonella is grossly overrated. We pamper the human body's immune system too much. It's like a muscle—the more you exercise it, the stronger it gets which translates into a healthier population."

"Mr. Butler, while I deeply appreciate your generosity in our arrangement with the tally sheets, and all other things, monkeying with the salmonella testing could lead to dire consequences for the unsuspecting public who rely on at least some degree of integrity in the USDA."

Cal's blood simmered. *Why must things be so complicated? The bank has me so tied up that I can't borrow to re-equip the plant. Hell, at this point, I can't even afford to clean it!*

"Okay." Cal leaned back in his chair and twirled his fountain pen. "I understand the game, pal. I'm paying you a hundred dollars a day for your tally sheet calculations. Here's a new deal—I'll pay you an extra hundred a day during this fifty-one-day process. You said you wanted to be an entrepreneur. Now is your chance. That's an extra five thousand, one hundred in tax-free cash. Plus, it relieves you of the burden of leaving the lab's comforts. A classic win-win. What do you say?"

Wimpy crossed his arms and knitted his brows. A pained expression clouded his face. He closed his eyes and bowed his head. The wall clock ticked as the silence stretched. Cal stared at the inspector's greasy, thinning hair and his twitching mustache. *This is a game of high stakes chicken.*

Wimpy finally looked up and shook his head. "Mr. Butler, it is with great sorrow that I inform you I simply cannot go that far. I have weighed the benefits—very generous and much needed—against the risks. I'm afraid if we did this and our actions in this regard ever came to light, I would be reduced to eating jailhouse slop for a long time."

Butler clinched his jaw, bolted upright in his chair, and slammed his fist on his desk. "Goddammit, I've had it with you government bastards, and I've had it with your sorry ass. Don't you dare come in here looking for your usual handout and tell me 'no.' I'll have your fat ass sleeping in the federal pen tonight."

Wimpy's eyes flared, his face flushed, and his jaw dropped. Cal had always treated him with kindness.

"Don't look so surprised." Butler's laser stare morphed into an evil grin. "We're just taking care of business right now, you and me. That's what we do, isn't it? Let me show you something, big boy, which may change your mind regarding my little proposal."

The chairman rotated his laptop so Wimpy could view the screen. He clicked a file and queued up a real-time aerial image of the two men. The Sun King's gilded face and flowing locks dazzled on Butler's desk. Cal waved to the camera.

Wimpy stared at Mr. Butler in confusion. Cal pointed to the "smoke detector" suspended from a ceiling beam. "Wave to the camera."

Inspector Pepper looked up at the smoke detector and squirmed as incredulity etched furrows across his pudgy face. He focused on the laptop, held out his hand, and watched in real time as he wiggled his fingers.

Cal advanced to a video folder and started the extravaganza. There was Butler, sliding a hundred-dollar bill across his desk and Wimpy grabbing it and slipping it into his trouser pocket. Clear image, crisp voices, date and time displayed—slick as any CIA production. Cal advanced to the next video and a similar transaction. Over and over, hundred-dollar bill after hundred-dollar bill.

Cal grinned as he watched Wimpy slump and melt into the Seat of inquisition. "Let me know when you've seen enough, Pepper."

"I have seen enough." Wimpy spoke in a clipped cadence, his throat now dry. "Apparently, I have punched a tar baby. Your new procedure may actually be an acceptable testing method after all. May God save us."

Butler opened his top drawer, pulled out two crisp hundred-dollar bills and slid them across the desk.

Chapter 51

*B*ean rolled into the Git-N-Split parking lot on his way home. Three beers and hot boiled peanuts is what he needed. A new Indian girl worked the counter with a green silk dupatta draped around her head and a red bindi dot painted mid-forehead above her wide, dark eyes. So distraught over rotten chicken, Bean didn't notice the new girl and even failed to buy a lottery ticket.

He eased his truck across the parking lot, killed the engine, and took a respite from the crazy world. He could think in his truck. He got lost in the scenery across the highway while slurping boiled peanuts and tossing the hulls out the window.

Cows milled about in a verdant pasture beyond the fence. In the middle, a lone live oak stood dense and green with a broad crown and wide-reaching branches. Longleaf pines and hardwoods towered in the background.

What to do, what to do? What would Hay-suess do if he could speak English? He gnawed his fingernails, and his mind raced, replaying the dirty trick Wilbur pulled on him. *I'm such a sucker and a loser.* He thought about his options. His anger raged, and he punched the truck's dashboard until his knuckles bled.

What he wanted most was to go to Butler's house, coax him into the front yard, and whip his ass. And Wilbur's, too. Both would be easy, but reason prevailed. *Prob'ly get locked up.* The answer came to him during his third beer—*talk to Ruby.*

Bean kicked up dirt devils racing down the Garden of Eden's thoroughfare before pulling into his spot. He noticed The Ole

Man lollygagging outside, lunging one step with his walker then reaching back to roll his oxygen tank like an inchworm's rear feet.

I ain't got time for that geezer now.

Junior appeared with football in hand. "Diddy, Diddy, kin we throw the football 'fore it gets dark?"

"Sorry, Son, not now. Daddy's got some real important bidness. Where's Mama?"

"She's in the beauty parlor. Her last patron just left."

Bean performed his ritual of stripping to his skivvies at the door and leaving the noxious clothes in a pile on the landing. Instead of heading straight to the shower, he slipped on some shorts, stomped barefooted through the kitchen and barged into the Flying Cloud with Junior on his heels.

Barefooted Ruby reclined in her styling chair with Li'l Bit in her lap while Tootsie swept. They gawked as Bean ducked and entered, camo-capped and shirtless. A rectangular blob of belly hung over his beltline. Tootsie turned her head like she'd seen something X-rated.

"Ruby, we need a pow-wow."

"Well hello to you too, Punkin'." She pinched her nostrils and spoke like a robot. "P-U. Darlin', you need to shower 'fore we talk."

Li'l Bit held her arms out. Bean scooped her up, kissed then cradled her.

"Honey, this cain't wait. I got important bidness."

"Lawd, we gonna have to talk outside or else I'll have to spend a fortune on aromatics."

"Fine, let's go."

"Okay. You look serious. Did you get fired today?"

"No, I ain't got fired." He cut his eyes toward Tootsie then tilted his head toward the door. "Come on, Ruby—outside."

"Okay, okay." Ruby struggled to stand, plopped Li'l Bit in her pen, brushed her pink muumuu and guided her feet into her slippers. "Tootsie, when you finish sweepin', go on home, and I'll see you in the mornin'. Junior, you look after Baby and no trouble, you hear? We'll eat after while. You kin have fruit cocktail 'til then."

Ruby headed for the exit. "Come on, Bean. Lawd, hep us all. What on earth did ya do this time?"

He stepped back to the refrigerator, snagged a Bud, and followed Ruby outside. They plopped down on NASCAR Central's bench seat. The Ole Man's head peeked above his windowsill.

Bean shook his fist, and *poof*, The Ole Man was gone.

Elvis ventured to the end of his chain and barked. Bean raised his finger. "Calm down. Sit." Elvis squatted and observed.

He pinched some Red Man, crammed it home, and turned his cap backwards. He leaned forward and rested his forehead in his palms. "Ruby, a bad thing happened today. Wilbur calls me to pick up three pallets o' chicken condemned by the inspectors. They was all wrapped with yellow tape. I tote 'em to a truck at the dock so they could be took off and burnt. So far, so good, right? Just another day at Majestic."

The sun was sinking behind the Garden of Eden tree line. He lit a cigarette and smashed a mosquito. "After the shift, Wilbur wants me to work overtime. Lo and behold, them same three pallets is on the truck at the dock, but the 'CONDEMNED' tape is missin'. 'Course, the inspectors is all gone home by now. Wilbur tells me to take 'em to the nugget line, and there, wouldn't ya know, the amigos and señoritas is waitin' to process that rotten chicken. It's the same thing that's happened before, and I swore I weren't gonna do it again."

Ruby's eyebrows knitted. "Why didn't you tell Wilbur you wasn't gonna do it?"

"I did. I told him it weren't right, and he said I'd be fired on the spot if I didn't do it. I got almost ten years seniority ridin' here, health insurance, everything. You keep remindin' me o' that, remember? Wilbur lied and said it weren't the same chickens and that could be my excuse. So, I deliver the bad chicken and the Mexicans' is grindin' it up then, get this, Wilbur comes back to my station. Says I'd go to jail if I said anything. Said he'd swear I was in on it. You believe that crap?"

"Lawd, hep us!" Ruby's jaw dropped, and she covered her mouth. "I just remembered. Today, a patron told me two people died over in Valdosta from sal-vanilla. Rumor is, *could* be bad chicken. She wondered 'bout Majestic Chicken. Course, I didn't say nuthin', but it ain't no secret that the place has done got nasty."

Bean laughed, guzzled some beer, and massaged his dangling gut. "Joker calls it a 'open secret.' You get it? How could it be a secret if it's open? That fella' comes up with the stupidest stuff."

"Forget Joker for now, please. Wha'chu gonna do?"

"I don't know." Bean drew on his cig and grimaced. "I could call the gub'mint somehow, in secret, and report it. But then whut? Put us all outta bidness. Remember what Butler said—rat on him, shut him down, and what does that do for my work buddies? Folks at Majestic Chicken is my second family—"

"Sometimes I think they is yo' first family."

"—and I have to think 'bout the consequences."

"*Consequences?* I ain't never heard you use that word before. Tell me this, what are the consequences if mo' people die and it turns out to be your plant and you knew 'bout it?"

"I guess I could get in trouble if I *don't* say nuthin', but Wilbur says if I *do* say sump'n, he'll claim I was in on it. Since I'm in on it, he said I'd go to jail. Speak up or not, either way, I go to jail. I might better go hide in the woods 'til this thing blows over. Maybe go live with my sister in Miss'ippi."

Ruby rocked the seat back then rolled forward onto her knees. With a push-off from Bean's foot, she stumbled forward, turned and confronted him. "Look at me."

Fire lit her eyes, fire usually reserved for Junior.

"Listen to me." Hands on hips, head rocking in rhythm with her words, pink muumuu swaying. "People... could... die. Think 'bout them consequences. Innocent people."

"But I don't partickly want to go to jail. I hear Sheriff Roscoe is in Butler's pocket. Some o' the boys at Fat Back is related to him, and they faces get red every time Roscoe's name comes up."

"Okay, for a minute forget the people who gonna die. If jail is yo' biggest concern, think 'bout this. Since you know 'bout it—and you do 'cause ya just told me—are ya mo' likely to go to jail if ya say sump'n or if ya say nuthin'? Why they gonna throw you in jail for speakin' up to stop it?"

Bean turned his head, launched a rocket into the dirt, and shook his head. "They shut us down, everybody at that plant will lose they job, me included, and I gotta live with that every day o' my life."

"Butterbean Sweat! We Christian people. They comes a time when you got to stand up and be a man and do the right thing. Are you a chicken or a rooster?"

Bean rubbed his temple. "Since you was up, get your man a Bud and let me think."

"You pray on it 'til I get back. And quit bitin' your fingernails." Ruby lumbered up the steps and opened the door. "Junior," she boomed, "put that ice cream back 'fore I..."

Bean rocked in the seat, eyes closed, stroking his week-old stubble. He was at a crossroads the likes of which he'd never faced. He removed his cap and massaged his burr head, forced to think harder than he preferred. Time flew by—or did it stand still?

"Here's yo' beer." Ruby startled him. "Did you pray on it?"

He popped the top, swilled, and stared at her. "I would o' prayed, but I didn't know who to pray to. If there is a God, he ain't nice. We could have avoided an operation on Baby's foot if we'd started her treatments earlier. But no, we couldn't afford it, and now it's too late. The doctor says she's gonna have to have an operation and that's *if* we can raise the money. Why would I pray to a God who would do somethin' like that to us?"

"God didn't do that to our baby. We did. You talk 'bout *consequences*. Li'l Bit's clubfoot was caused by you and me."

Bean choked on his beer. "*Me? Me?* What did I do?"

"You heard that nurse say it was 'cause a my bad eatin'." Ruby's voice cracked. He nodded. "Did you forget she said second-hand smoke can do it, too?"

Bean inhaled and pointed his finger, ready to protest. He held his tongue, shook his head, and pulverized his cigarette in the dirt.

Mascara tears streamed down Ruby's cheeks. She lowered her head, sniffled, and raised her chin. "God done forgive us both 'cause I prayed hard for that, and that's how He works." She dabbed her eyes and blew her nose. "He can turn things around for us. Li'l Bit could be president of a company one day, or… it's like Isaiah says, it's one o' them things we cain't see but we got to be certain of. You got to have faith and don't never give up."

"You always come up with some Bible this or that to 'splain everything."

"You got to trust Him. He's got a reason for everythin'. Don't you talk bad 'bout God. It's blasphemy."

"Then tell me this—if God created Heaven and earth, what was goin' on before that? Where did God live before he created Heaven?" Bean took a long swig of beer. "Who created God? I wanna meet that guy."

Silence prevailed as Ruby stared down on him, grinding her teeth and shaking her head. "You is hard-headed. Okay, Mr. Smarty Britches, we gonna go meet with Preacher Bobby and you can ask him them questions. He'll know. I'm gonna call him in the mornin' and make an appointment."

"Call him if you want, but I ain't meetin'. He don't know any more than I know. Face it, Ruby, nobody really knows."

Ruby's face flushed and her fists balled up. "You listen to me, Butterbean Sweat." She pointed to Heaven. "When Judgment Day comes, you better be on His side. If you ever talk to our young'uns like that, I suwannee, you better pack your bags and find another place to sleep."

"Don't get your panties in a wad, Baby. That ain't helpin' my situation none."

"Then wha'chu gonna do?"

"I ain't got no choice." He fired up another cig and spewed smoke, letting her chew on his words. "I got to somehow tell the gub'mint."

Ruby smiled. "Punkin', sometimes you is stupid, and sometimes you is *so* smart. I'm proud o' you. I think you made the right decision."

"Damn thing is, them bad chickens is sittin' in my freezer at work right now. I know they'll ship 'em first thing tomorrow to get rid o' the evidence. So I guess it's now or never."

"Who you gonna call?" She didn't wait on his answer. "I got a good lawyer in mind on one o' them 'frigerator magnets."

"I ain't callin' no lawyer on no 'frigerator magnet. He'd get me tangled up in it, and my name would leak out. Next thing you know, he'd say we owe him a bunch o' money."

He toed out his cig and cracked his knuckles. "Nawsir. I need to call Cuz. He works for the gub'mint, and they the ones that need to know. I'll tell him we ain't payin' no money and my name stays secret."

"Then call your cousin, the traffic court judge, and we'll put it in God's hands…"

> *This is how it went down, how it came to pass.*
> *Bean got up his guts, grew some chestnuts.*
> *Called his Cuz, caught him at supper.*
> *Told the sal-vanilla tale…I don't want no jail.*
>
> *No, I won't charge, Cuz reassured.*
> *Your name may be used, please understand.*
> *For if they take this matter seriously,*
> *they'll want it first hand.*

But I'll make sure, Cuz promised,
best I can, they protect the identity of their man.
Cuz said good-bye, said he'd get back.
Ruby comforted Bean, you done the right thing.

Three hours later, inside the Sweat trailer,
sat the USDA and FBI, old Cuz by Bean's side.
The whole sordid tale was told again.
Damn! No wonder people died.

The chicken is ready to ship, Bean warned.
Row three of the freezer, number six pod, so help me God.
The paperwork, Bean cautioned, won't match the facts.
They'll make it look hunky-dor-ee, I gar-ron-tee.

Anything else, Mr. Sweat?
No, I done said a ton.
We'll take it from here.
We'll be there before the sun.

Cuz and the G-men left. Bean drank Bud until there was no more. Exhausted beyond measure, Ruby's hero crashed into bed in his clothes and slept stone cold until thousands of headless, feetless carcasses came to life...

Naked, gutted Majestic chickens. Bloated by steroids. Sal-vanilla blisters bubbling neon green. The mutant freaks flap out of their disassembly line shackles and chase him. Why me, for God sakes? Chase Butler. They corner him and close in, spewing blobs of sal-vanilla...

"Roll over." Ruby pushed and pulled. "You twitchin' like bacon in a fryin' pan."

Chapter 58

Bean eased into Git-N-Split before sunrise. Butterflies fluttered over Ruby's sausage biscuits in his stomach. He had to get to the plant to see what was happening but couldn't be too early. Might look suspicious.

"Mornin', Paw-tell. Couple o' Marlboro one hundreds in the box, *compadre*."

"Good morning to you, guv'nor. Two boxes. No need to say brand, you are Marlboro man. Veddy good. How many lottery?"

Bean pouted. "I ain't playin' this mornin'. I'm kinda in a hurry."

"No lottery? You must be veddy sick today, my friend. Hey, we need more worms. Got plenty night crawlers. Need red wigglers."

"Yeah, okay, I'll bring 'em," Bean mumbled as he strolled out, tamping a cig box against his palm.

He monitored his watch while driving to the plant, kneading the butt of one burning cig after another between his lips. He drove slower than he ever had. Co-workers passed him, something he'd normally never allow.

His Chevy joined the queue on Majestic Road, his heart in his throat as he eyed the plant. He spotted black GM Suburbans with black tinted windows. *Oh, shit! Sump'n big's goin' down.* A man wearing an FBI cap and holstered pistol guarded the front entrance. Another guarded the delivery dock. Bean rounded the curve skirting the employee lot and gawked at his co-workers huddled outside the plant entrance, backs facing him.

He pulled into his parking space, hopped out, trotted toward the crowd, and spotted PJ and Joker. PJ waved, and Bean weaved his way through the dumbfounded throng. Latino and Oriental chatter filled the air.

"Come on, you missin' it. Where you been?" PJ chided as he grabbed Bean's shoulder. "This ain't good. Inspectors and the FBI are crawlin' all over the place. They won't let us in. An FBI guy walked out a minute ago and said the plant is closed 'til further notice."

Bean flushed. A plant closing was what he feared most. *Act natural.* He watched in horror. Neon yellow tape cordoned off all doors and loading docks. Delivery parking was crammed with eighteen-wheelers full of clucking cargo. Truckers paced and threw their hands into the air.

Men in blue sweatshirts guarded each entrance, "FBI" emblazoned in yellow across their chests and backs. Guns and cuffs dangled from their shiny black belts.

"Come on." PJ motioned to Bean and Joker. "Let's walk around and check the rear loadin' dock."

"I'll tell ya what's goin' down," Joker announced as the three amigos set out. "Majestic Chicken is goin' down, that's what, and like a sack o' shit. And I can promise ya something else—If I don't get paid today, I'm gonna put a pop knot on Butler's head big enough to hitch a trailer to."

"Look." PJ pointed at Butler's office. "They got that building shut down, too. That's where they print our checks. By the looks of it, I wouldn't count on a check today. Or ever again."

Ever again! A vice gripped Bean's heart. *What have I done?*

They turned the corner. Black Suburbans surrounded the loading dock, and USDA Ford Tauruses flanked its side. Agents scurried, loading plastic bins into the back of the SUVs. The three *gringos* watched until agents closed and padlocked the bays and wrapped the area with crime scene tape like kids rolling a house on Halloween.

The *gringos* shuffled back to the mob. All eyes studied the front entrance. G-men appeared, and crowd chatter subsided to whispers. Bean's mind swooned. *What about our paychecks? Are we ever gonna work again? What about Butler's revenge?*

Commotion erupted at the front entrance. An agent walked out gripping Wilbur's arm, the same agent who'd visited Bean's home last night. Murmurs rustled through the crowd. Wilbur limped along with shoulders slumped, head bowed, and hands cuffed. They tucked him into a Suburban.

Two more agents emerged, each holding a defiant arm of DNR corporal Mutt Hightower as they ushered him into another Suburban. "Lookie there," PJ pointed, "they bloodied his nose."

Workers gasped as two agents emerged, each gripping a handcuffed arm of the cussing Calvin Butler Jr. The agents pushed him toward an SUV. Murmurs and chatter escalated among the local chapter of the Chicken Workers of the World. Butler jerked away from his captors, turned to the crowd, and yelled, "FUCK YOU, SCUMBAGS!" Agents restrained him.

One worker started clapping, and viral applause spread through the crowd. Butler lifted his cuffed hands skyward and shot two birds. An agent folded him into the back seat of another Suburban, slammed the door, and flipped *him* the bird.

The Suburban convoy drove away in single file with the Tauruses bringing up the rear. Two agents stayed behind to guard the plant, now eerily quiet. Workers mumbled and looked at one another in bewilderment.

"Come on," PJ said, "let's go talk to them FBI guys to see what's goin' on." Bean stumbled along, quiet for a change, in his own secret world of misgiving and disbelief. PJ spoke in hushed tones with an agent. The *gringos* walked back to the eager throng, which engulfed them.

"We need an interpreter," PJ announced. *"Habla Inglés?"*

"Sí." Rio, the lung gunner, squeezed through the mob. PJ spoke a few sentences and Rio echoed in Spanish...

"The plant is closed for today...

"He does not know if or when it will re-open...

"He does not know if or when we will get paid...

"That's all he knows. He says we should all go home."

Confused and angry workers cursed in various languages. Bean and his displaced comrades gradually piled back into their vehicles and drove away.

Bean tried to drown his woes that night in a river of Bud. "What if they find out I blew the whistle?" he asked Ruby repeatedly, each repetition delivered with a bit more slur. "How we gonna live without no paycheck? Without no health insurance? What I done to all my people? I knowed I should o' just kept my mouth shut."

He lingered at the dinette table and waited for his fleeting moment. When the coast was clear, he stepped to the kitchen, reached to the back of the highest cabinet, and grabbed his pint of Jim Beam bourbon.

After taking a good slug, he quickly returned the bottle. The bourbon burned from gullet to gut before it kicked in.

He fell into bed drunk and sobbing. Ruby peeled off his boots. "This here..." he mumbled. "This here is the worst day o' my whole damn life."

Chapter 59

The rising sun streamed through slits in the blinds onto the half-moon crack of Bean's butt. Budweiser hung heavy in the air. He stirred and called for Ruby.

"Baby, I'm so thirsty, I'm fartin' dust. Bring me some water, and see if I got any Bud left in the icebox."

"You ain't gonna drink today. Gettin' so drunk you fall in bed with your boots on ain't helpin' our cause none. You settin' a horrible example for our young'uns." Shuffling in sweat pants and tank top, Ruby fetched water and aspirin. He peed, drank, and buried his head under the pillow for more slumber.

Ruby scooped up Li'l Bit at lunchtime, barged into the bedroom, and plopped her onto the bed. She came to life and crawled on him like a puppy. Hugs and kisses. Bean started their favorite game. *Pat-a-cake, pat-a-cake, baker's man...* "Baby Girl, Daddy loves you more'n huntin'and fishin' put together."

He sat on the edge of the bed, queasy at first then knocked back Ruby's Alka-Seltzer milkshake.

"You hongry, Punkin'? I made my hero somethin' special."

"Hongry? Is a pig's ass pork? Let's eat!"

They claimed their seats around the red Formica-topped dinette table. Bean, Ruby, and Junior shoveled it in like competitors at a Coney Island hotdog contest—fried catfish, collards, cat-head biscuits with red-eye gravy, and sweet ice tea. Li'l Bit pinched biscuit pieces and shared with Slippers. Apple pie warmed in the oven and filled the trailer with heavenly scents of buttered cinnamon. Vanilla ice cream stood on à la mode alert.

Bean finally pushed back and belched. "I'm pot full." He hobbled to the couch where he crash-landed for a nap. Junior carried Li'l Bit out to play while Ruby cleaned the kitchen.

"Ruby, they gonna find out it was me. I just know it. Then what's gonna happen? Them workers gonna string me up unless Butler's DNR thug gets me first. We may *all* have to move to Miss'ippi and stay with my sister."

"You done right, Punkin', and we ain't gonna run. We just need to pray on it real hard, and He will show us the way."

"Pray? You prayed the other day and look where that got us. The plant is closed, and everybody's out of a job, includin' me..."

He moaned then dozed, and Ruby tiptoed in her tube socks to the Flying Cloud. He awoke and tuned-in with one eye to watch the preview of tomorrow's NASCAR race then floated in and out, trying to keep his hung-over head as still as possible. His mind churned as he snoozed...

Lounging in his Chevy at work, scarfing beef jerky and scratching a lottery ticket... mob noise! Plant workers form a ring around his truck, closing in and wielding clubs, chains, and evisceration knives. Camo-clad PJ leads the way with his 12-gauge at the ready...

"Bean, Bean." Ruby shook his shoulder with telephone in hand. "Wake up. PJ's on the phone."

He awoke but couldn't sit. Ruby handed him the receiver. "Whut up? No, they ain't called yet... Does a one-legged duck swim in a circle? I'll be dogged. The bank? Yeah... Yeah..." A smile spread across his mug. "That's good news, ain't it... Whut's gonna happen next... Okay, see you."

Bean hung up and stared into space, a grin stretching his stubble. Ruby threw a punch to his arm. *"What'd he say?"*

"Somebody's officially callin' employees, tellin' us all to come back to work on Monday. Says we'll get paid then. The bank stepped in and worked a deal with the gub'mint to keep the plant open. They puttin' in a man to run it. An outside crew is workin' all day tomorrow cleanin' up the place."

"Hallelujah!" Ruby hugged his neck then opened her hands to Heaven. "This is a blessin' from above. Ain't nobody lost they job. You see what havin' faith in the Lawd will do for ya?"

The next morning, in light of the good news, Ruby cajoled Bean into church. He piloted her red Lincoln down the highway to Everlasting Baptist. They slowed and read the advertising sign on wheels before turning off into the gravel parking lot...

I HATE THIS CHURCH
-SATAN

Bean pointed to the sign. "Look what Brother Bobby Earl's preachin' today. Here we go, we in for some hootin' and hollerin'. Ruby, you check the young'uns in. I'll get us a seat in the back."

Ruby joined him on the pew, and he leaned into her. "Junior's gettin' too old for youngun's church. If I got to sit through this, so does he."

"*Shhh*... You right, he's old enough to hear the Word hisself, first hand."

Bobby Earl let fly a fiery, hour-long sermon. Bean mostly napped but took away one important message—*there ain't no air conditionin' in Hell.*

After the benediction, the family loaded into the Lincoln. Bean announced in a flow of divine inspiration, "Okay, everybody. We celebratin' our good luck by goin' to the boo-fay at Ryan's."

"How many times I got to tell ya," Ruby corrected, "it ain't luck. It's Providence. It's the Lawd's will for that plant to get cleaned up and stay open."

Either way, luck or Providence, it called for strapping on the feed bags. Ryan's Family Steakhouse was one of a dozen all-you-can-eaters within a fifty-mile radius. The Sweats and their extended families patronized them on a regular, rotating basis. A clever, unwritten family ethos dictated rotation so as not to run any one restaurant out of business.

Bean needed a smoke upon arriving home. He stretched out on the bench seat to digest and to scratch Elvis's back. He played the usual cat-and-mouse game with The Ole Man—*peek-a-boo, I see you.* His hound darted and danced while he took target practice with Red Man projectiles. *Kinda like dodgeball.*

Ruby rushed out to the stoop with phone in hand and beckoned him with curled finger. "It's a lady name o' Heloise. Says she's callin' for Majestic Chicken."

"'Bout time they called." He pushed Elvis, rolled to the ground, bounced up, and answered the phone. Ruby eavesdropped.

"Yell-ow… Fair to middlin'. You? Yeah… North Georgia? Yeah… You kiddin'? Great day in the mornin'. Yeah… Ain't that a peach? Yeah, I'll be at work tomorrow mornin'. See ya."

He handed the phone back to Ruby. "Darlin', would you hand me a Bud?"

"Bean, don't play games with me. No beer 'til you tell me what that lady said."

"Oh, that lady? She said that the plant has been sold to a company outta north Georgia and everybody is s'posed to go to work like normal in the mornin'. Says they have a good reputation. They're s'posed to run a clean plant and pay higher wages *and* overtime."

"Butterbean Sweat." Ruby yelled as she lunged off the step with open arms and bear-hugged him. "Look what you done. You the bravest and smartest man I ever knowed. Do you now understand 'bout God's favor? Just for once do you get it?"

"Maybe," he mumbled. He thought about God's favor. *Bank steppin' in. New company ownin' the plant. A clean plant. Pay raises and overtime. All happenin' so fast.* He remembered watching some country on TV that was under a mean dictator's thumb but a people's revolution boiled under the surface. It came together in a perfect, unstoppable storm, and the dictator was booted fast as a flash fire in a greasy skillet.

"I'm down to one beer and cain't buy no more 'cause it's Sunday. Let's see whut He can do 'bout dat."

Ruby the teetotaler took up the challenge. "I may even take communion my own self to celebrate God's favor." She ambled across the road in her Sunday muumuu and knocked on the door of the Mexicans' trailer. After some muted conversation, she sauntered back across the road with a plastic cup of sangria for her and two Tecates dangling from a plastic six-pack loop.

The lovebirds sat in the yard on the rotting bench seat, clinking cup and can and giggling like high school prom dates. "It's a new day," Ruby proclaimed. "Short o' winnin' the lottery, it cain't get no betta."

A Ford Taurus cruised down the dirt road and stopped in front of their trailer.

"That's the gub'mint guy from the other night." Bean pointed. "He's got some other feller with him. I knowed it was too good to be true. They need to leave me the hell alone…"

The driver killed the engine, doors opened on the Ford.
Two men emerged and walked toward Bean and Ruby, Oh Lord.

"Hello again, good folks," said the one they'd already met,
"this is Mr. So & So from USDA. Don't worry, he's no threat.

"Seems your whistleblowing, Mr. Sweat, led to this important bust.
There is reward money for people like you, from a special trust.

"We at USDA thank you for taking a stand.
Here is your check for twenty-five grand."

Stunned, in shock, Bean took the check.
Seconds later, Ruby's mascara was a wreck.

The Grand Notion, at the same time it did hit.
In unison they cried, "Operation for Li'l Bit!"

PART VI:
RETURNIN' THANKS

Chapter 60

Frosty the Snowman flashed in the Sweat's front yard. Glistening corkscrew icicle lights dangled from the roofline. Red and yellow lights blinked on an artificial Christmas tree in the bay window.

Bean and Ruby whispered across the dinette table. Li'l Bit nestled in her crib, and dim light gleamed beneath Junior's door.

"Okey-dokey, Einstein." Ruby passed Bean another Bud. "I'm all ears."

He patted two rubber-banded stacks of hundred-dollar bills totaling $25,000. Notes and ciphers, a calculator, wadded paper balls, and a pencil lay strewn across the sea of red Formica. "We only got one shot to get this right, and I done figured it out."

He snatched one of the stacks, closed his eyes, and fanned the greenbacks under his nose. "Best smell on the whole planet. Now I know how Dale Earnhardt feels."

"Dale ain't got nuthin' on you, Punkin'."

"Listen up, now. Fifteen grand for Li'l Bit's surgery…" Bean counted the money and checked off each item. "… and two grand for leg braces… two grand to get your Lincoln out of hock… and another grand for tires and service—*a rip-off*—and forty-two hundred for bills, including paying off this here dinette set."

Bean crossed his arms and grinned at Ruby. "We got eight hun-ert dollars leftover."

"Okay, Mr. Santy Claus, wha'chu got in mind?"

"Whut 'chu say we do some shoppin' at Walmart then go to Jakyll Island for Christmas?"

Ruby shrieked and clasped her hands under her chins. Tears welled then flowed. "Oh, Bean. You know I always dreamed o' spendin' Christmas on Jakyll. You my prince." She boo-hooed and hugged him. They had often talked about their honeymoon on Jekyll Island, a half-day's drive east to Georgia's seashore, but the children had never seen the ocean.

Junior appeared in the hallway in his tighty-whitey underpants. "I heard ya holler, Mama. You okay?"

"Oh, Angel, I'm fine." She held out her arms as Junior shuffled into her embrace.

"If you okay, Mama, why ya cryin'?"

"Let's tell him," Bean said.

"Tell me *whut?*"

Ruby unlocked her bear hug and dabbed her eyes. "If we gonna tell him, we need to get Li'l Bit up and give 'em the news at the same time."

Bean popped up. "I'll fetch her." A moment later, he reappeared cradling Li'l Bit. She settled onto his lap, rubbing her dazed eyes.

Junior pointed. "Look at all that money!"

Bean grinned. "Okay, ready to tell 'em?"

"Tell us *whut?*"

"Who wants all the fried shrimp they kin eat on Jakyll Island for Christmas?"

Junior jumped up and down like a pogo stick, hollering, "Yipeee!"

Li'l Bit made joyful noises, cackling, clapping, and bouncing on Daddy's knee. "Da-da." She squirmed away and crawled to Junior who dropped and rolled on the carpet, hugging her. Mascara streamed down Ruby's cheeks.

Bean leaned forward with eyes aglow. "Santy Claus is comin' to Jakyll this year. We'll get us a room right on the beach. We gonna spread some sheets on the sand and get us a huge bucket o' fried shrimp and hush puppies and we'll eat right there with our toes in the ocean—don't let the crabs bite your toes, *ho, ho, ho.* We'll swim anytime we want—"

"Kids," Ruby interjected, "we gonna return thanks at church before we take this trip."

"—and we gonna fish off the pier and play putt-putt golf and—"

"Jesus is definitely at work here."

"—eat ice cream 'til we're sick. We'll have one o' them fancy bathtubs at the motel. Hey, who wants to eat beans and take a bubble bath?"

Zebra-striped suitcases, Grampa's Army duffel, and Junior's ninja backpacks piled up on Sunday morning. Rods and reels, tackle box, dog food, diaper bag… the mound mushroomed. Ruby bagged Vienna sausage, crackers, venison jerky, 'nilla wafers, chocolate chip cookies, and more.

Bean dug hundred-dollar bills from his pocket when alone and wafted their sweetness under his nose.

"Okay, everybody," Ruby hollered, "we got to keep movin'. I don't wanna be late for church. Bean, you better go check on The Ole Man."

Bean removed his cap and scratched his noggin. "You sure you done the right thing by gettin' the gub'mint to haul The Ole Man away?"

"I told ya, after a week o' prayer and a half day o' fastin', the Lawd come and give me the answer. You cain't get no higher direction than that. The poor Ole Man's starvin' and ain't gettin' the doctor care he needs. He's all alone, his trailer's filthy, and he's dyin' right in front of us. The Lawd said we have to act."

"You sure that gub'mint lady is gonna show up after church to get him."

"I believe so. We talked on the phone 'bout every day for a week. She'll be there," Ruby assured. "He needs to go to church one mo' time. Once they put him in a rest home, he may never see the inside o' church again. But remember, don't tell him. He'll pitch a fit. Let the gub'mint break the news."

Ruby whisked Li'l Bit into the bedroom. Moments later, she strutted the catwalk clutching Li'l Bit as they modeled matching jolly-face Santa sweatshirts. Jubilant whoops echoed through the trailer. Bells jingled on the laces of Ruby's sneakers and Li'l Bit's lone sneaker—a pink bootie covered her clubfoot.

Ruby looked at Bean and pleaded, "Please, not camo pants, honey."

Bean patted his full pockets. "The only safe place for money."

Bean and Junior piled the bags into the Lincoln. They fetched The Ole Man, and Bean shoved the wheelchair through the dirt. He unstrapped the tank, handed it to The Ole Man, and plunked him into the back seat.

"*Ooowww*. Dammit, son, you killin' my leg and watch that toe."

Junior crawled in beside him. "Careful o' that leg, half pint."

Bean collapsed the wheelchair and lifted it. "Watch out, Junior, this is gonna have to lay on top o' you."

Ruby carried Li'l Bit, and they scooted into the front. They settled, and she motioned Slippers to hop into her lap. Bean locked the trailer door and sat on the Lincoln's trunk to close it. He grabbed the rods and reels, crammed the reel ends beside Ruby's feet, and guided the rods past her shoulder, over The Ole Man's head and out the cracked-open back window. Neon corks bobbed around The Ole Man's head, and fishhooks danced with his oxygen tube.

The Ole Man swatted the rods. "Son, what the hell you doin'? Them hooks better not poke a hole in my tube."

"Quit worryin', will ya, Ole Man? Ain't you never seen a fish-hook before?"

"Ain't you never learnt how to pack a car?"

"Y'all hush," Ruby said. "Y'all like a couple o' cats scratchin' at each other."

Driving over, Ruby turned to Junior—"No Santy Claus if you mis-behave."
At Everlastin' Baptist, the sign declared, "A Free Thinker is Satan's Slave."

"Look!" A live manger scene starring Betty Lou and poor Elmer
with his hunched back.
"Jesus For President," extolled the bumper sticker on the preacher's
Cadillac.

Bean wheeled The Ole Man, said adios, and parked him on the
front row,
then ambled toward the rear in search of Ruby, heigh-ho.

Last week's tally on the whiteboard below the picture of heaven:
attendance of eighty and offering of two hundred seven.

The bulletin announced a birthday party for Jesus in Fellowship Hall.
The choir straggled up—all comers welcome—not practiced a'tall.

Led by choir director Jenkins and a pianist, many a hymn the con-
gregation did sing.
Followed by Fellowship Time, mingle and greet, spread the Word,
Christ is King.

Jenkins took the floor and broadcast anniversaries and birth-days. Church members stood one-by-one to update illnesses and hospitalizations. A young woman with thick eyeglasses announced, "My brother is 'bout to finish chemo, and they think he might o' kicked it."

"Amen and praise the Lawd!" Hugs broke out as the pianist cranked up another stanza.

"Any more announcements?" Jenkins queried. "Then please turn to the back of your bulletin, and we'll have a moment of silence as we pray over thirty-eight prayer requests…"

Bean pointed out one prayer request to Ruby—"For Li'l Bit Sweat's foot." Her lower lip trembled.

"Other announcements?"

A Deacon stood. "I'm very happy to report that by the grace o' God, our district's mission in Africa has now distributed three hundred Bibles, tryin' to bring Christ to the savages in the deepest and darkest jungles. Can I get a witness?"

The crowd exploded with chants and applause while the pianist plinked background harmonic notes.

"Does anybody else have anything to be thankful for? Tell us about it, beloved."

The Ole Man's hand shot up.

Ruby elbowed Bean. "Praise the Lawd," she whispered, "I'm glad The Ole Man is thankful for somethin'."

"Yes, brother in the wheelchair," Jenkins called. "Do you have something to be thankful for?"

The Ole Man cleared his throat before his voice boomed. "I ain't got nuthin' to be thankful for, but I know who does." He torqued in his chair and pointed his bony finger in Bean's direction. "Butterbean Sweat, right back yonder, got twenty-five thousand dollars in re-ward money, and I think he's got it all in the pockets of his britches right now!"

Chapter 61

A collective "*awe*" rose in the sanctuary. Everyone turned to stare at Bean's and Ruby's flushing faces. Preacher Bobby Earl jumped up and maneuvered across the stage, peering around heads to bear his gaze down on the Sweats.

"Amen, brother," Jenkins shouted. "Praise the Lawd. Sounds like we gonna' need us a wheelbarrow." Laughter exploded.

Bean flared his eyes at Ruby. "Did you tell The Ole Man?"

She shrugged her shoulders and whispered, "I ain't told him nuthin'." Bean rolled his eyes and crossed his arms over the bulges in his pockets.

At this news, fire got a'hold of the preacher,
as if this was the day of his arrival,
like he'd been airlifted into a tent revival.

"It is writ that it is easier for a camel to pass through the eye of a needle,
than for rich folk to enter the Kingdom o' Heaven," he declared with thunder.
"Money will enslave you, don't make that blunder."

"Should we give back, or should we hoard? We look for an answer from above."
Suddenly the sanctuary lights blinked! "A miracle! A sure sign of God's love."

"Praise the Lawd, hah! But even right here in Your house, we got to watch out for the Devil hisself... aaargh!"

Bean looked up, astonished at the preacher choking his own neck—*aaargh*. Bobby Earl's eyes rolled back, and his face flushed crimson. The stranglehold tightened, his purple tongue rolled out, and he staggered. Parishioners' eyes bulged, jaws dropped, fingers pointed.

In dramatic fashion, Bobby Earl struggled with one hand to pull the other away like a professional wrestler gradually overpowering a headlock...

"Did you see that, brethren? The Devil hisself just dug his meat hooks in me. Wa-wa-what, Lawd? You wanna speak through me, Jesus? Yes, brethren, the Lawd now verily speaks directly unto thee through me."

Bean elbowed Ruby. She put her *shhh* finger to her lips...

"If anybody in this room has come into an unexpected windfall, be it re-ward money or whatever, I now guide ye. I have writ in Deuteronomy, each o' ye must bring a gift in proportion to the way I have blessed ye. The standard ten-percent tithin' rule applies only to normal wages. That rule don't apply to things like re-wards. They come only through My hand, and should be returned to Me, thy Godhead, the rightful owner. Re-ward money is held in trust for Me, like the song says, for I giveth in the first place. Return thy fruit to Me, its rightful owner, so My work can be done here on earth, so My people can help folks that ain't got none."

Preacher Bobby convulsed then slapped his own face and waggled his head. "I am back, brethren. The Lawd has released me to do His work. Ushers please come forward."

The collection plate was coming around, coins clanging on brass.
All eyes focused on Bean,
hand in his pocket fingering the green.

"Which do you choose?" the Preacher roared,
"Heaven and e-ternal bliss beyond your wildest imagination?
Or is bein' bullwhipped by the devil in the everlastin' flames o' Hell
your destination?"

With prodding from Ruby, Bean pulled a hund-o
and dropped her in.
Ooo's and ahh's rang forth. Amen, brother. Amen.

Offertory concluded, a stem-winder Bobby Earl did preach.
The evils of the internet, a world wide web of sin.
The devil lives inside that computer, just a-lookin' into your soul
with a grin.

Sermon and hymns concluded, time for altar call.
The preacher beckoned sinners forward for salvation, come one,
come all.

Mascara trickling down her face, Ruby stood for the walk and
summoned Bean.
He shifted and squirmed. "Not today. Ain't no way."

Chapter 62

A rare spell of silence permeated the Sweat Lincoln as it pulled away from Everlasting Baptist. Ruby crossed her arms, set her jaw, and stared out her side window as they motored along. She finally spoke with fury in her voice. "Butterbean Sweat, I ain't *never* been so embarrassed. Why didn't you walk with me to the altar?"

Bean peeked in the rear-view mirror at Junior's curious eyes. "Don't want to talk 'bout it right now."

Ruby glared at him. "That's the problem. You hardheaded and *never* want to talk 'bout it."

He clinched his jaw and sighed. "Okay. You wanna talk, let's talk. The Ole Man somehow found out 'bout the money, and we jest got skint for a hun-ert dollars. Great, now preacher's baby gets new shoes."

"You ain't listenin' to a word I say. Forget The Ole Man—I don't know how the ole snoop found out. Forget Bobby Earl, he shouldn't o' acted that way. Focus on this…" She pointed her finger toward Heaven. "… a lot o' people prayed hard for Baby's foot, and now she's gonna get it fixed. God has blessed us. Can you not see that?"

Bean glanced in the rear-view at the children's frowns. "Don't want to talk 'bout it now."

Ruby scowled as the Lincoln zigged and zagged toward the paradise of merchandise. *Cain't get to Walmart quick enough,* he thought, *that place cheers everybody up.*

Junior poked her shoulder. "Come on, Mama, it's Christmas."

Bean poked her. "Yeah, Baby. It's Christmas, and we're goin' Walmartin'. Santy Claus is ridin' his sleigh to the beach. Reindeers'll be wearin' sunglasses."

Li'l Bit giggled. Ruby remained mute as she re-upped her mascara. The iconic blue and white sign with yellow starburst beckoned on the horizon, and an endorphin shot fired through Bean. *Yeah, baby!*

Ruby broke her silence. "I'm gettin' me a scooter 'cause my feet is killin' me. Li'l Bit can ride in the basket. Just drop me and Baby off at the front door. Let's meet in our usual spot."

The Lincoln crawled toward the entrance. Ruby snapped her fingers and pointed. "Look! There's Santy Claus and somebody takin' pitchers. Change o' plan. When we finish, meet right over yonder so we can have a pitcher took of the young'uns with Santy."

Li'l Bit clapped. "Eee-Taws."

Ruby turned. "She said it again. Did y'all hear that? She said 'Santy Claus.'" Ruby reached over the seat and squeezed Li'l Bit's leg. Everybody laughed. Mama was happy so the coast was clear for everybody to be happy.

At the entrance, Ruby's sneaker bells jingled as she maneuvered her legs out the door. She hoisted Li'l Bit from the back seat while cradling Slippers with the other arm.

"Watch them fishin' poles," Bean hollered as she closed the door with her foot. As soon as they crept away, Bean reached for his chew and jammed home a wad. "Son, hep me find a parking place." The Lincoln crept up and down rows amid their eagle-eye recon.

They spotted a strip of dirt skirting the drainage ditch. With ease garnered from driving his lift, Bean paralleled the Lincoln into a tight spot. "Man, I ain't never had to walk so far jest to give the man my money. But Sugah, I got us a surprise." Bean popped the trunk and dug out matching green #88 Dale Earnhardt Jr. NASCAR T-shirts. "Santy Claus dropped these off early."

"Holy smoke, Diddy, this is the best present ever."

"Instead o' changin' right here, we'll jest wear 'em over our Sunday school shirts. Son, we need to look our Christmas best in Walmart. Bean jimmied the fishing rod tips inside the car and locked up while Junior stumbled around like a drunkard, crowing over his T-shirt.

Father and son trudged across the concrete tundra and entered the neon gates of retail heaven.

Kinetic energy charged the air in the bustling babble of commerce.
Every man toting a wallet, every woman a purse.
The crazies were out, like the bar scene in Star Wars,
and butt crack galore peeked above sagging pants and underdrawers.

Bean loved the rhythm of Walmart life. It appeared frenzied and disjointed at ground level, but he knew if he could rise to the clouds and look down, he'd see a fluid puzzle. Sure, nutcases wore their wild costumes but most folks weren't crazies. They were his people, imperfect like him, but each special in some way and each with a soul. Walmart was his bastion of civilization, the essence of life itself, a place to see and be seen, away from the screwy, messed up chicken plant. *Unlike dead chickens, everybody's alive here.*

In sporting goods, the boys loaded up with shark hooks and sinkers,
all the while scoring one another's stinkers.
He planted Junior in electronics to try a video game,
then snuck off to lingerie to buy Ruby something to fan his flame.
A pink negligée/panty set, them ought to be a hit.
He held up panties big as a parachute, them ought to fit.

They met outside amongst the sidewalk hustle and bustle and the *ting-a-ling* of Salvation Army bells. A children's choir sang *Silent Night* with sacks of potting soil as backdrop. Bagged surprises filled Ruby's scooter and Bean's buggy.

"You gonna have to pick me up, but let's get the Santy Claus pitcher first."

They staked their place outside the ropes. Li'l Bit's eyes grew wary as they watched the tipsy, glassy-eyed Santa sitting on his throne. An elf in pigtails ushered children in and encouraged smiles as the photographer clicked away.

"Who do we have here?" Santa's helper asked.

"This is Junior Sweat, and Li'l Bit Sweat is in her Daddy's arms."

The elf hailed, "Come on, Little Bit, let's go see Santa." Bean handed her over. She squirmed and looked back at her parents in horror.

Junior stepped up and hugged Santa. His elf spoke in hushed tones as St. Nick sipped from his Styrofoam cup. She set Li'l Bit on his lap. Santa boomed for all to hear. "HO, HO, HO, if it ain't Junior and Little Bit. Let's find out what they want for Christmas." He spent his obligatory half-minute listening to Junior prattle off a rambling list, from Nintendo to G. I. Joe, a baseball bat to a yellow cat. Li'l Bit's bottom lip pouted and trembled as Santa struggled to hold her. She started sobbing.

Ruby covered her mouth, and her mascara streaked. Santa's helper glanced at Ruby, love broke out, and the elf started crying, too. Bean fought to hold back his tears. He wiped them away and tried to think of something else so he wouldn't boohoo in public.

Ruby climbed off her scooter, shoe bells jingling, and rushed to Baby with outstretched arms. Li'l Bit lunged toward Mama, and the camera clicked.

Unlike all other trinkets in the bags, that treasured photo would stand the test of time.

Chapter 63

Junior stumbled around inebriated with euphoria as Diddy loaded gifts onto the tarp he'd laid on the ground beside the car. He stared at Diddy's #88 T-shirt, proud to show off his identical one.

"Don't you peek," Diddy warned, but Junior couldn't resist. *Look at all them presents.*

Mission complete, Diddy wrapped the tarp like a giant burrito and ran ropes through the metal grommets. Junior helped Diddy cinch tight and tie the laden tarp to the Lincoln's roof, one rope through the rear windows and one through the front.

"We got to leave them windows cracked, son, 'cause o' the rope."

"It's okay, Diddy, we got to leave 'em cracked anyway for the fishin' poles."

Mama inspected. "Lawd, Honey, you reckon that'll hold?"

"We golden, Darlin'. Me and Junior got it covered. Saddle up."

Junior hopped into the backseat behind Mama. He reclined and watched Diddy's head from an angle—that familiar, comforting mass of pink flesh, curled-up ears, and a tint of rust in his buzz cut. Diddy's head rotated left and right as he navigated traffic, his cheeks jiggling as he chatted with Mama.

Junior glanced over at Baby Girl. Her head was tilted back, and her eyes were closed. *She's tired.* He watched as her little head bobbed with each breath. *I love you, Baby. You gonna be fine. I can tell from Mama and Diddy. They so happy 'bout your operation comin' up after Christmas.* He grinned at the peaceful sight.

He laid his head back and relaxed. Air whistled through the windows, and the rope at his head vibrated and buzzed. He traced the shapes of stark white clouds as they floated across the baby-blue sky… a deer… a hamburger. Most were the shape of Mama's beauty parlor cotton balls.

He closed his eyes. *I need to keep playin' like I believe in Santy Claus. I think I seen a Nintendo in one o' them bags.* His stomach growled. "Diddy, when we gonna' eat?"

"Soon as we hit Willacoochee. We'll get us some GooGoo Clusters and some pee-can logs, too. Hey Mama, pee-can logs count as fruit, don't they?"

The Lincoln sailed merrily down the highway cruising toward the beach. Fishing rods reached for the sky, and the tarp flapped to beat all hell. Elvis's Christmas CD blared through the speakers behind Junior's head.

"TURN HERE!" Mama shouted.

Diddy yanked the wheel, and the tires screeched as they turned off the highway.

"Let El Gringo fly this here sleigh

to yonder Willacoohee boo-fay!"

Epilogue

Six television satellite trucks parked on the street in front of the Middle District of Georgia Federal Courthouse. Reporters and camera operators tested their equipment at the bottom of the granite steps.

A reporter for an Atlanta station postured in front of his camera then spoke frenetically. "Three defendants stood for a bail bond hearing today in the case of the United States of America versus Majestic Chicken Company. The individual defendants are all employees of Majestic, including Calvin Butler Junior, its chairman and CEO.

"The U.S. Attorney is pressing felony conspiracy charges alleging the defendants knowingly sent adulterated food to market—in this case, salmonella-tainted chicken from the Majestic Chicken plant. According to our legal experts, manslaughter charges may be forthcoming if the government can link the six recent salmonella deaths in the region to tainted Majestic chicken.

"The judge has just denied bail for two of the defendants—plant manager Wilbur Smith and part time employee Corporal Mutt Hightower of the Georgia Department of Resources. But in a surprising turn of events, the judge ruled that the alleged ringleader, Calvin Butler Junior, may remain free on bond until trial."

Commotion ensued as a throng of people pushed through the doors. "This may be Calvin Butler coming now."

The camera panned to the steps. Butler strutted down wearing a Cheshire cat smile, flashing a "V" for victory. An army of Kilroy & Russell lawyers cocooned him with Sheriff Roscoe and B.S. Birdsong guarding the flanks.

"There he is... MISTER BUTLER, MISTER BUTLER—"

"Out of my way, bastards."

About the Author

Jameson Gregg, a Mississippi native, is a graduate of Ole Miss and Mississippi College School of Law. Certain offbeat college jobs influencing his worldview include Mississippi River tugboat deckhand, traveling circus promoter, and taxi driver. His time spent as an iceman in a chicken plant 35 years ago provided inspiration for *Luck Be A Chicken*.

Jameson practiced law for 20 years in Georgia's Golden Isles in the state's second oldest law firm before shucking his esquire duties and assuming the role of scribe. He is an award-winning humorist, and his works have been published in literary anthologies, magazines, and newspapers. He lives in the Georgia mountains with his wife, Maureen. This is his first novel.

www.JamesonGregg.com

Acknowledgments

Writing a book is a team sport, and I owe thanks to many people.

The following trusted readers critiqued early manuscript drafts: Linda and Mark Mosely, Ron Adams, Marion Moore, and Lawton Tollison. Each offered insightful feedback, pointed out strengths and weaknesses, and provided much appreciated encouragement.

Great Southern Publishers of St. Simons Island, Georgia, crafted a splendid pre-book author website. Dr. Carrie Stempler acted as a valued consultant on societal topics. Mary Lou Cheatham, author of seven books, coached me on nut-and-bolt issues of the trade.

Members of Stonepile Writers Group in my adopted north Georgia mountains served up many good suggestions in our monthly critique sessions. Hats off to Atlanta Writers Club, Northeast Georgia Writers Group, and the annual Dahlonega Literary Festival for providing a steady supply of fine speakers, workshops, and seminars.

I am grateful to the Babcocks of Deeds Publishing in Atlanta for believing in this book and in me.

Raise your can and cup to Butterbean Sweat. He is fictional, of course, but he represents a compilation of all us bubbas out there. *Gentlemen, start your engines.*

Above all, I am forever indebted to my beautiful and brilliant wife, Maureen, who played an integral role in this project from concept to final proof. A woman more dedicated to her man you shall not find. As to any parts of the book that you may find slightly off-color, please know she edited those with one eye closed.